HELL'S
GATE

HELL'S GATE

A NOVEL

Stephen Frey

ATRIA BOOKS
New York London Toronto Sydney

ATRIA BOOKS

A Division of Simon & Schuster, Inc.
1230 Avenue of the Americas
New York, NY 10020

First Atria Books hardcover edition August 2009

ATRIA BOOKS and colophon are trademarks of Simon & Schuster, Inc.

For information about special discounts for bulk purchases, please contact Simon & Schuster Special Sales at 1-800-456-6798 or business@simonandschuster.com.

The Simon & Schuster Speakers Bureau can bring authors to your live event. For more information or to book an event contact the Simon & Schuster Speakers Bureau at 1-866-248-3049 or visit our website at www.simonspeakers.com.

Manufactured in the United States of America

10 9 8 7 6 5 4 3 2 1

Library of Congress Cataloging-in-Publication Data

ISBN 978-1-4165-4965-9
ISBN 978-1-4391-6555-3 (ebook)

For my wife, Diana, who is quite a fly fisherwoman.
I love you, sweetheart.

HELL'S
GATE

part I

1

A S FAR BACK as he could remember Hunter Lee had known his fate lay in the law. In being an attorney. In being a litigator.

It was a predestination he'd always found mysterious because he was an unassuming man outside a courtroom. A humble man. A man others had to make an effort to get to know, not a man who got to know others.

But Hunter turned into a different person when he came before the bench. Once he stepped through the dark-wood doors of justice he became gregarious, aggressive, and unfailingly persuasive. His key success factors inside a courtroom: He was always more prepared than the other side; he knew the answer to every question he asked; he had an uncanny ability to develop personal connections with jurors and hostile witnesses; he wasn't hesitant to use his rugged good looks and smooth southern charm to convince any woman sitting on the fence to see things his way; and he never lost his temper. He might turn up the volume once in a while, but he was always in complete control.

Over a decade, Hunter had won nearly a billion dollars in damage claims for his clients. In the process, he'd made his firm and its seven senior partners a fortune in contingency fees. People told him constantly to start his own firm so he could keep all those fees for himself, but he never had. He was still with Warfield & Stone, the same New York City firm he'd joined after graduating second in his class from the University of Virginia law school thirteen years ago.

During recruiting season of his final year at Virginia, he'd been drawn to Warfield & Stone's reputation for shunning publicity despite its long list of front-page cases and high-profile clients, drawn to its aura of secrecy. He was also impressed by the fascination his classmates and professors had with the firm and the near-celebrity status he attained on the grounds by being the only Virginia graduate the senior partners of Warfield & Stone wanted.

Hunter had gotten over his wide-eyed desire to be associated with such a prestigious firm a long time ago; that wasn't why he'd stayed. He'd stayed because he felt an enormous loyalty to the man who'd recruited him so hard out of Virginia. The man who was now Warfield & Stone's managing partner and a legend in the legal community.

Nelson Radcliff.

Hunter stood before the polished plaintiff desk to the judge's right, still wearing his sharp, pin-stripe suit coat despite the heat of the packed courtroom. Even though the four attorneys at the defense desk had removed their coats hours ago when the judge said it was all right to do so. For some time he'd been gazing down at a single piece of paper lying on the desk, as though hypnotized by the typed words on it and the heavy, unique signature beneath the words. Finally he brought his dark, penetrating eyes to those of the white-haired judge.

"Your Honor, I call Mr. Carl Bach."

"The plaintiffs calls Carl Bach to the stand," the uniformed bailiff announced in a booming voice.

A stocky, middle-aged man with a neatly trimmed, brown mustache rose from his seat in the middle of the third row. He excused himself in a low whisper several times as he struggled toward the center aisle over and around several pairs of knees. Finally free, he moved purposefully down the aisle to the witness stand, careful not to make eye contact with Hunter.

As Bach swore to tell the truth, the whole truth, and nothing but the truth, Hunter thought back to how he'd honed his skills in those intimidating amphitheater classrooms at Virginia. By the end of his second year he'd gotten so good he could usually argue either side of an issue and win, so good none of his classmates would volunteer to take him on in mock court even with mountains of evidence on their side. Professors had to *force* other students to oppose him. That was what distanced him so remarkably from everyone else, his professors would tell the litany of firms seeking his services. That was what caught the attention of the big New York and Washington firms even faster than his gaudy GPA.

What caught the attention of Nelson Radcliff.

It was Hunter's father who had decided what his career would be early on in his childhood, even before Hunter really knew what a lawyer was. Robert Hunter Lee would be an attorney, his father would announce every evening as the family sat down to dinner. A New York City litigator, he'd specify during the meal. Case closed, he'd say over dessert. Night after night, as far back as Hunter could remember.

Hunter had never questioned the decree. He'd simply done everything in his power to make it come true, everything he could to make his father happy.

As Carl Bach lowered his right hand and took a seat in the raised wooden witness chair, Hunter focused on his target. "Mr. Bach, please state your occupation for the record."

Bach rolled his eyes and gave Hunter an aggravated shake of the head, making it clear to everyone that he thought these proceedings were a charade. That they were a ridiculous way to spend a blistering hot summer afternoon in a stuffy Bozeman, Montana, courtroom with a broken air conditioner.

"I'm the chief operating officer of the Bridger Railroad," Bach answered stiffly. "I'm the second most senior executive at the company behind the CEO, George Drake."

"Mr. Drake also owns the company, correct?"

"Correct."

"Is Mr. Drake here today?"

"No."

Hunter gave the jury a puzzled look. As if it surprised him that Drake would miss such an important proceeding, as if it was arrogant of Drake not to be here and, therefore, a personal affront to them.

He moved out from behind the plaintiff desk and headed toward the witness chair, leaving behind the piece of paper he'd been studying. "As the COO, you're an important person at the railroad." It was an obvious point, but saying so for all to hear might put Bach off guard, might make him feel a connection to a hostile attorney, might cause him to drop his defenses at a critical moment. "A *very* important person."

"Ah . . . yes." Bach stroked the tips of his mustache with the stubby thumb and forefinger of his right hand. "Certainly."

"A person who should be up to speed on all important company matters. Especially matters related to the day-to-day operations of the railroad, especially as the *chief* operating officer."

Bach stole a wary glance at the jury, recognizing that he'd been deftly maneuvered into a tight corner right off the bat.

And the jury watched Bach silently remind himself that this tall, handsome attorney from New York with the deliberate manner and the intense eyes had a big-time reputation for a reason.

"Well, no one can really—"

"How big is the Bridger Railroad, Mr. Bach?"

"When you ask 'how big,' what exactly do you mean?"

"Let's start with how many miles of track you operate."

Bach pulled a white handkerchief from his shirt pocket and dabbed at the tiny beads of sweat forming on his forehead. "One thousand six hundred and forty nine miles of main line. Four hundred twelve and a half miles of yards, spurs, and sidings." The stocky man with the bushy mustache gave Hunter a smug look. "Give or take a few feet."

A chuckle rustled around the courtroom.

"Thank you," Hunter said politely. Good. Bach was giving specific answers. He'd taken the bait, felt he had to prove himself after being called out. Now the jury would expect crisp, specific answers to every question. In a few minutes Bach wouldn't be so specific, and the jury would wonder why. "Is all that track in Montana?"

"Most of it. We go a spitting distance into Idaho, Wyoming, and the Dakotas, but that's it."

"So you connect with other railroads."

Bach nodded. "With the BNSF and the Union Pacific, with the big boys."

Hunter furrowed his dark, arrow-straight eyebrows. "The Bridger is what's known as a short-line railroad. Is that correct, Mr. Bach?"

"A Class II railroad," Bach answered, using the official term. "As defined by the federal government," he added confidently, clearly believing there couldn't be a land mine buried anywhere in this field of questioning.

"Meaning?"

"Meaning," Bach continued, his voice taking on a professorial, condescending tone, "that we have annual revenues between $20 million and $280 million."

Hunter turned to the jury and let out a low whistle. "Wow. Two hundred and eighty million." It was so easy it was almost unfair, especially with the help he'd gotten from his anonymous benefactor. "That's big." To a New York jury that amount wouldn't sound very impressive. In Bozeman, Montana it sounded like the gross domestic product of most European countries. "*Very* big."

"Well, actually," Bach spoke up quickly, realizing he'd been backed into that same tight corner once again, "it isn't that—"

"Mr. Bach," Hunter interrupted, "I don't want to keep you up here on the stand any longer than I have to. I know you're a busy man, and I know it's warm in here." Hunter broke into a friendly smile as he made eye contact with several jurors. Longest with an older woman wearing a faded blue dress and matching hat who was sitting all the way to the left of the jury box. He still hadn't won her over. He could tell that by her rigid posture, stiff upper lip, and cold expression. "Made a lot warmer," he continued, allowing his southern drawl to turn thicker and more potent, "by the fact that you're on the *hot* seat."

This time the courtroom erupted into a loud laugh. Even the older woman in the jury box cracked a thin smile.

The judge, too, Hunter noticed. Which fit. He'd been worried at the start of the trial that a Montana judge might make it difficult for a New York lawyer carrying a big reputation into his courtroom, but that hadn't turned out to be the case at all. The man in black had been completely fair, which Hunter had found was true about most Montanans. They were tough—because Montana was a tough place to live—but they were fair. Which was refreshing. It might help with the size of the award, too.

Hunter raised a hand, requesting silence, subtly taking control of the proceedings. Then he made a slow, sweeping gesture toward two children sitting in the front row just behind the plaintiff desk. Both of them wore stark, black eye patches.

"We all know why we're here," Hunter said firmly when the laughter faded, his voice turning stern as he moved toward the children. They were sitting between their parents, their tiny, dimpled chins buried self-consciously in their narrow chests. "We're here because fourteen months ago westbound Bridger Freight 819 tragically derailed just outside the small town of Fort Mason, Montana. I say 'tragically' because the four tank cars that jumped the tracks that May afternoon were filled with liquid anhydrous ammonia, a common fertilizer. As we heard the experts testify, those four tank cars derailed near the Murphy General Store off SR 72 and suffered catastrophic fractures when they smashed into several boxcars sitting on a siding. Those fractures allowed the liquid inside the tank cars to escape, and, when liquid anhydrous ammonia hits air, it explodes into a gas."

The courtroom had gone deathly still. The judge was leaning forward on the bench, peering over his black-framed glasses. The reporters standing shoulder to shoulder in the back had ceased scribbling on their notepads. Those in the audience who'd been fanning their faces with newspapers had stopped fanning. Everything had come to a halt and everyone was staring at Hunter. They'd heard it all before during the past few days, but not like this, not so compactly and so dramatically. It was as if Hunter had magically transported them to the accident scene just as the train went roaring past and they could see for themselves how the tank cars had careened off the rails and slammed into the boxcars on the siding, then tumbled over and over. It was as if they could see for themselves the steel cars rip apart as if they were made of balsa wood, see for themselves how the liquid inside the cars burst into a huge, deadly, billowing cloud. It was as if they were watching the Zapruder film for the first time, as if they were watching Jack Kennedy reach for his throat with both hands, watching half his head blown off with the last ghastly shot. But Hunter was doing it all without a projector and an eight-millimeter film. He was making the jury appreciate the horror of the tragedy without any visual aids, making the jury appreciate why he was so good. He was making those twelve people sitting in judgment understand why the families who'd sought his services had actually gone to church to pray that he would represent them.

"Into a *monster*." Hunter's voice resounded throughout the courtroom. "A monster seeking water anywhere it could find it because that's what anhydrous ammonia does. It sucks water out of everything it comes into contact with. Like it did from the skin, lungs and eyes of those unlucky people in its path that terrible spring day in Fort Mason." Hunter pointed at the children in the front row. "Like it did from the eyes of these innocent children, blinding them as their lenses dehydrated like puddles beneath the Sahara sun."

"Objection!" One of the railroad's four attorneys shot up from his seat, unable to restrain himself any longer. "Mr. Lee's grandstanding, Your Honor. I mean, is there a question anywhere in our future?" The young man slammed the desk with his fist, totally frustrated. *"Objection!"*

"Overruled."

"Four people died when the gas singed their lungs bone-dry and ten were blinded, including these poor children sitting before us. Fortunately just in one eye for them." Hunter's expression turned sad, and he shook his head. "I can't believe I just said 'fortunately.' I'm sorry," he murmured, nodding solemnly to the little boy and girl, then to their parents. "Very sorry."

"Objection!"

"Overruled." The judge glared down at the railroad attorney. "Now, sit."

"Your Honor, please. This is—"

"I said, sit down, sir!"

Hunter glanced at Carl Bach. He was sweating profusely. "Those are the facts, Mr. Bach," Hunter said quietly, "and they are not in dispute. What is in dispute is who bears the blame. Was the engineer going too fast? Were the tracks the train was roaring down that day in desperate need of repair? Did the senior executives of the Bridger Railroad know the tracks were broken? As brittle as dead aspens in February?" Hunter pointed toward the witness stand as he scanned the jury. "Did Mr. Bach know those tracks were broken? Or," he said, gesturing toward the four attorneys at the defense table, "is it as *they* would have you believe, as their experts would have you believe? That the tracks had been tampered with and that was what caused the train to crash? That, in fact, the Bridger Railroad was a victim in this horrible tragedy, too?"

Hunter caught the judge's subtle hand signal. There needed to be a question soon. The objections hadn't been well received, but the point had been made. Enough orating.

"We've heard about chevrons in the rails, street gangs out to satisfy their hunger for random violence, even the possibility of foreign terrorists conspiring to murder the residents of Fort Mason." Hunter gave the railroad attorneys a did-you-really-think-anyone-would-buy-that-one look, slowly pivoting so that everyone in the courtroom could see his skeptical expression. "We've heard all manner of possibilities from that army of attorneys over there. One for each of the tank cars that derailed, now that I think about it," Hunter added, as if the fact had just dawned on him. Which, of course, it hadn't. "Ironic, huh?"

A murmur raced around the courtroom, full of hatred for the railroad. It was a reaction that told Hunter he now had everyone squarely in the palm of his hand, even the older woman in the faded blue dress and matching hat. It was a reaction that told Hunter his father had been absolutely right to guide his son into the law.

The railroad attorneys blurred before him. How could his father have been so sure of himself? Harboring not the slightest doubt about repeating his decree at the dinner table night after night. Filled with a sense of purpose and conviction completely uncommon to the man, according to people who'd known him well. *What had he known?*

"Mr. Lee," the judge urged under his breath, "get on with it. Please, sir."

A sincere "please" from a judge? Had Hunter heard the man in the black robe right? His partners back in New York would never believe him. Where he came from judges ran courtrooms with iron fists, not polite requests. When the hell had he made this deal with the devil?

Then it hit Hunter. Maybe he hadn't made the deal, maybe his father had. Maybe that was how his father had known his younger son was predestined for the law.

"What we haven't heard is the truth." Hunter moved back toward the witness stand, shaken by the thought of his father sitting across the negotiating table from the devil. For several moments he stood before Carl Bach, staring down at the senior executive, fighting the images racing through his mind. "Did you know those tracks needed to be fixed?" he finally managed to ask.

"No," Bach responded, his calm demeanor belying the anxiety etched into the lines on his forehead and cheeks. "In fact, they might have been fine. They probably were fine," he added quickly. "The cause of the accident could easily have been a hot box in one of the car's braking systems; a bad loading job in the coal cars ahead of the first tanker; or a shift in the load on the trip through South Dakota while the Burlington Northern had control of it. We just don't know, Mr. Lee." Bach spread his arms, appearing baffled. "No one knows. We dug through that accident scene for a week and nobody could figure out what happened. Us, the state boys, the federal agents. I spent two days over there myself. There was just too much damage to the cars and the tracks. There was lots of speculation, but nobody could ever say for sure what happened."

Bach scanned the courtroom, searching for compassion, searching for just one friendly face. "What I do know is that all the main-line tracks in our entire system had passed their regularly scheduled maintenance check the week before. With flying colors," he added. "With no exceptions and no maintenance orders filed. It's a stringent program we rigorously execute and document. You had access to all those records, didn't you, Mr. Lee?"

Bach had obviously been drilled on how to answer this question by his lawyers, but he'd practiced the response so many times the words sounded scripted now. Maybe the jury would pick up on that. Hunter was confident they would, because ultimately, juries were damn perceptive.

"Yes," Hunter agreed, finally pushing his distractions to the side, at least for the time being. "Your attorneys were very helpful in getting me those files."

"Good. I told them right from the start that you were to have everything you wanted as fast as possible. All the records, all the files." Bach's expression filled with sympathy for the two small children sitting in the front row. "The challenge, Mr. Lee, is that we can't possibly patrol every mile of track we operate every second of the day." Implying that the tracks had indeed been tampered with. "What happened was a tragedy, *is* a tragedy, is a *damn* tragedy. But there's bad people out there doing bad things more and more often these days. It's awful, but it's an awful reality, too."

Hunter nodded thoughtfully. "Yes, I see what you're saying." He paused. "But a question or two about what you just said, Mr. Bach. To set the record straight before you step down. Okay?"

Bach looked at Hunter suspiciously. "Yeah, sure."

"You just told the judge and the jury that all of those one thousand six hundred and forty-nine miles of main-line tracks are subject to a monthly maintenance program."

"Yes . . . I did say that," Bach agreed hesitantly.

"What about those four hundred twelve and a half miles of yards, spurs and sidings?" Hunter asked, boring in on his target. "Give or take a few feet here and there, of course. What about them?"

Bach shifted uncomfortably in the witness chair. It was obvious from his body language that he didn't like Hunter repeating the exact number of yard, spur and siding miles the Bridger Railroad operated. It was obvious that the precision coming back at him was unsettling.

One of the railroad's lawyers shifted in his seat, Hunter noticed out of the corner of his eye. Then another one ran a hand through his thinning hair.

"What *about* them?" Bach asked.

"What's the maintenance program when it comes to the yards, spurs, and sidings?"

Bach cast an SOS glance at his legal team. "Uh, it depends."

"On what?" Hunter was shooting questions at Bach faster now, speeding up the pace as he steered the COO into no-man's-land.

"On how much the tracks are used, on how old they are, on when they were last checked. On lots of things," Bach said, as if his answer should be obvious. "I mean, we're very diligent when it comes to those tracks, too, but we can't check them as often as we check the main lines. It wouldn't be cost effective."

"Cost effective?"

"And it isn't necessary," Bach spoke up quickly, realizing how callous "cost effective" had sounded in front of people who'd suffered so much. "Our trains go up to sixty, sometimes seventy miles an hour on the main lines, but on sidings the engineers are specifically ordered not to exceed fifteen, so those tracks don't take nearly the wear and tear. And, if there is a problem with a siding track, what happens won't be so bad because the train is going slower. We're solid on this with all our people, we've never had a problem. Our safety record has been outstanding. Other than what happened in Fort Mason last year," he admitted in a low voice.

"The train in question was going over fifteen miles an hour that day. Right, Mr. Bach?"

The COO bit his lower lip. "I believe so."

"How fast was it going?"

"We don't know for—"

"*About* how fast?" Hunter interrupted. He glanced at that piece of paper lying on the plaintiff desk, hoping Bach would catch the look. "Come on."

"Objection!" shouted one of the railroad attorneys. "The question calls for speculation on the part of the—"

"Overruled," the judge snapped. "We heard the experts testify. *Your* experts."

"Around forty miles an hour," Bach answered when the judge pointed at him. "Maybe fifty," he went on, almost in a whisper. "But it's a main-line track so the engineer wasn't even going as fast as he could have been."

"It's a double-track main line at that point in the system, right?" Hunter asked. "Meaning two trains can pass each other at that point west of Fort Mason. Correct?"

"Yes," Bach agreed deliberately, as if he suddenly realized he had a problem. "It's a double-track main line there," he confirmed, choosing his words carefully. "Then there are the siding tracks alongside the double main. The tracks those boxcars were sitting on."

"Why are those siding tracks there?"

"The Brule Lumber Mill is about a half mile away, back in the woods. The sidings are a staging area for the mill. The long-haul freights drop cars off there, then the local switcher takes them to the mill. And vice-versa."

"I see." Hunter rubbed his chin thoughtfully. "How far out of town on the west side does that double main go?"

"Huh?"

"How far west of town does the double main line go? When does it switch down to one track?" Hunter rested a hand on the railing that boxed in the witness chair on three sides. "What's the next big town west of Fort Mason?" he prodded when Bach didn't respond right away.

"Gordonsville."

"Okay. How far is Gordonsville from Fort Mason?"

"About thirty miles."

"Does the double main go all the way to Gordonsville? Are there two separate tracks from Fort Mason to Gordonsville?"

"No."

"Then how far does it go?" Hunter moved slightly to his right, blocking Bach's view of his attorneys. "Mr. Bach?"

Bach let out a measured breath. "Four miles."

"Four miles!" Hunter thundered, backing off a few steps and folding his arms across his chest. "That's all? You call that a main line? Isn't that really just a glorified siding, Mr. Bach? Just a place one train can idle while another one passes on the real main line?"

"It's a main line!" Bach shouted. "A *damn* main line, even if it is only four miles long."

"Has that four miles of track always been classified as a main line?" Hunter demanded.

Bach's eyes opened wide, his expression went blank, and his chin tilted slightly up. "I uh, I . . ." His voice trailed off.

"*Well?*"

"What's the point?" demanded one of the railroad attorneys, jumping to his feet. "What's this all about?"

"*Has it always been classified as a main line?*" Hunter fired again. "And I'm warning you, Mr. Bach, be careful about answering this question. Very careful."

"Yes!" Bach hissed, his knuckles going white as he clenched the arms of the witness chair. "It's always been classified as a main line."

Hunter stared at Bach for several moments, eyes flashing. The courtroom had gone deathly still again.

As if on cue, one of the dark-wood doors at the back opened, making what seemed like a huge racket in the stillness of the courtroom as it creaked on its hinges. Hunter didn't bother turning his head as an attractive young woman in a short dress slipped into the room and squeezed between two reporters. He didn't need to look; he knew what was happening. He kept his eyes riveted to Bach's, and he saw in Bach's forlorn expression exactly what he wanted to see. That it was over, that Bach was done, that suddenly Bach didn't want any more of this fight.

The woman had slipped into the courtroom as if she wasn't anyone special, which she wasn't. Except to Carl Bach and Hunter Lee.

"Are you sure you want to stick with that story?" Hunter strode toward the plaintiff desk and the piece of paper he'd been staring at before calling Bach to testify. He picked it up, then retraced his steps to Bach's shocked, terrified expression and slipped the memo into the COO's trembling fingers. "*Are you absolutely sure?*"

"I . . . I . . ."

"That's your signature on the bottom of the page, isn't it?" Hunter asked, his voice dropping to a whisper.

Bach swallowed hard.

"*I didn't hear the question!*" one of the railroad attorneys shouted, pounding on the desk. "*Please repeat the question! What's on that piece of paper? Speak up, will you!*"

"Do you recognize that woman who just walked into the courtroom, Mr. Bach?" Hunter's voice dropped a notch lower, so not even the judge could hear him.

Bach shut his eyes tightly and turned his head to one side, as though he was lashed to a post before a firing squad and the order had already reached "Aim." He nodded.

"You don't want to keep going, do you?"

The executive hung his head. "No."

"We can't hear the questions," came a chorus of voices from the defense desk. All four railroad attorneys were standing now. *"Your Honor, please!"*

"Mr. Lee," the judge said, "please speak up."

Another "please" from a judge? His father must have done one hell of a job on the devil. Of course, the devil always got something in return. "I'll ask you again," Hunter said quietly to Bach, backing off a little, offering the COO a horrible choice. His career—or his marriage. "The question you want to answer, not the other one. The one—"

"Ask me," Bach begged, unable to get the words out fast enough. "In Jesus's name, please ask me."

Hunter took another step back. "I'm going to ask you one more time, Mr. Bach." His voice was strong and clear again so everyone in the courtroom could hear him. "Was that four-mile stretch of track always classified as a main line?"

Bach stared straight ahead for what seemed like an eternity, eyes fixed on something in the distance only he could see. Then his lips began to quiver and his head to shake, almost imperceptibly at first, then with conviction. "No." He buried his face in his hands. "It was classified as a siding before the accident. We changed the track's maintenance classification to main line the day after those tank cars derailed." Bach began to rock back and forth in the chair. "Then we changed all the maintenance records from before the accident to make that four miles of track look like it had always been classified as a main line." Bach slumped down. "The train shouldn't have been going that fast," he mumbled. "It shouldn't have been going over fifteen miles an hour on that track, it shouldn't have been on that track at all. Those rails were rusty and cracked, they needed to be replaced. I saw it myself a few weeks before the accident. But we've been trying to save money everywhere we can." He gasped. "We've got *so much* debt on our books, and we're so damned strapped for cash. I mean, we're almost bankrupt."

Hunter gazed at Carl Bach for several moments, watching the other man's tears come streaming down, thinking about how he'd just destroyed a man's career and wondering if he should feel some sense of remorse. Hadn't Bach deserved to be asked that terrible question, hadn't he deserved that terrible choice? Shouldn't people be held accountable for the awful things they did and wasn't that all he was doing? Wasn't that justice?

Hunter motioned to the judge. "I rest my case, Your Honor."

A few minutes later the judge had delivered his instructions to the jurors and they were shuffling out of the room, some of them casting hateful looks in Bach's direction as they left. They were headed to an anteroom to deliberate on how much money they would award the eight families who'd retained Hunter Lee. The litigator from New York City had lived up to all of his advance billing, to his big-time reputation.

When the last juror had disappeared, Hunter realized that he was thirsty. But, unlike the judge and jury, he had to exit the room like everyone else. Through those dark-wood doors at the back of the room, and the pack of hungry reporters who were already starting to shout questions at him.

As Hunter pushed his way through the chaos, a small man holding a letter-size envelope stood directly in his path. He didn't look like a reporter, Hunter thought to himself as the distance between them closed. He wasn't holding a pen and notepad.

"Robert Lee?" the man asked over the din of voices as they came together.

Hunter's eyes narrowed. "Yes."

"Robert *Hunter* Lee?"

"Yes."

The small man smiled thinly and pressed the envelope firmly to Hunter's chest. "Congratulations, Mr. Lee. You've been served."

2

L IKE EXPERIENCED ASSASSINS, they left nothing in their control to chance. They did extensive reconnaissance; they reviewed every option from every angle once the information was in their hands; then they made their selections with respect to location, time of day, time of year, and weather conditions. All of which were chosen with the objective of, together, inflicting maximum possible damage.

The location they'd decided on tonight was a remote, three-thousand-foot-high ridge in southwestern Montana.

It was perfect for many reasons.

First, it had excellent cover. It was blanketed by a sea of thigh-high, paper-dry grass, which, importantly, grew right to the edge of the winding road hugging the base of the ridge's steep slope like a baby clinging to its mother. Dotting the sea of grass were sizable islands of ponderosa pine and Douglas fir, also very dry.

Second, despite the isolation of the area, the road at the base of the slope was paved—one of the few county roads in the area that was—and it connected to wide, even more smoothly paved state roads at either end. So it provided excellent access, a quick getaway, the ability for a vehicle to travel at a relatively fast rate of speed, and, most important, it facilitated combustion.

Third, the ridge was steep at the base, then leveled off as it neared the crest. This topographical feature was critical for the blistering ignition they sought.

Fourth, up and over the ridge's crest was an abundance of thirsty timber. Stretching for fifty miles toward Canada from the top of the ridge's north face was an army of pine trees, standing in formation, and on the rugged, up-and-down floor of the terrain lay their dry, fallen comrades. Five miles north of the ridge was the town of Big Cat, a lonely outpost inhabited by several hundred hearty Montanans. Between the ridge and Big Cat were a few small farms nestled beneath the thick canopy. As big as this fire could quickly become, the people living on those farms didn't stand a chance of containing the blaze without assistance from the outside.

Fifth, most of the roads in the dense forest between the ridge and Big Cat were terrible, nothing more than twisting, turning, barely maintained pothole-pocked logging trails. Getting equipment into the area over them would be a time-consuming, potentially deadly proposition. Potentially not even worth trying because you never knew what a fire would do. Fires rode the wind. When the wind changed directions—as it often did in Montana—so did the fire. Sometimes with a vengeance if the gusts were sudden and the tinder in the new direction was explosive.

If there was a blowup, people on those roads could become trapped because they wouldn't be able to turn around quickly and get out. So instead of fighting the fire in the middle of the woods, the Forest Service might decide to draw a perimeter on the south side of Big Cat and make a last stand there. Which was the perfect scenario, because by the time the flame front reached Big Cat, it would probably be a megablaze. A fire with flames hundreds of feet high moving at speeds of up to fifty miles an hour. If that happened, the Forest Service might not even try to save Big Cat.

They'd selected a perfect time to make their move: four in the morning. A perfect night: a moonless, black sky aglitter with pinpoint-size lights that barely illuminated the breathtaking landscape. A perfect time of year: late July. It was hot as hell, even at this early hour of the morning. In fact, it was the hottest July on record.

Most important, the weather conditions were perfect: There had been no rain for weeks, and there was a steady seventeen-mile-an-hour breeze blowing up the ridge with gusts exceeding twenty-five. Other than hot and dry conditions, wind was the most vital ingredient in the creation of a megablaze.

As with any high-risk operation, much could go wrong despite their level of preparation and attention to detail, but the perpetrators took pride in knowing they'd dialed back the odds of failure as close to zero as possible. They were confident everything would go off without a hitch. They'd been doing this since mid-June in other locations around Montana and other parts of the Northwest with excellent results. Which made them feel very good about their chances of success, about achieving their goal of inflicting maximum damage.

The driver pulled the semi-truck to a squeaky, hissing stop and cut the lights. Then he fished a cell phone from his pocket and pressed the IC button as he climbed out of the cab. "Echo Six, you there?"

He glanced around furtively while he moved toward the rear of the trailer. Man, it was lonely out here. On the other side of the truck was that steep south face of the ridge, and on this side was a wide, sweet-smelling, clover-filled meadow surrounded by a dense pine forest. There were probably animals peering out at him from the cover of the trees around the meadow—most animals saw much better than humans did at night—but he hoped there was nothing dangerous. Just squirrels, raccoons, coyotes, deer, and maybe an elk or a moose.

Unfortunately there were also bears in the area. Black bears as well as some of their massive grizzly cousins.

But even more deadly than the grizzlies were the mountain lions that prowled these lonely ridges. Specters of the hills, as they were known around here. A lot of people thought the lions hadn't made it this far south again, but he knew better. He'd seen one slink into the woods at the edge of his high beams a few weeks ago only a few miles from here. He'd never see a cat until it was too late, until its fangs were impaled in his throat. They were that good at stalking their prey. Well, he'd just have to count on luck for the next few minutes to stay safe. Which unnerved him. He hated counting on luck for anything.

The wind moving through the trees framing the meadow made a low wail, and a shiver crawled up his spine despite the heat of the night. He'd always found Montana to be an eerie place, and he wasn't the kind of man who was easily rattled. But being out here in the middle of nowhere in the dead of night convinced he was being stalked by apex predators brought home all those uneasy feelings.

"Echo Six, Echo Six. Come in, damn it!"

A few seconds of static followed, then came the positive response. "Loud and clear, Batman, loud and clear. You in position?"

A wave of relief washed over him. It was good to hear his partner's voice. He'd never liked the guy much, but suddenly he wanted to hug the bastard. "Yeah."

"Ready?"

"I've got a few minutes of setup, then we'll be good to go," he answered, releasing the lock on the trailer's back door and pulling up. The door rose with a loud clatter. He hoped that would scare off anything out there in the darkness that meant him harm. "How we looking?"

"Nobody around. It's all clear."

With a groan, the driver picked up a thirty-foot length of thick steel chain lying in the back of the cargo bay like a coiled python. "What about behind me?" he asked, dropping the shiny silver links to the pavement at his feet.

"All clear there, too. As of a few seconds ago, anyway. That's what Tom—I, I mean, that's what Thunder reported."

"Okay. I'll check back one more time when I got the things on, then we go. Yell at me right away if you see anybody."

"Sure, sure."

"And keep the fricking line open," he snapped, his eyes darting around. "You hear me?"

"I hear you, already. Roger out."

"Yeah, yeah," the driver replied sarcastically. There was no need for all the formality. It wasn't like this was a top-secret, enemy-soil operation—which he'd been a part of many times as a Green Beret. It was funny how people got caught up in things sometimes. "Talk to you in a few."

He leaned down, picked up one end of the chain, wrapped it around the truck's bumper, and hitched it back over on itself with a thick bolt and screw he'd pulled from his pocket. Then he grabbed the coil on the ground and moved straight back away from the truck, playing the chain out until it lay in a straight line on the road behind the big rig like a fishing line trolling behind a boat. Then he repeated the process with the other three coils of chain in the back of the truck until they were stretched out behind the trailer parallel to the first one.

As he dropped the end of the last chain to the ground, his head snapped to the left. He was sure something out in the meadow had moved. Not too far away, either. He had excellent eyesight and, despite the darkness, he was almost sure he'd spotted something. A few blades of grass moving against the wind, the flick of an ear, the flash of a tail. He leaned forward, peering into the night. He knew not to stare directly at a spot when he was scanning for something in the darkness, but rather to look a few feet right or left of it. He knew from his training that this technique gave him the best chance of picking up collateral movement. But he saw nothing.

He hustled for the cab, irritated with himself. He'd been alone on night maneuvers in places a lot more hostile than this, but he'd never had these kinds of creepy feelings. "Echo Six, Echo Six," he called into the phone again, his voice bouncing with each stride. "This is Batman. I'm ready to roll, I'm ready to roll."

"I copy, Batman. You're all clear. I just checked with Thunder, and it's all good behind you, too. Let's do it. Do it, do it, do it."

The driver hopped up behind the steering wheel, slammed the door shut, flipped on the headlights, revved the engine a few times, and rammed the truck into gear. Though the road ahead was twisting and narrow, he quickly accelerated to thirty, to forty, then to forty-five. He had experience driving big rigs, and he knew exactly how far he could push this one without rolling it. He could have gotten the damn thing up to fifty, maybe even sixty, but there was no need to risk it. Forty-five was plenty fast enough to get what they wanted.

Which were sparks. Lots and lots of sparks.

The four chains tumbled along wildly behind the trailer, igniting an impressive fireworks display in the darkness above the pavement, a myriad of white and orange flecks of fire that rode the gusts swirling crazily behind the truck. Most of the sparks blew into the dry grass at the base of the ridge, and, within minutes, an uneven fire line several hundred yards long had broken out along the base of the ridge. Moments later it erupted into a full-fledged flame front and raced for the crest, blown up the slope by the strong breeze streaming across the meadow from the south.

By then the truck driver and his accomplices were long gone.

3

THE TWELVE-YEAR-OLD BOY awoke with a start, heart pounding. He'd been dreaming about a six-engine, fully loaded hundred-and-ten-car coal drag rumbling down the track in front of him as he sat in the back of his mom's Ford pickup petting their old hound, Jenny. He loved watching those Bridger freight trains power through the narrow valley when he was allowed to ride along into Big Cat on errands with his mom.

At the beginning of his dream, he and Jenny had been watching from a safe distance away as the long train cruised down the single-track main line that cut through town. Then, suddenly, he was standing in the middle of the shiny steel rails and the lead locomotive was bearing down on him, horn deafeningly loud, headlight blindingly bright. But for some inexplicable reason he couldn't move, he couldn't jump out of the way. It was like he was wearing cement sneakers.

David breathed a heavy sigh of relief when he realized where he was—safe and sound in his bed at home. He was still coming out of the nightmare, still experiencing that spine-tingling chill, but now he knew where he was. Now he knew that those awful images his mind had conjured up weren't real.

He leaned over and glanced down at his younger brother, Billy, who was asleep in the lower bunk. The little punk. He was just nine years old, but he snored like a fat old man in a rocking chair. Like their grandfather did when he came to visit from up north in Whitefish. He knew why Billy snored so loudly. He needed his tonsils taken out. He also knew that their mom didn't have the money for the operation, so it wasn't really Billy's fault. Still, it was a pain in the ass listening to him every night.

David was about to put his head back down on the pillow, proud of himself for no longer needing to cry to his mother after a nightmare, even after one about his dead dad. Then he noticed a strange orange glow filling the window. He glanced quickly at the clock-radio on the dresser, which was against the far wall of their cramped bedroom. It was five-thirty in the morning, according to the neon-red LCD. His eyes shot back to the window. The orange ball outside was bright and the first thought that rushed through his young mind was that their house was being invaded by aliens.

Then he smelled smoke.

"Oh, *Jeez!*" David jumped down from the top bunk, shook his little brother wildly by the shoulder, then darted out into the hall. *"Ma, Ma, wake up!"* he shouted, bursting into his mother's bedroom. *"Fire, fire!"*

Billy staggered groggily into the room a moment later, still rubbing sleep from his small eyes.

Their mother was already out of bed, struggling into her dusty jeans. "Go open that gate at the end of the paddock!" she yelled, searching frantically for her boots. "Open it up and make sure it'll *stay* open. Tie it off if you can find some rope. Wait for me there. I'll get to you as soon as I can. If the fire gets too close, and I'm not there yet, run for town. Don't wait for me, boys. Run for Big Cat and go right to Mrs. Spencer's place."

"But, Ma!"

"Go, David, and take care of your brother. Don't let Billy out of your sight!"

"But, Ma, I—"

"Go on!" she shouted. *"Get!"*

The two boys raced back into the hall, then tore down the steps to the first floor and out the front door onto the house's narrow wooden porch. Flames crackling high into the night were churning down the slope, already close enough to the house for the boys to feel the searing heat. Off to the right, the fire had nearly reached the old wooden barn. They could hear the five horses inside their locked stalls going wild. Whinnying and snorting, they were panic stricken.

"We gotta go to the barn!" David shouted. "We gotta get the horses out!"

"But Ma said to open the gate to the paddock," Billy yelled back. "So they can run into the woods."

"There won't be no horses left to run into the woods if we don't get them outta the barn first. If we don't get them outta their stalls."

"But, David, Ma's gonna be—"

"Come on!" David grabbed his little brother's arm and pulled him down the porch steps. Then they raced along the familiar path to the barn with Jenny loping behind them, tongue out. It seemed strange for it to be lit up at night, but the rippling glow made it easier on their bare feet. They could see the cones, pebbles, and sticks.

Billy reached the barn first—he was fast for a kid only going into fourth grade—and hurled it open.

David was right behind him. He reached for the light switch over Billy's shoulder and flipped it on. The smoke was already so thick inside the barn it was difficult for them to see more than a few feet ahead, even with the string of overhead bulbs turned on. Still, they waded into the haze, hands over their mouths and noses, intent on saving their horses so their mother wouldn't have to.

David reached the first stall ahead of Billy and waved for his brother to come up. "I'm going to the last stall and work back this way. You open this one," he yelled, pointing past the frightened horse, "then the next one up. But after you open this one, don't come back inside!" he yelled above the roar suddenly coming from the far end of the barn as the fire burst into the building through the roof. "Stay outside, little brother, don't come back in the barn. Open the next stall from the outside, then stay right there. I'll get the other three open. When we got 'em all open, we'll run back to the house and get Ma. Then we'll open the gate at the end of the paddock so the horses can get into the woods. Okay?" He grabbed Billy's wrist as the younger boy reached for the stall latch, thinking about how his mother had warned him not to let Billy out of his sight. But they both knew the barn like the backs of their hands; the little guy would be fine. In two minutes they'd be done with this and back to the house. Ma'd be pissed that they'd disobeyed her orders, but she'd be proud of how brave they'd been. "Don't do anything stupid."

They gazed at each other for a few seconds.

"You hear me?" David shouted.

Billy nodded, then shoved David's hand from his wrist, slammed the latch back, raced into the stall and around the wild-eyed mare, threw open the stall's gate to the paddock, and hustled her outside by her halter.

It was the last time they ever saw each other alive.

4

KATRINA MASON WAS fifty-one years old, but she looked ten years younger. Her shoulder-length, light brown hair was still its natural color; her skin had a youthful luster to it, she had a spring in her step; there were no age spots on her hands; and she only had a few faint wrinkles at the corners of her eyes. She was a petite five-two and in excellent shape because she worked out almost every day. Even at her age she could jump rope for twelve minutes straight and jog three miles in under half an hour. It was no surprise to anyone that she'd won the Missoula 10K lady's senior division two of the past three years.

When her father died, Katrina had inherited the family's twenty-thousand-acre ranch, which sprawled across both sides of the Big Hole Valley south of Fort Mason. She'd also inherited nearly five hundred thousand acres of prime timberland, most of it in Montana. Her father was a widower and Katrina had no siblings, so everything was hers. The only requests her father had made in his will were that he be buried on one particularly beautiful spot of the ranch, that Katrina never sell the ranch while she was alive, and that it stay a working ranch. She'd honored all three requests and gone a step better than he'd asked on the last one. She managed the ranch herself—and lived on it.

It was clear in the will that her father hadn't intended to burden her with his requests. She could have hired a professional operator to manage the ranch if she'd wanted, to manage the thousands of cattle, sheep, and horses as well as the people who worked the spread on a day-to-day basis. But she hadn't. She'd flown back from New York City the day after his sudden heart attack, moved into the sprawling main house, and taken charge, even before the will was read.

Katrina usually worked at least twelve to fourteen hours a day six days a week. She was an accomplished horsewoman and sometimes spent all day outside, riding with her ranch hands to distant points of the spread to check fences or round up strays. But most days she worked on the operation's complicated finances from dawn to dusk at her father's old desk. The inheritance tax on the ranch had been brutal, and she'd been forced to take out a large loan to pay off the IRS.

Keeping the books balanced was no easy task because revenues from cattle and sheep sales didn't usually cover operating expenses. Income from selling timber made up the difference most months, and the ranch was worth millions as a development property. Still, meeting expenses was a constant challenge for Katrina. And if she was going to honor her father's last request, developing the property wasn't an option.

"Hello, Mr. Callahan."

Dale Callahan touched the brim of his white Stetson as they stood in front of the ranch's main barn. "Hello, Ms. Mason."

The barn was a three-story wooden structure painted a dull, dark red with white trim. There were five other barns scattered around the twenty thousand acres, but this one was only a few hundred yards from the main house, and it served as the ranch's center of operations. Unfortunately, time and the tough Montana weather had taken its toll on the structure. It needed to be replaced.

"Thanks for coming so early." It was just after six in the morning. "I appreciate it." Katrina gestured through the dim light toward four saddled horses and three ranch hands milling around the far end of the barn, letting them know that this meeting shouldn't take too long. "We're heading out in a few minutes for an all day ride across the ranch."

"No problem," Callahan answered. "I had to be up early anyway. I'm heading over to Billings to look at a new headquarters site, so this worked out fine."

Dale Callahan owned a food service company—Callahan Foods—which operated cafeterias in schools, corporations, hospitals, and assisted-living centers throughout the Northwest. It prepared all the meals and ran the cafeterias on a turnkey basis. The company also had a contract with the federal government to feed firemen while they were on the line fighting forest fires. Callahan Foods was based in Billings and growing fast.

"How are your dogs?" Katrina asked politely.

In his spare time, Callahan bred and raised yellow Labs on his property on the east side of Fort Mason. The sign at the end of his driveway claimed the dogs were champions, but Katrina had never heard of them winning anything at any shows outside the area, certainly not outside the state. Most of them ended up as house pets or hunters, not show dogs.

His expression brightened. "Fine." He loved talking about his dogs. "I've got a couple of pups I think might finally get me to New York. To the Westminster Show at Madison Square Garden, you know."

"That's great."

"You should think about buying one. You could use a dog out here."

Katrina had no use for a yellow Lab. She didn't hunt birds and yellow Labs weren't much for herding cattle or sheep. "Maybe I will, Dale. I'll let you know, okay?"

"Sure you will." Callahan glanced around. "Well, you weren't real clear on what you wanted to talk about last night when you rang, Ms. Mason."

"Please call me Katrina."

"If you'll call me Dale."

"Okay." Katrina nodded. "Look, I want to talk about Callahan Foods."

Callahan's posture stiffened. "What about it?"

"I hear it's doing well, *very* well."

"We make a few bucks," he said modestly. "We keep our heads above water."

"I hear you do a lot better than that, Dale."

He smiled evenly. "You know how people like to—"

"I want to buy a piece of the company," she spoke up. "Our family's always supported Montana businesses." She watched him shift self-consciously from foot to foot. "What do you think?"

"Well," he said, chuckling nervously. "That's a nice offer, Katrina, but I'm not sure I need a partner right now."

Katrina signaled to the ranch hands that she wouldn't be much longer. "I've heard a lot of good things about Callahan Foods, but I also heard you're a little short on working capital." She was taking a chance. She didn't really know if he needed cash, but it was what George Drake had told her to say. "Which happens sometimes when a company grows as fast as yours has." These were more of Drake's suggested lines. "You know, Dale, you might lose some chances to grow if you don't take outside money. You've got to strike while the iron's hot."

Callahan leaned down and plucked a long blade of grass. "What's that supposed to mean?"

"Banks get nervous." Katrina had a good relationship with the president of Callahan Foods' main bank, but she wasn't sure if Callahan knew that. "Sometimes bankers don't like it when companies grow fast, and they won't lend you the money you need right when you need it the most. I know it sounds crazy, but it's true. My father always used to warn me about that."

Callahan slipped one end of the blade in his mouth and chewed on it. "There's lots of banks," he mumbled.

Okay, so he knew about her connection. There wasn't any mistaking how his demeanor had changed. She could see it in his expression, hear it in his voice. "I'm sure we could work out something fair, Dale. I just want a little stake. You'd keep control of the company, you'd keep running it. I promise I won't interfere. Heck, I've got more than enough to do around here to keep me busy." She shrugged. "That sounds like a pretty good deal to me."

"How much were you thinking about investing?"

"A million, maybe two."

He turned his head and spat out the blade of grass. "I thought you had to take out a big loan when your dad died," he said. "To pay off the IRS."

"I did," she admitted, "and it was a *bitch*."

Callahan leaned back and his eyes widened a little, as if he was surprised at her language.

"But I've taken care of the situation, and it's all good now." She just hoped Callahan didn't know the president of the bank that was lending money to her. Then he might know as much about her as she knew about him.

"Uh-huh." He checked his watch. "Oh, Lord," he exclaimed loudly, as if he was surprised at what time it was. "I gotta go. I'll get back to you on this, okay? I really appreciate it, Katrina." He shook her hand, then jogged to his Cadillac.

After Callahan had roared off in a cloud of dust, George Drake stepped out of the barn and moved behind Katrina. "Well," he muttered, rubbing her shoulders, "what did old Dale have to say?"

She turned and put her arms around Drake's neck. "It wasn't what he said, George, it was what he didn't say." She kissed him on the cheek, then pulled back. "Look, I know you and Dale have had problems in the past."

Drake stared off in the direction Callahan had driven off. "Yeah, so?"

"Well, I was thinking he might be able to help you with your situation, with the problems at the railroad."

"How?"

"He's done pretty well for himself over the past few years. A lot of people respect him around here. If he came in on your side, he might be able to sway public—"

"Dale Callahan will never help me," Drake interrupted gruffly. "Besides, I don't want his help. The hell with him."

Men, Katrina thought to herself. They couldn't get past grudges. "Why don't you reach out to him, George? Ask him to lunch or something and try to bury the hatchet. I know you two have had problems in business in the past, but after all, that's what it is. Business. If there was some kind of incentive for him, maybe you could convince him to help you. He might be able to get the town back behind the Bridger Railroad."

Drake's expression darkened. "I can assure you that will never happen, not as long as I own the Bridger. And I intend to own it for a long time."

"Fine." George Drake was one stubborn man. Of course, maybe she didn't know the extent of the issues between Drake and him, either. "Any word from Bozeman yet?"

Drake shook his head. "No, but we'll be fine," he said confidently. "Even if we lose the case, the jury won't give those bloodsuckers Hunter Lee is representing very much."

"I heard Mr. Lee was impressive."

Drake clenched his jaw. "Yeah, I'd still like to know how those families hooked up with him."

Katrina gazed at the Bitterroot Mountains in the distance. "So would I," she said in a low voice so Drake couldn't hear her. "So would I."

5

THE ENVELOPE HUNTER had been served with as he was coming out of court yesterday lay on the hotel room desk. It didn't look like any big deal, it didn't look like something that was going to change his life forever. Inside was a single piece of folded paper, and there wasn't much printed on it. But Hunter had learned long ago that the most effective punches were compact ones. Long, looping hooks rarely connected with much effectiveness. They looked impressive, but they didn't usually do any real damage. It was those stiff, lightning-quick jabs straight to the chin that caused the knees to buckle and the eyes to roll back.

There were only a few words on the paper, but every one of them packed a power punch. Inside the envelope was official notice that Anne, Hunter's wife of eleven years, had filed for divorce in Connecticut.

The morning sun filtered into the hotel room through a narrow slit between the heavy, floral-pattern curtains. Hunter had pulled them together across the wide window last night while he was watching a late movie, while he was desperately trying to fall asleep. While he was trying to do anything but think about where Anne was, what she was doing, and who she was doing it with. He usually slept six or seven hours a night, but last night he'd managed only an hour or two. He'd tossed and turned, unable to stop thinking about disloyalty and dishonor, and how he'd never cheated on her once in eleven years.

It wasn't just what was printed on the paper that hurt so badly. What hurt almost as much as the words was the way she'd delivered them. How she'd served him as he was coming out of court, right after he'd rested an important and emotionally draining case. As he was transforming back into a civilian twenty-five hundred miles from home, twenty-five hundred miles from his den in their Connecticut house, which Anne had always referred to as his cave—an accurate description because it was where he went to escape, to be completely alone in an environment he loved. Dark wood, comfortable furniture, soft light, and pictures of good times, it was the place he retreated to for a few hours with a smooth bottle of scotch after destroying a man's career the way he had Carl Bach's yesterday. But he couldn't do that out here in Montana. At least, not in this cold, impersonal hotel room. So he still hadn't made his peace with what had happened to Bach, even though the man had admitted his guilt under oath.

Anne had known exactly what she was doing by serving him out here, by serving him as he was coming out of the courtroom. She'd known he was emotionally drained and vulnerable. She'd done it to hurt him as much as possible.

Well, her tactic had been pretty damn effective, he was forced to admit, but she was going to get hers. He hadn't been completely taken by surprise.

And at least he wasn't being stupid about it, he wasn't going into denial. He'd already spoken to one of the best divorce attorneys in Connecticut.

Hunter swung his feet slowly to the floor. He'd never done anything to Anne except give her what she wanted. Neither of them had come from money, but he'd worked his fingers to the bone to make a good life for her. Which had also included giving her that spot in society she'd always craved, one he'd never cared about. He'd given it all to her with no complaints, and now she was giving him his marching orders. Apparently she wanted to spend all that money he'd made with some-one else.

He moved in front of a full-length mirror hanging on the closet door and stood there for a few moments in his boxers, staring. Taking stock of the man staring back.

He was thirty-eight, six feet three inches tall, with the dark, wavy hair of his Italian mother, God rest her soul. Dark hair, which had only recently started to shimmer with a few silver flecks. He was tall and broad-shouldered, like his Scottish father. A little chicken-legged like him, too. Fortunately, he hadn't inherited the sloppy paunch his dad had grown by his late thirties. To fight that ugly gene, Hunter ate healthy at every meal and worked out at least two days a week, most weeks three. He patted his stomach. No six-pack abs, but no spare tire, either. He still had a thirty-five-inch waist, which was darn good for a man his age and height.

His gaze fell slowly to the carpet. But not good enough for Anne.

It wasn't like he hadn't had his opportunities, his chances for affairs. On the plane to Bozeman this past weekend a pretty blond flight attendant had flirted with him every time she passed his aisle seat. She'd refilled his wine glass without his having to ask, and touched him on the forearm and shoulder suggestively while they made small talk. As he was passing the cockpit door on his way off the plane, she'd slipped him her number, which was scribbled on the back of a tanning salon card. Beneath the number the card read: Call me any time you're out here. Tina. He'd tossed the card in a trash can on his way out of the airport, but he still remembered the number. It would take a year to forget it because he had an amazing memory. Outside a courtroom, that memory wasn't always an asset.

The point: He'd thrown the number away, as he had all the others. Apparently Anne had kept a few, maybe more than a few.

"Don't give away your heart next time," he muttered, sitting down on the end of the bed, then lying back. "No matter what."

He grabbed a pillow and held it to his chest as he stared up at the ceiling. Anne was probably sipping a hot cup of her favorite Colombian blend right now as she sat curled up in her robe in a chair on the wide back deck of their three-story, gray stone house back east. As she leafed through thick catalogues full of expensive clothes before hopping into her Mercedes and heading out for a morning of shopping or to the club for tennis and a swim. Like she did almost every day. They had no children so she had no responsibilities. She could go anywhere she wanted any time she wanted. He pictured her smiling to herself over the rim of that steaming cup of coffee, thinking about the alimony payment her lawyer was going to demand.

Hunter rubbed the overnight stubble on his strong chin. More likely, now that he thought about it, she was lying in bed in a Manhattan hotel room beside that man. That *damn* man. He almost certainly wasn't the only man she'd ever had sex with behind Hunter's back. He was just the only one Hunter knew about.

How many affairs had Anne hidden from him over the years? Hunter wondered. How many other men were strutting around Connecticut and

New York chuckling at their no-strings-attached good fortune? Anne was attractive. At forty-two, she still corralled those hungry, sidelong glances from college lifeguards at the club as she lay out by the pool in her string bikini—a bathing suit officially banned by club rules. Of course, no one told her she couldn't wear it. The men wanted her to wear it, and the women were too afraid she'd come after their husbands if they said something. Anne was vindictive as hell and everyone knew it. Hunter only wished he'd figured that out before they'd tied the knot.

She was a passionate, creative lover who'd try anything once. Who'd wanted him to try some things—including drugs—but he hadn't. It occurred to Hunter as he stared at the ceiling that there'd been more than a few times Anne hadn't explained her whereabouts during the day. Not very well, anyway. But he'd always trusted her, he'd never pushed when she ignored his questions or laughed them off. Which was just plain stupid, he realized. He was a litigator, for Christ sake. He was a man who ought to know better than to accept flimsy excuses from anyone, even his wife. He had a front-row seat for life's deceits and deceptions every day, he constantly saw how awful people could be to each other. Even husbands and wives, *especially* husbands and wives. He should have known better, shouldn't have lived in denial for so long. Well, at least he'd taken that one positive step. He couldn't wait to see the look on her face when she saw what he had waiting for her.

He hadn't called her yesterday after she'd served him, he hadn't wanted to give her the satisfaction of seeing his name pop up on her cell phone screen, then ignore him. At least he'd won that battle. Well, there'd be another one. A much bigger one he'd win, too. He took a deep breath. He just needed to have patience.

He shut his eyes again. Could he ever take her back? If she admitted that this divorce thing was stupid and that, of course, she still loved him? That it had all been a desperate cry for attention? Could he ever swallow his pride and bury the pain? At least, hide it? He tossed the pillow he'd been grasping at the TV sitting inside the armoire across the room. How could you love and hate the same person so much at the same time?

A soft knock on the door distracted him from his torment.

Hunter rose to a sitting position on the bed and stared across the room. He wasn't expecting anyone. He checked the clock on the nightstand. It wasn't even seven o'clock yet. Maybe the hotel was thinly staffed and the maids had to start their rounds early. He'd forgotten to hang the "Do Not Disturb" sign on the knob last night.

He slipped into the shirt hanging over the desk chair, then padded to the door and peered through the peephole. When he saw who was outside, he straightened up slowly then reached for the knob several times, pulling his fingertips away just before they made contact each time. Nothing good could come of opening the door, so why was he even considering it?

The knock came again, a hesitant rat-tat-tat. As if the person on the other side of the door wasn't sure anything good could come of this, either.

Finally, Hunter pulled the latch-lock back and opened the door. "Hello."

Carl Bach stood in the hallway. He was unshaven and looked as if he hadn't gotten much sleep last night, either. And, if Hunter's memory was serving him correctly, Bach was wearing the same clothes he'd been wearing in court. But as crisp and corporate as he'd looked yesterday, he was awash in wrinkles this morning.

"What do you want?"

"I'm sorry to bother you so early like this, Mr. Lee."

"I saw who knocked. I opened the door."

"May I come in?"

Hunter shook his head. "Let's talk here."

"Okay."

"How did you find out what room I was in?"

Bach's heavy eyes rose slowly to meet Hunter's. The bags beneath them looked like purple half-moons. "Welcome to Montana, Mr. Lee."

Hunter thought about asking again, but it seemed obvious that Bach wasn't going to reveal his source. Not that it mattered much. Most likely, Hunter would be out of Bozeman by tonight. Maybe not headed back to New York, but definitely out of Bozeman. "What do you want?" he asked. He'd put this man in a bad jam yesterday, but being a litigator was his job, and the people who'd been killed and blinded by Bach's negligence deserved justice. He had to keep reminding himself of that. *What do you want?*

"How'd you get a copy of that memo?" Bach demanded. "The one you shoved at me on the stand yesterday. The one I'd sent to the head of track maintenance. The one that proved we'd changed the maintenance classification on that four-mile stretch west of Fort Mason from siding to main line. Who gave it to you, huh, *who*?"

Hunter raised an eyebrow. Bach was out of line. His tone of voice was completely acceptable. "Welcome to Montana."

Bach stared at Hunter intently for a few moments, then his expression relaxed and he nodded contritely. "I deserved that one, didn't I?"

"I don't know who gave the memo to me," Hunter admitted, checking for a gun beneath Bach's sports jacket—a handle protruding from his belt, or hanging from a shoulder holster and making an impression in his suit coat. It seemed like everyone in the state was armed. Hunter had been told by several people, proudly, that the only places civilians couldn't carry loaded weapons in Montana were courts, banks, and bars. So maybe Bach was looking for revenge, trying to find out who'd ratted him out so he could get even. "It showed up in my office in New York City three months ago. It came by regular mail, but there wasn't any return address." In fact, Hunter had been trying to find out the identity of his anonymous benefactor since the day he'd opened that mysterious letter, since the day he'd realized he held the key to the case in his hands. Since he'd understood that he really didn't have to do much more work as long as he could prove the document was authentic. He'd proven that quickly, but had no luck finding out who'd sent it. "By the way, do you remember that woman who walked into court yesterday?" Hunter asked.

"How could I forget?"

If Bach was about to go postal, Hunter wanted to limit the damage if possible. "The only thing I asked her to do was get a sample of your signature so I could match it to the one on the bottom of the memo. So I could make sure you were the one who sent that document to the head of Bridger's track maintenance. Whatever else she did, she did on her own." Hunter hesitated. "Because she wanted to."

Bach gazed up at Hunter for several moments without speaking. "I may not be as smart as you, Mr. Lee," he finally said. "I doubt many people are. But I'm not stupid, either. Don't insult my intelligence like that."

"I—"

"You could have gotten a match on my signature from any one of the hundreds of documents you requested during the discovery process. You sent that woman to see me that night in the bar because you wanted something else over me. Don't lie to me. At least have the courtesy to tell me the truth."

"Look, I can't—"

"My wife left me yesterday," Bach interrupted again, his voice cracking. "Ida and I have been married for thirty-two years."

"I'm sorry," said Hunter, his voice subdued, the irony of the situation not lost on him. One wife leaving her husband because he hadn't been good enough, the other one leaving because her husband hadn't been bad enough. "I tried not to put you in that spot. I gave you a choice."

"My wife isn't stupid, either, Mr. Lee. She figured out what was going on right away."

Hunter had been worried about that, about Bach ultimately losing on both counts.

"Then George Drake calls me last night," Bach continued. "As I'm sitting at a bar near the courthouse staring at the bottom of a scotch glass. He's the owner of the Bridger Railroad."

"I know who he is."

"I was sitting on the same damn stool I was sitting on when you had that girl come up to me and make me feel like a million bucks. That night I did a bad thing."

"We're all human." For some reason Hunter felt sympathy for this man. He kept telling himself that people would still be alive if Bach had done his job, but it was hard to hate him, because it seemed as if he was about to crumble. Unless you were an iceberg, it was tough to watch anyone fall apart in front of you. Even a man like Carl Bach. "Don't beat yourself up for it."

"Drake fired me last night," Bach went on, ignoring Hunter. "He's making me the fall guy. He's going to tell the world this morning that he didn't know a damn thing about bad rails or falsifying documents. He's going to tell everyone that I did it all on my own because I was worried about some stupid stock options he gave me when he hired me away from the Union Pacific a few years ago. He's telling everyone I was worried that my options were going to be worthless if the Bridger Railroad lost the case, so I covered up the truth." Bach was glassy-eyed. "But it's a lie. He knew everything, he was behind it all."

Hunter nodded grimly. "I'm sure he was." George Drake had a reputation as a snake in business, and an even worse one as a human being. Hunter had checked Drake out with the investigation firm Warfield & Stone always used, a no-nonsense team of ex-FBI guys down in Washington, D.C. who could uncover anything about anyone. If you'd snuck a cigarette in your high school bathroom, they'd find out. "George Drake is not a good person."

"You think I don't know that?"

"Well, I—"

"Look, the day after the accident last year he told me, no he *ordered* me to do everything." Tears were streaming down Bach's cheeks. "He ordered me to change the records so it looked like that four-mile stretch of track west of Fort Mason had always been classified as a main line. He said if I didn't, he'd fire me. I needed my job, Mr. Lee. I've got kids in college." The ex-COO buried his face in his hands. "I feel so bad for the people who died, for the kids who got blinded. I really do."

Hunter wanted to reach out and comfort Bach, but for some reason he couldn't. "I'm sure you do, Carl." Using Bach's first name was the best he could do right now. "I wish I could help."

"No one can," Bach whispered. "I can't bring those people back from the dead, I can't give those kids their eyesight back." He lowered his shaking hands from his face. "I don't blame you, Mr. Lee. It was your job, and you did a good job. Those people deserve whatever they get today."

Hunter didn't answer. He'd never been good at accepting compliments.

Bach shook his head and his gaze dropped to the carpet. "I got so drunk last night I called that girl. The one who showed up in court yesterday, the one I ruined my marriage with. Can you believe I did that?"

People got desperate when they got lonely, Hunter knew. That was what made people human. He'd seen it so many times. Hell, one of the first things he'd thought about after being served—after his mind cleared enough that he could think about anything but killing Anne—was calling Tina, that flight attendant. He almost had called her twice last night as he lay on the bed, but somehow he'd kept his fingers off the phone. Thank God, too. If he'd called her, he would have been no better than Anne. And if Anne's attorney used an investigation firm half as good as the one Warfield & Stone used, he'd be looking at a huge monthly alimony payment.

"Yes, I can believe it."

"Do you know what she said when I called her?" Bach whispered.

Hunter pursed his lips. This wouldn't be pretty.

"She told me I oughta be ashamed of myself. She told me my wife was a saint for sticking with me because I was nothing but a washed-up middle-aged loser who didn't give a damn about anybody but myself. Who didn't care about killing people or blinding children." Bach managed a caustic laugh through his tears. "Then she told me I didn't know what I was doing in bed. She said I was the worst partner she'd ever had."

Some women really knew how to get inside a guy's head. Hunter started to say something, then stopped. There wasn't anything to say.

"Know what the worst part about it is?" A muffled sob escaped Bach's lips. "She's right on both counts."

Hunter grimaced. It was almost too much to watch a meltdown like this one outside a courtroom.

Bach tried to wipe the tears away with the cuff of his shirt, but they were coming too fast now. His cheeks were soaked again in seconds. "You really don't know who sent you that memo?" he asked.

Hunter cleared his throat, still unnerved by what was happening in front of him. "No, I really don't." He could tell Bach didn't believe him, but it was the truth.

"Would you have called that woman to the stand?" Bach asked. "Would you have had her tell my wife in court that we had sex? Is it really in you to do that?"

There was no good way to answer that question. "We'll never know, Carl. I wouldn't have wanted to, I can tell you that."

Bach stared up at Hunter for several moments, then trudged down the hallway. "Oh, Mr. Lee?" he called, turning back around after a few steps.

Hunter had been thinking about Anne, wondering how she could possibly have done what she had to a man who'd loved her so much. "Yes?"

Bach reached beneath his jacket to the small of his back, smoothly produced a small black pistol, and aimed it at Hunter's chest.

Hunter gazed at the end of the barrel, struck instantly by the fact that the gun wasn't shaking and that Bach had stopped crying, aware that Bach must have come to a momentous decision in the last few seconds. Which didn't bode well for either one of them. Hunter was struck by all that even before terror rushed through his body like it never had. "Carl," he pleaded softly, trying not to show fear. "Don't do this."

Bach stared at Hunter for what seemed like an eternity. The way he'd stared off into the distance yesterday in court when he'd been faced with his awful choice. Finally, he smiled sadly, lifted the pistol, pressed the end of the barrel firmly to his right temple.

And fired.

6

THIS WAS THE DC-3's fourth pass over the Big Cat Fire, as the blaze had already been tagged by the Montana Fire Jumpers even though it was only a few hours old and still three and a half miles south of the remote town.

It was the fourth pass and Paul Brule was getting impatient. "Come on, Booker!" he shouted over the roar of propellers spinning outside the open jump door. "Make the call!"

Ken Booker flashed a pissed-off look at the son of a senator with the blond, movie-star looks who seemed like he always had something to prove. Or maybe there was some truth to the gossip going around Fort Mason. Maybe Paul Brule really had a death wish.

"Come on, Paul!" Booker shouted back. "Gimme a break!"

Paul flipped down the wire mesh face mask of his helmet. "If you don't give the order, Booker, I'll jump anyway."

"Oh, you gonna fight the fire by yourself?"

"You're damn right I will!" Paul yelled, making a move for the door.

Booker blocked his way. "Easy, there, Paul." He stole a glance at the other nine Jumpers in the back of the plane—seven men and two women—and saw fear in their eyes. With the wind as strong and un-predictable as it was today, they knew how dangerous this mission could be.

Which was the thing about Paul. He understood the danger, too, even better than the others did. He'd seen firsthand how out of control it could get down there on the ground, and what happened when it did, but it didn't scare him at all. He never seemed scared of anything. Maybe he really wasn't. Maybe he was looking for fear, maybe that was what got him off. "One more pass," Booker pleaded. "Please, Paul!"

Four minutes later Paul and the other nine Fire Jumpers were out of the plane and falling toward earth. Toward hell on earth.

7

FOUR MEN SAT in front of a wide, flatscreen television. It was secured to the living room wall of a cabin built on a bluff overlooking the Lassiter River with the town of Fort Mason barely visible in the distance. They sipped fine whiskey as they watched a local reporter tick off the latest developments on the Big Cat Fire. They watched her shake her head in disbelief at the unusually high number of major forest fires plaguing the Northwest this hot summer. Particularly Montana, California, and Colorado. The men were sipping fine whiskey while they watched—though it was just seven-thirty in the morning—because they were celebrating. They didn't care what time it was. The Big Cat Fire was turning into a megablaze before their eyes. They hadn't counted on causing so much damage so fast.

One of the men leaned back in his chair and took a long swig from his glass when the broadcast broke for commercial. He was the driver, the man who'd created all those sparks on the road hugging the base of the remote ridge. "It's already burned six hundred acres and the sun's barely off the horizon. Wait till it really gets hot."

The guy who'd been on the IC with the driver leaned back in his chair, too, grinning. "They're gonna have to call in five hundred people to fight this thing."

"More like a thousand," murmured the man in charge, the man with the most to gain in all of this. "It sounds like there's a flame front heading east toward Wyoming now, too." He pointed at the TV. "Toward Yellowstone Park. The Forest Service can't let the fire get to Yellowstone. That would be a disaster, too much in lost admission fees. Worse than that, too much bad publicity back in Washington." He made the sign of a cross on his chest, even though he wasn't religious. "They've gotta keep it out of Big Cat *and* Wyoming. They have to fight it on two fronts now. Hell, they might have to bring in fifteen hundred people."

"Yeah, and it'll—"

"Shut up," the driver snapped as the commercial faded. "Here we go."

The four men listened intently as the young reporter confirmed that a flame front had broken off from the main blaze's right flank and was heading east toward Yellowstone. Then came shocking news. There was a casualty. A nine-year-old boy had burned to death in a barn trying to save his horses.

The man in charge glanced out the big bay window to his left, toward Fort Mason. "Casualties of war," he murmured, "casualties of war."

The driver shut his eyes tightly. A nine-year-old boy. He'd never thought it would come to this.

8

NEITHER BOOKER NOR Paul had spotted an area of open ground big enough for the team to land on near the new flame front—the one that had broken off and was headed toward Yellowstone. So the team was forced to leap from the DC-3 over a thickly forested area. Which wasn't unusual. The primary reason for the Fire Jumpers' existence was so the Forest Service—the federal agency responsible for fighting the country's forest fires—could quickly deploy assets into remote areas. In Montana, and a lot of the Northwest, those areas were often covered by dense woods.

To protect themselves when they slammed into the upper branches of towering ponderosa pines and Douglas firs, Fire Jumpers wore helmets and jump jackets—Kevlar-padded, full-body overalls with high, stiff collars. Even with all the armor, crashing into an eighty-foot pine tree could still hurt like hell. In some instances, it could even be fatal.

The parachutes they used didn't help much when it came to avoiding trees. They were big and bulky and provided little maneuverability after deployment, unlike their smaller, easy-to-steer cousins common at air shows and Super Bowl halftimes. But the ice cream cones—as the big parachutes were nicknamed—were durable. They could easily carry the firefighter and his or her equipment safely to the ground.

Despite the tough landings, history proved that the "chute" phase of an operation was much less risky than what Jumpers faced after they landed. Since their inception in 1947, the Montana Fire Jumpers had lost only two people during the trip from the plane to the ground. They'd lost twenty-nine on the ground fighting fires.

As he'd hurled himself from the plane, Paul had spotted a pinpoint of open land, a golf-green-sized clearing east and up the slope of target center. He knew instinctively as soon as he saw it that he might just be able to reach it by waiting to yank his rip cord until close to the point of no return—that critical moment when the chute no longer had time to deploy before he slammed into the trees. That he might be able to avoid a "let-down," as the clumsy rope descents from trees were called by the Fire Jumpers.

By streamlining his body as he dove—holding his arms tight to his sides and keeping his feet together—Paul could steer himself through the air. He didn't just drop straight down, even with the jump jacket and all the equipment strapped to him. But once he pulled the rip cord, he'd lose most of his maneuverability—and the rush. And slicing through the sky at 140 miles an hour was one killer rush, though not like the one he got at two hundred miles an hour when he was jumping in his sleek competition suit.

He started ticking off the seconds, going past the pull-thousand count his training would have him rip on. The ground felt as if it was rushing up at him as he hurtled toward the tiny clearing. It was a strange illusion he experienced every time he plummeted toward the ground after diving from a perfectly good airplane. He experienced it so strongly sometimes that he almost believed he was stationary in the air and that beautiful, mostly blue ball ironically called earth was rising up to snag him and bring him home. Either way, he was running out of time, racing toward the point of no return and the moment when it wouldn't matter if he ripped the cord or not.

The senior guys back at base wouldn't approve of what he was doing. Waiting so long to pull the cord was strictly against procedure, and they'd probably take him off the duty list for a week. Maybe dock his pay, even strip him of his team leader rank. Mutter about that death wish behind his back, too. Well, screw them. If he could reach that clearing, he could help the other Jumpers on his team that much faster. Then quickly organize them and get them fighting the fire that was torching his beloved Montana.

"Wait!" he yelled as he dove, his mouth and nose running like faucets. "Longer, just a little *longer!*" he shouted, bracing himself for what would feel like reentry on the space shuttle and a ride on the biggest, baddest bull at the rodeo, combined. That moment when the chute opened and filled with air. *"Now!"*

He leveled out, spread his arms and legs so he was in a belly-flop position—to slow down as much as possible—then ripped.

When he'd recovered from tossing around beneath the chute like a rowboat in a hurricane, he was still able to steer himself a little during the last few hundred feet to the ground. Enough to barely avoid snagging his boots in the treetops towering above one side of the clearing as he blew past them.

A couple of rolls on the hard ground—filled with crazy, blurry images of sky, trees, grass, and rocks—and he was on his feet, straining against the ropes as the big white canopy flapped in front of him. He'd probably have to rescue that rookie female Jumper from up in a tree, he figured as he fought for control of the chute. It wasn't unusual for rookies to suffer temporary paralysis the first time they found themselves dangling high above the ground.

When the chute was under control, Paul yanked off his helmet. For a split second he saw another ice cream cone settling into the treetops a few hundred yards down the slope. Then it was gone and there were no signs of the others. The rest of his team was probably strung out between here and that chute he'd just caught sight of. All of them were probably struggling down from trees as fast as they could because there was no way any of them could have made it to this tiny clearing. He hoped no one was hurt.

"Nice jump."

Paul whirled around. Struggling to her feet a car length away was Mandy Winslow, the rookie Jumper. She'd been fourth off the plane. He hadn't heard her land because his head was still plugged into his birdcage of a helmet. "Uh, you, too, Jumper Winslow."

"Thanks." Mandy's auburn hair tumbled to her shoulders as she lifted off her helmet. "You're fast. I was trying to catch up. Almost got you, but not quite."

It was their first jump together, the first time she'd been assigned to Paul's team, the first time he'd ever had any real interaction with her. Now that they were up close and personal, he saw she had a pretty face. Very pretty, he realized, stealing a second glance. He looked away when he realized she was searching his eyes right back, cursing himself for wasting time. Montana was on fire.

He unhitched the emergency chute from his chest and dropped it on top of the main, trying to figure out how Mandy had made it to the clearing. She'd only been a few seconds behind him out the jump door, but those few seconds were an eternity when it came to jumping from a plane. She would have had to fall faster than him to make it here. Up to now, he'd been pretty sure he was the fastest around.

He watched her roll up her chute as he peeled off his bulky jump overalls. Maybe she'd waited even longer than he had to rip the cord. Which would have taken a lot of guts, because he'd shaved it damn close to the point of no return himself. She'd have to have some heavy training to pull off a stunt like that, maybe even military. He dropped his jump jacket on the growing pile of equipment, refreshed now that he was down to his nylon pants and cotton shirt, then stole another glance at her. Maybe *she* had a death wish.

Or maybe she simply didn't know what she was doing. That was what really bothered Paul, because that could put other lives in danger, not just hers.

"Let's go," he ordered loudly when she was out of her jump jacket. "*Now.*"

She nodded at the pile. "Should we bring anything?"

"No, this'll be base. We'll clear in both directions across the ridge from here. Looks like the fire's headed right for us." Paul motioned across the valley toward a thin plume of smoke rising from the face of the opposite ridge. The fire was still small—he couldn't see any flames—and it didn't seem to be moving fast. If the wind didn't pick up much, they ought to be able to corral this part of it quickly. Unfortunately, from what he'd seen up in the DC-3 before jumping, the Forest Service was going to need a major force to put out the megablaze roaring toward Big Cat. "We've gotta round up everybody first. After that, we'll come straight back here. You won't need anything until then."

"Not even my tent?"

She was referring to her fire-retardant tent. When deployed, the tent looked like a tinfoil sleeping bag. The tent kept a Jumper safe from fire up to a temperature of five hundred degrees, then it burned to a crisp. Just like everything else in a megablaze's path.

"You won't need it, Jumper Winslow."

"But in training they told me never to—"

"You won't need it, *Jumper Winslow*," Paul repeated tersely. "Come on."

He turned and headed down the hill, running in the direction he'd seen that parachute settle into the treetops a few moments ago. They eased up as they reached the edge of the clearing and moved into the trees, searching for the other eight team members as they trudged over the dead, brown pine needles that covered every inch of the forest floor. It was like walking on dry sand.

After a few strides, Paul stopped and dug the toe of his boot into the layer of needles. It was six inches deep. He'd never seen it like this before.

Typically, Montana Fire Jumpers didn't drop from the sky to fight megablazes. That didn't make sense. Their limited air force couldn't deliver enough people or hardware to fight flame fronts like the one roaring north toward Big Cat. The Fire Jumpers' mission was to quickly take on smaller fires before they got out of control, like the right flank of the Big Cat Fire heading toward Wyoming and Yellowstone. So they didn't become megablazes; so the Forest Service wasn't forced to send in a large force with heavy equipment; so it didn't have to spend millions to support an army big enough to beat a megablaze. Fire Jumpers were the cavalry of the Forest Service's arsenal. Quick and agile, they were set up to quell a skirmish, but they couldn't do much about a well organized, full-scale frontal assault.

The Jumpers typically put out a blaze by cutting a fire line, which involved clearing a swath of ground in the forest ahead of the flame front. By doing so they took away the fire's fuel source rather than extinguishing the flames with water or chemicals. It was safer, and, many times, it was more effective. But in order for the fire line to be effective, the team leader had to anticipate the direction the fire would burn, then deploy his people far enough ahead of the flames to give them time to clear the line. Fire Jumpers cleared a line by hand with chainsaws and axes, and it was backbreaking work carried out in brutal conditions. But that was a Jumper's life during a fire season. Long hours, terrible conditions, intense physical challenges, little praise, and danger everywhere. Along with more camaraderie and self-satisfaction in a summer than most people experienced in a lifetime.

Of course, the fire could end up going in a direction the team leader hadn't anticipated, couldn't have anticipated without divine intervention, because of sudden wind changes. It became like a roadblock on a highway the bad guys had avoided, and all the work went wasted. Or the wind might strengthen, enabling the fire to jump the line. Or the Jumpers might not have time to finish the line if the winds strengthened quickly.

So many possibilities, so much uncertainty.

But the worst risk, by far, was that Fire Jumpers could go from hunter to prey in an instant. They could suddenly find themselves being chased by an inferno racing toward them at speeds of up to fifty miles an hour and packing temperatures of fifteen hundred degrees. So many things could go wrong, yet the Fire Jumpers' record over the past sixty years was remarkable. They'd lost relatively few people while extinguishing countless small fires that could have turned into megablazes. In the process they'd saved thousands of lives and immense property damage.

The slope turned steep as Hunter and Mandy headed down the ridge. Steep enough that at times they were forced to grab low-hanging branches to keep from falling.

"Wait," Paul said loudly, stopping to scan the forest canopy. He watched the treetops above them sway against a powerful gust, then caught a faint whiff of smoke. "Jesus." It was a warning, like the first time you heard that ping in your car engine. Except that this was an imminent life-or-death warning.

"What's wrong?" Mandy asked, pinning her hair back with bobby pins. "What is it?"

Paul gazed down the ridge, too focused on gathering data to answer. Thanks to the topographical map of the area he'd studied on the plane, he knew there was a wide stream at the bottom of this ridge. But it wasn't in sight yet because they were still too far up on the ridge to see it. He'd hiked this forest many times—the Gallatin National Forest—but, as bad luck would have it, not through this specific area. And, unfortunately, as he'd been scrambling to get his team and their equipment into the DC-3, he couldn't find anyone who knew this particular valley. Not even the vets up at Jumper HQ in Missoula had much on it. He saw from a records check on the base computer that there hadn't been a fire in this area in at least thirty years. Which was a terrible omen, he'd realized grimly as the plane had raced toward the drop zone. It meant that tons and tons of dead wood lay beneath them and in the fire's path. All that dead wood was perfect tinder to create a huge blaze. A recipe for disaster.

Now, standing on the ridge, his worst fears were confirmed. There was fuel everywhere—downed, bone-dry limbs just waiting to burn. There were lots of dead standing pines, too. Trees that had grown too slowly and lost their battle to reach the sun, but hadn't fallen yet, trees that would send the fire shooting up into the forest canopy. Then there was that thick blanket of dead pine needles beneath his feet stretching in every direction as far as he could see. He shook his head. This could get very bad very fast.

"Paul, what's going—"

"The wind's picking up, Jumper Winslow." He didn't have to be so formal—it was up to him now that they were on the line—but it was best. It was best to keep that distance between them, especially since he'd caught more than a professional interest in her searching gaze back at the clearing. "Could be twenty klicks sustained. Gusts to thirty I'd say, given how the trees are blowing over. Looks like it's still coming right at us." He waved to a group of his team members moving toward them through the forest from the left. Six of them were hustling along as fast as they could under the weight of chainsaws, axes, and shovels. "I don't like this. Check out all the dead wood." Paul gestured around. "It's everywhere, and the needles are *so* thick." He kicked up a bucket-sized clump with his boot. "This is trouble, real trouble."

"So it isn't true?"

Paul's husky blue eyes flashed to the colorful specks in hers. "*What* isn't true?"

"That you have a death wish. Why would you care about trouble if you did? In fact, you'd look for it."

He stared at Mandy hard, testing her will. People always had a tough time holding up against his gaze. There was something about the intensity of it, he'd been told many times. Something unsettling, something that made most people look away quickly. Even the older guys at HQ in Missoula couldn't stare back for long. Making a rookie blink ought to be a piece of cake.

But it wasn't.

"Who told you that?" he demanded when she kept staring back at him.

"Nobody." She shrugged. "Everybody."

He narrowed his eyes, intensifying his gaze, still trying to win. As soft as she was to look at, she was tough inside. She didn't give away her sources, either, which was good. But he still wasn't convinced she was that good a skydiver, even if she had made it to that tiny clearing as the fourth Fire Jumper off the DC-3. And he needed to see what happened when things got dicey on the ground, when a megablaze came roaring at her.

"Paul! Hey, Paulie!"

Paul's eyes flashed toward the voice, toward the big man who was leading what had now become a group of seven Fire Jumpers hustling through the woods. They'd just picked up the next-to-last team member. "Hey, Duff!" he yelled back. "Hurry up."

Duff Sparks was an eight-year veteran of the Fire Jumpers. A tall, strapping Montanan with a long red beard, he lived by himself in a small cabin west of Fort Mason, reportedly without running water. He'd never made team leader and the word around the base was he was getting pissed off about it. He had a temper, too. Paul had seen Duff make hamburger of a guy's face with a couple of sharp rights at the Grizzly Saloon in Fort Mason one night for making a crude comment about his girlfriend. The guy had deserved something for what he'd said, but not having his face smashed in so badly he needed two reconstructive surgeries.

"I got seven of us," Duff gasped, bending over to suck in air when he reached Paul. "Including me. We got everything off the equipment chute, too." Duff and the other team members with him were still wearing their jump jackets. It was the most efficient way to transport gear before setting up base, but it was hard to make good time wearing them. "We're missing Mitchell," he reported, "now that I've found you and Winslow."

Duff was using an in-charge tone, Paul noticed, as if he was the team leader. He wanted that promotion badly. "What number was Mitchell off the plane?"

Duff's eyebrows rose. "Um, Jeez. I don't re—"

"He was eight," Paul interrupted, not so subtly making several points. Duff's memory wasn't great, sometimes he didn't think clearly during chaos, and he wasn't very smart. "Nine and ten, raise," Paul ordered, looking over Duff's shoulder.

Two men in the back of the group reached for the sky. They were the last two off the plane.

"Seven raise."

The other female Jumper in the group raised her hand.

"Direction down?"

All three pointed in the same general direction, back over their left shoulders. Down the ridge and to the left, where they'd landed.

Duff should have already asked these questions, he should never have left the area where Mitchell most likely went down. You never left someone alone out here, never. It was more proof of why he'd never be a team leader, more justification for Paul's no vote at the last promotion meeting in May.

"Show them the way back to the clearing, Jumper Winslow," Paul muttered to Mandy. He bent down and with a quick rip pulled back a Velcro strip keeping closed the pocket on the lower right leg of Duff's jump jacket. "When you get to the clearing, Duff," he said loudly, "get started on the fire line." He pulled out a long length of coiled rope from Duff's shin pocket and slung it over his head and one shoulder as he stood up. "In both directions across the ridge as far as you can as fast as you can. Jumper Winslow will show you what I mean," he said, jabbing a thumb in Mandy's direction.

"Hey, I don't need no woman telling me—"

"Just *do it*," Paul snapped, sticking a finger in Duff's face, actually grazing his bearded cheek.

This was no time for pettiness and insecurity, but if Duff wanted a fight, well, that's what he'd get. Right here, right now, right in front of everyone. Paul hesitated a few seconds, giving Duff a chance to throw the first punch. He even stuck his chin out to give Duff a better target, to make the challenge obvious.

But the big man didn't engage. Duff knew how many guys Paul had decked in the past few years, most everyone in these parts knew about Paul's fight record. His one-two combination came at you so fast you couldn't defend yourself. You might block the first punch, but not the second. Paul didn't fight often, and it took a lot to get him to go to violence. But when he finally did, the other guy hit the ground hard and fast.

"Get going, Duff," Paul ordered when the other man backed off a step. "*Now!*"

Dominance restored, Paul took off past the team in the direction the three Jumpers had pointed. If seven, nine, and ten had all landed along the same general line, it was a good bet he'd find Mitch on this bearing, too.

As he ran, Paul tried to look up—he assumed Mitch was trapped up in a tree—but the slope turned too steep for him not to watch every step. So he had to stop and hold on to a branch each time he yelled Mitch's name and scanned the bottom of the canopy. Which was thick in here, making it dim even though the sun was well above the horizon.

It seemed as if there were more standing dead trees the farther down the slope he went which meant more fodder for the fire. This place could explode, literally. He'd seen that happen once before, a few years ago up near Kalispell. A Jumper only a few feet away from him had taken a direct flame burst from the explosion and had his jump suit and skin burned off in a matter of seconds. The poor guy spent three excruciating days in a Bozeman ICU before dying.

"Mitch!" Paul shouted at the top of his lungs, smelling smoke. "Mitch!" The treetops above him were *really* swaying now. Gusts had to be reaching thirty-five, maybe even forty miles an hour at this point. *"Mitch!"*

As he swerved to avoid the base of a large ponderosa, the slope turned even steeper, almost straight down. He fell, unable to keep his balance even with his incredible coordination, tumbling out of control down the slope until he slammed into the trunk of another huge ponderosa twenty feet farther down the ridge. His right side bore the brunt of the impact, but, even as he desperately tried to suck in air, he was glad his head hadn't taken the hit. He might have broken a rib or two, but that was better than being unconscious as the fire raced up the ridge.

"Paul."

He barely heard the feeble voice. It had to be Mitch. He tried to answer but could manage only a groan. "God Almighty," he muttered, tasting blood. Was it from a cut in his mouth or oozing up from his lungs? "Mitch," he hissed, his voice still not very loud. There was no way the other man could hear him.

"Paul!"

With a huge effort Paul made it to his feet. "Mitch," he gasped again, leaning against the tree he'd just slammed into. "Mitch!" Things were finally coming into focus again. *"Mitch!"*

"Up here, Paul."

Paul staggered around to the other side of the tree. As he looked up, he heard chainsaws roaring to life higher on the ridge. Duff was getting started on the line. At least something was going right.

"*Here!*"

Paul's eyes flashed to the left, and he finally spotted Mitch. The other man was sixty feet up, wedged into the tree, one leg twisted at a frightening angle. "I'm coming!" Paul shouted as loudly as he could, then bent over and spat blood. "Don't move!" He smiled wanly. You had to have a sense of humor out here, even at times like these.

"Funny, Paulie!" Mitch managed to yell back. "Real funny."

Paul lifted the coil of rope from over his head and shoulder gingerly, grimacing as a bolt of pain shot through his chest. With a stiff effort, he tossed the loops over the lowest branch, which was fifteen feet up this massive tree. A few loops dropped back down at him from the other side of the branch, and after snagging them, he lashed one end of the rope around his waist. Then he began walking himself up the trunk by pulling on the other end. He climbed slowly, step by painful step, groaning loudly until he reached the thick branch. He pulled himself up onto it and rested for a few moments before repeating the process using the next branch up, doing it twice more until he was forty feet up and he could climb from branch to branch without using the rope, because the branches this high in the tree were close together. When he'd caught his breath, he coiled the rope around his waist and began climbing again.

"Don't look down," he whispered to himself. Heights didn't bother him—as long as he had a parachute strapped to his back. "I'm coming, pal."

"It hurts, Paul, damn it hurts."

Mitch was only a few feet above him now, and Paul could plainly see that the leg was broken in at least two places. The middle of the thigh and down by the ankle. Mitch couldn't possibly have gotten himself out of this. It was as though he was wrapped inside the tree, and the tree was wrapped back on him.

"I'm coming."

"Holy Christ!" Mitch shouted. "You better move your ass!"

"Hey, I didn't climb up here for my health," Paul snapped. "A little appreciation would work."

"No, no," Mitch gasped, pointing. "Look."

At first, Paul saw nothing but blowing branches. Then there was a violent gust, and suddenly he understood. Through a break in the trees and only for a flash he saw what Mitch was yelling about. Huge, black clouds were billowing from the treetops at the bottom of the valley. The flame front had raced down the opposite slope in no time. Which meant it could be up here in no time, too.

Paul scrambled up the last few feet, trying not to stare at Mitch's leg. He didn't want Mitch to see his reaction and scare the man more, but, God, those fractures were nasty. He reached into his pocket and grabbed a pint of rotgut whiskey he always carried in case of emergency, then unscrewed the black metal top and held the bottle out. "Drink," he ordered. "As much as you can as fast as you can."

Mitch grabbed the bottle and turned it upside down, guzzling a quarter of it. "Jesus!" He pulled the bottle from his mouth and wiped his wet lips with a sleeve. "That's awful." His entire upper body shook involuntarily as the liquid coursed down his throat. "*Really* awful."

Paul grabbed the bottle back and took a healthy swig himself, then restowed it in his pocket. "Ready?" Without waiting for an answer he yanked Mitch's shattered leg from the tree's grasp.

"*Jeeeesus Christ!*" Mitch screamed, grabbing his thigh. "Gimme that bottle again!"

"No time. Get on my back." Paul pulled Mitch's rope from his lower leg pocket, then pivoted on the branch so the other man could crawl on. When he was aboard, Paul lashed Duff's rope—already on his waist—around himself and Mitch at the torso several times, then finished off the crude harness with a tight knot at his chest. "Hold on, pal." The smoke had gotten thick fast, and he could hear a low roar coming from down in the valley. The fire must have already skipped over the stream. It must have exploded into a megablaze. "I don't know if the rope'll hold. You gotta grab my shoulders."

"I don't know if I can," Mitch gasped weakly. "I'm fading, man."

"You can do it! You *will* do it!"

"I can't do this to you. Get out of here, save your own ass. Don't worry about me."

"*Grab my shoulders!*"

"All right," Mitch groaned. "I'll try."

"Don't try! *God damn it do it, Mitch!* Do it for your wife and that pretty little baby girl she just had. Do it for them if you can't do it for yourself. You hear me?"

"Yeah," he gasped. "I hear you."

"You don't and I'll kick your ass when your leg heals."

"Okay, okay."

When they'd made it down to forty feet above the ground, Paul pulled Mitch's rope from around his shoulder and tied it off to the branch. There would be no more climbing down from here. As hard as it had been to climb up, sliding down the rope would be easy and save a lot of time. And time was of the essence.

"Ready?" Paul yelled over his shoulder as he finished the knot. He dropped the coils and breathed easier when the end hit the ground with a coil to spare. "Here we go!" When Paul's boots hit the needles, he collapsed with Mitch on top of him. His shoulders, arms and chest seared with pain, but there was no time to rest. He could hear and smell the fire roaring up the ridge.

"Help us up, Mitch." Paul groaned. "You gotta push with that one good leg."

But there was no response.

Paul shot a quick glance over his shoulder. Mitch's eyes were closed. Paul hoped he was just passed out.

By grabbing the trunk of the huge tree, Paul was able to struggle to his feet with Mitch still roped to his back. He took a deep breath, then crawled and scratched at anything to get traction, shouting at the pain shooting through his chest.

It took several minutes, but he finally made it up the twenty feet he'd tumbled down on his way to slamming into the big ponderosa. The slope wasn't as steep here and they could make time. What he had to worry about now was getting his breath and not getting lost. The smoke had gotten thick, and the only thing he could do was trust his balance and a sixth sense he'd always had in the forest to guide him up the ridge. They might miss the clearing, but at least going up was going away from the fire.

Sweat poured down Paul's face as he stumbled ahead, Mitch's limp, heavy body lurching from side to side on his back. He searched through the gloom for any sign of the clearing, listened for the sound of chainsaws roaring above the wind and fire. Suddenly he thought he saw someone off to the right beckoning to him, just as the top of a tree to his left exploded. *Christ*, the fire was right on his ass.

He ducked between two trees, holding Mitch to his back as best he could, searching for the figure he thought he'd seen. But the haze was too thick.

Then he saw her again. He was sure this time, he told himself, as a tree to his right exploded and the fire's advance scouts danced across the canopy.

As Paul glanced up at the flash and the flames shooting horizontally across the treetops, the toe of his boot hit something hard and he sprawled face-first into the pine needles. Mitch landed on top of him like a ton of bricks, and lightning bolts of pain shot through Paul's chest. He tried to make it to his feet, tried to move, tried just to spit the pine needles from his mouth, but he had nothing left. Not even for Mitch's baby girl.

"Get up!" Mandy shouted, rolling Mitch and Paul on their sides. "Come on, Paul, get up!"

Paul gazed up at her, his head spinning. It was a labor just to breathe.

Mandy whipped a knife from her belt and slashed the rope binding Mitch and Paul together. Then she yanked Paul to his feet, and, together, they half-carried, half-dragged Mitch to the clearing, to what was now a village of small silver tents. They threw Mitch inside an empty one and zipped it up, then Paul rushed Mandy to hers. Finally, he dove for his.

Just as the massive flame front hit the clearing.

9

STRAT LEE PULLED his rusty pickup truck to a squeaky stop on the winding county road's crushed-gravel shoulder and leaned forward, resting his thick forearms on the steering wheel as he gazed through the cracked windshield. The entire face of the steep ridge to his right was seared black all the way to the crest. It looked like the surface of the moon. Worse than that, now that he thought about it. It looked like hell.

He glanced to his left at the lush meadow of clover surrounded on three sides by a pristine pine forest. Above the trees at the far end of the meadow, mountains rose majestically in the distance. A Montana postcard to his left, devastation to his right. He'd found ground zero of the Big Cat Fire. It didn't take much of a detective to figure that out. Figuring out who was responsible was where it got tough—and tricky. Strat could think of at least three people who had a big incentive to see these forests burn, and you didn't want to screw with any of them. Each of them stood to make a great deal of money, and he figured they wouldn't think twice about offing some pissant whistle-blower if they knew he was making trouble for them.

Strat checked the truck's dashboard for his cell phone, rummaging through several open packs of Camel cigarettes, a box of shotgun shells, an unpaid traffic ticket for a blown head and taillight, an old fly-fishing reel, and a road map of southwest Montana. He wanted to see if his brother, Hunter, had called. Hunter was a New York lawyer, the family star, and yesterday he'd rested a big case against the Bridger Railroad over in Bozeman. Strat was anxious to hear if the jury was in. As different as he and Hunter were, they were tight. Screw-with-him-you-screw-with-me tight.

He finally found the phone beneath an empty Styrofoam coffee cup and quickly checked, but there was no word yet. No missed calls or unheard messages registered on the tiny screen.

As Strat climbed out of the truck, he slipped the cell phone into his jeans pocket. He wanted to hear from his younger brother for another reason, too. Hunter hadn't sounded like himself when he'd called from his hotel room in Bozeman last night. The case had gone fine, but Hunter seemed preoccupied by something else, even down about it. And Hunter rarely got too emotional about anything.

Strat had thrown one cast in the water during the call. A nonspecific "Everything okay, Hunt?" near the end of it, but he hadn't gotten a bite. Strat knew better than to try again.

The first thing Strat noticed about the road were the scratches on the blacktop's surface. They weren't deep, but they were wild. All over the place with no pattern to them. As he knelt and ran his fingers across them, he saw that in certain places the grass at the edge of the gravel was chopped off almost to the ground—as if it had been mowed—but it was still its natural late-July brown. In other places it was thigh-high, and, again, still its natural color. In still other places it was almost thigh-high, but it was singed black.

He stood up and moved off the road when he heard a vehicle coming. It was an SUV, a shiny, black Escalade with tinted windows and flashy chrome wheels. It rolled slowly past him, then sped up and roared off.

He stared after it for a few moments, then turned and sprinted for his pickup.

10

EVEN ABOVE THE roar of the fire, Paul could hear someone yelling. He unzipped his tent a few inches and peered out into an almost indescribable scene. A chaotic orange, white, and red world of searing flames, some soaring over two hundred feet high.

For a few moments everything was a blur, then he saw why Mandy was yelling. A huge burning branch had broken off a tree on the perimeter of the clearing and landed beside her tent. The end of the branch was pressing down against the tent and threatened to destroy it. The fire-resistant material was already beginning to smolder.

Paul ripped the zipper of his tent down and scrambled across what seemed like the floor of hell. He felt his face starting to blister right away. With a Herculean effort he lifted the branch a few inches and managed to move it away from her tent, then he raced back to his.

When the roar outside abated, Paul peered out again. The fire was gone. It had blown past them in no time on the wings of forty-mile-an-hour gusts, he saw as he struggled out of his tent and stood. As his eyes adjusted, he saw that the flame front was already approaching the top of the ridge.

He moved out into the desolate landscape, relieved when Mandy unzipped her tent and crawled out, too. Then he shook his head sadly as the realization sank in. This place would never be the same. At least, not in his lifetime.

11

"ALL RISE!" THE bailiff called in a loud voice as the judge appeared at the chamber door and climbed the steps to the bench. "Judge Timmerman presiding."

Hunter rose up behind the plaintiff desk, his mind still on Carl Bach, still on the tragedy he'd witnessed a few hours ago. He couldn't help thinking there was something he could have done. He'd never felt as helpless in his life as when he'd watched the poor son of a bitch put the barrel to his head and pull the trigger. The absolute dejection and desperation in Bach's eyes the instant before the awful explosion would haunt Hunter for the rest of his life.

The judge motioned for everyone to sit down, then he waved for Hunter to approach the bench.

"Yes, Your Honor?" Hunter asked when he reached the judge.

"I want to thank you for being available now, Mr. Lee. I know it's been a tough morning for you. I know what happened to Carl Bach, but I didn't want to keep the jury here any longer than absolutely necessary. They have families. I hope you understand that."

"Of course, sir."

"I didn't want you to think I was being unfair."

"Not at all."

The judge gave Hunter an appreciative smile, then nodded for him to step back. "Has the jury reached a verdict?" he asked when Hunter was behind the plaintiff desk again.

"We have, Your Honor," the forewoman answered in a strong voice, rising from the seat in the jury box closest to the judge.

"What say you?"

"Guilty, Your Honor."

A murmur rumbled around the courtroom, but there weren't any shrieks of surprise. The verdict hadn't been in doubt in anyone's mind since Carl Bach's testimony yesterday afternoon.

"Have you come to agreement on the size of the award?" the judge asked.

"We have, Your Honor."

"What say you?"

Hunter took a quick breath. He was pretty sure one to two million was in the bag, but anything more than that might sound preposterous to people out here.

"We award the plaintiffs," the woman answered, hesitating a moment before announcing the number, *"forty million dollars."*

As the courtroom exploded into chaos, Hunter's eyes shot quickly from the judge's shocked expression, to the opposing attorneys' despair, to his clients' elation. *Forty million dollars.* It was unbelievable.

12

FROM FORT MASON it was a long way across southern Montana to the city of Billings. After leaving Katrina's ranch early this morning, Dale Callahan had gone north up to Missoula where he'd picked up the interstate. From there, he'd driven east past the old mining town of Butte, through Bozeman and Livingston, which were north of Yellowstone Park, and finally on to Billings. It was well over three hundred miles point to point, and, even though Callahan didn't have to make the trip very often, it was getting old. Fortunately, he only had thirty minutes left today.

Callahan was headed to Billings to take another look at a site on the city's south side where he was planning to move Callahan Foods' headquarters and its main plant. The company currently operated out of an old, cramped building on the north side of Billings which had quickly become too small and didn't have good access to the interstate. After looking at the new site, Callahan was headed downtown to meet with members of the city council to squeeze them for some low-interest, tax-exempt financing. On his last trip over here, he'd threatened to move Callahan Foods out of Billings to Fort Mason. A move out of Billings would mean lots of lost jobs and a public-relations nightmare for the local officials. Callahan didn't really intend to move the company, but he wanted those cheap loans so he was going to play the game.

He was supposed to be back in Fort Mason by seven-thirty tonight, so it was going to be a hectic day if he was going to make it home in time. He smiled. He'd make it. He liked that other thing too much to miss it.

He could have flown to Billings and saved a ton of time, but, as much as his friend Big Bill Brule and Big Bill's son, Paul, loved being up in the sky, Callahan hated it. He hadn't minded planes so much as a younger man, but now that he was in his early fifties, he hated them. He'd heard all that stuff about planes' being so much safer than cars a hundred times, but statistics wouldn't help as you were hurtling straight toward the ground at five hundred miles an hour screaming your bloody fool head off. Nah, he'd take a car crash any day. At least there'd be a body to bury.

Typically, Callahan put his Caddy on cruise control and listened to a book on tape as he drove across southern Montana, but today he'd driven in silence. He'd been thinking about his early morning meeting with Katrina, wondering why she suddenly wanted to buy a piece of Callahan Foods. He was suspicious that she knew so much about his need for working capital. Everybody knew Callahan Foods was growing fast, and fast-growing companies usually ate up cash because they needed to build more facilities and buy more inventory, but Katrina seemed to have a clearer picture of the situation than that. It was almost as if she had inside information.

He was watching a herd of pronghorn antelope—speed goats, as they were known in Montana—in a field off to the right when his cell phone rang. He glanced at the screen and saw that it was his chief operating officer, Brian Jones, calling for the third time since he'd left Katrina's ranch. Jones was a damn good executive. So good Callahan only had to be at headquarters over here in Billings once every few weeks, which freed him up to spend most of his time finding new customers. Callahan had taken the other two calls, but he ignored this one. Whatever Jones was calling about could wait.

Almost as soon as the call from Jones ended, the phone rang again. This time Callahan answered right away. It was Butch Roman, and Callahan wanted to talk to Butch. Butch owned and ran a large construction company that was going to build Callahan's new headquarters in Billings.

"Hey, Butch."

"Hi, Dale, how are you?"

"Good."

"You heading over to Billings?"

"Yup. I'm gonna put the screws to some local politicians." Callahan chuckled. "I'm looking forward to it, too."

"I bet you are," Butch agreed. "Listen, when are you planning to break ground on the new plant?"

"Let me get through today, let me make sure I've got the tax-exempt bonds locked up, then I'll tell you. I'll call you on the way home this afternoon."

"Yeah, okay. What about that big new house of yours over there? When are you going to start building—"

"Before we get into that," Callahan interrupted, "let me ask you a question. What do you think of Katrina Mason?"

There was a long silence, then Butch finally answered. "I wouldn't trust her as far as I could throw her."

13

ONTANA'S NICKNAME WAS perfect. Big Sky Country. It seemed as if that pristine, azure blue stretched majestically and mystically above and beyond in every direction forever.

Hunter sat on the open-air back deck of The Depot—Fort Mason's only decent restaurant—admiring that beautiful sky as late afternoon slowly gave way to evening. He'd just finished his third beer, and, since he hadn't eaten anything today, the alcohol was affecting him quickly, already softening the hard edges. As much as he preferred the periphery when he wasn't in court, he liked an ice-cold beer, too. It didn't make emerging from the background any easier for him, didn't usually make him more outgoing, but it gave him a different perspective. One he liked.

The Depot stood atop a rise at the east end of town. From the back deck, Hunter had an unobstructed view of the wide Lassiter River as it snaked away from two distant peaks standing side by side like twin sentinels. As it snaked smoothly toward him through a nearly unbroken sea of trees, then flowed past The Depot and on into town.

Hunter had been to Fort Mason several times in the past year to prepare for the Bridger Railroad case. Each time he visited he was struck by its isolation. It was a man-made island surrounded by that dense sea of trees. The thick woods were ringed by rugged mountains rising up five miles outside of town to the north, east and south. Mountains that formed an almost perfect semicircle around the town, if you looked down at them from above.

After leaving the Bozeman courtroom, he'd rented a car and driven the 170 miles west, past Butte and over the Bitterroots. He'd come at Strat's request, really at his *urging*. His brother had never pushed him so hard to do anything. Of course, it hadn't been a difficult decision. After all, what was there to go home to?

"Hello, brother!"

Hunter smiled at the sound of Strat's strong southern accent booming onto the deck from behind him. The remoteness of the place had been creeping up on Hunter, affecting him, making him even warier than usual, especially as he continued to be haunted by Carl Bach's suicide.

"Hello back." Hunter rose from his chair, turned around, and hugged his brother. He didn't display affection in public very often, but he made an exception in this case. "Have a seat." Hunter gestured at the table's other chair, then checked his watch. Right on time. Which was one thing about Strat. If he told you he'd be someplace at a certain time, he'd be there. "Want a beer?"

Strat laughed as he sat down. "You'll never learn, will ya, Hunt?" He waved to a pudgy, middle-aged waitress leaning against the brick wall by the door. "Beer doesn't do a damn thing for me anymore. Hell, I could drink a whole case of it, and I wouldn't feel a thing. And what's the point of drinking if you don't get a buzz?" He pulled a half-full pack of Camels from the pocket of his tattered green flannel shirt and tapped one out, then tossed the pack on the table and lit up. "Kate, I'll take a—"

"I know, I know," she interrupted in a spicy tone as she made it to the table. "The usual. Grey Goose straight up, tall glass." She put her hand on Hunter's shoulder. "How about you, handsome?" she asked, her voice turning friendly. "Another beer?"

"That would be—"

"Now wait just a damn minute, Kate," Strat cut in, dropping the match into an ashtray and taking a big first puff. "Is that any way to treat your best customer? Calling my little brother handsome right in front of me? You never call me handsome."

"First of all, you aren't one of my best customers," she retorted. "You always order lots of drinks, but I can't remember the last time you left me more than a few bucks for a tip. *Second of all*," she continued, raising her voice when Strat tried to protest, "this guy's gonna need bodyguards to keep the women away from him while he's in town. Heck, he might even give Paul Brule a run for his money." She pointed at Strat. "And don't give me that grumpy look. At least I didn't say why I never call you handsome. Gimme a little credit for that."

"Ah, you're gonna give my brother a swelled head," Strat muttered. But Kate was already heading back inside. "Well," he said, taking another long drag off the cigarette as he watched her go, "you can't really get that big a head, anyway."

"Why not?"

"Because there aren't that many good-looking women in Fort Mason."

Hunter cringed. Strat often said exactly what was on his mind at exactly the moment he thought of it. He had since he was a kid. Fortunately, The Depot wasn't busy tonight. They were the only patrons on the deck and Kate was already inside, so there wasn't anyone to offend.

"How was the trip over from Bozeman?" Strat asked, leaning back in his chair against the white wooden railing ringing the deck and putting his boots up on the table. In the process, he rattled a flowerpot full of daisies sitting on top of the railing behind him so hard it almost fell off and tumbled the seventy feet down to the river's rocky bank. "How long did it take you to get here?"

Hunter smiled wryly. Sometimes people had a hard time believing he and Strat were from the same gene pool. He and Strat had even joked when they were kids back in Virginia that maybe they weren't. Strat had the jet-black hair of their mother, but that was where the physical similarities ended. He was short and squat, with forearms and calves that were disproportionately large for his body, and he had their father's gut now that he was forty-one. It was noticeable even with his shirt untucked, as he always wore it. His hair was long in the back and on the sides, and he always sported a hat. Tonight it was a grimy, tan Stetson. He was bald on top, which he didn't like people seeing, and he had a face like a pug. Not as flat a profile, but he had a slight underbite and his natural expression was pissed off. There was nothing he could do about it, either. Unless he *really* smiled, he still looked mad. And he could never have worked in an office and survived, Hunter knew. Strat had the smarts for it but not the patience. He had to see progress on the job every day. Office politics would have driven him insane.

"Damn it, did you hear me, little brother?"

Strat cursed a lot, for no particular reason most of the time. He didn't do it any more when he was pissed off than he did during normal conversation. He just did it.

"It took about three hours," Hunter answered as Kate put their drinks down on the table, then turned and headed right back for the door to get food for a table she was serving inside. "It wouldn't have taken nearly as long if the speed limit in Montana was still 'reasonable and prudent.' But since you guys gave in to the Feds and dialed it back to seventy-five, I kept it under eighty."

Strat waved. "As if anyone really keeps it under eighty on the interstates out here. And we didn't give in to the Feds," he added firmly. "They *made* us change it."

Which wasn't technically true, but Hunter nodded anyway. He had no desire to get into a states' rights debate with Strat. Strat had been fighting that battle since he'd been old enough to understand federalism and what the Civil War was about, ever since he'd decided that Virginia was the center of the universe. Which was why Hunter found it fascinating that Strat had never returned to Virginia since moving out here, not even to visit.

"So, how are you, brother?" Hunter asked. It was best to run fast from this topic. Otherwise Strat might start ranting about the "damn liars in D.C." and then they'd be on it for the rest of the night. "Why'd you want me to come here to Fort Mason so bad?"

"All in good time." Strat picked up his glass and took two healthy gulps of vodka, giving no indication whatsoever that he had any problem swallowing it. He didn't pat his chest, didn't cough, didn't grimace as the alcohol rushed down to his stomach. "All in good time."

Vodka straight up with no ice, no mixer, no problem. Hunter grimaced just watching his brother swallow it. "Ever think you might be abusing alcohol?"

"Did I spill some?" Strat asked, grave concern suddenly clouding his face. "My God, don't scare me like that, Hunt." His concerned expression quickly gave way to a smirk. "I'm getting old."

Hunter watched Strat finish off another third of the glass. "Seriously," he said, amazed and concerned at his brother's ability to down straight vodka. He'd never worried about Strat's drinking before, but he'd never seen anything like this, either. "Seriously, maybe it's time for AA."

"AA's for quitters," Strat shot back. "I've never been a quitter, and I never will be. Besides, if some pansy-ass do-gooder tried to start a God damn AA chapter in Fort Mason, I'd be standing in line to shoot him. A *long* line. Drinking's a way of life out here, and I'm not talking about a few beers a few nights a week." Strat held up his hand when Hunter tried to interrupt. "Tell me about the Bridger case. What happened?"

Hunter raised an eyebrow. "As plugged in to this town as you are, I can't believe you don't already know." Strat had been living in Fort Mason for twelve years, so he was almost a local. If not for that southern accent, he might be. "Right?"

Strat held up his glass, tipped it toward Hunter, and nodded. "Salute," he said respectfully, finishing what was left. He put the glass down and signaled to Kate for another. She was leaning against the bricks by the door again, staring at Hunter. "Okay, then let's see how accurate the Fort Mason rumor mill is. I heard the jury gave you *forty* million bucks this morning. Ten for each of those damn tank cars that blew up." Strat raised one eyebrow back at Hunter. They had that genetic trait in common. It was one of the few. "And you guys get a third, right? That's over thirteen million." He hesitated. "So, how's the mill working?"

Hunter took a long guzzle of beer. It was just past eight in the evening, but it was still hot outside and the chilly amber liquid tasted good. Maybe it wasn't a vintage celebration champagne, but it was doing fine as a substitute. "Pretty well, Strat. And I'm surprised because most rumor mills don't."

"Then it's true? Forty and thirteen?"

"Yeah," Hunter admitted, glancing around. He didn't want anyone hearing. "Forty and thirteen," he echoed quietly. "That's right."

"*God damn!*" Strat broke into a proud smile, putting a dent into his naturally angry expression. "Jesus H. Christ," he muttered. "That's what you are, you know that? You're Jesus H. Christ."

"Hey, don't—"

"In a courtroom, at least, to those damn families, definitely." Strat rubbed his eyes hard as if he couldn't wait for his next drink, as if it was driving him crazy not to have alcohol in front of him. "To hell with Jesus Christ, you're God. Do you realize what that kind of money means to people out here? To people anywhere."

"Well, I—"

"Those families might as well change their names to Rockefeller." Strat leaned forward and slapped Hunter on the shoulder. "And you're getting thirteen million of it. Damn, little brother, that's a good day's work. I mean, let the big dog eat. Maybe Dad was right to make you be a lawyer after all."

Even after so long, Strat remembered how their father had announced the decree night after night at the dinner table. "The *firm* is getting thirteen million, Strat, not me."

"So, what's your piece?" Strat asked. Kate was nearing the table with his next vodka. "You know, Kate," he said loudly as she put the glass down on the white linen tablecloth, "my little brother's good looking *and* rich."

"Oh, I know," she called over her shoulder as she walked away. "Everybody knows. Thirteen million rich just today."

Hunter didn't like Kate knowing about the settlement and thinking he'd made thirteen million dollars today. He liked flying under the radar, liked his place on the periphery. Especially when it came to money.

"So," Strat spoke up, "what *is* your share of the thirteen million?"

Hunter took another healthy gulp of beer. "I don't know yet."

"Well, what do you think it'll—"

"*I don't know.*" There were places he wouldn't even go with his brother, even with the person he was closest to in the world. At least, he wasn't going there right now. Plus, he wasn't sure what his share would be. Which was damn frustrating, and one reason he wasn't as elated about the size of the award as he might be. Bach's suicide was putting a dark cloud over everything, too.

Strat took a careful sip of vodka, leaning down to the table and pressing his lips to the rim without picking the glass up, because it was filled right to the top. "It's tough to watch a man kill himself," he said once he'd steadied the situation. "Isn't it?"

Strat had said the words quietly, but they rattled around in Hunter's brain like rocks in a tumbling tin can. He tried not to let his expression change, but surely Strat had seen the shock register. They knew each other too well for him not to recognize something like that, and Strat had obviously said it out of nowhere to get a reaction. But how could he have known?

"Tough to see a man so screwed up in the head he can't handle the thought of taking one more breath," Strat continued. "So screwed up he'd rather face the abyss than another day on earth. Especially tough to watch it when maybe you had something to do with it. Whether that's fair or not." He glanced off into the distance. "Yup, tough to watch a man put a bullet through his head and splatter his brains all over a wall."

Hunter followed Strat's gaze out at the Lassiter River and to the twin sentinels reaching for the azure sky in the distance. "It seems like such a big state," he murmured, indirectly answering the question. It didn't surprise him that Strat knew about Carl Bach's suicide. News of it had been all over the radio. But it did surprise him that Strat knew the details, knew that his brother had witnessed the tragedy. The police had promised to keep him out of it, and Hunter hadn't heard his name mentioned on the radio coming over from Bozeman. But Strat still knew. God, it seemed like everyone knew everyone else's business out here. That was one thing he didn't like about this place.

"Size-wise it's a damn big state, brother. About as big as California and Texas." Strat raised his glass, obviously happy at what he was going to say. "But there's less than a million people in Big Sky Country, and God damn it, I love that. I hope we never top a million. Hell, I hope it goes down to just two people." He broke into a big smile that almost erased his naturally pissed-off expression again, and held up two fingers, then pointed at Hunter. "Me and you."

"Only a million?" Hunter had always assumed there were more. It seemed like there *had* to be more people here than that because the territory was so big. He'd gotten a real sense for that on the long drive over from Bozeman today. "Is that really all?"

"Like I said, *less* than a million. I think there's like twenty-six million people in Texas and around thirty-five in California, but there's under a million here. Bozeman's our biggest city, and it only has about a hundred thousand people in it and a lot of them are pilgrims. Outsiders, I mean. It's our one cosmopolitan city," Strat said sarcastically. A curious look came to his face. "By the way, why was the Bridger trial in Bozeman? Why wasn't it here in Fort Mason?"

"The railroad claimed they wouldn't get a fair trial here," Hunter answered, still staring out at the beautiful landscape. "They figured they'd be found guilty before they even set foot in a Fort Mason courtroom, and the state agreed. The railroad was probably right, too."

"Well, it didn't help much in the end, did it?"

"I think it did," Hunter disagreed. "I bet I could have gotten sixty million down here," he said confidently. Which was easy to say in hindsight and probably an estimate helped by the beer. "Maybe fifty."

Strat's eyes flew open. "Jeeeeesus Christ."

"Hey," Hunter spoke up. "Does the river go between those two mountains?" He pointed at the twin peaks in the distance. "Is that the pass?"

"Yup." Strat took a long guzzle of vodka. "It's called Hell's Gate."

Hunter's eyes flickered from the mountains to Strat. "Why's it called that?"

Strat puffed on his cigarette a few times before he began. "The Lassiter River Valley starts about a hundred miles southeast of here. Most of the way to Fort Mason the valley's pretty wide. The mountains are a ways back from the riverbanks on both sides so there's lots of flat, open ground. At least a half a mile on each side, even more in some places. And the slopes to the peaks are gentle, easy to hike, you don't have to climb at all until you get near the top. It's a lot like the Madison Valley once the Mad gets away from Yellowstone." The look in Strat's eyes intensified as he went to his glass again. "But about twenty miles the other side of those two peaks, the valley starts getting narrower and the slopes up to the peaks get steeper. A little on both counts at first so you barely notice at first, but then it gets to happening quick." He waved at the peaks with the hand holding the cigarette, leaving a smoke trail. "For the last quarter of a mile on the north side of the river the bank's only about thirty feet wide. There's just thirty feet of ground you can walk on before the mountains start going up real sharp. On the south side, the mountains come straight up out of the river at least a thousand feet. There's nowhere to walk on the south side." He gazed at the peaks. "You ever talk to any Injuns on your trips out here, brother?"

Hunter had been staring at his beer, thinking about Strat drinking straight vodka like it was water. "No. In fact, I haven't seen many Native Americans out here."

"That's because there aren't many to see. What's left of them have been shoved onto reservations or into corners of the state where you won't notice them."

"It was a terrible thing," Hunter said softly. "No doubt, Strat, but what's that got to do with—"

"They knew as soon as they saw the first white one of us all those years ago what was going to happen," Strat interrupted. "Yes, sir, they knew all right, but they still tried to stop the stampede, at least delay it." He took another guzzle of vodka, then a few puffs off his Camel. "And Hell's Gate was one of the best places in the West to do it. The Lassiter was a major route for settlers back then. Those wide, level banks were like a superhighway for folks coming out here to start a new life, for people headed to the West Coast. Until it got to Hell's Gate, anyway. At that point it turned into the perfect ambush spot. Before all those poor pilgrims made it into this valley we're sitting in right now, they had to run a gauntlet. They had to run that last damn quarter of a mile where it's so narrow, where it's like the narrow part of a funnel. And there was nowhere to hide when the Blackfoot started shooting at them. It was run for the pass or dive into the river, which wasn't a great choice."

Kind of like Carl Bach's choice yesterday, Hunter thought. "The settlers were sitting ducks," he murmured, shaking his head as he imagined the chaos and the carnage. "It was a kill zone."

"The Blackfoot used arrows at first," Strat continued. "Then they got rifles and it turned into a real slaughter. As the word spread, the settlers would band together for protection, sometimes into groups of hundreds. If the Injun scouts saw that, they'd build a big bonfire at the end of the funnel, right where the river comes through the mountains, just before the valley spreads way out again, and they'd light it a few minutes before the lead wagons got to it. The horse and oxen teams pulling the wagons went crazy when they saw the fire and a lot of people ended up getting trampled. Or drowned," he added. "The Blackfoot didn't even have to shoot a lot of them."

"Good God."

"They say there were times back then when you couldn't walk that last quarter of a mile to Hell's Gate without stepping on bones or bodies. The government cleaned it up around the turn of the century, after the war with the Injuns was over, but you can still find bones out there pretty easy if you dig." Strat stared into the distance for several moments. The sun was close enough on the horizon behind them that it was turning the faces of the twin peaks a brilliant gold. He raised his glass toward them. "And that's why they call it Hell's Gate."

14

PAUL CLIMBED OUT of his beat-up Explorer with a groan. He was pretty sure he had a hairline fracture in at least one of his ribs, but he wasn't going to a doctor. He hated doctors. Besides, there wasn't anything a doctor could do for a broken rib except tell him to stay off his feet and get some rest. You're welcome for the advice, now go pay my assistant two hundred bucks. That didn't seem like much of a deal.

Paul knelt and ran his fingertips across the wild, shallow scratches in the pavement, then glanced at the grass by the side of the road, noticing how some of it was burned and some of it wasn't, how some of it was thigh-high and some was chopped off right at the ground. He rubbed his chapped lips as he gazed up the road, following the scratches until the pavement disappeared around a bend. This was where the fire had started. God, if only he could have been in the trees watching.

He'd wanted to see this place for himself, wanted to see if he could figure out what had happened and come up with some answers on his own. The investigators would be out here tomorrow morning first thing, combing the site for clues, but he didn't have any faith in them. It was the end of July, Montana had been burning since early June, and they still hadn't come up with anything. Maybe they were on the take. It seemed like everybody else was.

He shook his head. There were just too many damn fires breaking out all over Montana and the rest of the Northwest this year. Too many to explain them away as being started by careless campers or lightning strikes.

Ultimately, the Forest Service had brought in nine hundred fire-fighters and dropped chemicals and water from planes to save Big Cat. They'd barely prevailed, managing to stop the flame front at the outskirts of town. But everything between the ridge rising above him here and an uneven line a few hundred yards south of Big Cat had burned. Two thousand acres of pristine Montana forest and several farms had been incinerated, and that nine-year-old boy was dead. Murdered, if Paul's theory was right. The men and women who'd rushed to the scene had stopped the fire with a heroic effort, but there'd been an awful cost.

The fire line that had broken off from the main blaze and gone east—the one that had roared past Paul and his team of Jumpers on its way up the ridge this morning—was still burning out of control, still heading toward Wyoming. It had turned into a megablaze, too. Fourteen hundred more firemen had been brought in to fight it, but the location was so remote it was hard to get manpower and equipment to the scene, and the winds hadn't died down as everyone hoped they would. This fire had already scorched four thousand more acres, and they were calling in people from Wyoming and Idaho because it was getting wider and hotter by the hour. Paul had heard from command in Missoula that the higher-ups had made a decision to do *whatever* was necessary to stop it before it got anywhere near Yellowstone. If it didn't die down overnight, he and everyone else from Fort Mason would be on planes at 6:00 A.M. to go to war.

"This is ground zero," Mandy spoke up, coming around the front of the Explorer. She pointed at the lush meadow to the left, then at the scarred face of the ridge rising steeply on their right. "Not much doubt about it, huh?"

At first, Paul hadn't wanted her to come. But she'd insisted, claiming she wanted to learn, and now he was glad she'd tagged along. It was a long trip over here from the base in Fort Mason, and it had been nice to have company. She'd done most of the talking on the way—about nothing in particular—but it was better than listening to the same old songs on the radio. "No, there isn't, Jumper Winslow, not much doubt at all."

"No, there isn't, Team Leader Brule," she repeated in as deep a voice as she could muster, making it obvious she was imitating him. "Not much doubt at all."

Paul glanced up into her eyes, into an obvious devil-may-care expression. "Is there a problem?" he asked, brushing a few pieces of loose gravel from the knees of his nylon fishing pants as he stood up.

She put her hands on her hips. "Do we have to be so formal all the time?"

He spread his arms. "Well, I just—"

"The name's Mandy," she said, holding out her hand and breaking into an easy smile. "It's nice to meet you, Paul."

He glanced down at her slender fingers and manicured nails. In the truck on the way over here he'd gotten several whiffs of a pleasant perfume; she'd put her hair up in a sexy way with a red ribbon; and she'd worn a cute top and a pair of snug jeans. The whole effect was nice. Nicer than he wanted to admit. "Okay, okay, I get it."

"Yeah, sure you do."

"The thing is," Paul spoke up, "rumors get started real quick around the base. I've seen it happen before. You think that fire came up the ridge at us fast this morning? That was nothing compared to how fast rumors spread around the base. I just don't want—"

"You don't want any of your macho Jumper buddies thinking you might have more than a professional relationship with a woman in the outfit," she interrupted. "Right?"

It wasn't about any macho buddies he had. In fact, he didn't have any real buddies. He was a loner when it came right down to it. It was that he didn't want *anyone* in the Fire Jumpers to think he was having an affair with a subordinate. That could put his job in jeopardy. "Yeah, sure."

She took a step closer to him. "See, I understand," she said, her voice turning gentle. "I'm sure it's hard for you."

"What the . . . what are you . . . I mean . . ." He couldn't remember the last time he'd been tongue-tied. He wasn't a guy who ran his mouth, but when he did say something, he didn't waste time getting his point across. "What's that supposed to mean?"

"You know, being a senator's son. Being the son of the man who owns the Brule Lumber Mill, which is Fort Mason's biggest employer."

"You're crazy."

Mandy nodded at the Explorer. "How old is this heap?"

"I don't know. I bought it used a few years ago. It's an '02 or '03, I think. Who cares? What's your point?"

"It's dented and dinged, and it looks like it could fall apart any time. That's the point. That's what's important to you."

"Why's that so important to me?"

"You want people to know you aren't living off your father. You want everybody in Fort Mason to understand that you're making your own way in the world, that you aren't suckling at the family teat like your older brother, Jeremy." She smiled smugly. "See? I get it."

She was smart. "Ah, you don't get anything."

"That's why you wouldn't let anybody call the newspapers today and tell them how you saved Mitch's life. Which," she interrupted herself, "has to be one of the bravest things ever. He would have burned to death up in that tree, and how Godawful would that have been? Watching hell come at you but not being able to do anything about it. But you didn't let it happen, you wouldn't let it happen, you willed it *not* to happen." She shook her head. "Mitch told me all about what you did before they choppered him off that ridge. He told me how you climbed up to where he was in the tree, gave him whiskey, pulled his leg out, then lugged him down on your back. It was superman stuff. You got an S painted on your chest or what? I mean, I heard the stories about you, but, well, I'm a show-me kinda gal. Guess what? I'm a believer now."

"I did what I was trained to do," Paul said firmly. "What you would have done in the same situation. What any of us would have done."

"Except that hardly anyone else *could* have done that," she argued. "Including me. And, if they had done it, they would have wanted it spread all over the front page in big bold letters. Including me," she admitted. "But you? No way. And it's because you figure people would think the only reason the press was into it was because you're Big Bill Brule's son. That they'd think the reporter stretched the truth and the editor splashed it on the front page so the next time they wanted an exclusive out of your dad, he'd give it to them."

She wasn't just smart, Paul realized, she was *very* smart. "Like everybody else hasn't figured that out," he said as convincingly as he could. "You want a medal?"

"Nope, I just want to be friends. No more Jumper Winslow this and Jumper Winslow that, at least when we're by ourselves. I understand when we're on the fire line or around the base. But not here, okay?"

Paul stared at her hard. Maybe she was right, maybe he was going overboard with the formality. And maybe he was doing it because he was starting to like her in more than a professional way. He took a deep breath. How stupid was that? A relationship with a woman who reported to him. And what if she really did only want to be friends? Like she'd just said. What if he was misreading the signals? God, she was hard to figure out.

He was about to change the subject when he thought he saw something over Mandy's shoulder, something moving in the woods at the edge of the meadow. But when he looked harder, he realized it had just been his imagination, just a branch swinging in the breeze. Still, it had sent a shiver up his spine and suddenly he wanted to get out of here. He'd seen enough. "Come on," he said gruffly. "Let's go."

"But we just got here."

"I know, but—"

"All the way from Fort Mason and we're going to—"

"Now." Paul took her by the hand and led her toward the passenger side of the Explorer. *"Mandy."*

Then it hit him. Why maybe he didn't want to figure out who was burning Montana. Why it might be the last thing in the world he wanted to figure out. "Jesus Christ," he whispered. He glanced up at the blackened ridge one more time, then slammed her door shut and hurried back around the front of the Explorer to the driver's side.

15

OW DID YOU know I was there when Carl Bach shot himself?" Hunter asked, gazing at the Lassiter's surface. It was glittering silver in the long-shadowed evening light. The beauty of the river combined with the beer and seeing his brother again had dimmed the awful images of what he'd witnessed a split second after Bach had pulled that trigger. But when Strat mentioned the suicide, the image had hurtled back at him and it was more vivid than ever.

"Same way I knew about the Bridger Railroad settlement," Strat answered, slurring his words. "You said it yourself. When you really get down to it, Montana's a damn small place."

Slurring his words, but at least he'd slowed down on the intake, Hunter saw. Strat was on his third tall vodka, but he'd only taken one swallow from the last glass since Kate had set it down on the table a few minutes ago. "Hell's Gate sure is impressive," he said, gesturing at the twin peaks in the distance.

"It really is." Strat picked up his vodka, then put it back down when he noticed Hunter watching. "It's dangerous, too."

"Why? Because kids climb up there and get into trouble?"

Strat shook his head. "They could do that lots of places around here. There's peaks just as steep and even higher than those on the north side of town." Strat picked up his glass again. Try as he might, he couldn't keep his fingers off it. "Remember on the phone last night we talked about all the fires we're having out here this summer?"

"Sure." Hunter had read about the fires back in the New York newspapers even before he'd come out to Bozeman for the trial, and he'd seen video of the blazes on national newscasts. But he'd been too focused on the Bridger case as well as one other case in Boston to pay close attention. Last night, Strat had gone into detail about the number of big blazes that had broken out in Montana this summer and in other states across the Northwest. And, along with details of Bach's suicide, he'd heard about the Big Cat Fire on the radio during the drive over to Fort Mason this afternoon. "I remember."

"Well, Hell's Gate creates a nasty wind tunnel. Sometimes we get sustained winds of forty to fifty miles an hour through here in the summer, with gusts up to seventy. Not often, but it happens. The Forest Service and the local fire people are real concerned about that because if a big blaze ever broke out east of town and the wind was screaming through Hell's Gate from the east, they aren't sure they could stop it. Not before it blew through town, anyway."

As he looked out over the landscape, Hunter imagined a massive wall of flames like he'd seen on some of the news videos racing toward town. It would be terrifying, to say the least. "Jesus."

Strat took several gulps of vodka. "Yeah, well, I'm not sure Jesus could stop a fire like that. I'm not even sure his father could."

Hunter scanned the area between Hell's Gate and town. "Hey, what's that clearing off to the left of the river over there?" he asked, pointing. It was one of only a few islands of open ground spotting the ocean of trees.

"That's Dale Callahan's farm. He owns a big food services company that's headquartered over in Billings, I think, but he lives here. He raises dogs in his spare time. Other than his business, his dogs are his passion."

"Oh, yeah?" Hunter had been thinking about getting a dog. It would be a lot more loyal than Anne. "What kind does he raise?"

"Yellow Labs."

"Does he raise them just as a hobby, or does he sell them?"

"He sells most of them, but he keeps some as show dogs."

"Have his dogs ever won anything?"

"Nothing big," Strat answered. "Nothing outside the state, I don't think. Supposedly, he had a real winner at one point, a dog he thought was going to take him all the way to that big Madison Square Garden show in New York. But the thing got killed before it was even a year old."

"That's too bad."

"Yeah, it was run over by a Bridger Railroad freight late one night after it got out of the kennels on Callahan's spread. A couple of big Bridger locomotives made mincemeat out of it. That was what I heard anyway."

Hunter grimaced. "That's terrible."

"Yeah, Callahan was pretty upset about it."

Hunter gazed at Callahan's farm, thinking about walking across a remote Montana field on a cool autumn afternoon with a big yellow Lab at his side and the smell of wood smoke from the chimney of a far-off cabin drifting to his nose. He thought about golden aspens ringing the field and mountains rising to meet an azure sky in the distance. He thought about a man and his dog enjoying a wonderful moment no one else would ever know about.

"Hunter."

Hunter looked over warily. Strat usually called him "Hunt" or "brother." Strat only used his full name when he was about to say something important. "What is it?" Hunter asked deliberately, making it clear with his tone that he knew something significant was heading his way.

Strat leaned back, spread his arms and gave Hunter a why-the-aggravation-tone expression. "Hey, what's wrong?"

"Nothing. What are you talking about?"

"It's just that you seem a little out of sorts. You did on the phone last night, too. I was wondering if you wanted to talk about it."

Hunter sat up in his chair and crossed his arms tightly. It was what he always did when he felt uncomfortable in conversation. Unfortunately, Strat would recognize the reaction immediately, and now it was simply a question of whether Hunter would fess up. He wanted to talk to someone about it, about how Anne had left him, but he always found it hard to be open about issues that were close to the heart. Even with Strat.

"Something's bothering you," Strat pushed. "I can tell, I can always tell." He pulled the brim of the Stetson down slightly to shield his eyes from the sun's rays, which were streaming brightly around the side of the building. At this time of year the sun didn't set until after nine o'clock, so it had a few minutes of life left in the day. "Don't lie to me."

"*Lie?* Hey I—"

"Okay, that was a little much," Strat acknowledged. "I'm just worried about you. I care about you, Hunt. You know that, *damn it.*"

How could they possibly be from the same parents? Hunter wondered, still amazed at their differences even after all these years. Strat had no problem expressing his feelings, he never had. On the other hand,

Hunter couldn't remember the last time he'd told Strat he cared about him. Or the last time he'd told Anne he loved her.

Of course, he couldn't remember the last time she'd said it to him, either. Most mornings he was gone before she got out of bed; most nights when he got home she was out with friends or already asleep; and they rarely saw each other on weekends. Dinner parties that they had to go to as a couple or out by the club pool—that was about the extent of the time they spent together. So there weren't many opportunities to say it even if either one of them had actually wanted to. But, way back, when they'd cared about each other—at least when he thought they had—he'd been the one to say he loved her first. Which was how he'd known it was real for him. She was the only one he'd ever felt so strongly about that he could say the words first. Now he couldn't remember why he'd felt so strongly, why he'd wanted to say those words to her. Which was the real tragedy in all of this. It made him feel as if he'd wasted the last eleven years of his life.

"I know you do," Hunter said quietly, gazing at Hell's Gate. He started and stopped twice before he finally got it out. "Look, Anne filed for divorce yesterday."

Strat took a long drag on the first cigarette of a new pack he'd pulled out from beneath his Stetson. "Why doesn't that surprise me?"

"She had me served as I was coming out of court." Out of nowhere Hunter felt heat at the corners of his eyes, and he hated the thought of Strat seeing his emotion. "As I was trying to get past the reporters," he added, his voice straining. He coughed several times, trying to make it seem as if he had something stuck in his throat. "Right after I'd rested the case."

"Which doesn't surprise me, either." Strat scratched his scruffy chin, careful not to burn himself with the cigarette he was holding in that hand. "That woman's a damn piece of work, brother. I'd like to call her something else . . . but I won't. Out of respect for you."

A piece of work, Hunter thought. That was the understatement of the year, and Strat didn't know half of it. Hunter let out a measured breath. The emotion had passed, thank God.

"I warned you before you married her," Strat muttered in an I-told-you-so tone. "You could see it in her eyes. She has those crazy eyes."

"Ah, that's a bunch of—"

"Oh, yeah, she does." Strat took an extra-long puff. "Like some of those stallions out on Katrina Mason's ranch do. Before we bust 'em and get a saddle on their backs the first time."

Strat wasn't just drinking a lot, Hunter noticed, he was smoking a lot, too. He didn't go more than a few minutes between lighting up. "You did warn me," Hunter admitted. "I wish I'd paid—"

"That's it!" Strat slapped the dirty knee of his faded jeans. "She's cheating on you," he said loudly. "That whole production yesterday in the courtroom was a preemptive strike to get you back on your heels." Strat flicked his cigarette butt over the railing and watched it flutter down to the Lassiter. "What was her official reason for divorcing you?" He put two fingers up on both hands to make quotation marks. "Irreconcilable differences?"

It was almost as if Strat had read what was on the paper inside the envelope the guy had shoved at his chest yesterday. What the hell was the deal out here? Weren't there *any* secrets? "Who's Katrina Mason?" he asked, trying to change the subject. He'd done enough thinking about Anne for a while. She'd get hers and so would the guy. He just needed to have that patience. "You mentioned her a minute ago. Something about getting saddles on her horses."

"She's kind of the town matriarch," Strat answered. "By default, I guess."

"What do you mean?"

Strat smiled as if Hunter ought to be getting something that was obvious, and he was enjoying himself immensely because Hunter wasn't. "Uh, Katrina *Mason*, Fort *Mason*."

"Oh, *I* get it. The town is named for her family."

"Right," Strat confirmed. "Katrina's great-great-grandfather was a cavalry officer in the 1890s, and he was the commander of the fort that used to be where the town square is now. They had to build the fort to wipe out the problem at Hell's Gate. When the Injuns were mostly killed off, the army tore the fort down, but General Mason stayed. The town took on his name, and he got a lot of land around here from the government for his years of service in the cavalry. Katrina has a big spread south of here in the Big Hole Valley, and she owns something like half a million acres of timber. Mostly in Montana, I think."

Hunter whistled. "So she's loaded, huh?"

"I don't know about that, Hunt. I heard she had to take out a big loan to pay off the inheritance taxes when her father died."

"That damn inheritance tax thing—" Hunter interrupted himself when he noticed a tall, slim woman with long raven hair sit down alone at a table near the far corner of the deck. He was about to pick up his beer to hide his stare when Strat kicked him in the shin. "What the hell?" Hunter snapped, turning quickly to glare at his older brother.

"What are you doing?" Strat demanded under his breath.

"What do you mean?"

Strat nodded subtly at the woman. "You know what I mean."

Hunter stole another glance at the woman as she ordered a drink. She was about his age, maybe a little younger, and striking. A woman who'd stick out in any crowd. "Is she a local?"

"Jesus." Strat fired up another cigarette, irritated. "What did we call it when we were kids? Oh, yeah, yeah, the grip."

The grip. God, how long had it been since Hunter had heard that one. It was what he and Strat called it when a guy saw a girl for the first time, and he couldn't take his eyes off her because for whatever reason she was different for him than the rest. She might not even be the best-looking one of a bunch, but for some reason he found something about her so compelling he had to meet her. Which was the way Hunter had felt about Anne the first time he'd noticed her. He'd even tried to explain the grip to her a few weeks after their first date, but she didn't seem interested. In fact, she seemed put off when he'd explained that the woman didn't neces-sarily have to be the best looking one of the group. Fortunately, he'd been able to change the subject quickly and save the date.

"Yeah," Hunter agreed, "that's what we called it."

"Well, don't let her grip you," Strat advised, leaning over the table. "Get her out of your mind fast."

"Why?"

"She's crazy as hell. She's twice as crazy as Anne."

"What do you mean?"

Strat leaned even farther over the table, motioning for Hunter to do the same. "Nobody really knows for sure, but we think she was a faith healer in San Francisco or a commune leader in Portland. One or the other, or something weird like that. Know what I mean? Anyway, she moved here about three years ago. We figure she's running from the IRS. She's never had a job, but she lives in a nice pad we hear she paid cash for. It's over near Callahan's farm," Strat went on, gesturing in the direction of the clearing. "She always wears nice clothes, clothes you can't get in Fort Mason, and she drives a Beamer. It's a few years old, but it's a Beamer." He pointed at Hunter. "And here's the kicker. She doesn't have an account at either bank in town. In fact, nobody's ever even seen her go to an ATM."

"That makes her crazy?"

Strat didn't answer. He leaned back slowly and tugged the brim of his Stetson a touch lower over his eyes.

"Hello."

Hunter turned toward the smooth voice. The raven-haired woman was standing right in front of him. "Hello," he said politely, standing up and taking her hand.

She was even more striking up close, taller and thinner than he'd first thought. Not rail thin, but definitely slim beneath her form-fitting designer jeans and strapless top. Her long black hair was darker than his, and it shimmered with silver highlights like the surface of the Lassiter. Her eyes were a deep mahogany, but there was a light in the middle of each dark pupil that burned intensely. He couldn't tell if it emanated from them or was a reflection, but it was powerful and unwavering either way. She had one of those beautiful, high-cheekbone smiles that made you smile yourself, and her sinewy fingers were soft but her handshake was firm.

"I'm Zoe Gale," she said as their hands parted, "but I probably didn't have to tell you that."

"What do you mean?"

Zoe nodded at Strat. "I'm sure your brother's already told you all about me. What he thinks he knows about me anyway."

Hunter felt his heart beating fast, as it did as he was about to begin questioning an important witness. "How did you know he and I were brothers?"

She touched his forearm gently. "Oh, Mr. Lee, you're a smart man. Surely you've figured out by now that there aren't any secrets in Fort Mason." She put a finger to her chin and looked up at the darkening sky. "Well, not many anyway."

He smiled a comfortable smile that came to his lips effortlessly. "Call me Hunter." It was as if he was in court, he realized. Where everything came effortlessly. "Please."

"Mmm. So, it's certainly a pleasure to meet a celebrity."

"Oh, I'm not a—"

"Anyone who wins forty million dollars for poor families in Fort Mason is most certainly a celebrity," she assured him. "Of the highest order." She paused. "How long will you be here, Mr. Lee?"

He liked that she was still calling him "Mr. Lee" even though he'd asked her to call him Hunter. He wasn't sure why, but he did. "You know, I believe I'll stay here long enough to get to the bottom of a secret or two."

Zoe brushed his arm with her fingers again. "That sounds divinely delicious."

He liked the way she said delicious. "Mmm." And divinely.

"I certainly hope that's long enough for us to see each other again." She touched the back of his hand lightly. "It was charming to meet you." With that she turned and walked back to her table.

"Well," Hunter said, sitting down and turning to face his brother after he'd watched her walk all the way back to her table, "if that's crazy, I'll take it."

Strat pointed his cigarette at Hunter. "Be careful, little brother, real careful. You hear me?"

"I appreciate the older-brother advice, Strat, but I can take care of myself at this point." He saw that Strat was about to make what Hunter assumed would be a snide comment about his younger brother being unable to hold a marriage together as proof of the need for advice, but held back. Presumably because Strat was being sensitive to the situation. Maybe the man was finally growing up, Hunter thought, sneaking another look at Zoe. What he saw didn't make him happy. Zoe had company. "Hey, who's that?"

Strat looked up from beneath his hat. "Well, well, speak of the devil."

Hunter's eyes raced quickly back to Strat's. "What do you mean?"

"That's Dale Callahan." Strat pointed toward the open ground short of Hell's Gate. "That's the guy who owns the place you asked me about, the one who raises yellow Labs."

"Are they an item? Zoe and Dale, I mean."

"Why?"

"You know why." Hunter forced himself not to sneak another glance at Zoe. "Is Callahan a bad guy? Is that why you called him the devil?"

"Sorry, brother, just the opposite. He's got a great reputation around town. I don't know him that well, but every time I've talked to him he seems like a good guy. My boss, Butch Roman, knows him real well. He says a lot of good things about Dale, and Butch doesn't say a lot of good things about many people." Strat hesitated. "Of course, Roman Construction's made big bucks building plants and warehouses for Callahan Foods over the last couple of years, so maybe Butch isn't as objective as he might be."

There was something very compelling about Zoe Gale. Hunter could feel the grip taking control. "She sure is pretty."

Strat rolled his eyes. "Don't get involved with her, Hunt." He took a puff off the cigarette. "We'll probably both regret it if you do."

16

THE BRULE LUMBER Mill and its fourteen buildings sprawled out across thirty-two fenced-in acres on the banks of the Lassiter River a few miles west of Fort Mason. With over five hundred workers, it was by far the town's largest employer. Every day it churned out plywood, two-by-fours, four-by-fours, and so on. A vast assortment of building products shaped by the mill's many saws and presses out of the massive logs transported to the plant by a seemingly endless convoy of trucks. Logs from towering conifers that had been felled, stripped of their branches and hauled away from forests throughout Montana, Idaho, and Wyoming.

The mill was founded in 1939 by Paul Brule's grandfather, Grayson Brule. The son of first-generation Scottish immigrants, Gray—as his nickname became soon after birth—had walked out of his parents' cramped Brooklyn apartment one steamy July morning when he was sixteen and never returned. He hopped a freight train west and ended up in Butte, Montana, where he sweated in the mines for a month. Fed up with spending most of his day underground for very little pay, he headed farther west to Missoula and took a job as a lumberjack. The pay wasn't much better and the work was even tougher, but at least he was outside where he could enjoy the beauty and wildness of a West he'd heard so much about back in New York City. It was a beauty and a wildness that hadn't been exaggerated, he realized when he saw it. It never occurred to him that by chopping down trees he was destroying that splendor, because, after all, there was so much of it. There always seemed to be another immense mountain chain and more tall trees as far as the eye could see.

There always seemed to be another barroom brawl, too. Gray spent a couple of nights in local jails during his first few years in Montana, but not for anything serious.

In the summer of 1938—when Gray was twenty-one—the wildness, which until then had brought him nothing but problems, delivered what would lead him to his fortune. By that year he'd risen to the rank of foreman in the Great Missoula Logging Company, and for the month of June he and his crew of twenty lumberjacks were working outside Fort Mason. Five large canvas tents and a crudely built stone grill served as camp while they systematically clear-cut a wide swath of the Fort Mason Valley in the shadow of Hell's Gate. At the time, that area of the valley was owned by a wealthy Philadelphia banker who was leasing logging rights to the GMLC.

One Saturday evening, Gray was walking along the town's narrow, muddy main street with one of his crew and, on the spur of the moment, he headed into the Grizzly Saloon for beers and a few hands of poker. It was a game Gray had come to excel at in the smoke-filled front street bars of Missoula. His father had told him over and over as a child never to let life control him, but to control it. He took the advice to heart and applied it to everything he did, including gambling. He figured out quickly that if you only used the cards you were dealt, your odds of winning weren't much different than those of the players sitting on either side of you. So he learned to cheat. He got damn good at it, too. To help, he always carried nines of the popular decks with him, nines being strong but not obvious cheating cards.

After a few beers at the bar, Gray moved to a table at the back and sat down with four other players, one of whom was a giant of a man reputed to have a quick temper and a liver the size of a cantaloupe. At six-two and two hundred pounds, Gray was good-sized himself, but the man sitting opposite him was six-six and 250 pounds, with biceps the size of cantaloupes, too. One thing led to another, and, by the time Gray had a pile of chips in front of him, accusations were flying. Accusations that grew loudest after Gray won a particularly large pot with four nines. It seemed to the other men at the table that Gray won his biggest pots on his deal and that nines were usually involved, but they couldn't prove anything.

Things finally overheated and the game ended with a lot of shouting, fist slamming, and threats of revenge. Gray left with five hundred dollars in his pocket and a date for a fight in the morning. He caught a restless night of sleep back at camp, arose at six in the morning, and headed for the Grizzly Saloon at nine. He figured he didn't have any choice but to fight because the giant knew where his camp was and they were only halfway through their work in Fort Mason.

When he arrived that morning along with several men of his crew, Gray found an excited mob awaiting. They whooped, hollered, and tossed their caps when he turned the corner onto Main Street. No one had been brave enough to fight the giant bully since the man had moved to town a year ago. The crowd wasn't anticipating much, but at least this would get their blood up before they had to sit in church and listen to how sinful they were. The giant was on the street in front of the bar waiting, too, shirt off. His muscular physique glistened in the blazing morning sun as he loosened up with an impressive shadowboxing display.

The fight started immediately, as soon as Gray appeared. There were no preliminaries: no bell, no announcement, no referee with rules. Just a lunatic man-mountain sprinting down Main Street, veins in his massive neck and forehead bulging, obsessed with exacting some pain for his losses of the night before and the cheating he was certain he'd been a victim of.

What the man had no way of knowing was that one of Gray's best friends back in Brooklyn was a Chinese kid who'd taught him how to fight martial-arts style. Gray easily avoided the giant's initial charge—he simply head-juked one way then stepped the other—and the big man went tumbling past. On the giant's second, shorter rush, Gray delivered a quick, downward kick to the bottom of the guy's left thigh—which sent the big man's kneecap spinning to the back of his leg. A split second later, before the giant even had a chance to fall, Gray delivered a lightning chop to the neck. The guy fell to the dirt of Main Street like a sack of seeds and was pronounced down and out. Literally. He was as down and out as a man could be, because he was dead.

Fortunately, Gray had a hundred witnesses who swore to the constable on Main Street patrol that he'd been acting in self-defense. There was a brief police inquiry into the incident, but Gray was never arrested and the matter was dropped a few days later. Logging below Hell's Gate went on uninterrupted and executives at the GMLC never heard about what had happened, the Montana rumor mill not being as efficient in those days.

It turned out that the giant was married to a beautiful, blond twenty-year-old girl from Philadelphia named Sara Covington. It turned out her father was the one leasing those acres beneath Hell's Gate to the GMLC.

And it turned out the giant had been an abusive husband and had threatened to kill Sara if she ever told her father what was going on. When Mr. Covington heard the truth about the battering his daughter had been suffering, Gray Brule became an instant family hero. For Sara, Gray was a knight in shining armor. For Gray, Sara was a princess. They were married three months later and Gray's days as a lumberjack were over. So were his days as a front street poker player.

A few weeks into their courtship, Gray presented Sara's father with plans to build a lumber mill on the banks of the Lassiter. In addition to the land in the shadow of Hell's Gate, Mr. Covington owned hundreds of thousands of acres of mature forest on the east side of the pass. Forests that lined large tributaries to the Lassiter. These trees could be harvested, then floated downriver to the mill, saving significant transportation costs. Why not grab the wide margins other mills in Montana were getting? Gray suggested in a letter to Covington. Even undercut the market on price initially to ramp up sales? Given the advantage they had in captive raw materials and transportation, the mill would be extremely profitable.

Within a week of receiving Gray's letter, Mr. Covington approved the formation of the Brule Lumber Mill and invested a hundred thousand dollars. The first building went up in April 1939 and the company was an instant success, turning a healthy profit in only its third month of operation.

William "Big Bill" Brule gazed proudly at the black-and-white, silver-framed photograph on the credenza beside his desk. It was a picture of his parents—Grayson and Sara—in their late sixties. They were holding hands as they stood together before the living room fireplace of the old house, the house Big Bill had been born in and enjoyed so many wonderful years in as a child. The photo on the credenza was the last he had of his parents together. Several weeks after the picture was taken, his father had died of a heart attack, and his mother died of a broken heart only a month later. It had been a long time since their passing, but he still missed them, especially his father. Big Bill cited many role models from all walks of life in the political speeches he gave, but he had only one true hero: his father.

Grayson had turned control of the mill over to Big Bill in 1979, a few years before the photograph on the credenza was taken. Big Bill had run the operation with an iron fist until 1998, when he won his first State

Senate race. He remained the company's CEO, directing business from Helena when the legislature was in session, until he won his United States Senate seat in 2004. At that point he turned the company over to Jeremy, his older son. Running the mill from Helena was one thing, but running it from Washington, D.C., was quite another.

Jeremy Brule was thirty-three, four years older than Paul. He was a mediocre businessman at best, but when he was distracted by his vices he was terrible—drinking and gambling, mostly, but he chased prostitutes, too. Big Bill would rather have made Paul CEO, even back when Paul was only twenty-four. Paul was that much more capable than Jeremy at everything, he always had been. And Paul *never* gave in to pressure, he just got stronger. Jeremy wilted when things got hot. But Jeremy was family, and it was better to have your blood running your company than somebody who wasn't. At least, that was what Gray Brule had always preached.

Big Bill gazed at another picture on his credenza, one taken of him standing between Paul and Jeremy when they were children. Big Bill grimaced. If his father had known Jeremy as an adult, he might not have preached that blood speech so hard.

Unfortunately, Paul had wanted nothing to do with the family business. He had a boulder on his shoulder about being given anything; he wanted to make his own way in the world. Wasting his time as a Fire Jumper, Bill thought grimly as he stared at the photograph of his parents. And, to some extent, Paul had probably turned his back on the family business because of their relationship—or lack of it. Though why it had gotten so bad in the past few years was a mystery to Big Bill.

He and Paul rarely spoke now. When they did, the conversation was brief. Paul never seemed angry, just impatient. It seemed like he wanted to get off the phone or back in his beat-up Explorer and roar off as soon as possible. They'd made plans to have dinner at The Depot several times over the past year when Big Bill was back from Washington, but Paul always canceled a few hours ahead of time with no explanation. He'd asked several times what was wrong, but Paul always shrugged and claimed there was no problem. Paul had never been much of a communicator. He'd never been much of a liar, either.

Big Bill leaned back in his leather desk chair. His expansive office was on the fourth floor of the Brule Lumber Mill's main building. From the window behind his desk he could see most of the operation, and all the way down to the Lassiter. The plant didn't have logs delivered by river anymore, but the employees still cleared the property all the way to the banks because they knew Big Bill loved the view. He wasn't CEO now, but he maintained an office here because it was a good place to conduct business when he was in town, when the Senate was in recess, as it was now for the summer. He felt energy here the way he did in Washington. And, for all intents and purposes, he still ran the company.

As he put his hands behind his head and locked his long fingers, he caught a glimpse of himself in the mirror hanging above the couch against the far wall. At six-four he was taller than his father. He had been since he was fifteen, which had earned him his nickname. He gave himself a quick, winning smile, unable to keep from admiring himself. He was still 220 pounds, exactly what he'd weighed the day he'd graduated from Dartmouth over forty years ago. The pounds were distributed a little differently on his frame, but he was still in good shape for a man in his seventh decade. Good enough shape that even young women took notice of him as he strode quickly along Washington's corridors of power in what he called his "Montana Gait" with his staff trailing behind him, struggling to keep up. The strong jaw, full head of silver hair, broad shoulders, and sharp suits helped corral those looks, too.

Sometimes the young women didn't just look, sometimes they followed him and gave him their telephone numbers. For them the aphrodisiac wasn't that he still looked good for his age, though of course that didn't hurt. What attracted them so strongly to him was the aura of power he so naturally projected. He knew that, and he used it.

He didn't call many of them, just the very pretty blond ones. He'd invite them to an intimate dinner at his exquisitely decorated Georgetown town house with a beautiful view of the Potomac River. And, despite the secluded location and all that it implied, they rarely turned him down. He never went anywhere in public with them, and didn't have more than three dates with any woman no matter how beautiful or passionate she was. He didn't want them mistaking the evenings for a commitment. The great thing about it: He wasn't doing anything wrong, he wasn't doing anything the *Washington Post* could drag him through the muck and mire for even if they did have a reporter camped outside his door. He'd been a widower for fourteen years.

He'd only made one exception since he'd been in Washington, only dated one young woman more than three times and been seen in public with her. Her name was Joanna Preston, and the whole thing had turned out badly. *Very* badly. Big Bill took a deep breath. Joanna had been *so* beautiful and *so* passionate, which was why he'd made the exception. He shook his head. Men could be incredibly stupid when it came to beautiful women, and unfortunately, it turned out that he was no different. Well, at least he'd learned. He'd never break his three-date rule again or be seen in public with one of them. *Ever*. Like his father always used to say: When you lose, don't lose the lesson.

He wouldn't take any of them back to Montana again, either. As he had Joanna. No matter what. Thank God for good friends, he thought, clenching his jaw as he spotted himself in the mirror for a second again before quickly glancing away. This time he didn't smile back.

"Come in," Big Bill called, answering a knock on the office door, glad to be distracted from his thoughts of Joanna Preston.

"Dad?" Jeremy leaned into the office. "Got a minute?"

"Yup."

Jeremy shook hands with his father, then took a seat in front of the desk. "When'd you get in last night?"

"Around midnight."

Big Bill kept a Cessna at the Bozeman airport when the Senate was in session because Bozeman offered the most commercial flights to and from major destinations outside the state. That way he could get off the airliner, jump right into his little plane and fly it to the small Fort Mason field. He could come and go with relative ease and didn't have to drive long distances, which he absolutely hated doing. Plus, he loved to fly. There was so much more to see when you flew, even at night.

Joanna had loved flying, too. She'd punched Big Bill's ticket into the mile-high club, but he'd gladly give up that experience if he could just turn back the hands of time. Then he wouldn't have to live with that nagging voice in the back of his head whispering to him that this might be the day he started paying. That this might be the day when everything unraveled.

"The flight from San Francisco was late," Big Bill explained, thinking about how his friend Dale Callahan had gone white as a sheet when he'd suggested taking a trip up in the small plane last spring. Dale hated to fly so much. He grinned a little as he pictured the terrified expression on Dale's face. He'd always found it good therapy to think of something amusing right on top of remembering something terrible. "Two damn hours late."

"That sucks. Where were you?"

It was ironic. Jeremy always took an interest in what he was doing;

always sympathized with how hard his father worked for the country; always showed how much he cared. Paul never asked about anything, never showed he cared at all. Despite that indifference—maybe because of it—Big Bill wanted Paul's attention much more than Jeremy's. It was difficult to admit, but it was true.

"China. I was over there with three other senators. Officially, it was a glad-handing mission to one of the provinces. We sat down for some meetings with a few local bigwigs, and we cut a ribbon at some factory opening. But we were really there to make sure they weren't breaking any of the export agreements they'd signed with us. We were getting some behind-the-scenes information from our State Department guys on the ground, too. Some hush-hush crap."

"Damn, Dad, it's amazing what you're involved in."

"Yeah, I guess it is."

Big Bill wasn't really listening. He was focused on the fact that Jeremy looked fatter than he had the last time they'd seen each other. The older boy never had been an athlete like Paul, he'd always had carried a few extra pounds even as a teenager. He was blond like Paul, but at five-eight, he was six inches shorter and just about the same weight. Dumpy was the adjective that most often came to Big Bill's mind when he thought about his older son. Plus, Jeremy was a whiner when he didn't get his way or work ate up too much of his time.

Paul never complained. Paul was a man of action.

"Yeah, the political stuff was cover," Big Bill continued, "but . . . hey, have you put on a few pounds?"

"What?"

"Have you gained weight? What are you up to now?"

Jeremy's proud smile disappeared. "Jeez, Dad, I—"

"Come on, really, what do you weigh?"

"I don't know. Around one-eighty, I guess."

A crock, Big Bill figured. Jeremy was probably pushing two hundred. "So, what'd you want to see me about?"

"I was hoping," Jeremy said in a subdued voice, "that we could catch up a little before we got into the business stuff. I haven't seen you in—"

"I've got lunch at the Lion's Den with Dale Callahan in forty minutes," Big Bill cut in, recognizing the hurt in his son's eyes. But the boy was a good actor. It was about the only thing he did better than Paul. "Don't worry, you and I will have time. How about dinner tonight?"

"I'd like that." The smile reappeared on Jeremy's face. "I really would."

"Good. Now give me the update. What's the deal?"

Jeremy's smile faded again, but this time his happiness was replaced by fear. "It isn't all good news around here, Dad."

Big Bill was checking a stock quote on his computer. "What do you mean?" Jeremy had always been a sky-is-falling kind of guy, so Big Bill didn't bother looking away from the screen.

"We've got a problem." Jeremy let out a sigh and put his hands to his face. "I can't find any more trees, Dad, and we've only got about thirty days of timber inventory left on site. Maybe less," he added.

Big Bill's eyes flashed from the screen to Jeremy. *"Thirty days?"* This wasn't a problem, it was a catastrophe. The sky really was falling. *"Are you serious?"*

"Then we won't be able to make anything," Jeremy went on, his voice shaking, "because we won't have anything to make it out of. Then we'll have to shut down the plant."

"Why's this the first I've heard of it?" Big Bill demanded, his face getting red.

"I didn't want to bother you, Dad. I thought I could take care of the problem myself, but I guess I—"

"Jesus Christ!" Big Bill roared, the gravity of the situation sinking in. "I'll tell you something, Paul would never have let it get this far."

"What?"

Big Bill groaned, regretting what he'd just said instantly. Maybe it wasn't fair to constantly compare him to Paul, especially to his face, but it was impossible not to. Big Bill wanted both of his sons to be alpha dogs— like their father.

"I can't believe you said that to me!" Jeremy shouted. "Paul didn't want anything to do with this place. He turned his back on you and the mill, but you're still—"

"I'm sorry. All right? *Christ!*"

Big Bill was trying to stay calm, trying not to panic, but it was tough. The Brule Lumber Mill had some big loans out, money he'd borrowed to fund his Senate campaign. Plus, he'd borrowed more money to fund what had turned out to be some pretty stupid technology investments. Even though technically it was the company borrowing the money, he was personally guaranteeing the loans. If the mill couldn't pay them back, he'd have to, and he didn't have enough in his personal accounts to make the banks whole. Not nearly enough.

The mill had always been his cash cow, and he'd assumed it always would be. If it suddenly stopped producing, he might go bankrupt. Unlike his dalliances with younger women, a personal bankruptcy was definitely something the *Washington Post* would drag him through the muck and mire for. Of course, if the mill stopped producing, the *Washington Post* would be the least of his worries. There'd suddenly be five hundred people out of work in Fort Mason without much chance of finding another job. Any one of whom might get liquored up one night and decide to vent his frustration on the person who'd axed him.

"Thirty days?" Big Bill asked again, mad as hell at Jeremy. Almost as mad at himself for feeling the sweat break out all over his body, for hearing the strain in his own voice. He'd always prided himself on being a cool customer, on being able to handle stress no matter how bad it was. Maybe he wasn't as cool as he'd thought. Of course, he'd never faced anything like this before. "What the hell's going on? Why can't you get trees?"

"Over the last few months, groups have been locking up the timber supply all over the Northwest and Canada," Jeremy explained, his voice still shaking. "It's weird."

Big Bill's eyes narrowed. He had an idea who one of those groups might be. "Is it Integrated Papers?"

Jeremy shook his head. "They've gotten some of it, but it's mostly independent partnerships and limited-liability companies that aren't related. At least, it doesn't look like they're related." He took a deep breath. "It seems like every damn tree from here to the Arctic Circle is gone, and it happened so fast. It doesn't make sense, Dad. They've locked up lease rights on trees that won't be ready to cut down for five years. It's crazy."

"Call them," Big Bill ordered. "See if you can make some deals."

"I've tried, but I can't get through to anybody. They all give Delaware numbers, but I call and I don't get any answer."

Big Bill swiveled around in his chair and gazed down at the river. This was what happened when you let somebody run your company who didn't have that street fighter instinct. He swallowed hard. And when you broke those rules about dating you swore you'd never break.

Maybe it was time to call that friend of his out east. A man who suddenly owed him a big favor.

17

I WANT TO KNOW *how the hell Hunter Lee got that memo!*" George Drake yelled. He was a short, thin man who walked with an obvious limp because of a hip injury he'd suffered in a terrible car accident as a boy. Drake was small in stature, but he had a set of lungs on him any lion would have been proud of. And he had a temper to match the pipes. "That memo from Carl Bach to the head of track maintenance that blew the whole damn case for me. The one that proved Bach was behind everything. That little rat bastard," Drake hissed.

Charlie Hall made certain his expression betrayed no emotion, even though he wanted to slug his boss for being so heartless. Hall was chief financial officer of the Bridger Railroad and of Drake's other big company, Bridger Air. He'd been Drake's money man for eight years, and he knew how to get his point across without sending his boss into orbit even when Drake was already on a rampage. Most of the time, anyway.

"Speaking of Carl," Hall said calmly, "we should send flowers to the funeral."

It was a subtle but poignant reminder that the "little rat bastard" had committed suicide by blowing his brains out in a hotel hallway. Hall and Bach had been friends, often ate lunch together, and Hall was pretty sure Drake was the real rat bastard in all of this. He was pretty sure Drake had given Bach the choice of committing fraud or being fired, too. Bach had two kids in college and another one about to get there, so what the hell was he supposed to do? It seemed pretty clear that it was Drake who'd set off the terrible chain of events that had ultimately ended in Carl Bach's suicide.

The critical questions for Hall at this point: How could he stick around? How could he stay loyal to a man who didn't care about anything but himself and the balance in his bank account? Who treated human beings the same way he treated rails, ties, and boxcars? "It would be a nice gesture." Hall had been pondering those questions for two days but hadn't come up with any answers yet. Not ones that made any sense or ones he wanted to admit to. "And it would look good to the public."

"Yeah, sure," Drake grumbled, gazing out the window of the limousine as they headed away from O'Hare Airport. They'd flown to Chicago this morning to attend an emergency meeting called by the railroad's lead bank. "Go ahead and send them. What I also want to know," he kept going, his voice growing strong again, "is how these damn people in Fort Mason found a lawyer like Hunter Lee. I mean, does that make sense to you, Charlie?"

It was an interesting question, Hall reckoned. How had eight blue-collar families from a forgotten dot on a Montana map hooked up with one of the most talented litigators around? How had they gotten him to take what he must have figured at first blush was a small-potatoes case? Was it just coincidence, or was there more to it than that? But no one had been able to figure out the connection.

"I hear you, George." It didn't look like they were ever going to find that connection now that the case was over. "As far as figuring out who slipped Lee a copy of the memo, well, you've got to start by looking at who had motive."

"Okay," Drake pushed, "who had motive?"

Hall made an aggravated face, as if what he was about to say was obvious. "There's a few executives you've fired along the way who'd love to see you go down."

Drake rolled his eyes. "*A few?* There's more than that, Charlie." He waved, aggravated himself now. "But how would they get to the files? Security knows not to let anybody who's been fired into our facilities. And for all his faults, Carl Bach was a careful guy when it came to sensitive files. He kept all that stuff under lock and key. He certainly wouldn't have wanted that memo to get out, either, so he would have been extra careful about it. Even if some of the people who work for me now wanted to see me go down, they wouldn't have been able to get to the files."

It was Hall's turn to roll his eyes. As smart as Drake was, he could be damn naive at times. "People get creative, George."

"You're barking up the wrong tree," said Drake dismissively. "Who else?"

Hall spread his arms. "The trial's over, George. What difference does it make?"

"It does."

"But why?"

"It *just* does."

Drake was figuring the trouble wasn't over, Hall assumed. He was figuring whoever had slipped the maintenance memo to Hunter Lee was out there planning more trouble for Bridger Railroad, or Bridger Air, or both. Ultimately for George Drake. That was why Drake was still intent on figuring out how the memo had gotten into Hunter Lee's hands. If he could figure that out, he could figure out who was planning more trouble for him and stop the guy dead in his tracks. Drake was good at stopping people dead in their tracks.

Hall gazed out the window. He and Drake had worked together for eight years, and they'd talked to each other almost every day over that span. Most days they spoke to each several times or attended meetings together. Despite all those years and all the ups and downs they'd been through together, it still didn't feel to Hall as if they were friends. It still felt as if they were just business acquaintances. He'd never even been to Drake's house over in Missoula, not once, never even been invited to come over. So why the hell was he still in business with the man? After all the thinking Hall had done, he could only come up with one answer. Drake paid him extremely well. Which wasn't much of an answer.

"How about Big Bill Brule?" Hall suggested.

Drake's eyes moved slowly to Hall's. "Go on."

"Come on, George, it isn't that hard to connect the dots."

"I want to see if you're thinking the same thing I am."

Hall shrugged. "The Bridger Railroad takes Katrina Mason's timber out of Big Bill's hands, away from Montana, and away from his mill out on the Lassiter to mills farther west or in the Southeast. Without the Bridger, Katrina would have to send her timber to those guys by truck and she wouldn't make nearly as much doing it that way because shipping by truck would cost a lot more. Without the Bridger, she might sell it to the Brule mill." Hall hesitated. "We've heard Big Bill's got a supply problem. We don't know how bad it is, but it would make sense that he'd want to lock up those hundreds of thousands of timber acres Katrina has in Montana. If the Bridger Railroad wasn't around, it'd be a lot easier for him to do that, for him to convince her to sell him her timber. Even though supposedly they can't stand each other," he added. "I mean, she's still gotta keep that big ranch of hers going and that takes cash and lots of it. Cash from the sale of trees. Slipping that memo to Hunter Lee would be a damn good way for Big Bill to get what he wanted, for him to force Katrina to sell her timber to him." Hall could see that Drake was riveted to what he was saying. "The railroad was on the edge financially even before this lawsuit," he muttered. "I know the insurance company's gonna pick up a good piece of the settlement, but not all of it. We're in an even deeper hole now."

"Yeah, but how would Bill Brule get that damn memo?"

"He knows everyone in Fort Mason, everyone in the damn state for that matter."

Drake picked up a bottled water from the console along one side of the limo and took several frustrated gulps. "Who else?"

Hall took some time getting up his nerve to make this suggestion. "What about Dale Callahan?"

Drake's eyes snapped to Hall's, but he said nothing.

"He's one of those guys you fired."

Drake had fired Callahan from his position as senior marketing officer of both Bridger companies three years ago. It had been a messy corporate divorce because Callahan had a contract, and details of the suits and countersuits had been followed closely by the state newspapers. Both men hadn't held back their hatred for each other in their comments to reporters as the fight went on. Callahan had ultimately settled for an unspecified amount, and they'd both agreed in the final documents not to publicly criticize the other. But it was common knowledge that they despised each other.

"Then there's that other thing with Callahan," Hall continued.

"What other thing?"

Hall took a deep breath. God, Drake could be so obtuse, or at least seem to be when it was convenient. Or maybe he really thought that his CFO hadn't heard all the rumors. "The dog, George, the dog. That yellow Lab Callahan thought was going to take him to New York and win him a blue ribbon at the national show."

"I had nothing to do with that dog being killed," Drake snapped. "The damn thing got killed by my train, but I didn't have anything to do with it getting out of its kennel or onto the tracks."

"I'm not sure Callahan believes that." Hall wasn't sure he believed it, either, but he wasn't about to say anything.

"He can believe what he wants, but I had *nothing* to do with it." Drake shook his head as though it was absurd to think that he would stoop to that level. "Who else had motive, Charlie?"

Drake didn't like hearing bad news, but sometimes you had to level with him. Of course, you had to pick your spots, too. "How about Butch Roman?" Hall suggested.

Butch Roman owned the other big company headquartered in Fort Mason: Roman Construction. It was second only to the Brule Lumber Mill in terms of local population employed, and it built almost anything. From small homes to mansions to commercial space to factories to office buildings, Butch Roman would take on the project if the deal was priced right. In the last ten years Roman had expanded his business so that he was building across the entire Northwest, even as far away as California, and he brought a lot of his supplies into headquarters from the Midwest and the West Coast on the Bridger Railroad.

"Butch thinks you're charging him way too much to bring his supplies in from the outside," Hall continued. "He's called me a dozen times in the past few months to bitch about it. He got pretty jacked up on a few of those calls, too."

"Butch can be a real horse's ass," Drake agreed. "That's his personality."

"Especially when he feels cornered, and you've got him in a tight one. Katrina Mason's only other choice to get her timber out of Montana is by truck. Well, that's Butch's only other choice to get supplies *into* Montana. He knows it, you know it. The Bridger Railroad is cheaper than trucks, but Butch still feels screwed. He made that clear to me in no uncertain terms during those calls. He just hates being put in a box."

"But that doesn't explain why he'd want to shut my railroad down," Drake argued. "As you said, whether he likes it or not, I'm still cheaper than trucks."

This answer might actually send Drake into orbit, but Drake had asked the question and he needed to hear the answer. "Maybe Butch figures the Bridger Railroad goes into bankruptcy if we lose the suit. Then he buys it on the cheap from the banks and operates it himself. I hear he's been talking to an investor group from out east about that, about buying the Bridger Railroad with him."

"*What?*" Drake turned quickly toward Hall. He'd been gazing at the Chicago skyline, which had just come into view. "Where'd you hear that?"

Hall didn't want to be specific, not even with Drake. Break a confidence once in Montana and no one would ever talk to you again. "Around."

"Don't play coy with me, Charlie."

"A friend of mine over in Billings told me. He was talking to an outfitter who got it from a fishing guide. The guide overheard some chatter while he was taking a couple of execs from out east down the Big Horn on a fly-fishing trip. I guess they thought a fishing guide wouldn't understand what they were talking about, or wouldn't care. Obviously they didn't understand Montana."

Drake stared at Hall darkly.

Hall had one more thing to tell Drake. This one was really going to fry his boss's brain, but he had to get Drake thinking realistically. The senior credit officer of the bank in charge of today's meeting had made clear to Hall on the phone this morning that it wouldn't be pleasant. Unless Drake was willing to inject a significant amount of additional equity into the railroad or put up other assets he owned as collateral for the loans to the railroad, the bank was going to put Drake on the clock. They were going to give him a short window to make things right, then they were going to force him into bankruptcy. At that point, Butch Roman would get the railroad if he and his investors came to the table with a fair offer. Losing the lawsuit had been the last straw for the banks.

"Look, George," Hall said, "at least Bridger Air's doing well. That contract you inked with the Feds two years ago to fly firefighters from hot spot to hot spot is paying big dividends." Hall shook his head. "We almost don't have enough planes at this point because of all the fires breaking out this summer."

18

KATRINA SAT BEHIND her father's old desk in the study of the ranch's main house getting ready to work the numbers. Balancing the books was taking more and more time lately. She'd enjoyed her ride across the ranch after her early morning meeting with Dale Callahan yesterday, but it seemed like those days were few and far between now. Running the ranch was turning out to be far more difficult than she'd ever imagined.

Butch Roman sat in front of her still wearing the white construction hat he'd shown up in an hour ago, smacking on spearmint-flavored gum. Butch had grown up the hard way, pulled himself up by his bootstraps. He was originally from one of Fort Mason's poorest neighborhoods, and he'd never graduated from high school. At fourteen he'd taken a job with a construction company in Missoula by faking his age and convincing the foreman he was sixteen, then toiled in the field for twenty years before building a house for a friend on his own time. The day after finishing it— the day of his thirty-fourth birthday—he'd quit his job as foreman of a crew in Dillon, Montana, and founded Roman Construction. He'd never looked back.

Now in his early fifties, Butch still put his nose to the grindstone every day. The only speed he knew was full, and people who got in his way were sorry, whether they meant to cut across his path or not. There were rumors that he'd killed an Idaho man a few years ago over an unpaid eight-thousand-dollar invoice, but nothing had ever been proven. Butch was a touch under six feet tall, had tight curly brown hair, a square jaw, a bushy mustache, and boxer's hands—big and powerful with thick fingers. One of his claims to fame was that he'd never worn a suit a day in his life. And, though only a few people in town knew it, he was the founder and largest supporter of a new soup kitchen that fed at least a hundred low-income families a day. He drove a plain Chevy pickup truck, lived in a modest home, and never told anyone what he was worth. Not even his personal banker really knew.

"I really appreciate you doing this for me personally." Katrina could smell the spearmint. God, he smacked that gum hard. "I hear you don't usually do these kinds of meetings anymore."

"No, I don't," Butch answered gruffly. "Usually I have one of my guys do the estimates." He shrugged. "But, hey, you're Katrina Mason."

Katrina had always liked Butch's directness. It made doing business with him extremely efficient. "Look, this new barn's very important to me." She'd asked Butch to come to the ranch today to talk about Roman Construction replacing the worn out main barn with a new one. They'd spent the last hour walking around the old barn so Butch could give her an estimate. "It'll really improve the operation. Will you do it for me?"

"Yeah, I will." He put his notebook on the desk and leaned back in his chair. "It'll be six hundred grand."

"That's pretty steep." She hesitated, considering the pros and cons. The price was high, but Roman Construction was unquestionably reliable. Butch would hit whatever timetable he laid out. "Okay, I'll pay it. One more thing, though. I need it done before winter, before the snows hit."

"Then it'll be eight hundred grand."

"No, no. You're not gonna—"

"Eight hundred grand, Katrina. That's my offer if you want the barn finished by November 1."

"Seven," she countered.

Butch shook his head. "If I say it'll get done by November 1, it'll get done by November 1. The other two companies you could go with will tell you they'll get it done by then, but they won't. They'll leave you and your sheep and your cows and your horses out in the cold when the snows roll in. You know it, I know it. The price is eight hundred thousand dollars," he said firmly.

She could tell he wasn't going to budge. She'd known him a long time and she recognized the body language. "All right," she agreed deliberately, making certain he could see her frustration.

"I'll need 50 percent down to get started, too."

Katrina rolled her eyes. This was ridiculous. *"What?"*

"You need to write me a four-hundred-thousand-dollar check if you want me to get started."

"I thought you were doing pretty well. Should I be worried that—"

"It isn't *my* credit that's the problem," Butch interrupted. "It's yours."

She gazed at him hard, then opened a drawer, pulled out a big blue book and wrote the check. "Here," she said, ripping it from the book and holding it out. "Satisfied?"

"I will be when it clears." He took the check, folded it over once, and slipped it into his shirt pocket. "My contract people will be in touch with you," he said, picking up his notebook off her desk and starting to get up. "We'll have something to you by—"

"Wait," she said, motioning for him to sit down. "Please."

He eased back into the chair. "What?"

Butch had a reputation for being tight with information. He wasn't into the rumor mill the way a lot of people out here were. He didn't mind getting information, but he rarely gave it back out, so this was a long shot. Still, she had to give it a try. "You've done a few buildings for Dale Callahan, right?" she asked. "For Callahan Foods."

"We built a big warehouse for him over in Boise last year with full refrigeration and freezer capability," Butch said proudly. "And it looks like we'll be doing his new headquarters in Billings as well as a big production plant for him in Sacramento."

"He's going all the way into California now?"

"Yup. Just like me. Dale's not the only guy I'm building for on the West Coast these days."

"Did you get 50 percent down from Dale?" Katrina asked.

Butch shook his head. "Nope. Look, I've got another—"

"I heard you were working with an investor group out east to maybe buy the Bridger Railroad if it goes bankrupt." Katrina could tell by Butch's expression that she'd gotten his attention. "That true?"

Butch smiled thinly and stood up. "Why?"

"The Bridger Railroad carries a lot of timber for me," she answered. "I want to make sure it stays in business."

"Is that it, or are you trying to get information for someone?"

"Who are you talking about?" she asked defensively.

"You know who I'm talking about." Butch touched the brim of his construction hat. "Like I said, my contract people will be in touch with you. Thanks, Katrina."

When he was gone, she tossed the checkbook back into the drawer, frustrated. She'd been hoping to keep her relationship with George Drake a secret. Clearly that had been a pipe dream.

19

FOR THE LAST six hours they'd been fishing one of Strat's favorite stretches of the Lassiter River. The picturesque spot was twenty miles west of the Brule Lumber Mill, and it was remote, far off the beaten path. As if there really was a beaten path anywhere near here, Hunter thought, grinning. But the more time he spent in Fort Mason, the more he liked it and the more he was getting comfortable with its isolation.

The last two miles to the river, Strat and he had careened through first light along a rutted logging road. A few times, when they'd hit what felt like a pothole the size of the Grand Canyon, Hunter was sure Strat's old pickup was going to disintegrate, or at least blow a tire or two. It hadn't, but Hunter had banged his head on the roof a few times—being tall wasn't always an advantage. Amazingly, the crap on the dashboard had stayed put. Everything except an unpaid ticket for a blown headlight and taillight that had tumbled into his lap after they'd hit the worst bump. The ticket was a year old, Hunter had noticed as he tossed it back up on the dashboard. But that was how things were in Fort Mason, he was coming to find. People moved at their own pace.

They hadn't seen anyone since leaving town. In fact, the only evidence of civilization Hunter had noticed thus far this morning were jet exhaust streams painting thin white ribbons across a cloudless sky. Other than that, the only significant sightings involved wildlife. A herd of mule deer grazing in a small meadow filled with colorful wildflowers; a huge bull elk with a massive rack still covered in velvet that had burst from the forest in front of them as they were speeding down the logging road and almost turned the day into a disaster; a moose dredging up underwater plants along the far bank of the river; and a curious coyote with a crooked tail who kept checking on them every hour or so. As well as an assortment of eagles, osprey, Canada geese, mergansers, and mallards. But they'd seen no large predators, no bears or cats.

Which was fine with Hunter. He'd heard plenty about bear and cat attacks, and he had no desire to experience one, to even come close to experiencing one. Strat kept mumbling about at least seeing a grizzly this morning, but Hunter figured his brother was just saying that because he was a Montanan now and Montanans were supposed to be tougher than anybody else around. And because there was still some sibling rivalry left in Strat, even after all these years.

"Hey, brother," Strat spoke up as he tilted the straw hat he was wearing forward over his face to protect it from the blazing rays. It was ninety-six degrees and the sun hadn't even reached its apex yet. "You really should move here to Fort Mason."

They were relaxing on top of a smooth flat boulder that overlooked a deep pool, flyrods lying on the rock face beside them. At the beginning of July, state wildlife officials had forbidden any fishing on the Lassiter after noon because of the summer's hot temperatures. The Lassiter was a blue-ribbon catch-and-release trout river, and as the water warmed in the afternoon, large trout had a tough time recovering from a fight. The twenty-inch-plus browns and rainbows needed cold water flowing over their gills to regain their strength after being released back into the water. The shallows became like bathwater when the sun was high overhead, which made it very difficult to resuscitate the fish.

So, now that it was past noon, Hunter and Strat were kicking back, taking in the day before heading home to Strat's old trailer, which was parked in a small, weedy clearing in the woods off an isolated dirt road a few miles north of Fort Mason. As they relaxed, they watched big rainbows take caddis flies emerging on the surface near a tangled mess of branches protruding from the middle of the river. The rising fish were setting off ever-expanding circular wakes as they gulped newly hatched insects with their gaping white mouths. Hunter doubted that he and Strat ran any risk way out here of crossing paths with a ranger who'd cite them for fishing past the cutoff time, but he respected Strat's respect for the environment. Besides, they'd both had an excellent morning. Each of them had landed a couple of big fish.

It was obvious that Strat loved Montana, maybe more than Virginia now. Which made Hunter wonder why he hadn't dropped the Virginia accent. Strat was smart enough to know that it would get in the way out here, but, of course, he could be a stubborn son of a bitch. Maybe somebody had made fun of the accent when he first moved to Fort Mason, and Strat had vowed to himself never to lose it. Or maybe it was that he still loved Virginia, too. Maybe he was holding on to the twang because it was his one last connection to his childhood. Mom and Dad were gone and most of their friends had moved away from the old town.

"Seriously," Strat kept going as he reclined on the boulder and slid the hat back over his face. "You should move here."

It was at least the fifth time Strat had pushed Hunter to move to Fort Mason since drinks at The Depot last night, but it was the first time Hunter had actually considered it. "Why, Strat? Because Anne filed for divorce, and now I've got nothing but an empty, single life back east as I hurtle toward my fortieth birthday?" Up until now Hunter hadn't responded to the uproot-and-move suggestion, just changed the subject.

Strat let out a low chuckle from beneath his hat. "I couldn't have said it better myself, brother."

"Thanks for sugar-coating it."

"Sure. Oh, by the way," Strat spoke up, "we refer to it as *out* east in Montana."

"Huh?"

"When we talk about the East Coast in Montana, we refer to it as *out* east. Not back east."

"But that's where most everybody came from," Hunter pointed out. "Where *you* came from. So it should be *back* east."

"Nevertheless." Strat adjusted his hat. "And don't get off the point, which is that you should move here. Come on, no more excuses, brother, just do it."

It wouldn't do any good to remind Strat that he was the one who'd gotten them off the point, or to argue about whether it should be "out" east or "back" east. For the last hour, Hunter had caught Strat stealing quick gulps from a flask he kept sneaking out of his fishing vest. Not that Strat was ever really open to changing his mind or admitting to a mistake, but that would never happen with alcohol in his system. Well, at least he'd held off until eleven, Hunter thought ruefully.

"I've still got my law practice in New York." Hunter watched the rainbows gulp flies a little longer, then lay back on the boulder, too. For a damn rock it was pretty comfortable. "I've gotta think about my partners."

"Screw those bastards," Strat grumbled.

"Huh?"

"They're screwing you."

"How do you figure?" Hunter asked. "You got a mole in the payroll department at Warfield & Stone?"

"I don't need a mole."

"Then how—"

"Any time a person won't tell me what he makes, or what his cut of a deal is, I figure it's because he doesn't think it's enough and he's pissed off about it. Don't get your boxers in a bunch, brother," Strat continued quickly, anticipating a comeback. "That's just my experience."

Unfortunately, Strat was right. Hunter was starting to get irritated about it, too. On one hand, he realized he was a lucky man when it came to money. He made a lot more than the average Joe. On the other hand, he worked hard for it. Seventy-hour weeks weren't uncommon, and that didn't include his three-hour-a-day round-trip commute or the weeks he spent out of town for trials. Weeks Anne was having a lot of fun, he now realized. Which was probably why she'd always encouraged him to go for longer if it would "help win the case."

And pay ought to be relative no matter how many dollars were in the pie. It ought to be distributed in direct proportion to success, in proportion to what you did for your firm. The seven senior partners were taking huge bites of Warfield & Stone's pie and they weren't sharing the wealth with the next level down, with the twenty partners on Hunter's level who were doing most of the work. In fact, two of the senior partners—Sam McCabe and the founder's son Harry Stone—were barely bringing in any fees at all, but both of them had taken ten million in cash out of the firm at the end of last year. Hunter had made seventy-five million for the firm last year, but he hadn't taken ten million out. Not even close.

Hunter sat up quickly and looked around, checking in every direction, suddenly uneasy, suddenly feeling as if one of those dangerous predators he'd heard so much about was lurking in the underbrush. This was the one part of Fort Mason's isolation he'd never get used to.

"What's wrong, Hunt?"

"Nothing."

Strat laughed. "You hear a twig snap?"

"Funny."

"Relax, everything's fine."

Which was exactly what Nelson Radcliff had said when Hunter and the old man had met last March in the managing partner's spacious corner office overlooking Park Avenue. After the firm's year-end distributions were made and the other nineteen partners on Hunter's level had unanimously elected him to go to Radcliff and tell him how frustrated they were at how the senior partners were screwing them. They'd elected Hunter because he was Radcliff's protégé, and, therefore, they felt he stood the best chance of convincing the senior partner to change the pay structure.

Hunter had always been close to Radcliff, ever since the managing partner had recruited him out of law school. In fact, it was more than a mentor-protégée connection, it was closer to a father-son relationship. Which made it tougher—not easier—to approach Radcliff about money. But Hunter had forced himself to do it and been proud of himself afterward.

After talking in the office, they'd gone to lunch and Radcliff had smiled at him over coffee, told him how the other senior partners thought of him as the odds-on favorite to be the next managing partner. It might be a few years until that happened because, after all, he was only thirty-eight, but it was almost sure to at some point because of all the business he was bringing in. Because of the way he carried himself around the office, too—with sincere concern for everyone including the paralegals and secretaries. And because of his reputation for being tough but unfailingly honest in a field littered with unethical attorneys.

Hunter remembered feeling good about their talk. Until he had a chance to really think about it on the long train ride home to Connecticut, until he remembered what a master manipulator Nelson Radcliff was.

Now, a few months after all of Radcliff's promises to change things, Hunter was certain this year would be no different. Except for Radcliff, the senior partners were doing even less business this year, relying even more heavily on their twenty younger partners to carry the load. Harry Stone was only making it into the office two or three days a week, and he hadn't landed a new client in a year. But the word from the Greenwich Country Club was that he'd cut his golf handicap in half this summer.

"What would I do out here?" Hunter asked.

"Start your own damn practice."

"In *Montana*?"

"Why not?"

The thing was, he probably could. Thanks to his track record, Hunter had more cases than he could handle these days. They were coming in from everywhere except the senior partners. Once in a while Radcliff tossed him a bone, but he was the only one of the inner circle who did. The cases Hunter was bringing in from his own network were the mega-money paydays—except for the Bridger case. That had come from Radcliff, though Hunter still wasn't clear how Radcliff had found it. He'd asked twice but hadn't gotten a satisfactory answer.

Despite being confident in his ability to generate business, it would still be a risk to go out on his own. A lot of clients would always want a big name New York City firm representing them. Hunter wouldn't get those cases hanging out his shingle on Main Street in Fort Mason, Montana, but there'd still probably be enough cases to make a living. Maybe even a good living.

"How many people are there in Fort Mason?" Hunter asked.

"Around six thousand in the valley," Strat answered. "Of that, around four thousand are inside the town limits. Why do you ask?"

There wouldn't be many eligible women in that group, Hunter figured. "Who am I going to hang out with?"

"Me."

"Great, there's one night a month."

Strat pulled his hat from his face, turned on his side, and broke into a wide grin. "Oh, you mean *women*-wise who are you going to hang with."

Hunter shrugged. "Well, sure. After all, I'll be a divorcee." A divorcee. God, that sounded terrible. It sounded like something your friend's mother and father were going through, not you. Out of nowhere, the image of who Anne had probably spent the last few nights with flashed through his mind again.

Strat's grin grew wider. "Hell, you'll have your damn pick, Hunt. They'll be hanging all over you. You heard what Kate said last night."

"Wait a minute, brother. You told me I wouldn't get a big head here because there aren't that many good-looking women in Fort Mason."

Strat's expression turned grave. "Is that what New York City does to people? Is that what it's done to you? Does a woman have to be good-looking for you to be interested in her?"

Hunter turned his head deliberately to look at Strat, trying to figure out if his brother was being serious. Even though he wasn't that hand-some, Strat had always managed to date reasonably attractive women.

"No," Hunter answered slowly, still trying to figure out where Strat really was on this issue. "I like a lot of women you wouldn't give the time of day to. Look, you're the one who always—"

Strat burst out laughing. "All right, all right, you aren't gonna find any centerfolds in Fort Mason, but how about Zoe Gale? She's pretty, huh?"

"Sure, but you told me to stay away from her. You told me she was big trouble."

"Yeah, I did," Strat admitted. "But I got to thinking about her last night, and I figure you need a challenge. That's probably why you wanted to marry Anne in spite of what we all told you. Because she was a challenge." He rolled onto his back again and stared up at a lone buzzard circling lazily across the deep blue sky above them. "For all her faults, Anne's pretty sharp."

"Yeah, she is."

During their first few years together, Hunter and Anne had often stayed up late into the night talking about politics and social issues. Hunter had enjoyed those discussions immensely, even when they'd gotten heated. Maybe even more when they got heated because the sex ended up being better the angrier they were. He pictured her body on top of his, pictured her arching her back, hands on his chest. She was a free spirit, a wild woman who'd often told him she thought sex was the only thing really worth living for. He took a deep breath and shut his eyes. He missed her. Which was hard to admit.

Hunter sat up and glanced around the area again. Which didn't do much good. You couldn't see more than a few feet back into the woods. It wasn't as if you were going to have time to react if a critter with long teeth and sharp claws suddenly came charging out at you. "You really think Zoe's trouble?" he asked.

"I think anyone who's name is Gale and has brown eyes might be keeping a secret or two."

Once in a while Strat came up with a lulu, so Hunter checked the buckle of his psychological seatbelt. Thing was, sometimes Strat's out-of-left-field observations ended up being accurate. He had a sixth sense about people. Of course, sometimes he could be way off, too. "Why do you say that?"

"Gale's short for Galanis," Strat answered. "In Greek, Galanis means 'one with blue eyes.' I looked it up. But Zoe's got brown eyes."

"Jesus Christ," Hunter mumbled, half-irritated, half-amused. "That's her capital offense, Strat? That's why you think she's so much trouble? Maybe she doesn't even know—"

"Translated," Strat cut in, "I don't think she's who she says she is. And," he kept going before Hunter had a chance to protest, "I think she kinda likes that little inside play. I think she kinda likes staring at us with those big brown eyes of hers thinking she's pulling one over on a bunch of dumb locals who don't know that her name means blue eyes." He nodded confidently. "She knows what she's doing. Oh, yeah, she's trouble all right. Of course, that makes her a challenge, and that's what you need."

Hunter had heard Strat call himself a local. It was the first time in all the years he'd been out here Hunter had heard that. "How do you know? How do you know she knows?"

"Yeah, she's trouble all right," Strat repeated, avoiding the question. His expression darkened as he watched the buzzard retrace circle after lazy circle in the sky. "Of course, nothing like the trouble you might get from George Drake after what you did to his railroad." He pursed his lips. "But you already know that."

In a strange way, Hunter had always hoped someone he'd sued would come after him. Bring it on was his attitude, but it had never happened. People thought a lot about it when they lost, and sometimes they got worked up about it after a few drinks, but nobody ever did anything. They'd already been to court and they didn't want to go back again, especially not to answer a criminal complaint. It turned out courtrooms were damn intimidating places. For good reason.

"I'm not worried about George Drake," Hunter said evenly. "He doesn't scare me."

"Really?"

"Nope."

"Well you banged up his company pretty good," Strat said, pointing up at the sky. The lone buzzard had been joined by four more. "From what I hear, the vultures are circling around the Bridger Railroad just like those guys up there are circling around some kill. Thanks to you."

Hunter glanced up at the birds, hoping the kill the birds were circling around didn't involve a bear or a mountain lion. A bear or a mountain lion that was still lurking in the area, still protecting that kill. "Oh, yeah?" He knew the railroad was struggling, but he assumed Drake was smart enough to have insurance policies in place to cover any major liability claims.

"Yeah." Strat was quiet for a few moments. "But he owns Bridger Air, too. That thing's probably doing pretty well right now. So, maybe he's not in such bad shape after all. Maybe you're right, maybe there isn't any reason to worry about him."

"What's Bridger Air?"

"It's an air cargo company," Strat explained. "It does okay." He held his hand out so his fingers were level to the ground and shook them slightly.

"But you just said it was probably doing well right now."

Strat slowly lowered his gaze from the buzzards to Hunter. "I did say that, didn't I?"

Hunter didn't like it when Strat played games. "Strat, what are you—"

"Bridger Air has a contract with the United States Forest Service to move firefighters around the country. Even to east of the Mississippi if they have a real big fire out there and they need more people on the ground. I hear he got a nice payment when he signed the contract, but that the real juice comes when the fires break out."

"What do you mean?"

"Drake gets a fat per-person fee every time one of his planes lifts off with firefighters in it, and the farther he has to take them the more he gets. So he gets this big per-body payment for each individual he flies to a forest fire, and suddenly there's lots of fires breaking out all over the Northwest this summer. Especially in Montana. *Lots* of them." Strat gave Hunter a curious look. "Yeah, you need to move here to Montana, brother. You *really* need to move here."

Hunter glanced at the pile of dead branches in the middle of the river and the trout feeding around it. He watched the circular wakes still magically appearing on the river's shimmering surface until everything faded to a blur when what Strat had said became clear. "So," he spoke up, "I take it you don't think Bridger Air signing that contract with the Forest Service and the number of forest fires going up so much this year is a coincidence."

"Brother," Strat answered in a quiet voice, "I don't think anything's a coincidence anymore."

"Do you really think Drake is setting the fires?"

"He sure gets paid a lot when fires break out."

"Is that why you want me to move here, Strat?" Hunter asked directly. "Do you want me to help you figure out if George Drake is setting the fires?"

"I want you to move here mostly because I miss you, Hunt." Strat hesitated. "And because I want you to help me figure out if George Drake is behind all these fires. Or if someone else is."

"Is this more than just a hunch on your part? That someone's starting all of these fires, I mean?"

"Yeah, it is, a lot more than a hunch, in fact. I've been doing a lot of snooping around in my spare time."

Hunter had been afraid of that.

"But I need help, your help, brother. I can't trust anybody like I can trust you, and I can't do all this alone."

"Did you come up with this conspiracy thing on your own," Hunter asked, "or did you have help?"

"I had some help, but I'm not going to tell you who it is that's helping me. Not yet, anyway. It's better for you that way. It's better for you not to know right now."

Something told Hunter that Strat was right, that he didn't want to know right now. "Why do you think Dad pushed me into the law?" he asked out of nowhere. "Why do you think Dad wanted me to be a litigator so badly, Strat?"

Strat thought for a few moments, then held up two fingers. "Two reasons. First, you're the best damn arguer on the planet. I've never seen anyone like you when it comes to that, and I don't mean you're loud or obnoxious or anything. I mean you've got this talent for making things sound so much more believable than the other guy. You've got this way of simplifying really complicated stuff so even I can understand it. You're amazing that way." He paused. "Second, you're relentless. Once you set your sights on something you never give up until you get it. You've been that way since you were a baby. It's the perfect combination for a trial lawyer." Strat smiled as if he was about to say something he'd wanted to say for a long time. "Let's be honest, Dad wasn't a real sophisticated man. It's kind of hard to be sophisticated when you're a ditch-digger, but give him credit. He understood what you were good at, then he figured out how you could take what you were good at and make a lot of money. Looking back on it, I'm surprised he even knew what a litigator was. But he didn't want you to be poor like him, so he did his research. He figured out that being a litigator was your best chance of getting rich. He probably felt bad because he couldn't give you all the things he wanted to, but he figured if he made you be a lawyer, at least that would be some kind of gift." Strat shook his head. "How much was it the other day in Bozeman? Thirteen million? I'd say Dad hit the jackpot, wouldn't you?"

20

THEY WERE DIVING into the big sky together again, but this time they were wearing sleek, royal-blue skintight jump suits, not Kevlar-reinforced earth-tone overalls. The chutes they were packing were small and highly maneuverable, not the ice cream cones they used for battle. This time they were jumping from fourteen thousand feet, not five. Most important, this time it was for fun, not to fight a fire. It was still dangerous, because any time you threw yourself from a perfectly good airplane you were asking for trouble, Paul figured. But at least they didn't need to worry about a wall of flames hundreds of feet high chasing them up a ridge at fifty miles an hour.

Burning to death had to be one of the worst ways to go, Paul had always thought. Excruciatingly painful, he'd heard from two guys who'd suffered serious burns. Hitting the ground at high speed wouldn't be nearly as bad. Everything would be over in an instant and there wouldn't be any pain. A lot of screaming on the way down, then a blackout. Which had made him wonder long and hard about his choice of professions. Maybe he ought to be a skydiving instructor, not a Fire Jumper.

It was his scheduled day off, and with some behind-the-scenes sleight of hand, he'd managed to free up Mandy, too. Fortunately, nobody from the Fort Mason Fire Jumper base had been called out to fight the blaze that had been roaring toward Yellowstone. The winds in southwestern Montana had suddenly turned around 180 degrees and the monster had been reduced to a mouse in no time when it was forced to go back the way it had come. There was nothing left in that direction, no fuel to feed on. Just six thousand blackened acres that looked like something from a picture book of World War I battlefields.

The megablaze had died of its own device, as monsters often did.

Paul signaled to Ronnie Childs, who was piloting the single-engine Cessna they were about to leap from. Ronnie was a once-in-a-while fishing buddy who operated a flight training school out of Fort Mason's small airfield. A crusty old codger who ran the school more as a hobby than a business. He was only there a day or two a week, and he didn't know many of the Fire Jumpers. Except for Paul, he didn't know any of them well, so he wasn't likely to tell someone about this afternoon's jump with Mandy. His school's small building was on the opposite side of the field from the Fire Jumper base so it wasn't as if he'd have many opportunities, either. Of course, this was Montana and Paul wasn't stupid or naive enough to think that word wouldn't leak. But he had his story straight if it did.

After Ronnie signaled back with a thumbs-up, Paul tapped Mandy on the shoulder and pointed down through the open doorway at the drop zone. It was the top of a wide, grassy, relatively flat ridge uncluttered by trees. The winds were light today so hitting it ought to be easy. Paul had chosen the ridge because it was clear of trees and because it was close to something he wanted to show Mandy, something he hoped she'd appreciate.

She pulled her goggles down and nodded, then they dove through the doorway side by side. Crisscrossing each other's paths while they raced through the clear air toward the ridge. Shouting and laughing as they veered close to each other, then away. As they somersaulted, spun, and spiraled toward earth, as they had the times of their lives.

At one minute down, Paul checked the altimeter on his wrist. They needed to rip soon. They still had time before that point of no return, but he didn't want to cut it too close. He still didn't know much about Mandy's background, and he didn't want any trouble. He could have checked out her résumé on the base computer, but he didn't trust résumés. People exaggerated their achievements on those things all the time, and you couldn't confirm or call foul on a résumé without a background check. The Fort Mason Fire Jumper budget was small; cut-rate background checks barely scratched a résumé's surface; and people were pretty sharp at hiding things. Translated: If you wanted to make sure your information was reliable, you checked it out yourself.

He was sure if he talked to her for a few minutes about it, he'd be able to tell if she knew what she was doing. She wouldn't be able to lie to him. But he hadn't brought it up. For some reason he wanted her to open up to him first.

He signaled to her that it was time to rip as they whipped through thirty-nine hundred feet, and he grimaced when he saw that familiar, devil-may-care smile light up her face. They were only fifteen feet apart so he couldn't miss it. He couldn't miss what she was thinking, either. She was challenging him, she wanted to see who'd pull the cord first. Well, there wasn't going to be any game of rip-cord chicken on this flight. He'd played it a few times before when he was younger, when he was her age, and it was a stupid risk. He'd seen a kid killed trying to be macho, and it was a terrible waste of a young life. They had only ten to twelve seconds left, and he didn't know if she realized that. There wasn't time to find out.

Paul pressed his arms firmly to his sides, pulled his ankles together, pointed his toes back—turning his body into a missile—and aimed. He was next to her almost instantly and deftly pulled her rip cord, then smoothly moved away before deploying his own chute. He'd executed the entire maneuver in less than three seconds.

"Are you crazy?" She was yelling at him before her boots even touched the ground. Before she pulled up on her control ropes at the last second and landed gently on the top of the grassy ridge ten feet from where he'd come down. "You could have killed us both."

"No chance," he muttered as he wrapped up the small chute and stuffed it into a nylon bag on his belt. He'd figured this was going to happen. "I had everything under control."

"That was ridiculous."

"Hey, I didn't know if you got my signal."

"Liar. You saw me smile."

"I was being safe."

"I know how to pull a damn rip cord!" she shouted. "And when."

"How would I know that?"

"I made it into the Fire Jumpers, didn't I?"

"So?"

"So?" She flipped her goggles off and came at him, dragging her chute behind her like a wedding train. "What's your problem?"

"I told you, I signaled for you to pull. You didn't."

"Who made you king of the air?"

"I was in charge of the jump."

"Who said?"

She was right in front of him, in his face. God, she was pretty, even with that furious expression on her face. "Me!" He could see the fire burning in her eyes. Not white hot, but almost. "I know what I'm doing. You're safe on the ground, aren't you?"

"That's the problem with all you guys in the Fire Jumpers," she snapped. "You've got this macho hang-up. You think women are completely incapable, that we need to be coddled and protected, that we all got into the Jumpers on the back of affirmative action. Because the suits in Washington want to make sure there's gender equality everywhere in government, even on a fire line in Montana."

"We can only take a certain number of rookies every year," Paul shot back, trying to keep his temper in check, wishing they hadn't hit this topic so early in their relationship. It was a hot button for him, and she'd pushed it hard. "You really think you're as qualified as some of those guys we cut loose at the end of rookie camp?"

There were twenty-five applicants for rookie positions at the Fort Mason base when camp had opened at the beginning of May. It was a grueling three weeks of physical hell loaded with full-gear hikes through the mountains, ten-mile runs, strength tests, simulated fire situations, and jumps. Twenty-five applicants—twenty men and five women—but only ten rookie spots were available, and by regulation the Fire Jumpers had to accept at least three women into the program at Fort Mason as long as the women could pass the minimum pull-up, push-up, and sit-up requirements. They had to accept them no matter how much more qualified any of the thirteen men who had to be cut were.

"Do you really think that?" He heard his voice rising, felt himself struggling to stay calm. *"Huh?"*

"You're damn right I do."

"You think you can do everything as well as that kid from Wisconsin we cut the last day? That kid who benched three-ninety and finished first in almost every run?"

Mandy glared at Paul. "He was a nice guy, and he was in great shape. I'll give you that. But he was a damn coward. He would have freaked out on the line the other day when that fire was coming up the ridge at us. You know it, I know it."

"Oh yeah?" Their noses were almost touching, fingertips grazing each other's cheeks as they made their points. *"Really?"*

"Yeah, really." Mandy's eyes narrowed. "You think that guy would have gone looking for your butt when that fire wall was blowing up the ridge?"

Paul stared down into her eyes for a long time, trying to make her back down, but for the second time in two days she didn't. Finally, he shook his head. "No, I don't," he admitted, putting his palms on her soft cheeks. "I think he would have run like a deer from a wolf pack." He leaned forward and kissed her on the lips. Damn, that felt good. He loved a woman who knew how to kiss, who *really* knew how to kiss. And Mandy sure did.

She smiled up at him as he pulled back, her frustration snuffed out as quickly as it had ignited.

Paul had never been taken by a woman so fast. For the first time in a long time he felt vulnerable. "I think you're about the best rookie we—"

But she didn't let him finish. This time she started the kiss. A deep, passionate kiss that lasted twice as long as his had.

21

H E WAS OUT scouting again, out searching for another location to cause maximum damage. At least he didn't have to drive a big rig today. Today he was behind the wheel of the black Escalade, and he was loving it. He'd never owned a nice truck like this, he'd never been able to afford this kind of style. Sometimes it was the little things in life that counted most. Not the thousands in cash he was being paid each week to torch the Northwest, but driving around in style. In a truck people gave those impressed looks to. Even if it wasn't his truck, it was his style. And those people giving him the looks didn't know it wasn't his truck.

It had been barely more than a day since he'd set the last fire, but the boss already wanted more. He was angry that Montana had played such a dirty trick on him, irate that the wind had turned around suddenly and extinguished the right flank of the Big Cat Fire when the flames could have done so much more damage. When so many more firefighters would have been called in if the winds had just kept blowing toward Wyoming for another twenty-four hours.

The man eased the Escalade to the side of the county road—just a lonely strip of packed dirt winding through the Bitterroot National Forest, barely wide enough for two cars to pass. He edged the big SUV into a small clearing and reached into the backseat for a fishing rod. It was his cover in case he ran into anyone, which wasn't likely because the area was so remote. He was twenty miles from the closest town and fifteen miles from the closest house. Which was important to him since that nine-year-old boy had died trying to save his horses from the Big Cat fire. He hadn't slept much since then. He groaned as he opened the door and jumped down from the driver's seat. But here he was, scouting out another target. Well, the only way to look at the kid dying was that he should have saved himself, not the dumb horses.

The boss was getting greedy, that was obvious, and it could become a problem. He'd literally started salivating as they'd all watched reports from the Big Cat Fire on the TV, started salivating at the thought of all those firefighters descending on one small town in southwestern Montana to fight a megablaze. At the thought of the Forest Service needing to move that many people into a small area in such a short time, then having to support them all.

The authorities had moved a total of twenty-three hundred people in to fight the two fronts of the Big Cat Fire, which was eight hundred more than the boss had originally predicted could be needed. But, as he sat in the cabin overlooking the Lassiter listening to the young reporter describe how bad the situation was getting on both fronts, he'd started calculating what it would mean to have three to four thousand people deployed, and what he'd earn off that big a deployment. Not just for a couple of days either, for a week. By noon, he'd already penned a huge figure into his bank balance, counted the chicks well before they'd hatched. When they didn't hatch, he was furious.

Yup, greed had set in. If they weren't careful, things were going to spin out of control, because greed was what usually tripped up a good operation.

The man moved into the woods and started checking for downed timber, depth of needle cover, ability for the wind to move through here. Everything seemed perfect. The only negative: no paved road. He couldn't drag chains behind a truck this time, so they'd have to use a more traditional way to bring hell down on this area of Montana. Which made the job a little riskier, but he could handle it.

Damn, for what the boss was paying him, he could handle anything. Maybe even a few more victims now that he was getting more comfortable with the idea of people dying, comfortable with there being casualties of war.

22

LET'S GET RIGHT to the point."

The straitlaced-looking older man wearing a conservative three-button charcoal suit and an aggravated expression sat at the far end of the conference room table. He was a senior vice president of Chicago National Trust, the agent bank for the Bridger Railroad's two-hundred-million-dollar revolving credit. As of this morning, the revolver was drawn down to the very last penny.

Along each side of the polished table sat representatives from the other financial institutions participating with Chicago National in the Bridger loan. There were people from two other Chicago banks, two New York City banks, and a North Carolina financial institution.

"We're worried about the Bridger Railroad," the senior banker continued. "We're worried about its ability to survive. Mostly we're worried about getting our money back."

"You're wasting your time worrying about *my* railroad." George Drake sat at the opposite end of the table from the senior banker. Charlie Hall was to his right. "You ought to worry about things like death," he suggested with a brash grin. "And taxes."

Hall cringed. Drake could be so damn arrogant. He didn't understand that this was a time for contrition, even groveling. Of course, Drake had never been in the path of a financial hurricane like this one.

"Mr. Drake, you're wasting our time with your silly—"

"Everything's under control at the Bridger Railroad," Drake cut in with a reassuring tone, "now that we've got the lawsuit behind us, now that we know what we're dealing with."

"I disagree," spoke up a woman from one of the New York banks. "Now you're in even more trouble, with all the money you're going to have to pay out."

"Our insurance company will cover the settlement," Drake retorted tartly. "All but a small piece of it."

"You call ten million dollars a small piece?" the man at the end of the table demanded. *"Really?"*

"They'll cover all but *two* million of it," Drake shot back. "Two million won't be a problem. It'll take Charlie a couple of days to find it," he said, motioning to his right, "but he will."

Hall nudged Drake's arm. He'd just gotten an email from the railroad's insurance company informing him that, under a clause buried deep in the fine print of the sixty-page policy, they were going to contest eight million dollars of what they were supposed to pay. The insurance company might not ultimately win, Hall figured, but that part of the payment could be held up in court for years. And the judge would order the railroad to pay now despite the trouble with the insurance company. Finding two million quickly was one thing, something he could probably handle. But finding another eight million on top of that would be tough, nearly impossible.

Hall handed Drake his BlackBerry under the table and watched him read the message. Piled on top of this disturbing news was the fact that the banks had obviously known about the insurance company contesting the payment before he and Drake had. Somebody was in cahoots; things were clearly going on behind the scenes. Bad things.

"You better get your facts straight, Mr. Drake," one of the bankers warned.

Hall had to give his boss credit. Drake hadn't blinked once while he was reading the email. He hadn't given away any indication that he was feeling the slightest bit of pressure. Drake was a cool customer, at least in public.

"Our understanding," the senior banker continued, "is that the Bozeman court will force you to come up with the money in ninety days if the insurance company contests. Where are you going to come up with another eight million dollars?"

"We'll get it," Drake replied calmly, adjusting the knot of his tie. "I told you, don't worry."

Hall glanced quickly around the table. The bankers were nervous as hell. They were like turkeys on the Wednesday of Thanksgiving week. He could see it in their eyes and their strained expressions. They were faced with the possibility of losing money from their huge, institutional coffers, and they were acting like a meteor the size of Texas was about to slam into earth and set off the human race extinction clock. Drake was facing the imminent loss of his entire railroad, but he was ice-cold calm. He'd probably lose his marbles in the limousine on the way back to the airport—he was never calm after a meeting like this—but he wasn't going to let anyone in this room see him sweat. Hall looked out the long window overlooking Lake Michigan from fifty stories up and smiled thinly. You had to admire that in a man even if you didn't admire the man.

"How are you going to get it?" the woman from New York wanted to know. "I can't go back to my credit people in Manhattan with a 'don't worry.' I need something more concrete."

A murmur of agreement raced around the room.

"I need specifics," she kept on, emboldened by the support. "Otherwise I'll have to—"

"How old are you?" Drake interrupted, sitting up as straight as he could, trying to make himself seem bigger than he really was.

"I don't think that's any of your—"

"How old?" he interrupted again. "It's a simple question."

The woman hesitated. "Thirty-one."

"And your title is what, vice president?"

The woman pushed her chin out defiantly. "That's right."

Hall shut his eyes, but he couldn't keep them closed. It was like looking at a car wreck on the interstate as you slowly passed by. You knew how horrible it was going to be to look, but you couldn't stop yourself from doing it. He knew where Drake was going with this. They'd had this discussion hundreds of times over the years. Drake was going to tell the bankers how worthless they were, how he figured their jobs could have been handed off to chimps from any city zoo and no one would have known the difference. The bottom line: Drake didn't know when to shut up and take his medicine. Or maybe he knew, but he couldn't control himself.

These people weren't going to make any decisions today. It usually took bankers weeks to make a "fast" decision. Drake would be so much better off just nodding politely and catching the express out of here, but it was no use trying to reason with him. He wanted to inflict some pain, wanted to stick the dagger in and turn it a little. They were sticking it to him, and he couldn't stand being the only one in the room to get stuck. He didn't get the whole pick-your-battles thing.

Well, Hall realized, maybe it was time to let him start learning that he was digging his own grave.

Drake chuckled sourly. "Think you're pretty important, don't you?" He sneered, staring the young woman down. "You know, there's probably fifty thousand loan officers like you around this country. Fifty thousand of you good-for-nothings pushing endless mounds of worthless paper from one side of your desk to the other. Hell, a monkey could do your—"

"I've heard enough!" the senior banker at the end of the table roared indignantly, banging the table and springing from his seat. It was an agile move that defied his age. "You've broken four covenants in the loan agreement. The cure period is sixty days, and it starts right now. On top of that, eight million has to go into the railroad to fund the settlement, and I want you to put at least another twelve million in on top of that. I want at least twenty million dollars of fresh cash into the Bridger Railroad by mid-September, or we're taking it over. And, Mr. Drake, think twice about scurrying for Chapter 11 bankruptcy cover. That might not help you much. Maybe in the short term, but the state of litigation in the loan agreement is clearly Montana." He laughed, a low, confident laugh. "Nobody likes you much in Montana since you killed those people in Fort Mason." The banker raised an eyebrow and smiled. "Why don't you drop some money into the railroad from that other company you own." His smile grew wider. "I hear you're printing cash at Bridger Air."

23

I T'S BEAUTIFUL," MANDY whispered, gazing at the majestic
waterfall towering above them, watching in awe as the whitewater
cascaded down and down, then rushed through the heavy mist rising
as though in slow motion from the deep pool at the bottom of the falls. "It
must be a hundred feet high."

For the last half hour Mandy and Paul had been hiking upstream
beside a wide, crystal-clear stream. They'd just rounded a sharp bend,
and the waterfall was still a fair distance away. But from here they had a
perfect, unobstructed view of it.

"A hundred and *thirty*," Paul answered, pulling a two-foot-long, cy-
lindrical fly-rod case from his backpack. He slid five pieces out of the case
and began assembling them, one on top of the next. "I found it two years
ago while I was in here."

"What's its name?"

He attached the reel to the butt end of what was now a perfectly balanced nine-foot piece of tapered graphite. "That's the great thing," he said,
feeding the bright green line from the reel through the guides on the rod.
"It doesn't have a name."

"Really?"

"It's not on any map I can find." From his pocket Paul dug out a small
box of dry flies—insect imitations tied mostly with feathers and wool that
floated on the surface—picked an 18 Adams and began tying it to the

end of the ten-foot monofilament leader. The leader was attached to the end of the fly line with a nail knot. "That's one of the cool things about Montana. There's still a lot of places that haven't been discovered. We can name it whatever we want to."

Mandy gazed at the waterfall for a few moments more, then turned toward Paul. "This is why we jumped onto that ridge? *This* is why we hiked all the way in here?"

Paul's spirits sank. He'd assumed she'd love to see this incredible example of what nature could create, that she'd appreciate this work of art. He'd assumed she'd rather spend the day like this than sitting around the base waiting for a fire call. But, judging from the tone he'd just heard, he'd been wrong. "Yeah," he replied uneasily. "This is why."

She walked to where he was standing, stared straight up into his eyes, then broke into a wide smile. "It's gorgeous, Paul. Thanks for showing me."

He wanted to smile back, but he was irritated, mostly with himself. This proved how easily she could already toy with his emotions.

She laughed.

That soft, comforting laugh he'd already come to crave.

"Have you shown this to anyone else?" she asked, gesturing at the falls. "Ever brought any of those hundreds of other girls who want to love you in here?"

"No."

"Why not?"

He shrugged. "I don't know. Just never thought about it."

She pulled him to her, pressing her lips and her body to his.

After a few moments he pulled back, grinning. "Well, this is real nice and all, but I gotta get going."

She looked at him like he was out of his mind. "Why?"

"I've got a date."

"*What?*"

Well, good. He could play with her emotions, too. "With a fish, Mandy. I've got a date with a fish." He motioned for her to step back away from the tail end of the pool they were standing beside. "This is the other reason I wanted to come up here," he explained, starting to false cast, moving the fly rod rhythmically back and forth between the ten o'clock and one o'clock positions, peeling more and more line off the reel with each cycle, waiting longer and longer for the line to load at each position. "I saw a huge trout over by that rock last time I was here." He pointed at the top of a dark stone jutting up through the surface off the far bank about forty feet away. "It looked like a real hog, but I didn't get a good spot on it because it spooked and went deep real quick. I want to see how big it really is. Fish that size don't usually move out of a large pool in a stream as small as this one, so the odds are good it'll still be here."

"Oh, I get it. This is the *real* reason we came up here."

She was looking for reassurance. Okay, he'd give her some. "Don't kid yourself, gorgeous. You know the real reason we came up here." But that was as much as she was going to get. For now, anyway.

"You don't intend to catch this thing and cook it for lunch, do you?" she asked worriedly, her upper lip curling. "This isn't one of those hunter-gatherer proving exhibitions, is it? Sorry to tell you, but I hate fish. And if you think I'm gonna kiss you again after you eat a fish lunch without using a scrub brush and bleach on your teeth, you're out of your mind. I mean, I love your lips and I love the way you kiss. Most guys are pretty bad, but you're different. Probably because you've had so much practice, which I don't really want to think about right now," she added in a strained tone. "But I'm warning you, Paul, if you eat some big trout in front of me, you aren't getting within ten feet of—"

"Will you please shut up," he said as politely as possible. She might not like fish much, but she sure was appreciating the way he could cast a fly line. It wasn't easy to do, and he could tell she understood that. "Otherwise there won't be any fish in this stream for a hundred yards in either direction."

"Sorry," she retorted sarcastically. "*So sorry.*"

"Was your dad a fly fisherman?" he asked, sending a final tight roll of line zipping over the pool, then letting the tiny fly flutter to the surface upstream of the rock.

"Maybe. But how would you know? Can you read minds or some-thing? I heard that about you. People in town say you've got that gift. It's almost like they're scared of you. But in a good way," she added.

"Oh yeah?"

"Of course, they say you've got that death wish, too. Which scares them, too. But in a bad way."

"Uh-huh."

"And people around the base say it."

"People talk a lot," he said, picking the line up off the water, false casting once, then putting the fly down above the rock again. "Mostly because they don't have anything else to do."

"Everybody seems to be impressed with your fists as well."

"I can take care of myself."

"I bet. Duff Sparks didn't want any part of you the other day. He's got three inches and forty pounds on you, but he backed right down."

At his core, Duff was a coward when it came to fighting. He'd take on someone he knew he could beat, but that was it. Paul wasn't going to say anything though. He was loyal to his team members no matter how he felt about them. "Yeah, well."

Mandy eyed the tiny fly as it drifted slowly past the rock, carried along the surface by swirling minicurrents. "Do you get in a lot of fights?"

Before Paul could answer there was a terrific explosion on the surface of the water. The tiny dry fly disappeared inside a frothy splash and the swirl of a wide speckled tail, then the green fly line stretched tight. Seconds later a glistening twenty-three-inch rainbow trout came flying out of the water like a missile launched from a nuclear submarine.

"Oh, my Lord!" Mandy shouted as the fish went three feet into the air, then dove back into the pool. "Did you see that?"

Paul chuckled. "See what?" Of course, he'd seen it. It was funny how people reacted that way sometimes when things went crazy.

A few minutes later Paul carefully lifted the three-pound rainbow from the cold water and slipped the barbless hook from its mouth. He held the heaving fish up for a moment so Mandy could see, then slipped it in the water again to recover, gently moving it back and forth so fresh water washed over its gills.

"What a rainbow," she murmured. "Those red markings on the gill plate and down both sides are so bright. I've never seen one like that."

"It's not as big as I'd hoped, but it'll do." Her knowing the fish was a rainbow was good—he hadn't mentioned what kind of trout it was he'd seen in this pool last time he was here—but knowing the term "gill plate" was impressive, damn impressive. "Now I'm sure your father was a fly fisherman," he said, releasing the fish and watching it swim slowly toward the depths of the pool and disappear. "At least, somebody in your family was. Most people wouldn't know a rainbow trout from a catfish. Even less what a gill—"

"My father was a fly fisherman," she admitted, gazing back at the waterfall and pursing her lips.

He'd hit a nerve, that was obvious. "What's wrong?"

"What do you mean?"

"I heard it in your voice. You know I did."

She shoved her hands into her pockets. "Another thing people say about you is you can't stand a complainer, and that's from people you respect at the base, not the townies. I don't want you thinking I'm a complainer."

"Complainers complain about things that don't matter, or things they could change if they really wanted to. What you were going to say didn't sound like that."

She shook her head. "No, I can't change it. Not now."

"Come on," Paul urged. "What's up?"

"Just another stupid little daddy-didn't-love-me story. Nothing you want to hear about, I'm sure."

Actually, he did. "Come on, tell me."

"No."

He put the fly rod down and moved to where she stood. "I won't think it's stupid, I promise."

Mandy ran her hands through her hair and moaned, frustrated with the bad memories boiling to the surface. "I have two older brothers. My dad took them everywhere while we were growing up. Hunting, fishing, you name it. Including out here to Montana on fly-fishing trips, to Missoula, actually. But he never once took me." She gazed at the waterfall, lower lip trembling ever so slightly. "I wanted his attention so bad." Her gaze turned distant. "He loved fly fishing. He died of a heart attack on a river in New Zealand last year fighting a ten-pound brown on South island. He went face first into the water just like he said he always wanted to. I hadn't talked to him in two years." Her chin slowly dropped. "You know, I'd read every book I could find about fly fishing, and at dinner I'd try to talk to him about what I'd read. He'd give me one of those forced smiles he was famous for, then start talking to my brothers about what I'd just brought up. It was so damn frustrating."

"That's tough." It was probably exactly how Jeremy had felt every night at the Brule dinner table.

"It was tough." She glanced at Paul. "Don't think I'm a complainer, okay?"

He waved her off, making sure that she understood he wouldn't. "Where'd you grow up?"

"Key Largo."

"Really?" So she was a Florida girl. He never would have guessed.

"We were rich," she said under her breath.

Apologetically, Paul noticed. As if it were a sin to have money. No wonder she'd figured him out so fast.

"My dad inherited *a lot* of money," she continued. "He managed it from his office overlooking the Gulf. In the mornings anyway. By one o'clock he was on his boat fishing the flats and the mangroves for jacks and tarpon. With my brothers, of course."

"Pretty nice life."

"I guess. I gave up on him at sixteen. Which was about the time both my brothers had headed off to college, and he was actually trying to talk to me, actually trying to start a relationship with me because he was lonely. But I didn't want to be his friend by then. At that point I'd met some people who were into skydiving, people who knew Casey Atwater."

Paul's ears perked up. Everybody who was anybody in the skydiving world knew the name Casey Atwater. Atwater was a world champion and a man who'd pioneered big jumps. Record-breaking jumps involving hundreds of people who formed massive shapes as they dove. "He runs a skydiving school down in Florida, right?"

Mandy nodded.

"You learned from him?" Paul asked.

"Yup." She laughed. "I had to lie about my age for the first couple of years because you aren't supposed to jump until you're eighteen. I think he was a little ticked off when he found out I'd done that, but he's such a nice man."

Well, there couldn't be any more questions about her skydiving skills if she'd trained with Atwater. He was the best around. No wonder she'd been able to make it to that tiny clearing when they'd jumped in front of the Big Cat Fire. Now Paul was embarrassed that he'd ripped her cord at thirty-nine hundred feet. "If you're family's rich, why are you a Fire Jumper?"

She looked at him as if he was crazy. "Same reason you are, silly. Because it's exactly what my father didn't want me to do."

Paul nodded deliberately. She was good all right, very good. "I guess I asked for that—" He stopped short when he thought he caught a movement up the slope in the trees on the other side of the creek. When he saw it again for sure, he grabbed her arm. "Stay here," he ordered. "Don't move."

He sprinted past her, then dashed across a shallow stretch of the stream halfway between where Mandy was still standing and the water-fall, trying to keep his eye trained on that spot as he headed up the slope. It was tough going because his chest still hurt from the collision with the ponderosa pine the other day, but he had to see what the deal was. Maybe he was being paranoid, maybe this was stupid, but it seemed like too big a coincidence for someone else to be out in this remote section of the Bitterroot Forest at the same time he and Mandy were. Way too big a coincidence.

As he reached a small rise and closed in on the guy, there was a sharp pop and a flash from up ahead and to his left. A millisecond later the nasty zip of a large-caliber bullet blew past his left ear.

He dove behind a tree, breathing hard. He hadn't been paranoid at all.

The man raced the last few yards to the Escalade, pulled the driver side door open, tossed the .44 Magnum on the passenger seat, threw the truck into gear, and tore off. Back the way he'd come two hours ago, suddenly wishing like hell he wasn't driving something so conspicuous. Maybe style wasn't so important after all.

24

"YOU HUNGRY?"

"Yup," Hunter answered loudly over the engine noise. "Starved."

"Good." Without warning Strat swung the old pickup into a rutted, gravel parking lot and skidded to a stop in front of a dilapidated wooden building. "Because, brother, you're about to have the best burger you ever tasted. I mean, *the* best."

"Yeah, sure." Hunter eyed the building skeptically, just glad he'd been able to avoid banging his head on the roof as the truck bounced across the lot.

The place reminded him more of a tool shed than a restaurant. The screen door hung from one hinge; the exterior looked as if it hadn't had a fresh coat of paint since the Carter administration; and there was a flea-bitten hound lying on the front porch. There were a bunch of cars in the parking lot, but most of them looked as if they hadn't had a fresh coat of paint since Jimmy Carter was president, either. Except for two shiny Cadillacs, which were parked next to each other off to one side.

"You have health inspectors in Fort Mason?" Hunter muttered, opening his door.

"Probably not," Strat answered, as though he didn't give a damn if they did or they didn't. He patted his stomach. "Welcome to the Lion's Den. A burger and a beer from the LD, and it's a good day to die."

Hunter wanted to ask if that meant it was a good day to die *because* of the burger and the beer—but he didn't. "Great."

When he'd climbed out of the pickup, Hunter glanced around for a Lion's Den sign but didn't see one. There wasn't even a sign indicating that cooked food was available inside. Either the burgers were as good as Strat claimed and the owner didn't need to advertise, or he didn't want anyone with authority knowing this was a restaurant. Based on the condition of the building and the hound, Hunter was pretty sure he knew which one it was.

When they came together in front of the truck, Hunter nodded down at Strat's shorts, which were still soaking wet from fishing. "You going in like that?" Strat never wore the old pair of rubber waders that lay crumpled up in one corner of the pickup's bed. Even when he fished in the winter he didn't wear them. He hated them, figured they were more dangerous than anything, because if he slipped in the river and they filled up suddenly with water, he could drown in seconds.

Strat put his head back, laughed loudly, and slapped Hunter on the back. "Brother, brother," he chuckled, "this is Montana. I assure you the management of the Lion's Den won't give a rat's ass about a little water on their sawdust floor as long as you order a damn burger and a beer." He grabbed Hunter's arm. "On second thought, leave the ordering to me. Now, come on."

Hunter followed Strat up the rickety porch steps, feeling a little silly for asking about the dress code. He glanced warily at the old dog as they passed by. It bared the few teeth it had left and growled, but didn't make a move.

Once inside it took a few moments for Hunter's eyes to adjust. It was bright outside, but dim in here, so his first impression of the place wasn't visual. It was the smell of ground sirloin sizzling on the grill. After six hours of fishing without any breakfast, he had to admit that the burgers smelled damn good.

When things came into focus, he shook his head and grinned. Sitting on a stool at the chipped Formica counter was Big Bill Brule. It wasn't as if the senator was stopping by for a quick minute on a campaign swing, either. He didn't have a camera crew in tow, he wasn't holding a wriggling baby, he wasn't smiling uncomfortably as he shook hands with a potential voter whose name he'd missed. Big Bill was here to eat. In fact, he probably ate lunch at the Lion's Den most days he wasn't in Washington, Hunter figured. The entrance to his lumber mill was only a half mile down the road. They'd passed it on the way here after going by the Murphy General Store.

Well, maybe Strat was right after all. Maybe this place did make a good burger. But the best ever?

Sitting on the stool beside Big Bill was Dale Callahan. Hunter recognized him immediately as the man who'd met Zoe Gale at The Depot while he and Strat were having drinks. He couldn't tell at The Depot if Zoe and Callahan were involved. It had seemed as if Callahan was trying to be romantic, but Zoe was avoiding his advances. Maybe it had been Hunter's imagination, maybe Callahan was just a touchy-feely guy with women and they were only friends. Either way, it irritated Hunter, which he realized was completely irrational. He didn't have any claim on Zoe, he'd only met her once briefly. And he'd never even been introduced to Callahan.

Hunter took a deep breath, remembering how he'd felt the grip slipping its fingers around him as he'd watched Zoe walk back to her table after they'd spoken, after he'd first noticed those gleaming points of light in her eyes. Maybe his reaction to imagining Callahan trying to seduce Zoe Gale was irrational, but men's reactions usually were when it came to beautiful women.

"Come here, Hunt," Strat called from the counter. "I want you to meet some folks."

Montana suddenly became even more puzzling—and a little scary. Apparently Strat knew Big Bill. Pretty well, too, judging by the friendly way in which the senator had slapped his brother on the shoulder for something everyone was getting a good laugh about. Which was wrong, just plain wrong. The idea that Strat had direct access to a United States senator was more than a little scary now that Hunter thought about it. It was downright terrifying.

"Hello, Senator Brule," said Hunter respectfully as they shook hands. He'd read a lot about this man before the trial. "It's an honor to meet you."

"The honor's all mine, young man." Big Bill's voice boomed throughout the small restaurant. There were four cramped booths along one wall and eight stools in front of the counter and every seat in the house was taken. "Congratulations. I heard you were spectacular in Bozeman. One lone ranger against the railroad's posse and you made them all look like rank amateurs." His expression turned serious. "The most important thing is that justice was served, that those families got closure and compensation. And don't let Carl Bach's suicide get you down, son," he said with conviction. "I've never seen a man shoot himself, so I don't know what it was like to watch Bach paint a wall with his brains." He held up a finger. "But I will say this. If he knew those railroad tracks were bad, he had it coming." Big Bill's expression went from serious to steely. "So the hell with him. You kept up your end of the bargain, you stayed true to your oath and did what was right. Committing suicide was probably the only brave thing Bach ever did, or the most cowardly. Either way, you shouldn't lose sleep over it. You're a hero, Hunter Lee."

Hunter had heard that Big Bill didn't suffer fools, and that he hated cowards. The reports seemed pretty accurate. "Thank you."

"Don't worry about George Drake, either," Big Bill added. "He won't try to get back at you for screwing him. Not even if he loses his railroad, not if he loses everything. He's a liar, a cheat, and a thief, but he's no killer. At least, I don't think he is."

Killer? Hunter had figured from the start of the trial that of all the people he'd ever sued, George Drake might be the first one to try to get revenge. The research Hunter's staff had done indicated that the little man was vindictive as hell. Nothing had ever been proven, but circumstantial evidence pointed to Drake using tough, even criminal tactics to even a score. But the research report hadn't mentioned murder, not even his people beating the crap out of someone. Using violence didn't seem to be Drake's style. He was more into framing an enemy or ruining them financially, and that part of the report had been put together by the investigation firm Warfield & Stone always used. By those ex-FBI guys down in Washington who could find out if you'd ever snuck a cigarette in your high school bathroom.

"Hell," the senator continued, glancing around and smiling as if he was on stage at a Washington cocktail party, "he probably doesn't even own a gun."

Strat and Callahan burst into loud laughter. Even the husky woman wearing a grease-stained, pink Guess sweatshirt who was cooking burgers on the grill behind the counter let loose with a few deep, shoulder-shaking hahas. Apparently you weren't much of a man in Montana if you didn't own a firearm. Hunter made a mental note of that in case he ever did move here. As adolescent as it sounded, he didn't want a repu-

tation as a man without a gun. For a lot of reasons, but one in particular now. He was suddenly worried that he might have underestimated
George Drake, particularly given what Strat had said about the man
earlier on the river.

Strat nodded at Hunter, then at Callahan. "Hunt, this is Dale Callahan. He owns a food company. It's based over in Billings, right, Dale?"

"That's right," Callahan answered, shaking hands with Hunter.
"That's over in the southeastern part of the state, Hunter, but I live here
in Fort Mason. My family moved here in the late 1800s from out east.
They wagon-trained it all the way from Baltimore, and made it through
Hell's Gate alive when a lot of people didn't." He winked at Big Bill. "I'm
sure there's some in these parts who wish we'd been in the group that
didn't."

Big Bill chuckled. "Screw them."

"Yeah, screw 'em *hard*," Callahan muttered, his expression darkening.

"Easy, Dale."

"Sorry." Callahan nodded at Hunter, forcing a smile. "We're all happy
for those families you represented. They deserved what you got them."

"Thanks."

Callahan was around fifty, Hunter judged. Of average height and
slender build with thinning brown hair, he wasn't a man who impressed
you with his physical presence the way the senator did. But Callahan
had a strong jaw, and he spoke with a preciseness that made you listen
carefully to each word he said. And he had an innate warmth about him
Hunter hadn't found with many people in Montana. It wasn't that people
out here were unfriendly. They were just wary, careful not to let you be a
friend too fast, probably because most outsiders didn't stick around too
long. Hunter hated to admit it, but Callahan was charming.

"I hear you're moving to Fort Mason," Big Bill spoke up through a
mouthful of cheeseburger.

"Oh?" Hunter's eyes flashed to his brother, but Strat was talking to
the woman behind the counter. He was probably ordering. "Who told
you that?"

"I heard it, too," Callahan chimed in before Big Bill could answer. "I
heard you were going to hang a shingle out on Main Street."

"Yeah," Big Bill agreed, wiping ketchup from his lips with a white
paper napkin. "In that vacant space between the washette and the fishing shop, right across the street from the Grizzly Saloon." He gestured

toward Hunter. "It used to be an antique store until Harriet Quinn died last March. She was the owner. It's been empty ever since, but like Dale said, it's a great location."

"It really is." Strat had finished ordering and was back into the conversation. "You should get a lot of walk-in business there."

Hunter thought about explaining to Strat that walk-in business didn't happen very often with the kind of law he practiced, and that attorneys who took walk-in business in his area were desperate. But this wasn't the time or the place. As much as they might go at it in private, they never embarrassed each other in public. They'd made that pact with each other a long time ago.

"Who told you I was moving to Montana, Senator?" Hunter asked, directing his question to Big Bill but staring at Strat.

Big Bill thought for a moment. "I believe it was Butch Roman." He pointed at Strat. "Your boss."

Hunter glanced at Callahan. "How about you, Dale?"

"Let me see." Callahan furrowed his brows. "I think Katrina Mason told me." He patted Big Bill on the shoulder. "Your good friend."

The senator rolled his eyes. "Yeah, right," he mumbled, finishing the last bite of his cheeseburger and standing up. He crumpled up his napkin and tossed it toward his plate, but it overshot the plate and fell to the floor on the other side of the counter. "Well, I've gotta go. I gotta get back to the mill and finish up a few things before I take off." He snapped his fingers. "Damn."

Callahan looked up. "What?"

"Oh, I promised Jeremy this morning that I'd have dinner with him tonight, but something just came up as I was driving here and now I've gotta leave town. So I've gotta remember to cancel with him. Otherwise he'll act like a little puppy dog who can't find his mother." Big Bill grimaced. "He'll act like that anyway, but it'll be a lot worse if I don't cancel."

"Where you going?" Callahan asked, standing up, too. He'd only taken a few bites of his burger.

"Scotland."

"*Scotland?* That's what *just* came up?"

"Yeah."

"What are you going there for?"

Big Bill smiled smugly. "A vitally important environmental conference with a couple of my Washington brethren."

"Uh-huh." Callahan pulled out his wallet and dropped a twenty on the counter between his plate and the senator's. "Let me guess. This conference is being held near a golf course."

"As I understand it, the hotel overlooks the seventh green." The senator winked at Hunter as they shook hands. "Nice to meet you, son."

"You, too, Senator."

"And don't be so quiet next time," Big Bill urged. "You're a smart man. I like hearing what smart men have to say."

"Welcome to Fort Mason." Callahan shook Hunter's hand, too. "You'll like it here."

Hunter and Strat sat down on the vinyl covered stools Big Bill and Callahan had just vacated as the woman behind the counter snatched the twenty dollar bill, then cleared the dirty plates away.

"Why are you telling everyone I'm moving to Montana?" Hunter demanded, watching the woman bend down to pick up the wadded napkin Big Bill had tossed at his plate.

"What are you talking about?"

"Come on, both those guys think I'm moving here. Soon, too. You heard them tell me how good that location on Main Street is."

"Well, it is."

"That's not the point."

"Then what *is* the point?"

Hunter clenched his jaw, frustrated. Strat could be damn evasive when he wanted to be. "Why are you telling people I'm moving here?"

"Dale said he heard it from Katrina Mason, and Big Bill got it from Butch Roman. How am I involved?"

"Well, where'd *they* get it from?"

Strat shrugged. "Beats the hell out of me, brother."

"If Butch Roman's your boss, that's a pretty direct connection."

"Hunt, I didn't tell him." Strat was a plumbing foreman for Roman Construction. "Heck, I don't see him that often. I used to but not anymore because the company's gotten too big. Hey, you aren't going to pin this on me."

"Fine." Hunter caught a glimmer of a smile flash across Strat's face. There was a lot going on behind the scenes, he was sure. Which didn't surprise him. After all, this was Montana. "Dale seems like a nice guy," he said after a few moments. He was disappointed about that. He'd been hoping the guy would turn out to be a prick so he'd feel better about competing with him for Zoe. "The senator, too."

"Dale is a good guy," Strat agreed. "Big Bill can be a pain in the butt sometimes, but he's a senator so I guess it comes with the turf. For the most part he's okay."

"What do you mean he can be a pain in the—"

"Of course, he was nice to you today."

"Why?"

Strat gave Hunter one of those do-I-really-have-to-explain-this looks. "Because you're a celebrity, a *big* celebrity. Come on, Hunt, don't make me keep saying it." Strat pulled some napkins from a holder beside a ketchup bottle and dropped them in front of Hunter. "You trying to remind me how you're a star, but I haven't made anything of myself? Is that what this is?"

"Of course not." Maybe this sudden bitterness was a product of drinking all morning on the river, or maybe he was just trying to switch subjects. "I just—"

"You talked to Anne yet? Since she served you, I mean."

Hunter glanced down. "Nah."

Strat adjusted his Seattle Mariners baseball cap. He'd switched to it from the wide-brimmed straw hat on the way to the Lion's Den. "Sorry, Hunt. It's none of my business. I won't ask again."

Now Hunter felt bad. In their younger days they'd always been able to read each other like a large-print hardcover. Apparently, Strat still could. "Ask all you want," Hunter muttered. "It's just that I've never been through a divorce, you know? It's a lot tougher than I thought it would be."

"Maybe you don't like being lonely after all these years of having someone," Strat observed. "Which is understandable. Maybe it's better to be with someone you don't like than to be lonely."

Sometimes Strat could be pretty profound. "How would you know?"

"I wouldn't, I'm guessing. I've always been lonely so it doesn't seem like a big deal to me anymore."

God, Hunter thought. It would have been impossible for him to admit that, to admit something that made him seem so weak, but Strat still seemed so strong. Maybe that was because he'd said it so matter-of-factly, without any hesitation. "Maybe I'm figuring out that I still care about her," Hunter murmured.

"Oh, Christ."

"I'm thinking about calling her."

"Don't do that, Hunt," Strat pleaded. "You'll end up being sorry. Come on, I—"

"Here you go, guys," the husky woman behind the counter interrupted, slapping two full plates of food down on the counter. It was the same fare for both of them: huge cheeseburgers and a steaming heap of golden steak fries along with ice-cold beers in twenty-two-ounce mugs. "That should help you get over your wife, Mr. Lee," the woman said pleasantly to Hunter. "If it doesn't, look me up. I can get you over her."

So that was why there weren't many secrets in Montana. People were always listening. "I will, Betty," Hunter answered, eying the nametag pinned to her blouse. And because people like him were always saying things where everyone could hear them. He made a promise to himself to be more careful in the future about what he said and where he said it. "You can count on it."

Betty giggled. "Okay."

Strat nudged Hunter's knee when Betty went back to the grill. "Be careful, brother," he whispered.

"Why? Is Betty trouble, too? Is she running from the IRS like you think Zoe Gale is?"

"Uh, highly unlikely. She's probably never made more than ten thousand bucks a year."

"Then what's the problem?"

"She'll take you seriously. She'll track you down, lasso you, hogtie you, and do unspeakable things to you under a full moon."

"Maybe that's what I need," Hunter retorted, staring down at the massive puck of meat in front of him. "How in the world do I even start on this thing?" he muttered.

"Hunt, Betty's been the number-one female calf roper at the Livingston rodeo for the last two years."

"Sure she has," Hunter said, reaching for the knife beside his plate. "No offense, but I doubt there's a horse in Montana that could carry her."

Strat grabbed Hunter's wrist. *"What are you doing?"*

"Huh?"

"What are you gonna do with that knife?"

"I'm going to cut my cheeseburger in half so I can eat it," Hunter answered, laughing. "Don't worry. Divorce is bad, but it isn't that bad. No suicide thoughts. Not yet, anyway."

Strat glanced around furtively. "Don't cut that thing in half, Hunt. That's not how you eat a burger at the Lion's Den, not even the Big Daddy Burger. Maybe in some fufu New York City linen napkin place you cut a burger in half to take the first bite," he said, feigning a snobby accent. "You'd probably eat the thing with a fork, too, but you don't do that here. Not in Big Sky Country. You don't cut it in half, and you don't use your fork to eat it. You pick up the thing with your hands, okay?"

"Have you lost your mind, Strat? Has it finally happened? We all knew it would sooner or later," but—"

"Pick it up and take a bite," Strat growled. "Don't embarrass me."

"Okay, okay," Hunter agreed, rolling his eyes as if he thought Strat ought to be in the back of a white van headed to the nearest asylum wrapped inside a straitjacket.

"Now remember." A slight smile invaded Strat's naturally irritated expression. "Eat hearty, brother, because you never know when you'll eat again."

That had been their grace ever since they'd been kids.

Hunter smiled back, nostalgia prodding him. Then he opened his mouth as wide as possible and pushed the burger in.

As soon as he started to chew, he understood. As much as Hunter hated to admit it, he was suddenly tasting heaven.

"Good Lord," Hunter finally managed to mumble when he'd swallowed the delicious bite of meat, melted cheese, and hot buttered bread. "That *is* the best cheeseburger I've ever tasted." He quickly opened wide and took another bite.

A slow but unstoppable grin began spreading across Strat's face until it had completely erased that naturally angry expression. He nodded at Hunter's glass of beer. "Now drink."

Hunter reached for the ice-cold mug. He couldn't remember the last time he'd seen every bit of Strat's pissed-off look completely gone. Maybe he'd never seen that, now that he thought about it. Maybe he'd just witnessed a miracle.

Perhaps there really was something inexplicable about Montana, he realized as the gulp of chilly amber malt chased the burger down his throat. Something that transcended rational explanation, something that people who hadn't spent time here couldn't possibly understand, as Strat had claimed was true ever since moving to Fort Mason so long ago.

Maybe, maybe not, but Hunter was going to find out.

"Pretty good, huh?"

Hunter glanced over at his brother. Strat's mouth was full of burger, too, but that hadn't stopped him from speaking and inadvertently spitting out a few crumbs in the process. Strat had never been a big proponent of manners. "Brother, when you're right you're right. I'll give you your due."

Minutes later, Hunter slid the last, lonely bite of cheeseburger around his plate to pick up what was left of the ketchup and mayonnaise that had dripped down his fingers, then eased it into his mouth and chewed slowly, savoring each taste. As skeptical as he'd been an hour ago, he was a true believer now. Each bite of the Lion's Den cheeseburger had been an explosion of taste-bud heaven, even better than the one before. Maybe Strat was right, maybe now it was a good day to die.

After he'd swallowed the bite, he finished what was left of his second beer. When the last drop of it was gone, he put the mug down beside his plate with a sigh. All good things had to come to an end at some point. It was a simple, sad, and unavoidable truth. He smacked his lips. "Why are the burgers here so good, Strat?"

"It's this mix of stuff they add to the meat before they make it into patties. Some spices and a special sauce, but I can't tell you what it is."

"You mean you don't know what it is, or you know what it is but you won't tell me?"

Strat gave Hunter a forced half smile as he stood up, his naturally angry expression back again. "Good question." He reached into his pocket for his cell phone, pushed a button, and put it to his ear. "Yeah?"

Hunter looked around while Strat took the call. It was after three and the place was almost empty. Empty except for a few guys in the far booth who didn't look as if they were going anywhere. Judging from the collection of empty beer pitchers on their table, they shouldn't be going anywhere. Not behind a steering wheel anyway.

"Okay," Strat said loudly. "Be there as soon as I can."

Hunter stared at the men in the booth even after he heard Strat end the call, at one of them in particular. He'd caught the guy sneering at him a couple of times during lunch, and now the guy was doing it again, giving him a sullen, I-hate-out-of-towners glare.

Finally, Hunter broke off the staring contest. "What's going on?"

"I got a problem at a job site," Strat explained, aggravated. "We've got an issue with a plumbing inspector."

"Oh."

"It's no big deal. The guy probably just wants money. Mr. Roman's a big believer in keeping the hands of progress greased and these inspectors get used to it. I'm the foreman on the job, so I gotta take care of it. The job's about an hour away, so I'll be gone a while."

"I'll go with you," Hunter volunteered, rising from his stool, too. "How about it?"

Strat shook his head. "You're staying here."

"What the hell am I going to do—"

"Hello, Mr. Lee."

Hunter turned around, recognizing the voice instantly. "Well, hello there." It was Zoe Gale. She was dressed in a cotton fishing shirt, jeans, and hiking boots. Not the comely outfit she'd been wearing at The Depot, but she still looked sexy. "Were you out in the woods?"

"No."

"Too bad." He could feel that familiar confidence building, the same way it did when he walked into a courtroom, the same way it had when he'd met Zoe at The Depot. It was as if his mind suddenly went crystal clear when she was around and he could think twice as fast as he normally could. He knew just what to say and just how to say it. "I was hoping you'd worked up an appetite."

She gave him an uncertain look. "For a cheeseburger?"

He gave her a sly smile, that usual urge to hang on the periphery replaced by his courtroom urge to play the leading role. "Oh, no, not for a cheeseburger."

"Ah." She moved a step closer to him and smiled her beautiful high-cheekboned smile. "I never have to work up an appetite for that, Mr. Lee. I'm always ready."

Hunter gazed at Hell's Gate from five hundred feet above the Lassiter River, gazed down at the dark, choppy water swirling past them far below, watched the waters flow between the two mountains forming the gorge. They were the twin sentinels he'd spotted from the back deck of The Depot beneath that gorgeous azure sky. Now that he was standing here, he truly understood what a deadly ambush spot it was.

From where Hunter was standing, it was obvious how easy it would have been for Blackfoot warriors to pick off settlers with their rifles, how easy it would have been to create havoc down there. Hell's Gate was an ideal killing zone, just as Strat had described. With a bonfire raging in front of them, deep current-laden waters to the left, a sheer wall to the right, screaming face-painted warriors closing in from behind, and a hail of bullets raining down from above, the settlers would have been trapped and defenseless. Like the easy targets at a shooting gallery.

Strat had described the site perfectly. A quarter mile upstream—to Hunter's left—the mountain on the other side of the Lassiter came up vertically out of the water to a height of a thousand feet. And it kept coming straight up out of the water until the river reached Hell's Gate, making that side of the river completely impassable for anything on two feet or four hooves.

Hunter craned his neck and leaned cautiously out over the edge of the cliff so he could see all the way down on this side of the river. As Strat had described, the bank down there was only about thirty feet wide before the mountain started coming straight up. That thin strip of land was occupied by a single main-line track of the Bridger Railroad today, but in the late 1800s the track hadn't been there and the thin strip of land was a leg of the settlers' best route through the Rockies for a hundred miles north or south of here. The settlers knew it—so did the Blackfoot.

Hunter turned away from the ghosts lurking below him. Zoe Gale was sitting on a rock a ways back from the cliff. The mountain on this side of the river stairstepped its way to the summit, as skyscrapers did in New York. A few hundred feet straight up, then back twenty to thirty. A few hundred feet straight up, then back twenty to thirty. All the way to the top. On this level there was a trail through a mini-cut of rocks leading back into the woods. That was how they'd made it out onto this plateau from Strat's pickup, which was parked on a logging road back in the woods.

"This is amazing."

"It's only my second time up here," Zoe said, "but it's as hard for me to look down there this time as it was then. It's hard for me to think about all the pain and suffering that went on. Especially the children's." She sniffed. "I'm sure the natives didn't show any mercy to the children."

This was why Zoe had been wearing jeans and hiking boots at the Lion's Den; why Zoe had happened to show up at the Lion's Den when she had; why Strat had asked about Anne right before Zoe showed up; why Strat had taken Zoe's BMW to his job site and given them his pickup—if in fact Strat had really gone to a job site. It was pretty obvious what was going on. This date was a setup. Strat knew that most of the women in Fort

Mason wouldn't interest Hunter, but he figured Zoe Gale just might. And getting them together quickly might be the deciding factor in whether Hunter moved here or not.

Hunter gazed at Zoe. He loved that raven hair and those silver flecks shimmering in the black tresses all around her face, loved the way her long hair was being blown sexily about her pretty face by the wind. He loved those laserlike pinpoints of light in her eyes, too. Mostly, he liked being alone with her in a place Dale Callahan couldn't possibly run into them.

"Do you really blame the Native Americans?" He could tell she was struggling with her answer. "For not showing any mercy, I mean." He knew how she wanted to answer, but she was conflicted because she knew what he was going to say. That whites had killed many more natives than natives had killed whites. "I can tell you that we didn't show much mercy to them when the roles were reversed, and we were coming into their country."

"You're right," Zoe admitted. "I just can't stand the thought of anyone hurting a child."

"It's windy up here." Hunter wanted to leave behind the issue of who had shown less mercy. This wasn't the time for it. "It's probably even windier at the bottom of the canyon," he observed, pointing down toward the river, "where it's even narrower." There were actually small whitecaps on the river's surface at the point where it moved through the gorge. "You can see the chop on the water even from here."

"It was really windy last time I was here, too. I don't usually remember things like that."

Hunter moved to the rock and sat down beside Zoe, making certain he kept a respectable distance between them. So, what *are* you doing in Fort Mason?

"What do you think I'm doing in Fort Mason?" She tossed her hair back out of her face defiantly. "I'm sure your brother's helped you form an opinion on that."

"Wait a minute," Hunter said, holding up his hands. "It sounds like you're mad at me for talking to Strat about you. But, hey, you're talking to him about me. I mean, come on."

"Your brother hasn't told me anything about you."

Hunter wasn't buying that for a second. "You mean he hasn't told you about my wife serving me with divorce papers right after court over in

Bozeman? He hasn't told you how he thinks I should move here to Fort Mason?"

Zoe couldn't hide her grin as she moved over on the rock so that her leg was touching his, so that the respectable distance he'd established was gone. "Well, he might have mentioned something."

"Yeah, I thought—"

"He might have mentioned that your wife had a wild side to her that you don't care much for, too."

This was getting very personal very fast. "He did, huh?" Hunter could hear the irritation in his voice, and he wondered if she could. "I don't know if I like that."

She gave him a pleading look, then stroked his cheek with her fingers. "He swore me to secrecy. Please don't give me away."

"Well, I—"

"There's no reason to be mad," she interrupted. "My interest is purely selfish, I'm not judging. I learned a long time ago that people who live in glass houses shouldn't even throw pebbles." She leaned against him lightly, shoulder to shoulder. "Let's be honest, we were both attracted to each other at The Depot, and I'm figuring you're a pretty quick character study. I doubt it takes you much more than a glance to size someone up, to decide whether or not you're interested in them. You *stared* at me." She put her face to his shoulder and caressed his cheek again. "You didn't like Dale sitting with me, did you?"

Her voice was soft and pleasurable, almost as soft and pleasurable as her fingers were on his skin. "What are you saying?" he asked, avoiding the answer. Besides, she already knew what it was.

She looked up, slipped a finger beneath his chin and gently turned his head so they were gazing into each other's eyes. "I have a wild side, Mr. Lee. You know I do. You knew it the first second you saw me, you didn't need Strat to tell you that. But you were still attracted to me. Weren't you?"

There was no denying it. To try would have been ridiculous. Disrespectful to her and completely insincere of him. If there was one thing he wanted her to believe of him, it was that he always told the truth. "Yes, I was."

"Is that going to be a problem? My wild side, I mean."

Hunter gazed deeply into her eyes, mesmerized by those points of light burning bright in the middle of her pupils. She was coming toward him, ever so slowly, like sap dripping down a maple tree. Their lips were getting closer and closer, and he knew he wasn't going to stop her. Maybe he wanted to experience that wild side, maybe he'd wanted to experience it for a long time. But not with Anne, not with someone who flaunted her wildness, but with someone who guarded it. Not with someone who didn't care who she experienced things with as long as she experienced them. With someone who valued the person she experienced it with as much as the experience itself.

"No, it won't be a problem," he said quietly, suddenly feeling more alive than he had in years. This was crazy, risky, stupid, and not at all him, but he liked it. No, he *loved* it. Maybe he was suddenly feeling so strongly because everything had been building up inside him for so long and here was that person who might be able to break the logjam. Or maybe it was the magic of Montana. Whichever one it was, at this moment he didn't care. "Not at all."

As their lips touched, his cell phone went off, piercing the cathedral-like quiet of the place.

"*Damn it.*" He stood up to dig the thing out of his pocket. He shouldn't answer the call, should have turned the damn phone off before they got here. But answering—at least checking the number—was a reflex action. "Sorry, Zoe," he muttered. Why did there have to be reception up here? Of all places, of all *times*? "I'll just be a few seconds."

Hunter checked the tiny screen. It wasn't a number he recognized, but the area code was 212 and that was New York City. Answering was a bad idea, a *terrible* idea, but if the call was from New York, he had to. He had partners who depended on him, and he took that responsibility seriously, much as he hated his compulsion to do so. They didn't do it for him all the time.

He listened for several minutes to the person on the other end of the line, speaking only at the end of the call to agree to her one request. When the call was over, he glanced down at Zoe. "I'm sorry but I have to go to New York right away."

25

THE INSIDE BAR of The Depot was furnished more formally than the back deck. A wide leather couch and several wingback chairs were arranged on an expensive Persian rug in front of a stone fireplace; tall stools with upholstered seats and backs stood before the dark-wood bar; western prints painted by Montana artists hung on the walls; Native American artifacts decorated the tables; and dominating one corner of the room was a massive stuffed grizzly bear rearing up on its hind legs—long canines bared, sharp front claws extended.

Jeremy sat on one of the stools nursing a gin and tonic, thinking about how it seemed as if there was some kind of stuffed animal or fish in almost every Montana bar he'd ever been in. He was thinking about how he'd been waiting for over an hour, too. It was obvious Big Bill wasn't coming. He'd tried his father's cell phone fifteen minutes ago, but the call had gone straight to voicemail.

This was the last straw. He'd taken as much of this crap as he could stand. To hell with his father, to hell with everything.

"Well, well, look who it is."

Jeremy turned in his seat. George Drake stood a few feet away, glass in one hand, lighted cigar in the other. His eyes were red, his speech was slurred, and he was swaying slightly from side to side. The drink he was holding obviously wasn't his first. "I'm surprised you're celebrating, George." He and Drake had never gotten along. Drake was a self-made man who never missed a chance to remind Jeremy that he'd been given everything while Drake had been forced to make his own way in the world. "Not with what that jury did to you and your railroad over in Bozeman." He gave Drake a cocky smile as Katrina Mason walked into the bar from the restaurant and moved to Drake's side. "What a shame."

Drake gestured at Jeremy with his cigar. "Look who I ran into, Katrina. Big Bill's fat, stupid son."

Katrina grimaced. "George, I don't think you need to—"

"What did you say to me?" Jeremy snapped, hopping off the stool. The bartender was in the stockroom getting another bottle of gin, so he, Drake, and Katrina were the only people in the room. "Huh?"

"Aw, now the spoiled little rich boy's getting mad."

Jeremy slammed his glass down on the bar, spilling most of what was left in it. He was going to teach George Drake a lesson. He had so much anger built up inside he couldn't wait to slam Drake's cheek with his fist. But as he grabbed the older man by the collars, out of the corner of his eye he noticed a hulking form move through the doorway leading to the restaurant.

A second later, Drake's bodyguard seized Jeremy and sent him sprawling to the floor in front of the grizzly bear. As Jeremy struggled to his hands and knees, he saw Katrina race from the room just as the big man delivered a swift kick to his soft belly, knocking the wind out of him. With a loud groan, Jeremy collapsed to the floor again. As he lay there gasping for breath, he expected the guy to finish him off, to pick him up and throw him into the wall. But suddenly it was Drake's bodyguard who was crashing into the wall, instead. Headfirst, just a few feet away from where Jeremy lay. Jeremy rolled onto his side and watched his brother, Paul, pick up the groggy bodyguard and deliver a lightning-fast, one-two combination to the guy's chin and cheek. The guy crashed into the wall again, then toppled to the floor beside Jeremy, unconscious.

Paul whipped around and pointed at Drake, who was taking cover behind a bar stool. "You ever send one of your boys after my brother again," he said evenly, "and I'll kill you. You understand me?"

Drake nodded, then shoved the stool at Paul and hobbled away as fast as his bad leg would carry him.

Paul deflected the stool, then leaned down to help Jeremy up. "You all right?"

Jeremy pushed Paul's hand away. "I don't need your help, little brother," he muttered as he made it back to his feet. "I don't need it, and I don't want it. Just leave me the hell alone."

26

HUNTER TAPPED LIGHTLY on the heavy wooden door even though he'd been told to go right in, even though the door was slightly ajar. His knock was a show of respect for the man who'd been running Warfield & Stone for the last eighteen years, the man who'd recruited him so relentlessly out of law school.

Nelson Radcliff.

"Come in."

As Hunter moved into the spacious office, Radcliff came out from behind his precisely arranged desk.

Radcliff was tall, silver-haired, and still in excellent shape for sixty-two years old. Physically, he reminded Hunter of Big Bill Brule. He was slightly slimmer, though still broad-shouldered and imposing. He was similar in stature but had a very different personality. He was much more reserved than the senator; he didn't constantly try to muscle his way into the center of every conversation the way Big Bill did. Most of the time Radcliff kept to the perimeter in social situations, as Hunter did. However, when Radcliff was in court arguing a case, he stepped into the leading role, as Hunter did.

Nelson Radcliff was the reason Hunter had joined Warfield & Stone. He'd felt an instant kinship with Radcliff on several levels, and the bond had grown stronger and stronger over the years. People commented constantly how alike they were, how their personalities and mannerisms were eerily similar. It was as if they were father and son.

"Congratulations." Radcliff shook Hunter's hand. "You did a nice job in Montana, son," he said quietly.

Outside a courtroom, Radcliff always spoke quietly. In fact, Hunter had never heard the managing partner raise his voice—other than in a courtroom to make certain the jury understood the point he was making or to evoke the truth from a hostile witness. Of course, at this point in his career, Radcliff didn't need to speak loudly because he carried such a big stick. One withering stare from the head of the conference room table during a partners' meeting and the entire room went silent. Radcliff had that rare gift, and he knew how to use it.

"Thank you, Nelson." Hunter was the only nonsenior partner at Warfield & Stone who called Radcliff by his first name, and Hunter was the only person at the firm Radcliff called "son." "I think the amount was fair."

"You might have gotten more if you'd fought the venue harder," Radcliff observed, moving back to his desk chair and sitting down, "if you'd gotten the trial to be in Fort Mason. But I suppose it all worked out. Shut the door, will you?"

All worked out? Hunter had made the firm thirteen million dollars in Montana. That was just working out? "Of course."

"And have a seat."

As always, Hunter had waited for an invitation to sit down. Though they never spoke about it, Hunter knew Radcliff appreciated the formality because it implied respect. If there was one thing Radcliff demanded of everyone at the firm, it was that. For the managing partner, respect was equal in importance to hard work and results. He'd never come right out and tell someone he wasn't kissing the ring properly, but people got the message. They got it from someone else at the firm, from a paltry bonus check, or from a demand to leave the premises immediately—personal effects to be boxed and delivered at a later date.

Of course, Radcliff rarely had to send messages anymore, either, because he was so feared inside *and* outside the firm. He was the most revered, sought-after litigator in New York. Second to no one, not even Hunter. When it came down to the two of them, Radcliff was still the mentor, Hunter still the protégé.

"Our share of the Bridger settlement was over thirteen million. Correct?"

"Correct." Hunter eased into one of two comfortable leather chairs in front of Radcliff's desk. From here he could see into the office buildings on the west side of Park Avenue which was forty-seven stories below them. "Thirteen point three million to be exact."

Radcliff raised one perfectly trimmed salt-and-pepper eyebrow. "Well, I wish your return to New York could have been under better circumstances. I was hoping you could have spent more than a few days with your brother after winning the case. I know how close you two are."

Hunter glanced down. "Strat's a good man."

"Of course he is, he's your brother." Radcliff tapped the desk several times impatiently. "Did Anne really serve you with divorce papers as you were coming out of the courtroom in Bozeman?"

It was as though Radcliff couldn't contain his curiosity any longer, as if he'd been making small talk up until now because he felt he couldn't ask the question he wanted to ask right away. It was as if he felt that there needed to be a period of reconnection before he could dive into the dicey stuff, even if that reconnection lasted only a few seconds. "Yes."

"Right after you'd rested the case?"

"Yes."

"That *bitch*."

Hunter's eyes flashed to Radcliff's. It was the first vulgar word he'd ever heard Radcliff utter. Along with his habit of speaking softly, Radcliff had a reputation for never swearing.

"Did she give you any hint this was coming?"

There were indications, but what good was it to talk about them now? "No," Hunter said deliberately.

"Did she give you any reason for wanting the divorce? Other than the boilerplate on the legal paper?"

Hunter shook his head stiffly, making it clear he didn't want to discuss it. "I appreciate you letting me use our conference room for the meeting today."

Radcliff waved. "Of course, anything to help. Maybe it'll give you home field advantage." The older man's expression turned curious. "It seems like a quick start to negotiations, doesn't it? I mean, she only served you a few days ago."

"She's making it clear to me that there's no chance of us getting back together." The call he'd taken at Hell's Gate had been from his divorce attorney's assistant. On the call, she'd told him that he needed to get back to New York right away. Anne wanted to wrap up a separation agreement as soon as possible and had promised, through her attorney, to be reasonable if they could get the process going immediately. "That's how I take it anyway."

"You're probably right." Radcliff raised one hand as if something had just occurred to him. "I need to warn you about something."

Hunter looked up. "Oh? What?"

"I asked Sam McCabe to sit in on today's meeting with your wife."

Hunter had figured this was the real reason he'd been summoned to the corner office. Not for the congratulatory handshake, as back-handed as it had been, but to make clear that the proceedings with his wife were going to be monitored. McCabe was a Warfield & Stone senior partner, the one who handled the firm's administrative and per-sonnel issues. One of the two senior guys who hadn't brought in any business in a long time, but since he handled the logistical side of the firm, at least he had some excuse. Radcliff wanted McCabe at the meet-ing to make certain the firm's interests were represented at a table that could get messy.

"Your most valuable asset is your partnership interest in this law firm," Radcliff said matter-of-factly. "Anne's attorney will try to grab a piece of it, make no mistake about it. So I want Sam there to steer your wife and her attorney toward your other assets. Sam will make it clear from the start how illiquid the partnership interest is, how your wife wouldn't be able to sell it without my permission, and how it might be years before she sees any cash from it. It'll be better coming from Sam than you, it'll be more convincing that way. I don't want another partner if I can avoid it," Radcliff grumbled.

It was a reasonable request, Hunter figured. Nobody wanted ex-wives and ex-husbands attending partners' meetings. "Okay."

"By the way, who is Anne's attorney?"

"Marty Friedman."

Radcliff groaned. "That's too bad. Marty doesn't care what he says or who he says it to. That doesn't get him many dinner party invitations, but it gets results for his clients." He hesitated. "Who are you using?"

"Delilah Priestly."

Radcliff smiled for the first time since Hunter had come into the of-fice. Even a thirteen-point-three-million-dollar fee hadn't evoked this kind of emotion. "Good choice. Delilah's beaten Marty a couple of times representing people I know. She'll understand the firm's sensitivity in the matter, too."

"That's why I chose her, Nelson. With the firm in mind."

Radcliff gazed at Hunter intently for several moments, then his expression relaxed into a smile. A pure, friendly smile. "You're a good man, Hunter," he said. "I don't tell you enough how much I appreciate what you do for Warfield & Stone, how much all of the senior partners appreciate what you do. I know you could have started your own firm a long time ago. I know people tell you to do that all the time, son."

"I've always been loyal to you, Nelson." Hunter pulled his cell phone from his pocket and began flipping the sleek, black gadget over and over in his hand. It was the most advanced cell phone on the market, and what it could do amazed him. "You've taught me everything I know, and I've always been grateful." Hunter watched Radcliff nod. The managing partner was clearly pleased by what he'd heard.

"Don't worry about the divorce, son," Radcliff said reassuringly. "I've already spoken to the senior partners about it. I promise it won't get in the way of you becoming our managing partner someday. They're all very supportive. They all know Anne's the one who's in the wrong here. You're a good husband."

That was ridiculous. Radcliff shouldn't have said anything to the other senior partners so fast, he shouldn't have jumped the gun like that. But Hunter managed to remain stoic. He just needed a little more patience, just needed to play the game a little longer, then he'd get his satisfaction. "Thank you, Nelson."

There was a long pause.

"Well," Hunter finally spoke up, starting to rise from the chair. "I better get down to the conference room. I'm meeting Delilah to go over a few things before the other side gets—"

"I have two daughters," Radcliff interrupted. "They're a few years younger than you."

"Kelly and Paige." Hunter eased back into the chair. "I know." In his thirteen years at Warfield & Stone, he'd only met Radcliff's daughters twice. There'd been so many years in between he hadn't recognized Paige the second time they'd seen each other. Radcliff was an intensely private man, especially when it came to his family. "They're very nice."

"I never had a son."

Hunter nodded. "I know."

"But I always wanted one. I've never told anyone that," he admitted, "not even my wife."

This was extraordinary, Hunter realized. Radcliff rarely touched on anything personal.

"Then you came along," Radcliff continued, his voice growing strained, "and suddenly I knew I had one."

Hunter felt a lump form in his throat, felt his breath grow short.

"The firm will do whatever is necessary to get you through this awful time, Hunter. Whatever is necessary," Radcliff repeated firmly. "You're one of my family now. Do you understand that, do you understand what that means to me, son?"

Hunter could barely believe what he was hearing. This was more than extraordinary, it was unprecedented. "Yes, I do."

27

DURING ALL HIS years in Montana, Strat had never been to Gordonsville. It was only fifteen miles west of Fort Mason, but in all that time it had never been a destination for him, never a place he was interested in seeing. As far as he was concerned, Gordonsville was someplace you passed through to get somewhere else. It was a town you stopped in for a few minutes to fill up your gas tank, buy a Coke, or pick up a pack of Swisher Sweets to smoke on the river after catching a nice fish. It wasn't a damn place you spent any more time in than you had to.

Okay, it had two nice restaurants instead of one and there was a four-screen Cineplex playing the latest movies instead of a single-screen theater playing a movie that had been released months ago. But so what? It didn't have the tight-knit feel or the character of Fort Mason. It didn't have the Lion's Den, Hell's Gate, the Lassiter River running right through the middle of town, or the history of a fort that had occupied the town square before there was even a town. And Gordonsville wasn't a big city that had things you were willing to drive a long way for like sprawling indoor malls, airports that could actually get you somewhere, and *really* nice restaurants. Things that cities like Missoula, Butte, and Bozeman offered.

The only interesting thing about Gordonsville was that it had a new Caterpillar factory. The word going around the area was that the Cat plant was paying fourteen dollars an hour to new hires—which was nearly thirty thousand a year—and that was for people who didn't have experience, who'd never operated big assembly equipment. The word was that they were paying foremen as much as forty-five grand a year to start.

"Lord, that's good money," he muttered, irritated that he couldn't find the place he was looking for.

He was only making thirty-four thousand a year, and he'd been with Roman Construction for seven years, three as a foreman. With his leadership skills he ought to be able to move into a job on one of the Cat lines right away. He'd heard from several people that they were short on experienced foremen. He'd feel disloyal to Butch Roman, but maybe he ought to head over there after his meeting today and fill out an application. He could use another eleven grand a year. He was getting damn tired of living in that rusty, leaky trailer in the middle of the woods; tired of eating whatever trout he could pull from the Lassiter for dinner even though you were supposed to release everything you caught. He was tired of eating franks and beans on the other nights, too, tired of thinking about how much Hunter made. Strat had always convinced himself that material things didn't matter, but it was getting tougher and tougher to make that case, especially now that he was starting to feel his age.

"Damn!"

Strat leaned over the pickup's steering wheel and squinted, frustrated. He'd been around the block twice, but he couldn't find the damn diner. He was starting to worry that he'd taken the directions down wrong or that he didn't have the right address. This was the problem with thumbing your nose at a town, then suddenly needing to know your way around it. Karma was a bitch, all right. Of course, getting that new prescription he'd been needing for his glasses for a year and a half might help, too. But new glasses cost money he didn't have. Everything seemed to cost money he didn't have.

"There it is," he sang out, wrenching the steering wheel to the right and zipping into a parking spot. "Finally."

He turned the engine off and pulled the keys from the ignition. He was thirty minutes overdue, and it was against his religion to even be a minute late. It was the height of arrogance to be late for a meeting, especially one you'd requested. It was terrible to waste another human being's time like that. On top of that, the woman he was meeting might already be gone, fed up with waiting. And she was his best lead.

Strat jumped from the truck, then hustled up the cracked steps and into the diner. A hostess wearing a checked polyester dress waved a menu at him, but he was past her quickly and pacing up and down the booth-lined aisles. After a few moments, he spotted the person he was looking for. At least, he hoped it was her.

"Mrs. Bach?" he asked as he slid onto the bench seat across from the middle-aged woman, keeping his voice low. "Mrs. Ida Bach?"

"Yes," she answered. "Are you Strat Lee?"

Strat took a relieved breath. "I am."

He glanced around, trying to tell if anyone was paying too much attention to them. One of the men in the booth across the aisle seemed like he was listening, but Strat figured that was probably just his paranoia kicking in. Of course, he felt like he had a right to be paranoid at this point. He was convinced there were people who'd be very interested in this seemingly innocent get-together. The question was: Who exactly were those people? He was pretty sure he knew, but he had to get more information before he'd get all the help he'd been promised. Before that person he'd mentioned to Hunter was going to jump in with both feet.

He leaned forward over the table. "Thank you for meeting me, Mrs. Bach."

"Call me Ida."

"All right . . . Ida. I'm sorry I was late, but I—"

"I would have waited all afternoon." Her lower lip began to tremble and tears welled up in her eyes as she gazed across the table. "All night, too."

Strat tried to make his expression sensitive. He knew how intimidating his natural one could be. "I'm sorry about your husband." Suddenly Ida seemed so sad, like maybe she'd been thinking about suicide herself. "Maybe we can do some good together. You know, make some people pay."

He'd been worried on the drive over from Fort Mason that Ida might have a change of heart, that she'd get scared or decide not to help because after all it was Hunter who'd pushed her husband over the edge in that Bozeman courtroom. Not that it was Hunter's fault, because ultimately a man had to be held accountable for his own actions and Carl Bach had done some terrible things. But, after all, Carl was her husband and Hunter was his brother.

Now that they were face to face, Strat could see that Ida wasn't going to let any of that matter. She just wanted to do the right thing, that was all. As sad as she was he could tell there was a fire in her soul, too.

Ida reached across the table and took Strat's hand. "I don't care about making people pay, Mr. Lee, I just want to stop the fires. I want Montana to stop burning. I don't want to hear about another little boy dying while he's trying to save his animals." Tears trickled down her face. "I can't take it anymore."

28

ANNE SAT DIRECTLY across from Hunter near one end of the long conference room table; to Hunter's right was his attorney, Delilah Priestly; and across the table from Priestly and to Anne's left sat Marty Friedman, Anne's lawyer. Sam McCabe was at the far end of the room, at the head of the table in the chair where Nelson Radcliff sat when he presided over monthly partner meetings.

McCabe was so far away it almost seemed as if he wasn't involved in the proceedings. Hunter realized that sitting so far away was intentional on McCabe's part, and he appreciated it. McCabe was basically a decent man. He wouldn't get in the way of a settlement.

But Radcliff might.

Hunter glanced at Anne, but she was looking down. She wouldn't make eye contact with him, she hadn't since she and her attorney had entered the room. She was wearing a low-cut top that didn't leave much to the imagination. He grimaced, watching Friedman take an eyeful. She didn't get it and she never would.

"All right," Friedman began, "let's get going. We all know why we're here. We're trying to get the ball rolling, we're trying to establish a general framework for the divorce so we can agree on the major points of a separation agreement. I don't think any of us expect to come away from today with too much in the way of specifics, but if we focus for an hour or two, it should set the stage for a good, fair process." He gestured at Priestly. "That sound right to you, Delilah?"

She nodded. "I think that's a good way to—"

"Let's cut the crap," Hunter broke in, leaning over the table. "What does my money-grubbing, soon-to-be-ex-wife want?"

"The house free and clear of all liabilities," Friedman shot back, "and everything in the house except your personal effects. We'll send you a list of those."

A lot of opposing spouses must take this same in-your-face approach, Hunter realized. Friedman hadn't missed a beat, hadn't seemed unnerved at all by it. Well, Friedman would have another missile screaming at him in a few minutes, and Hunter was betting the opposing attorney wouldn't take the impact of this one quite so calmly.

"We want her Mercedes, too," Friedman kept going, "as well as a lump-sum payment of a million dollars tax-free and alimony of twenty-five thousand a month for life with all the normal death policies in place to protect the annuity. Premiums on the insurance to be paid by you, of course," Friedman added as he sat back and gave everyone a few moments to digest what he'd just said. "Oh, yeah, and half your Warfield & Stone partnership interest. What do you think of that, Mr. Lee?"

"I think it stinks," Hunter answered. "I was told that your client would be reasonable if I got to the table quickly. I don't think anyone in their right mind would say she's being reasonable after hearing that list." It took every ounce of self-control Hunter had to stay calm. "It sounds more like a ransom demand for Bill Gates's kid than a property split."

Friedman shrugged. "So make me a counteroffer."

"Why don't we all stop and take a deep breath?" Priestly suggested, trying to defuse what had quickly become a tense situation. "Let's be systematic about this, Marty." She reached for a folder lying on the table. "First let's compare the personal asset and liability statements we've gotten from our clients so we're sure we're all singing off the same sheet of—"

"Here's my counteroffer," Hunter interrupted. "I'll give Anne a hundred thousand dollars in cash in exchange for a written apology admitting to each time she's ever had sex with someone other than me during our marriage."

Anne burst into a loud, caustic laugh and banged the table with her fist, shocking everyone. Even Sam McCabe came off his elbow with a start. "Forget it, Hunter," she hissed.

"Don't play this game," Hunter warned, pulling his cell phone out and flipping it over and over in his hand the same way he had in Radcliff's office. "You don't know how, Anne. You'll get burned."

"Ooooooh, you're so scary," Anne retorted, opening her eyes wide and putting her hands up as if something was coming at her out of the dark. "Here comes big bad Hunter Lee. Everybody watch out."

"And I do know how to play this game," Friedman asserted. "I'm one of the best in the business. Tread carefully," he advised. "Don't make me mad."

Priestly patted Hunter's arm. "Let me handle this," she urged. "Please."

"You sure you're as good as you think you are, Marty?" Hunter asked. "Are you sure you've judged your client's veracity correctly?"

Friedman gave Hunter a puzzled expression. "I'm not sure I know what you mean by that."

"It's a straightforward question. I'm wondering if you're really as good as you say you are. That's all."

"Oh, yeah." Friedman smiled like the cat who'd swallowed the canary. "You may be one of the best litigators around, but you're a babe in the woods when it comes to divorce. This is my game, not yours." Friedman shook his head as if what he was about to say was a shame but proved his point. "Look what happened to Michael Jordan when he tried to play baseball. He couldn't hit a Double A curveball to save his life, and it was pathetic watching him try. That'll be you if you take me on." Friedman gestured at Priestly. "Do as she says," he advised. "This'll turn out a lot better for you if you do. Trust me."

"Trust the opposing attorney." A grim smile creased Hunter's face. "Now that's an interesting concept. Naive, but it's interesting." How in the hell could anyone be a divorce attorney, Hunter asked himself. Being a litigator was bad enough, but a *divorce* attorney? God, he wouldn't be able to face himself in that morning mirror if that was how he made his living. "Okay, Delilah," he spoke up, "this may shock you, but I'm going to do exactly that, I'm going to take opposing counsel's advice. It's your show, and I won't interfere anymore." He aimed his cell phone at the wall to his left, at a spot where everyone in the room would have a clear view of what he was going to show. "But I think I ought to get some kind of discount off the fee we talked about earlier because it's going to be pretty easy for you to win this thing after everyone gets a load of this."

Hunter pressed a silver button on one side of the cell phone and a moment later a crystal-clear, three-by-three-foot color image appeared on the wall—accompanied by sound. As it became obvious who was in the movie and what was going on in it, there was a collective gasp from around the table.

Hunter looked away, unable to watch his wife and Nelson Radcliff have sex any longer.

Suddenly it sounded as if there were fifty people yelling at each other in the conference room, not just four. Marty Friedman was shouting at Anne that he was dropping her as a client immediately. Anne was shouting back that he was already fired. Sam McCabe was yelling at Hunter to turn the phone off immediately. Delilah Priestly was howling at Friedman. A red-faced Friedman was shaking his finger at Priestly and warning her at the top of his lungs to stop laughing at him or he'd throw her through the window. McCabe was warning Friedman that he'd face sanctions if he kept threatening Priestly. And Priestly was laughing louder and louder the redder and more animated Friedman became.

As Hunter gazed at Anne—and she gazed back—he understood for the first time that she really didn't love him anymore. It was all over her face. She wanted to move on, she wanted someone else. Maybe in all the years they'd been together, now that he thought about it, she'd *never* loved him. He hated to admit it, but, now that he was staring into those eyes, he understood the truth, the awful truth. She'd been using him ever since they'd met.

Hunter rose from his chair and headed for the door even as the others kept shouting, even as Priestly and McCabe yelled for him to come back. All he wanted to do now was get on a plane and get back to Montana.

29

IT DIDN'T TAKE long for the first few pine trees in the grove to torch. He'd scouted well again, made certain to locate another remote spot that would ignite quickly, located another fuse for another megablaze. A few dead trees that would burst into a freight train of fire, then race away into a vast, difficult-to-access forest full of downed timber and leaves on the wings of a consistent, twenty-mile-an-hour westerly breeze blowing straight in off the Pacific Ocean.

This time the flames were headed toward a big town. That requirement for the location had come directly from the boss.

The man moved quickly back toward the Escalade, orange flames reflecting in the glossy black paint of the SUV. In a few hours, there'd be another huge fire raging in the Northwest, this time in California. The authorities would have to call in at least three to four thousand firefighters to get this one under control. A lot of them would have to come from other parts of California and from other states because the locals wouldn't be able to handle this one on their own. All of those imported firefighters would have to get here somehow; they'd need to eat three times a day; they'd need a place to sleep, and they'd need a long list of supplies.

It was all working perfectly. Maybe greed wasn't such a bad thing in the end, maybe it wasn't going to torpedo them after all.

The man climbed in behind the truck's steering wheel as he watched the fire grow. They were leaving Montana alone.

But not for long.

30

HUNTER SAT IN a small room down the hall from the partners'
conference room staring at his cell phone. It lay on the round
table in front of him like a piece of evidence. All it needed was
"Exhibit A" penned in blue ink on a tag hanging from it by a white string.

He'd been sitting in this square, sterile room for an hour with nothing
to do—no magazines to read, no laptop to work on, nobody to call. He'd
been left with nothing to think about but those awful images of Anne and
Radcliff having sex, of his wife and the man so many said seemed like his
father entwined in all those positions. He was so bored he was actually
thinking about playing the clip again to remind himself of how much he
hated Radcliff.

He leaned forward and reached for the phone, then shook his head
and eased back into the leather seat. No way, no way in hell.

"Hunter?"

Sam McCabe was finally back. "Yeah?"

"May I come in?"

It was a silly question because McCabe was the one who'd pleaded
for him to wait here "for a few minutes while things got sorted out." After
he'd chased Hunter down the hall past several wide-eyed junior people
who must have picked up what was going on after all the screaming and
shouting coming from inside the partners' conference room. Hunter was
certain the intraoffice email rumor mill was humming by now.

"Of course, Sam."

McCabe was a small man with thinning brown hair who wore round, tortoise-shell glasses and sported a perma-tan even in the winter after years and years of sailing on Long Island Sound. Sailing was his passion. He loved it more than anything in the world, and if you weren't careful, he'd take up your entire afternoon telling you about it. Hunter had learned that lesson the hard way a long time ago.

"Mind if I sit down?" McCabe asked, shutting the door.

McCabe was meek to begin with, but this was ridiculous. Hunter gestured at the chair beside his. "Sure."

McCabe put a worn, brown notebook down on the table, then eased into the chair with a loud sigh. "Well, well, what a day."

"Yeah."

McCabe bit his lower lip. "I'm thinking there might have been another way to deliver your message, Hunter."

Hunter said nothing, he just stared at McCabe. Through him, really.

"I understand that you're upset," McCabe continued, his tone turning nervous. "You should be."

McCabe didn't mean that he "understood" in a personal sense. McCabe didn't understand how deeply it hurt to watch a wife in all those positions with another man on a wall in the partnership conference room, because he didn't care about his wife. Mrs. McCabe spent most of the year in West Palm Beach. As far as anyone could tell, McCabe was in West Palm two, maybe three weeks a year around Christmas, and most of that time he was out on sailboats without Mrs. McCabe. What McCabe meant was that he understood in a general sense that it wasn't optimal to have your wife screwing the managing partner, especially someplace a private eye might catch them doing it and record it all. It wasn't optimal for a husband, a wife, or a managing partner. In fact, it wasn't optimal for *anybody*. That's what he meant by understanding.

"What are we going to do about it?" Hunter had already decided he wouldn't work another day for Warfield & Stone. He wasn't going to line Radcliff's pockets with one more dime. Of course, he probably wouldn't have to worry about it. Radcliff would probably ban him from the building by the end of the day. "What's the deal?" he demanded bitterly. *"What's the damn deal, Sam?"*

"Please don't take this out on me," McCabe begged. "I'm just trying to get through this thing. God, I can't imagine how it is for you. I . . ."

I've always liked you, Hunter, I've always respected you. You know that."

Hunter sat up, rubbed his eyes for a few moments, then reached over and patted McCabe's arm. "Sorry, Sam, you're right." McCabe was simply the messenger. There wasn't any reason to make him feel bad. "I know you're trying to help."

"Thanks." McCabe pulled a folded, yellow piece of paper from his pocket. "I've been sent with an offer."

Here it was, the buy-off. It was how Radcliff handled anything unsavory in his life: with money. Even when it involved a man he'd called his son only a few hours before.

"I'm sure you were expecting this."

Hunter nodded. This was so cowardly of Radcliff. "I was."

"Okay, here goes." McCabe unfolded the piece of paper. "You get ten million in cash after tax. It's yours free and clear. I'll get all the necessary documentation from the IRS so we make sure it's after tax." The paper was shaking in his hands like a flag in a stiff breeze. "In return, you give up your partnership interest in Warfield & Stone and all copies of the clip." McCabe nodded at the cell phone lying on the table. "You're never allowed to discuss what happened here today with anyone, and you can't tell anyone that Nelson had sex with Anne. If you do, you owe Warfield & Stone the ten million back, *plus* another ten. If you keep a copy of the clip and it shows up somewhere, you owe us fifty million."

When McCabe was finished, Hunter picked up the cell phone and aimed it at the wall.

"Don't do that!" McCabe shouted, holding up his hands and turning his face as if like he was being attacked. "Please don't!"

Hunter stood up and tossed the cell phone down on the table in front of McCabe. He'd already bought another one and transferred all the numbers to it, anticipating what Radcliff would require. "He's not coming, is he?"

McCabe shook his head. "Would you?"

"I'd never get myself in this situation."

"No," McCabe agreed, "I don't think you would."

Hunter moved to the door, reached for the knob, then glanced back over his shoulder. "You tell that son of a bitch it's twenty million free and clear, not ten. If he agrees to that, he's got a deal." Hunter tapped his watch. "He's got fifteen minutes to agree or I call a reporter friend of mine at the *Post* and I tell him everything. And, Sam, I do mean *everything*."

"Hunter."

He'd been reaching for the knob again. "What?"

McCabe let out a labored breath. "Look, I don't usually say things like this, and if you ever told Nelson I did, I'd deny it." He took his glasses off and shook his head sadly. "Which I guess pretty much sums up the man I am."

Hunter turned around to face McCabe. The other man was struggling hard with what he was trying to say.

"You're right," McCabe finally agreed. "Nelson Radcliff is a son of a bitch. Hell, he's worse than that. We both know it." He glanced around furtively. "I pray to God this room isn't bugged. If it is, my career's over."

"Look, Sam, I'm—"

"You're a good man, Hunter," McCabe interrupted uncharacteristically. "You didn't deserve this."

Hunter hesitated. "Good men never do, Sam, but it still happens." He reached for the doorknob again.

"Hunter."

Once more Hunter stopped and turned back around. "What?"

"If you ever need anything, call me." McCabe hesitated. "I mean it. Anything."

PART II

31

IT FELT STRANGE to be on a plane and dressed casually. Hunter was wearing a loose-fitting golf shirt, a comfortable pair of khakis, and loafers with no-socks. It felt strange, but it felt good, too, especially the no socks part.

He'd always worn a suit and tie on trips because he was always on business for Warfield & Stone. He couldn't remember the last time he and Anne had flown anywhere on vacation—actually, he couldn't remember the last time he'd taken a vacation except for a day here and there to do personal business or to go fishing in New England. One of Nelson Radcliff's many mandates for his employees was that if you were on business for the firm, you wore a suit and tie even on a plane.

There were no exceptions to the rule and God help you if you didn't follow it. At one point, the firm's top associate was spotted coming out of LaGuardia Airport late on a Friday night wearing a Walkman, a backward-facing New York Yankees cap, a Rascal Flats T-shirt, cargo shorts, and flip-flops. He was on his way home from a trial in Texas where he'd been the star of the courtroom, the one who'd cracked the case when the partner couldn't. He'd won two million dollars for the firm, but thirty minutes after deplaning, he was out on his ass after a quick call from Sam McCabe. That was how fast Nelson Radcliff worked when you didn't follow his guidelines to the T, because he took it as a personal sign of disrespect.

Hunter hunched over and glanced out the window from the next-to-last row of the Boeing 737. They were descending into Missoula at the end of a short hop over from Salt Lake City, coming down through ten thousand feet. There were just a few high clouds passing over the valley so he could see the Clark Fork River winding its way out of town beneath them, glistening brilliantly in the bright sunshine.

When the river curled behind a ridge and disappeared, he eased back in the narrow seat and stared up at the red call button. For the first time in a week he was starting to feel like himself again, and Montana was feeling like home. More than Connecticut ever had, even more than Virginia had. The stress of the last two weeks was finally ebbing now that he was back in Big Sky Country.

The pain was still with him. It would be for a while, he figured, some piece of it probably forever. He'd come out of a nightmare on sweat-soaked sheets early this morning in his Manhattan hotel room, wide-eyed and shaking. In the dream Anne was showering in the men's locker room at the club with two young lifeguards. It was definitely going to take time to put the pain of the divorce and who Anne had been cheating with in the rearview mirror, but that's what he had now—time and lots of it. He couldn't think of a better place to spend it, either. The magnificence and mystery of Montana would distract him.

So would Strat. It had sounded on the phone last night when they'd spoken as if making Hunter get over everything was going to be Strat's personal mission. One of them, anyway. Strat was determined to find out who was torching Montana, too. Hunter grinned. Strat was a good man. A little rough around the edges, but ultimately he was even more loyal than Dale Callahan's yellow Labs.

Hunter shifted in his narrow seat. Sitting in the back of the bus was another new experience for him. Radcliff's second mandate for air travel was that everyone at Warfield & Stone, from the greenest associate to the managing partner, flew first class whenever they went on business. Not because Radcliff was a snob or because he was noble and wanted his employees to be rested when they arrived at their destination. Just the opposite. He wanted them on the clock constantly so they could bill as many hours as possible. He figured if they were flying first class and could spread out, they were more likely to work than if they were crammed into coach.

Of course, Radcliff wasn't naive. He knew his people wouldn't work harder in first class simply because they were loyal to the firm, so he spot-checked. Every so often he had McCabe call people right after they'd landed to find out what they'd learned in the air about whatever case they were working on. That call book-ended a report Radcliff had gotten just before the person being spot-checked took off from New York. Then Radcliff and McCabe would compare notes, and sometimes the lawyer in question didn't come back to New York. At least, not on Warfield & Stone's dime.

Maybe it was a good thing that he and Radcliff would never see each other again, Hunter figured, remembering the last associate who'd been fired by McCabe in a faraway city for not getting enough accomplished at thirty-five thousand feet. She was a nice young woman who'd fallen asleep after wheels-up because she was fighting the flu and had taken medicine. Hunter shook his head in disgust. Maybe leaving Warfield & Stone and divorcing Anne were blessings in disguise, as hard as it all had been on him. If he'd stayed and become the managing partner, he might have turned into Nelson Radcliff, he might have ended up firing people for falling asleep when they were sick. He might have ended up as despicable a person as Radcliff, or worse.

Now that he was on the outside looking in, Hunter could see Radcliff's faults. He could see how cowardly the old man was, too. Radcliff should have had the courage to show up for a final face to face with the one he'd called son for thirteen years, he shouldn't have sent McCabe to do his dirty work. Of course, Hunter thought ruefully, he probably would have strangled Radcliff with his bare hands if they'd been alone for even thirty seconds.

So maybe in the end it was better that Radcliff hadn't come down to the small room, maybe it was better that McCabe had shown up instead and acted as an intermediary. Thanks to McCabe, Hunter now had twenty million dollars parked in a numbered account at JP Morgan. Twenty million dollars. It was almost incomprehensible.

All that money and here he was crammed into the back of a plane. And he wasn't back here because first class was full; there were seats available up front. There had been on the New York to Salt Lake City leg, too. He'd checked on his way from the hotel to LaGuardia this morning, but he'd decided against sitting up there, decided he shouldn't fall into the trap of living the high life even with twenty million dollars in the bank.

Which seemed stupid now that the plane was about to land. It wasn't as if he'd be flying much after this, and how was he supposed to fall into a living-the-high-life trap in Fort Mason, Montana, for crying out loud? With everything he'd been through, he should have spoiled himself on the trip out. Maybe then he would have met that pretty brunette who was working first class. He'd been hoping Tina would be on this flight—it was the same airline—but she wasn't. He laughed, thinking about how he hadn't been with a woman in so long. He laughed because it was so sad, because laughing seemed better than the alternative. Maybe he'd give Tina a call sometime. Sometime *soon*.

"What's so funny?"

Hunter glanced over at the guy sitting in the middle seat. This was the first time they'd spoken, and, now that Hunter was focused on the guy, he noticed that he had a sharp, confident air about him. "Ah, nothing."

"Come on." The guy gave him a wide smile. "Share."

He had a disarming way about him, too, and not because he was laid back. He was relaxed right now, but Hunter sensed an intensity lurking beneath the surface. Zoe was right. It didn't take him long to size somebody up. It never had.

"I was thinking about a woman," Hunter admitted. It was a good thing Tina wasn't on this flight. She'd be paying a lot more attention to this guy. He looked like he ought to be headed to Hollywood instead of Missoula. He was that handsome, that charismatic. He was younger, too, in his late twenties probably. "She's a flight attendant, and I met her last time I came to Montana. It was a couple of weeks ago. I was flying into Bozeman."

"What was so funny about meeting her? Why were you laughing just now?"

Hunter wasn't going to own up to the real reason. "We had a nice conversation. She was fun. I liked her."

"Are you thinking about asking her out?"

"Well, she gave me her number."

"I bet she's pretty."

Hunter pictured Tina for a second. She wasn't as pretty as Zoe, but she was attractive. "She is."

"Which is how it should be."

"What?" That seemed like a strange thing to say. "Why?"

"You're a good-looking guy, so you should date pretty women."

Hunter smiled self-consciously. That had come out of nowhere and seemed like an awfully forward comment from someone he'd just met. *"Huh?"*

"That's nature, and I respect nature."

Hunter respected nature, too, but it didn't have anything to do with handsome men dating pretty women.

"I'll give you some free advice. Since you obviously aren't from here."

"Why do you say that?" Hunter wanted to know.

"About taking phone numbers from women you don't know in Montana," the guy said without answering the question. "Be careful doing it. It can get you in trouble." He flashed that grin again. "Because the chances are almost 100 percent that any halfway-attractive woman here is either married, engaged, or engaged to be engaged. At least there's a guy out there who thinks she is." He chuckled. "And most guys out here have guns. They usually shoot first and think about the consequences later, which could be a problem for someone like you." His smile grew wider. "And for me." He reached over and tapped Hunter's wedding band. "Your wife back in wherever you're from might not like it, either. Taking a phone number can get real expensive. At least, that's what I've heard. I've never been married but my friends who have and are on their second wives cry the money blues all the time."

What Hunter liked about the advice was that it hadn't been delivered in judgment. There'd been no edgy tone, no raised eyebrows, just honest counsel from one man to another. "I'll remember that." He started to say something more, then held back. This was so stupid. Hadn't he learned his lesson at the Lion's Den? People were always listening in Montana. But what the hell, he'd probably never see this guy again, and he felt like talking. "I shouldn't even be wearing it," he said, holding up his hand and gazing at the thick gold band, wondering why he still had it on. Force of habit or still trying to hold on? Even after he'd figured out the truth about the way Anne felt.

"Why not?"

"My wife and I are getting divorced." Maybe this was part of the healing process. Saying the words aloud to people you didn't know so they wouldn't sound so awful when you said them to people you did know. "We finished up our separation agreement a few days ago." In the end Hunter had given Anne almost everything Marty Friedman asked for—except the alimony. Which had shocked Anne—and Friedman. But why not be generous? He had twenty million dollars in the bank, and he didn't want anything that reminded him of her. That would just cause the pain to keep going. All he'd wanted were things from his study, from the place he went to recharge himself after a big case. "Now we just have to wait." Delilah Priestly had said it would take less than six months for the official decree to come through. "You know, let the system do its thing."

"You still care about her, don't you? That's why you're still wearing the ring."

Hunter folded his arms across his chest. "So, where you coming from?" It was better to change the subject than get irritated. The guy seemed to have good intentions, he'd just gone a little far with that last comment. Despite his confidence, he was still young, and he still had things to learn. Or maybe that hurt in his eyes made him not care about what he said.

The guy grimaced. "Sorry. That was pushing it," he admitted, holding out his hand. "I'm Paul."

"Hunter."

"I was in northern California the past few days fighting a forest fire," Paul answered when they finished a firm handshake. "I'm heading home."

Hunter's eyes flashed to Paul's. "You mean that big fire up near Mendocino?"

"Yup."

"Jesus." Coverage of the Mendocino fire had been all over the national news for the past few days. It had burned over sixty thousand acres and destroyed hundreds of homes. It would have torched an entire town except for a heroic, last-ditch stand by a huge firefighting force that had included planes and helicopters dropping tons of chemicals and water on the massive flame front round the clock for two days. "Is it out?"

"Pretty much," Paul answered. "There's still a mop-up crew on the scene making sure it's dead."

Now Hunter understood why Paul had that confident air about him. He faced death every time he went to work, every time he went into the woods to fight a fire. Hunter had been reading up on forest fires— at Strat's suggestion. He'd never realized how fast they could move, how quickly they could change direction, how dangerous they really were. If Paul wasn't confident, he'd be dead.

"My hat's off to you," Hunter said earnestly. "I've been reading about forest fires lately. I doubt most people understand what you guys do and how dangerous it is. You deserve a lot of credit."

"Thanks."

"Lightning started the one out there in California, right? That's what I read in the papers, anyway. And the thing is," Hunter continued, shaking his head, "what can you do about lightning strikes? They're going to happen. Hey, this forest fire thing is only going to get worse as the planet heats up. I mean, we can argue until we're blue in the face about whether global warming is an inconvenient truth or nature going through a cycle, but the bottom line is, the earth is getting hotter. A degree or two up in average summer temperature and the fires are going to get worse and worse. More and bigger. It's inevitable." He hesitated. "And lightning's the fuse, nature's fuse, but there's nothing we can do about it."

Paul stared silently at the back of the seat in front of him. "Lightning," he finally murmured. "That was the official word, wasn't it?"

It didn't sound as if Paul believed the official word. "What? You think it was something else that started the Mendocino fire?"

"I don't know," he answered tersely. "My job is to fight the damn things. I don't get paid to figure out how they start."

It was as if he wanted to say more but something was holding him back. Unfortunately, this didn't seem like the time to dig deeper, because Paul didn't seem like the kind of guy you got to know real well on final approach. Not well enough to ask him something as sensitive as how fires in the West were getting started if he had a suspicion it wasn't because of lightning. "How many people fought that fire in California?"

"Over four thousand. There were people in from as far away as Oklahoma."

Hunter finished his drink with a quick swallow. "Does the government put all you guys on commercial flights to get you to the fires?" He reached past Paul and handed his empty cup to the flight attendant as she made her last pass through the cabin. "And back home again?"

"Nope. We usually ride planes the Feds charter from a cargo airline that's based out here. I'm paying my own way home this time. It was gonna be two more days before I could get out of California because there were so many of us. I didn't want to wait that long."

Hunter smiled. "Got a girl at home, huh?"

"Maybe."

"Well, at least the taxpayers made out a little bit," Hunter observed. "At least the cargo airline didn't get paid for bringing you home."

Paul flipped a pretzel into his mouth as the plane banked hard to the left. "You'd think it would work like that, wouldn't you?"

"It doesn't?"

Paul shook his head. "They get paid for a round trip even if I pay for my own ticket home on a commercial flight."

"That's a hell of a deal. Somebody negotiated pretty well."

"Or got help negotiating."

That was an interesting take on things, especially since it seemed that Paul wasn't buying into lightning causing the fires. "What's the name of the cargo airline?" Hunter asked.

"Bridger Air."

32

STRAT HAD MET Ida Bach in Gordonsville so he'd have plenty of time on the drive over to see if he was being followed, but he hadn't noticed anything suspicious. Ida lived in Missoula, where the Bridger Railroad and Bridger Air were based, and it hadn't been too long a drive for her down to Gordonsville. It would have made more sense for them to meet in Missoula or Fort Mason or a directly in-between-on-the-main-road town like Boxwood. Not Gordonsville, which was out of the way for both of them. The interesting thing was that Ida hadn't once asked why he'd suggested Gordonsville. It was as if she understood the need for secrecy, as if she understood the need to meet in an out-of-the-way place.

Strat had driven to Missoula for today's meeting. Today's contact—the young man Ida had recommended that he meet with—worked for the Bridger companies and he couldn't take the time off to drive to Gordonsville. Strat hadn't told the guy exactly what the deal was when they'd set up the rendezvous over the phone because he was afraid someone might be listening, but the young man had agreed to meet anyway. The young guy had known Ida for a while and trusted her. She'd told him in confidence that he *had* to meet with Strat, that it was extremely important. Still, meeting in Missoula, so close to where George Drake was, made Strat very uncomfortable.

Strat had been sitting on a stool at the Rhino Bar in downtown Missoula for thirty minutes when Andy Kohler finally showed up. Red-haired and freckled, Kohler looked young enough to be in college, but he was actually thirty-two. He was a Bridger Railroad staff attorney who had reported to Carl Bach. Kohler spent most of his time working for the railroad, but he also did work for Bridger Air. George Drake regularly shared his executive staff with both companies because that saved money and saving every penny was critical for Drake, given how debt-loaded the railroad was.

Bach had taken Kohler under his wing when he joined the company two years ago. The young man was from out east and didn't know anyone in town when he'd first gotten to Missoula. Bach had taken him hunting and fishing and invited him over to the house for dinner once or twice a week. Which was how Ida had gotten to know him.

"Strat Lee?" the young man asked, a relieved look coming to his face when Strat nodded. "Whew. Glad I found you so—"

"Sit down, pal." Strat wanted to blast the guy for being half an hour late and for saying his name so loudly, but he didn't want to get the meeting off to a bad start. He needed Andy Kohler.

"I gotta get something to drink," Kohler said, waving to the bartender. "Man, I worked up a sweat walking over here. It's hot as hell outside. You want anything?"

"No." Strat grabbed Kohler's arm and pulled him down on the stool beside his before Kohler could order. "Look, kid," he growled impatiently, "I need a copy of the Bridger Air contract with the Feds. The one that covers what the company gets to fly firefighters to hot spots." The person who was helping him had specifically requested to see that document. Getting it might go a long way to getting even more help.

Kohler's expression turned incredulous. *"Are you kidding me?"* The young man shook his head hard. "Do you know what kind of trouble I could get into doing that? I mean, not only with George Drake and Charlie Hall, but I'd never work anywhere again. They'd put the word out on me."

"Didn't Ida talk to you?"

"Yeah, but—"

"Listen to me," Strat ordered gruffly, glancing around, "and listen to me good."

This was the critical moment. Ida was certain the kid could be trusted, she felt sure his heart was in the right place. But how could you ever really know? Someone might have gotten to him. Kohler probably didn't have much money, so he was vulnerable. It was a sad truth, but almost everyone had a price. For some, like Kohler, it was probably pretty low.

"All of these forest fires this year," Strat continued, twirling the tip of his index finger around, "in Montana, Idaho, Oregon, Colorado, and California. Like the one they just had over near Mendocino."

"Yeah? What about them?"

"I don't think they were all started by lightning or campfires. It's not like the newspapers are saying." Strat hesitated. "If you get my drift."

Kohler didn't get it right away, then his eyes flashed wide open. "You mean . . . you mean it's *arson*?"

Strat watched Kohler's eyes bug out, watched him make the frightening connection. "Do you know the contract pretty well?"

Kohler gazed intently at Strat. "Yeah."

"There's an annual fixed payment in it to Bridger Air, right?"

"I, I really shouldn't be going into details about—"

"Is there a damn fixed payment?" Strat demanded loudly enough that the bartender glanced up from a crossword puzzle he was doing. "Look, Ida told me you'd—"

"Yeah, there is,"

Good, the kid was finally answering. "Then Bridger Air gets a perbody transportation fee, right? A fee for every person it takes to a fire on top of the annual fee, right?"

"That's right," Kohler confirmed.

"In other words, the more people Bridger Air takes to a fire, the more—"

"The more money it makes," Kohler cut in. "That's right."

Strat wanted to make certain Kohler understood how bad this thing was. "You know there was a boy killed in that Big Cat Fire down south of here?"

"Yeah," Kohler said, his voice dropping low, "I heard about that. He died in a barn trying to save his horses. It was terrible." Kohler shook his head. "Are you saying that—"

"I'm not saying I know for a fact that there's a connection between that fire and Bridger Air," Strat broke in, anticipating the young man's question. "Or to any fire, for that matter. I'm not saying people are starting fires because George Drake or Charlie Hall are telling them to, not for sure, anyway. What I'm saying is, I want to find out. There's a couple of us who want to find out, including Ida Bach," Strat added, pulling the brim of his dirty gray Stetson slowly down over his eyes. "Look, there's other people who've got basically the same motive George Drake does. Maybe

Bridger Air isn't involved in anything, maybe it's somebody else who's behind all this. I'm just trying to find out who it is and right now process of elimination seems like the best way to do it."

"Who else are you thinking about?"

"Maybe somebody who feeds firefighters while they're on the line." A man like Dale Callahan, Strat thought to himself grimly. Callahan Foods had a huge contract with the Forest Service to provide three squares a day to every man and woman fighting a forest fire in every state in the Northwest. "Like people who'd make money rebuilding homes and businesses if towns were torched, like that town in California almost was." A man like his ultimate boss, Butch Roman. Strat couldn't believe he was even thinking about this possibility. Butch had been good to him for the last few years, but things were getting out of hand and the fires had to be stopped. No one could be above suspicion at this point. "Don't worry, Red," he spoke up, satisfied with the nickname he'd just tagged on Kohler because of the color of his hair. "I'm checking those people out, too. Not just George Drake and Bridger Air."

Kohler shook his head. "It makes so much sense. You start a fire and you create your own demand. It probably means millions of dollars in revenues when the fire's big and you're the one flying people in to fight it. Or the one feeding them all. At, what, twenty bucks a meal?"

"Try sixty." Strat had done his research. "Take the Mendocino fire, Red. Four thousand people, three times a day for five days at sixty bucks per." He scratched his head. "That's um . . ."

"Three million six," Kohler answered. "Three point six million dollars," he repeated. *"For five days work."*

"Plus there's add-ons for all kinds of other things that push the money way beyond that. Like bottled water, trash clean up, and on and on." Strat pointed at Kohler. "What's Bridger's per-body transport fee?"

Kohler thought for a moment, trying to remember the language in the contract. "It depends how far the fire is from Missoula, but it averages around two thousand bucks a trip."

"Okay. Let's say half the four thousand people who fought the Mendocino fire in California were flown in there at two thousand bucks a pop. What's that?" Strat knew the answer to this one, but he wanted Kohler to say it out loud. So it made a bigger impression on him. "Well, Red?"

"Four million dollars."

"*Four million dollars,*" Strat echoed. "I'd say that's a damn good incentive to start a fire."

Kohler ran both hands through his hair. "Jesus, I never thought about this."

"Neither," Strat pointed out, "did the federal government." Or maybe some prick in the Forest Service administration department was way ahead of everybody, and he was getting a nice kickback. "Now are you going to get me a copy of that contract? It would be a personal favor to Ida," he pushed when the young man didn't answer right away.

"Yeah, I'll get it," he finally agreed. "It'll take some fancy footwork to get into the files without anyone noticing, especially after that memo showed up at the Bridger Railroad trial over in Bozeman." His expression turned steely. "But I'll get it."

At that moment the door opened and a tall man wearing a plaid shirt, jeans, cockroach killers, and sunglasses stepped into the bar. As he sat down on a stool at the other end of the bar, Strat stood up and put a five down on the bar. It was time for them to get the hell out of here.

33

HUNTER STOOD IN the small baggage claim area of the Missoula airport, waiting impatiently for the black conveyor belt at his knees to start moving. Waiting for the bag he'd checked this morning at LaGuardia to emerge from an opening in the wall as part of a long luggage train. He hoped his bag would be the locomotive, or at least near the front of the train, so he could get out of here fast and meet up with Strat, who was supposed to be waiting for him outside. He'd tried calling his brother twice since the plane had landed ten minutes ago, but had no luck reaching him. He was starting to worry, because Strat was rarely late for anything. Hunter could have taken a quick look out the exit to see if Strat was there. The double doors leading outside were only fifty feet away. But he was afraid of what he might *not* find.

Hunter knew what Strat was up to in his spare time out here in Montana. They'd talked about it on the river that day for a long time before going to lunch at the Lion's Den. His brother was playing amateur private eye, trying to figure out if there was an arsonist in Montana. And if someone with a profit motive was starting the fires, he was trying to figure out who it was. Strat had been straight up with Hunter as they'd reclined beside the Lassiter about that being one of the reasons he wanted his brother to come to Montana, straight up about the fact that he wanted Hunter's help with his investigation, straight up about the fact that he wasn't asking Hunter to move to Montana just because he missed him.

They'd talked more about the fires last night on the phone. Strat had gone into more detail about who it might be if it wasn't George Drake, and how he was trying to follow up on certain leads he had. But he still hadn't come clean about the person who was supposedly helping him, and Hunter still wasn't sure he wanted to know who that person was. It was a dangerous game his brother was playing, and, as much as Strat figured he was bulletproof, Hunter knew he wasn't. No one ever was. Especially not against the kind of influence and power Hunter assumed Strat was up against if he was on target about what was going on. If someone was torching Montana for profit, chances were good that the guilty party had significant resources. And, if they were committing arson on a massive scale, it was likely the person with those resources would use them to destroy anyone on his or her tail.

Hunter went for his cell phone, then stopped. Strat knew what time he was landing. They'd gone over it twice last night on the phone. If he was outside, he was outside. If he was dead, there was nothing anyone could do about it. Hunter exhaled heavily. That wasn't much of a thought, just the old Hunter being too black and white, being too cold. Well, hell, Strat *better* be out there.

Hunter had shipped most of his stuff to Montana yesterday. He'd sent three large bags to the Lassiter Bed & Breakfast—a 1920s vintage mansion set on Fort Mason's town square. The B&B had seven comfortable, though less than private, guest rooms. Less than private because the walls were thin and supposedly the couple who owned the place liked to listen in on their guests at late hours. However, it was the nicest hotel in Fort Mason, and it was where Strat had recommended that Hunter store his fly rods until he made a decision about where to live permanently. Which shouldn't take long. And the couple was supposed to be harmless, just curious.

The rest of Hunter's scant, post-separation-agreement possessions were packed into a storage facility off Interstate 95 a few miles north of Stamford, Connecticut, behind the triple-locked steel door of a ten-by-ten-foot area identified as Bay Number 329. While he was unloading the van he'd rented to pick up his personal effects from the house, it had occurred to Hunter that Bay Number 329 would be a perfect place to hide a dead body. Like this naval intelligence officer he was friends with who worked at the Groton nuclear submarine facility had always told him that the circular, rarely visited insides of heavily wooded interstate cloverleafs were perfect places to hide bodies. Hunter had paid the naval officer on the side to help him work through technical issues of tough cases. It turned out the officer made more money under the table from Warfield & Stone than he did from the federal government. It turned out the officer was almost as disappointed in Nelson Radcliff and Anne as Hunter was.

When the conveyor belt began to churn and suitcases, bags, and gun cases from the Salt Lake City flight began surging through the opening in the wall, Hunter glanced at a stuffed grizzly bear inside a glass case near the exit. The bear was rearing up on its hind legs, baring its huge teeth and daggerlike claws. The pose reminded him of what Anne and her older sister had looked like to him at his ex–Connecticut home when they'd opened the door two days ago. Then they'd turned into hawks and watched carefully as he and his helpers had removed his things. Tailed him through the house like a bird dog on the scent as he carried out the few items he'd asked for during his last meeting with Marty Friedman. Anne and her sister had carefully checked each item off a typed list as it went into the van, and the sisters had shrieked with delight when the last item—a beautiful print of the University of Virginia that had hung in his study over his desk—was gone. He couldn't deny that he'd thought long and hard last night about Bay Number 329 and interstate cloverleafs as he'd drifted off to sleep in his hotel room.

But it was a waste of time to think about revenge. He had his twenty million dollars, and that was revenge enough. At least he'd gotten back at one of them.

He took a deep breath. *Twenty million dollars*. It really was incredible. He just wished he could sit down with his father for five minutes to thank him, and to ask him about negotiating against the devil.

"Hello, Hunter."

"Jesus!" he muttered, whipping around toward the voice that had startled him away from thoughts of selling souls and hiding bodies. "Well, well," he managed when he'd caught his breath. Zoe Gale was standing in front of him. "Um . . . where's—"

"Your brother called me a while ago," Zoe spoke up, smiling her perfect high-cheekbone smile. "He asked me to pick you up. He said he was tied up and couldn't get here in time. You know how he hates being late."

After Hunter had finished his call with Delilah Priestly's assistant on the plateau overlooking Hell's Gate, he and Zoe had hurried back to Strat's pickup, then sped straight to the Missoula airport. They'd barely said a word during the entire trip. He was distracted, and, as he'd realized during the flight back to New York City, she was probably upset. They'd been close to making a wonderful connection, but he'd switched gears in the middle of their moment to get back to New York. Zoe had probably figured he was running back to the East Coast to try to save his marriage, so of course she was angry and upset. After all, he'd said some things that would have led her on, and there was that near kiss.

They'd said a quick good-bye when she'd dropped him off last week, and he'd spent his time in New York City assuming their relationship had disintegrated before it even had a chance to come together. Apparently, he'd been wrong, which was wonderful. He loved being wrong when it meant he won.

Montana was turning out to be a tough place to keep a secret, but he was pretty sure no one out here knew he was suddenly worth twenty million dollars. He hadn't even told Strat about it, just told his brother that he'd reached an agreement with Anne. So his settlement with Nelson Radcliff couldn't be Zoe's motive, the reason she seemed so willing to get past what had happened last week on the plateau. Of course, everyone in Fort Mason thought he was worth thirteen million after the Bridger Railroad trial, so maybe money had been Zoe's motive all along.

Damn. Why couldn't he ever just stay in the moment and not try to figure out everybody's agenda? Why couldn't he just let happen whatever was going to happen and not try to protect himself?

Because he'd been a litigator for thirteen years, he answered himself. He'd seen how rotten people were to each other time and time again, how most people had ulterior motives and hidden agendas when it really came down to it. Because two of the people he'd been closest to in the world had just screwed him as hard as a person could be screwed.

"Well, thanks for—"

He didn't finish. He couldn't because Zoe pressed her body to his, slipped her arms around his neck, and kissed him deeply.

His first instinct was to pull back, but then he relaxed and took his own advice. He let go—for the moment.

"There," Zoe murmured when she ended the kiss. "We should have done that on the mountain. This isn't the most romantic spot for a first kiss, but so be it."

"It sure felt romantic to me," Hunter assured her, smiling. "Even if it is baggage claim."

"I have a suggestion."

Damn she looked good. "What?"

"Let's go back to our spot and pick up where we left off." She ran her fingers through his hair "I've got wine and cheese in the car."

"Sounds great."

Zoe slid her hands slowly down the front of his shirt. She was about to say something when she looked to one side and broke into a sly smile.

As if what she was about to say was giving her a big kick, Hunter realized.

"Oh, hello, Mr. Brule," she called.

Mr. Brule? Hunter followed her gaze. The guy he'd been sitting next to on the plane was standing thirty feet away, trying to seem inconspicuous. He had a hand to his face, rubbing his forehead. Hunter rolled his eyes. The Paul he'd been sitting next to on the way from Salt Lake was Paul *Brule*. Well, he thought grimly, the whole state was going to know about the divorce now. Here was another sledgehammer-to-the-forehead example of why you didn't talk about your personal life to anyone out here. Not if you wanted it to stay private.

"Hi, *Paul*," Zoe called loudly a second time when he didn't look over.

Paul slowly dropped his hand from his face and waved. "Hello, Zoe." He gave Hunter a quick grin. "So, we meet again."

"What?" Zoe was surprised. "You two already know each other?"

"Oh, yeah," Hunter answered. "We're on a first-name basis."

"I'm impressed." She pointed at Paul. "Not many people are with him."

"It's not as impressive as it sounds," Hunter cautioned. "What I really meant was we're on a first-name-*only* basis. We sat next to each other on the plane, but I don't believe Paul ever mentioned that his last name was Brule."

"I don't believe you ever mentioned your last name, either," Paul shot back good-naturedly, moving toward Hunter and Zoe.

"I didn't know yours," Hunter said, "but I'll bet you knew mine."

"Maybe." Paul picked Zoe up and twirled her around several times. "Hello, gorgeous."

She put her head back and shrieked. "Stop, Paul, *stop*."

He eased her back down to the floor beside Hunter. "Plus, I didn't want to intrude on this budding romance. Nice kiss, you two."

"Which I'm sure will be front-page news in the *Fort Mason Gazette* tomorrow morning," Hunter spoke up, a trace of tension creeping into his voice. He was certain Zoe's embrace with Paul was harmless, but he'd felt a twinge of jealousy watching Paul pick her up. Which was good. It meant he really liked her. "The top story."

"Oh, I'll be on the phone to Scoop Woodward as soon as I'm out of the airport," Paul confirmed, his expression turning serious. "You can count on that."

There was no *Fort Mason Gazette*. The town hadn't had a local newspaper in thirty years, but Hunter was betting there might as well be. He was betting Paul was going to make sure everyone in Fort Mason heard about the kiss.

"Sorry, Hunter," he said, smiling again. "I didn't mean anything personal. I just don't like throwing the family name around. I seem to get more sincere reactions from people when they don't know I'm Big Bill's son." He stuck his hand out. "Paul Brule at your service."

"Yup," Zoe said as Hunter and Paul shook hands again. "This is Paul Brule all right. *The* Paul Brule." Several people who were milling around waiting for their bags looked over right away, impressed.

Hunter caught a couple of their glances. It was amazing. It was like being with a movie star or a well-known athlete.

"The son of Big Bill Brule," Zoe went on. "Our distinguished senator. Some people think Paul might outdo his father someday. When he's finished his Fire Jumper days, they think he might be a senator, too, maybe even president. He's sure got the looks, doesn't he?"

"He does," Hunter agreed, trying not to seem envious.

"Ah, you couldn't pay me enough to get into politics because—"

"And Paul," Zoe interrupted, fluttering her fingers at him as she leaned against Hunter, "this is Robert Hunter Lee. New York City attorney extraordinaire."

"Oh, I know who he is. He's the slayer of the Bridger Railroad and the ogre, George Drake. He's our knight in shining armor, our Robin Hood. The man who takes from the rich and gives to the poor."

Paul's tone didn't sound a hundred percent sincere, Hunter noted. In fact, it sounded like Paul had that natural disdain for attorneys a lot of people did. Somebody who probably told that joke about five hundred lawyers at the bottom of the ocean being a good start as many times as he could. After his experience with Marty Friedman last week, Hunter was starting to feel that way, too.

"I did my job," said Hunter quietly but firmly. "That's all."

Paul stared intently at Hunter for a few moments, then nodded. "Yes, you did, and you did a great job. Those families deserved the best, and that's what they got."

Hunter nodded back. "Thanks." Paul Brule seemed tough but fair, a real Montanan. Which made that obvious hurt in the corners of his eyes even more of a mystery.

Paul grabbed two bags off the conveyor belt. "Well, I gotta get going. It was great meeting you, Hunter. Oh, by the way," he said, hesitating, "do you fish?"

"Yeah, I do."

"But do you *fly* fish?"

"That's all I do," Hunter answered. "I've got nothing against people who fish with a worm or a lure, it's just not for me."

"Well, you're a better man than me. I hate bait fishermen. It's cheating, and I hate cheaters." Paul hoisted one of the bags onto his shoulder. "Maybe we ought to go sometime."

"Sure, I'd like that."

"I'll give you a call." He glanced at Zoe. "Nice seeing you, gorgeous."

"You too, Paulie."

Paul grinned as he passed by them. "Yup, I gotta get out of here so I can get on the phone to Scoop Woodward. Gotta let him know about this hot, hot Fort Mason romance."

Hunter grimaced. Great. That was all he needed.

"Oh, Paul," Zoe called as he neared the exit.

Paul turned back. He was still grinning. "Yes, Ms. Gale?"

"Do say hello to Mandy Winslow for us. I saw her outside waiting for you. At least, I assume she's waiting for you."

Hunter glanced up to see Paul's cocky smile disappear. He chuckled. Well, good for Zoe. Strat had said she didn't take crap from anybody. Here was proof.

"She's such a cute girl," Zoe continued, putting her fingertips to her lips. "But my, my, an affair with a woman who reports to you? Now that's risky."

The smile slowly reappeared on Paul's face, but this time it was a conciliatory one. "Well played, Ms. Gale. Okay, I don't call Scoop Woodward if you don't either. Do we have an understanding?"

Zoe glanced up at Hunter. "Do we have an understanding, Mr. Lee?"

Hunter hesitated. "We do."

"Yes, Paul," she called, "we have an understanding."

Paul nodded, then turned and headed out the door.

When he was gone, Hunter took Zoe in his arms. "You know, you're an amazing woman."

She nodded confidently, a determined look in her eyes. Which made those bright points of light in her pupils even brighter. "You haven't seen anything yet, Mr. Lee." She took him by the hand and pulled him toward the exit. "Come on, let's go to Hell's Gate."

34

KATRINA MASON GLANCED up from her desk with a start. "What are *you* doing here?"

"Well, thanks a lot." George Drake dug his hands into his pockets hard. "That's a nice way to say hi to your man."

Katrina had been writing month-end checks, and she wasn't in a good mood. Ranch expenses were outpacing timber sales for the third month in a row. There hadn't been any livestock sales during that stretch. But there ought to be a good deal of cash coming from that revenue stream in August and September, so she wasn't really worried about the big picture. Still, she never liked it when the cash balance in the general ledger went down three months in a row. Piled on top of that frustration was the fact that apparently the man standing in her doorway was partly responsible for her cash problem. They were supposed to be a couple, and he hadn't even bothered to give her a warning about a rate increase. Maybe that should tell her something.

"Sorry," she said, closing the big accounting book. "It's just that you usually call before you come."

"I wanted to surprise you." Drake gestured at the ledger. "Do you still do all of your accounting by hand?"

"Yup. I do it the old-fashioned way, George. The way I like to do it."

"You ought to think about coming into the twenty-first century, honey. Maybe buy software that can do this accounting stuff for you. It would save you a lot of time. I can help you—"

"Please don't make another suggestion about how to run my ranch." She held up her hands. It seemed as if he dealt out these pearls of wisdom constantly, and, frankly, she was getting sick of them. *"Please."*

"Okay, okay."

Katrina stowed the ledger in a drawer of the credenza behind her. "Why did you want to surprise me?" she asked, locking the drawer with a key she kept on her personal chain. As she turned back around, she saw Drake eyeing the key. As if he found it offensive that she locked her books away in front of him.

"I figured we could go up to Fort Mason and walk around, then get dinner at The Depot. *And,*" Drake said loudly when she tried to break in, "I figured I had a better chance of convincing you to go with me face to face than asking on the phone. You get up so early most mornings I figured you'd tell me you couldn't go. Come on," he urged soothingly, "my treat."

"Did you call ahead to make sure Jeremy Brule wasn't going to be there?"

"Hey, now don't start—"

"How exactly do you intend to pay for dinner?" asked Katrina sarcastically.

Drake's expression soured. "Look, I know my railroad's having a tough time, but I don't think you need to make fun of it. What the hell's gotten into you tonight? This isn't like—"

"I guess you'll pay for it with that rate increase you tacked onto my bill this month for transporting my timber. Without even telling me, I might add."

He looked at her as if she was crazy. "What are you talking about?"

"I could use trucks, you know." She rose from her chair and moved across the room until she was standing right in front of him, hands on her hips. "Come on, George."

He held his arms out. "What?"

"You increased the rate for me to put my trees on the Bridger Railroad. By a *lot.*"

"One of my sales guys must have done it on his own," Drake protested. "Maybe Charlie Hall implemented an across-the-board increase. We're trying to find cash anywhere we can right now. I swear I had no idea. How much was it?"

"Enough."

"I'll find out what happened in the morning," Drake promised. "First thing. I'll make sure it gets fixed, I'll make sure it gets back to where it was."

"Uh-huh."

They eyed each other from close range for a few moments, then Drake moved to the window. "I heard Butch Roman was out here a few days ago," he finally spoke up, staring out at the main barn.

How could Drake possibly have known that? Katrina asked herself. Maybe he already had a mole here at the ranch. Well, that was what they said about him, wasn't it? That he was damn good at getting information, that somehow he always found a way to get it.

"So what?" she said defiantly. It didn't make any sense to deny it. That would only make him lose faith in her, and she wanted to keep him close despite what a lot of people thought of him. "I need Butch's company to build that new barn I told you about. He's the only one that can get it done before winter."

Drake's expression went from irritation to hurt. "You have him over here the day I'm in Chicago fighting to keep my railroad, the day I'm away. Does that sound fishy to you, Katrina? Because it sounds fishy to me."

"It was the only day Butch could do it."

"Why couldn't one of his assistants give you a quote?"

"I wanted to asked Butch about what was going on with the Bridger Railroad," Katrina snapped. "I was trying to get information for you, I was trying to help you. I heard he was working with an investor group out east, and I was trying to see if he was making any progress. Okay?"

"What's the deal?" Drake hissed under his breath. "Does everyone know Butch is working with a group out east to buy my railroad?"

Katrina headed back to her desk. "Little did I know you were gouging me on my freight costs the whole time. Maybe I should use trucks after all, or sell my trees to Big Bill."

Drake sneered. "You wouldn't sell your trees to Bill Brule even if you were losing the ranch, and he was the last person on earth who'd buy the trees. We both know that." He gritted his teeth and shook his head. "First you have Dale Callahan out here, then it's Butch Roman. Damn it, Katrina. Maybe I should be worried. I mean, they're both bachelors and they're both doing well." His eyes were flashing. "Hell, we've been seeing each other for three months, and we haven't slept together yet." He turned away from the window and stared at her for a few moments, then limped away. "Sorry I surprised you!" he yelled over his shoulder. "Sorry I tried to be romantic. I'll remember not to try again."

"George, stop!" But he didn't. "George!" Katrina shouted again, hurrying after him. Suddenly another lonely night didn't seem very appealing. "Wait!"

"What?" he growled when she caught up to him.

"I'm sorry," she said, grabbing his hand. "I get cranky when I pay bills."

After a few moments he nodded sympathetically. "Yeah, I can understand that."

"Look, I want to go with you up to Fort Mason. It sounds fun."

Drake's expression brightened. "Good."

"There's one thing I need to ask you, first," she said, grasping his hand tightly, not allowing him to head toward the door. "One thing I want to know before we go."

"What is it? What's wrong?"

She hesitated, uncomfortable about this. She'd seen symptoms of that temper she'd heard so much about, but she'd never been subjected to a full-blown storm. She was afraid this question might bring it on, but she had to know. "Did you have anything to do with Dale Callahan's yellow Lab being killed on the railroad tracks? His favorite one. The one he thought was going to be a champion."

Drake's eyes narrowed. "Did Butch Roman tell you that?" He was suddenly seething. "Butch and Dale are thick as thieves and Butch is all pissed off at me right now," he muttered, veins rising from his neck. "Did Butch tell you that? Well, *did he?*"

35

"HAVE YOU EVER smoked pot?"

Hunter chuckled, embarrassed by the question. "Of course. For God's sake, Zoe, I went to college. What do I look like? Some kind of square?"

She laughed. "You really want me to answer that question?"

They were sitting side by side on the plateau overlooking Hell's Gate, on the same rock they'd been sitting on when Hunter had gotten the call from Delilah Priestly's assistant. They were enjoying a second bottle of smooth Chablis as they watched the sun fall slowly from the sky.

"I guess not," Hunter murmured. He'd set himself up for that one, violating the rule he always followed in court about never asking a question he didn't know the answer to. "I probably won't like it."

"I think you will."

"Oh?"

"You don't look like a square at all. Not to me, anyway." She kissed him on the cheek. "But last time we were up here you told me your wife thought you were the biggest square in the world. That's why I asked."

"My soon to be *ex*-wife, you mean." He hadn't told her on the drive down. He'd wanted to wait until they were up here and they'd had some wine.

A quick flash of excitement streaked across Zoe's face, then her expression turned to one of compassion. "I'm sorry to hear that."

"You mean you didn't know?" He was testing, trying to find out how far the tentacles of the Fort Mason rumor mill reached. "You didn't hear about what happened in New York?"

"No. What?"

"My wife and I agreed to a separation agreement. Now we just have to wait for the state to approve the divorce. Which shouldn't take that long." She seemed to be sincerely surprised by the news. "My lawyer's assistant was the one who called when we were here last time. She was calling to tell me that my wife was willing to be reasonable if I was willing to wrap things up quickly."

"I wish you'd told me that. I kept thinking it was your wife who called."

So, he'd been right. That was the reason she'd seemed frustrated on the drive up to Missoula that day.

"I didn't think you were coming back," Zoe continued. "I figured she'd called to tell you she missed you, and she wanted you to come home. I thought you'd been lying to me about how you and she weren't getting along. I thought that was why you didn't say anything all the way up to Missoula." She patted his thigh and sighed. "I have to admit something."

"What?"

"It sounds terrible."

"What, come on?"

"I was happy when Strat called this morning and asked me to pick you up. I figured it meant you and your wife really weren't getting along. That's mean, I know."

"No, it isn't. I'm glad I'm here, I'm glad I'm here with you." He took a deep breath. "My wife doesn't love me anymore, Zoe. If she ever did," he added softly.

"Your wife's crazy."

He gave her an appreciative smile, then glanced at the sun. It was going straight down through the cut between the peaks forming Hell's Gate. "That's gorgeous."

"That's Montana."

He reached out and gently pulled on her chin until she was facing him again, like she'd done to him the first time they were up here. "Why the full-court press, Zoe?"

"What do you mean?"

"Why the trip back up here so fast? Why the wine and cheese?"

"I don't want anyone else to have a chance at you, Mr. Lee," she answered matter-of-factly. "A man like you doesn't come to Fort Mason very often."

"If Fort Mason's so bad, what are you doing here?"

She sighed. "Is this the third degree? Is this the lawyer coming out in you?"

"No. I'm just curious."

She turned and gazed at the setting sun. "You know, you have this effect on people."

He understood that she was avoiding his question, but he'd circle back to it later. "What do you mean?"

"You scare them, but in a good way."

Fascinating. Nelson Radcliff had always said the same thing.

"They figure you aren't a man to screw with, that it doesn't pay to get on your bad side," she went on. "They figure that they'd be smarter to get close to you than to be your enemy." She ran her long fingers through his hair. "I'll give you an example. Paul Brule called while we were on the way down here to set up a day of fishing with you."

"So? He said he was going to do that at the airport."

"Yes, but I figured he wouldn't actually call," Zoe explained. "At least, not so fast."

"Why?"

"Because Paul only ever fishes with two other people and everybody in town knows it. With some old guy who runs a pilot school out at the airfield, and some friend of his from college who only comes to town once or twice a year. And Paul hardly ever goes with the guy who runs the pilot school, he usually goes by himself. Like he usually does everything." Zoe hesitated. "It's interesting that he asked you to go fishing in the first place, and that he followed up so fast."

Hunter raised both eyebrows. "That's pretty cool."

"It is." She picked up the half-full bottle of Chablis and refilled his glass. "There."

"Thanks." He swirled the wine in his glass for a moment, thinking long and hard about the question he wanted to ask. "Tell me something."

"What?"

"Where are you from?"

She moaned and took several swallows of her wine. "Everybody's always prying. Why is that?"

"I'm not prying," he said firmly. "Like I said, I'm interested in you. That's all. You should take that as a compliment." She still wasn't talking. "Okay, I'm from Virginia. Now it's your turn. This is called getting to know each other. First I tell you something, then you tell me something."

Zoe gazed at Hell's Gate a little while longer before answering. "I'm from San Francisco. This is the only place other than San Francisco I've ever lived."

Hunter was about to follow up with another question, but she beat him to the punch.

"Why did your wife think you were such a square, Mr. Lee?" Zoe asked.

He smiled. "Because I haven't smoked pot since college. Because pot's the only drug I've ever used."

"Is that the only reason she thought you were a square?"

The subject was quickly becoming more personal than he'd anticipated. The tables were turning. Zoe seemed to have a knack for doing that.

"I'm waiting," she said.

Maybe it was stupid to open up so fast, but the heck with it. He was worth twenty million bucks, and it didn't matter what people in Fort Mason thought of him. It wasn't as if he had to make a living here, and he wanted to be completely honest with her, wanted her to understand who he was and where he was coming from.

"Come on," she pushed. "Tell me."

"No it isn't."

"What were the other things she—"

"Sexual things," he admitted.

"Involving you and her?" Zoe asked, standing up in front of him. "Other people, too?"

This time he took a long swallow from his glass. "You name it, she wanted it." He shook his head. "But I didn't."

Zoe stroked his cheek gently with the backs of her fingers, then reached for her top. "Did you ever make love to her in the great outdoors?"

Hunter's pulse quickened when she started unbuttoning it. He gazed at her fingers as they worked, unable to take his eyes off them.

"Well, did you?"

God, he'd always been so uptight about sex. Maybe Anne had been justified in looking outside their marriage for partners, looking for people

who were more exciting. But Nelson Radcliff? She had to have been trying to hurt him with that one—which meant she'd wanted to get caught,
whether she knew it or not. "No, I never made love to her outdoors," he
admitted as she slipped her top off and let it fall to the ground. She was
wearing a lacy black bra underneath. "I never made love to her anywhere
but in a bedroom," he answered, standing up, too, after she'd motioned for
him to do so. "I guess I was pretty boring."

"Well, outside is the first place we're going to do it." She kissed Hunter
deeply, even more passionately than she had at the airport. "Do you understand?"

"Yes." It felt incredible to let go of life's steering wheel, to be completely
controlled by this amazing woman. If only for a little while. "I do."

"Good." She reached between her breasts, undid her bra, and let it slip
down her arms to the ground as well. "Now make love to me, Hunter."

36

BIG BILL SAT in his office at the Brule Lumber Mill, gazing toward the Lassiter River through the wide window behind his desk. The evening landscape before him matched his mood: darkening by the moment.

"Dad."

Big Bill swung around in the big leather chair. Jeremy was standing in front of his desk. "Don't you knock anymore, boy?" The door to his office had been ajar, and he hadn't heard Jeremy come in. He'd been whispering to himself, as he found himself doing more and more often these days, and he was worried the boy had heard what he was saying. The subject matter he'd been mumbling about wasn't for his son's ears. It wasn't for anyone's ears but his own. "Jeremy?"

"No, I guess I don't."

"Well, in the future you better damn well—"

"What the hell do you want?" Jeremy interrupted rudely. "Look, I was in a meeting with the engineering firm up in Missoula all day about the new grinding line we're putting in. As if we're really going to need it now," Jeremy muttered, checking his watch. "Christ, it's eight o'clock, and I'm still working. And for what? To listen to this?"

"Sit down," Big Bill ordered. He was in no mood to hear his older son complain. "Now." He'd gotten back from Scotland late last night, and they hadn't had a chance to meet until now. Jeremy had been away from the plant all day and hadn't returned any of Big Bill's calls from Scotland. "What's the deal?" he demanded angrily, furious with the boy.

"What do you mean?"

"What do you *think* I mean?" It seemed as if a smug smile had flickered across the boy's face, as if somehow Jeremy was enjoying the dire situation the mill was in. But Big Bill wasn't sure if he'd really seen the smile or if it was simply his imagination playing tricks on him. Only an hour ago he'd finished a long meeting with Butch Roman at The Depot. He'd downed a lot of scotch while he and Butch had discussed several sensitive matters in a back booth. It was all he could do to drive himself back out here to the mill without hitting a couple of telephone poles on the way. "You find any timber yet?"

"Nope, and I looked hard, damn hard. I kept calling those Delaware numbers of the partnerships that sucked up all the trees. The ones on record as leasing the land now. But nobody answers. I even called some people on the West Coast I know, people I thought might put us on to who's behind the partnerships because they're in the timber markets every day. At least put us on to the people who snapped up the big parcels. But no luck with them, either."

Jeremy was a loser, plain and simple, and that wasn't the scotch talking. That was the scotch letting Big Bill be honest with himself. Damn it, he had to mend whatever bridge he'd destroyed with Paul. Paul was a winner, the one who always found a way to get things done, the one with a future. Paul knew a lot of people in the Northwest, people who considered him a hero, people who might be able to find them timber. Important people. Not the little people Jeremy knew. Jeremy only thought he knew important people.

Most significantly, Big Bill thought as he gazed at Jeremy, Paul could carry on the family legacy. Paul could be a senator someday, maybe even president. People loved Paul the instant they met him. The same way they didn't like Jeremy—unless, of course, he threw money around. But when the money stopped, it was the same old story.

"How many days of timber do we have left?" Big Bill demanded.

"Nineteen. I've managed to stretch it a little."

"*Jesus Christ!*" Big Bill yelled, pounding the desktop. "Nineteen days? You idiot. Do you understand what this—"

"Why don't you help me?" Jeremy shouted back, springing out of his chair. "Don't just sit there yelling at me. Use some of that God damn clout you have to help me solve the problem."

That was the problem. Big Bill had been trying to use his clout, but that wasn't working, either. The situation was quickly becoming critical. There was still that one person he could turn to, but using him might open up a whole different can of worms. He took a deep breath. Well, there wasn't any choice in the matter now. It was just a damn good thing he'd convinced the man to stop over on his way back from Los Angeles. "Don't let on to anybody except the purchasing people about how low we are on timber," Big Bill instructed. "Tell them to keep their damn mouths shut."

"It's pretty obvious that we've got a problem," Jeremy shot back. "It's not like we can hide our timber inventory, or lack of it. It sits in piles around the yard in plain view, and those piles are getting small. It's not like the employees don't notice how few trucks are coming in, either."

"Well, make up something!" Big Bill shouted. "Use your imagination, use whatever brain you have in there between your ears. *Do something!* Be a businessman."

Jeremy stared intently at Big bill for several seconds. "I'd need to be your son first," he finally said in a gravelly tone. With that he stalked out of the office.

37

HUNTER WATCHED IN awe as Paul Brule deftly handled a fly rod. The distance and accuracy of his casts were amazing, and when a trout struck, Paul didn't miss. He'd landed six fish in thirty minutes, and two of them had been rainbows over four pounds. Four pounds was a large trout in most any Montana river, but particularly in the smaller river Paul had chosen to fish this evening. Remarkably, he'd caught everything on dry flies. No dredging the bottom with nymphs, which Paul had made clear on the way here was the easy way to fly fish. Almost as easy as bait fishing, he claimed. Quite simply, Hunter was watching a master at his craft, and he was enjoying every second of it.

When they were teenagers, Hunter and Strat had taught themselves to fly fish on the slow, wide rivers of central Virginia after watching Saturday morning fishing shows and being fascinated by the sport's style and difficulty. They'd saved up enough money to buy a couple of cheap rod-and-reel rigs from a local hardware store by cutting lawns and doing odd jobs in the neighborhood, and fly fished for bass and bluegill, convincing themselves they'd gotten pretty decent at it.

After joining Warfield & Stone, Hunter made time to go fly fishing at least a day or two a year somewhere in New England to keep up his skills—the only vacation he took. But as he watched Paul work the narrow, rocky-bottom river snaking through the trough of this steep-walled, secluded canyon, Hunter realized how much of a novice he still was. Even with all of his years of fly fishing in Montana, Strat seemed average in comparison to Paul.

Hunter sat on a large rock that jutted out from the side of the canyon twenty feet above the river's surface. From here he had an excellent view as Paul moved to the bottom of the next pool upstream and began hunting. Paul systematically worked closer and closer to the prime feeding lanes at the top of the pool where the larger trout typically hung suspended from the bottom by a few inches waiting for big bugs and worms to come tumbling down out of the rapids. It was amazing to watch him snatch the line off the foamy riffles as smaller dorsal fins headed for his fly—a big Royal Wulff he'd told Hunter he'd tied last winter during a bad snowstorm—then lay it smoothly back down again on a different section of the pool. Paul was after the monster in the pool, and when you went after the monster, you did it patiently and methodically.

Finally, Paul sent the Royal Wulff shooting up into the whitewater at the base of several large rocks near the top of the pool. He landed the fly perfectly so it sat high on the water and was clearly visible with wings spread as it bobbed along atop the foamy water. Despite being tied with feathers and wool, it bore a striking resemblance to a real insect that had just hatched or fluttered back to the surface to die after mating. Almost instantly a long, speckled dorsal fin emerged and sliced toward the Wulff, then a massive white mouth engulfed it. Paul hesitated a moment before lifting the rod tip and setting the hook. The line went taut instantly and the huge fish dove, then came streaking from the water.

Hunter grinned as he watched the fight unfold, glad he'd picked this vantage point. The trout exploded from the surface three more times in rapid succession; Paul dropped his rod tip to keep tension on the line each time the fish burst from the water; the fish went for a submerged rock near the opposite bank of the pool after it jumped the last time; Paul expertly guided the huge fish away from the rock; the rainbow made a mad dash for the tail of the pool and the next set of rapids downstream; but Paul skillfully led the fish away from its target once again by applying firm pressure with the rod.

A few minutes later Hunter climbed down from the rock to where Paul was landing the stout fish. "How big is it?"

"A little under six pounds, I'd say."

Hunter liked that answer. Paul could easily have guessed that the trout was a little *over* six pounds, as a lot of people who stood just shy of six feet tall claimed to be a little over that height. But he hadn't. He'd estimated the weight of the rainbow without trying to impress anyone. Paul seemed as if he was straight up about everything. A man who was confident enough in himself and his abilities that he didn't need to exaggerate.

"Nice fish."

"Thanks." Paul knelt in the shallows and moved the rainbow back and forth, washing cold water over its heaving, scarlet gills. "You hooked some nice fish yourself this afternoon."

Hunter had caught a couple of browns over three pounds after Paul had offered a few hints. "Yeah, but nothing like this giant."

"For a guy who doesn't do it much, you're a great caster. You just need to catch a few more, then you'd be really good."

It meant a lot to hear that from an expert who didn't mince words. "Thanks."

"Guess you'll have that chance what with your divorce."

"Yeah, I guess I will."

"We'll have to do this again." Paul smiled. "Zoe probably told you that I usually fish alone."

Hunter had sensed a friendship developing between them quickly. He'd sensed on the way out here that Paul hadn't invited him along this evening just because he figured it was a good idea to make sure Hunter was a friend and not a foe. That, as Zoe had predicted, there was some of that going on, but it wasn't the entire reason for tonight's outing. "She did mention that."

"Zoe's a nice lady," Paul said, releasing the rainbow. He rinsed his hands off, then stood up and watched the fish head slowly back toward the deep water and disappear. "I like her."

The image of Zoe's exquisite body drifted back to Hunter. Last night they'd made love for an hour on that ledge overlooking Hell's Gate. It had turned out that she was even more passionate than Anne. Which had amazed him. "Me, too."

"She seems a little lost at times, but maybe you can help her with that."

"Maybe."

"Well," Paul said after a few moments, glancing up at a sky that was quickly turning dark, "how about a smoke?" He reached into a pocket of his fishing vest and produced two long, neatly rolled cigars. "We've only got a little bit of daylight left, and I don't want to be out here too long after dark. I saw fresh bear droppings around that bend," he said, handing one of the cigars to Hunter, then gesturing downstream. "And they weren't black bear droppings." Paul put the cigar in his mouth and lighted it. "If you get my drift."

Hunter peered downstream, straining to see if anything was moving down there in the fading light. He'd gotten Paul's drift all right. The only other kind of bear out here was a brown bear—also known as a grizzly.

Paul handed his lighter to Hunter. "Don't worry, I've got no desire to run into a grizzly. I'm not like some of these locals who'll tell you they'd love to stare one down in the woods. I'm no idiot." He took several puffs off his cigar, then sat down on the river's edge, boots still in the water. "It's pretty rare to see one," he said reassuringly.

"Have you?" asked Hunter, sitting down a few feet away and lighting his cigar, too.

Paul nodded. "Yup. I used to hunt grizzlies. Cats, too."

"Ever shoot any?"

Paul took a deep breath. "Oh, yeah. Up north I got two grizzlies, and I shot a big male cat not far from here. Only about ten miles west of this river, actually." His eyes took on a distant look. "Man, the paws on that thing seemed like they were as big a round as Frisbees, and the grizzlies' paws seemed twice as big as that." He glanced toward the top of the pool where he'd hooked the big rainbow. "I'm still sorry I killed them."

"Why?"

"I figured out that there wasn't any reason to take life like that, especially the lives of things as magnificent as grizzlies and mountain lions. They never did anything to me."

"Hey, you were just hunting. Like everyone else out here does."

"It doesn't matter. Those animals got it tough enough without some joker like me stalking them." Paul gestured toward the river with his cigar. "That's why I like fishing. You can catch something unearthly beautiful like that rainbow, feel its intensity, experience its desperation to live, then slide it back in the river and catch it another day." He grimaced. "I'll never forget that last bear I shot. It was lying there bleeding from the mouth and nose just trying to breathe until I blasted another 30–30 shell into its heart from up close. He still lived another fifteen seconds after that. It was amazing. I'll never forget the look in his eye, either. It was like he was asking me why I did it." Paul grimaced again, even more sharply this time. "I didn't have an answer." He bit his lip. "Maybe that sounds stupid, but . . . well . . ." His voice trailed off.

"It doesn't sound stupid." Hunter watched Paul struggle with the memory. "At least you figured it out. A lot of people never do."

Paul picked up a stone and sent it skimming across the river's surface. "I've never told anyone that." The stone skipped seven times before it finally ran out of steam and sank beneath the surface. "I guess this is what makes you so good at what you do, Hunter. You've got a knack for getting people to spill their guts."

"Maybe you wanted to tell somebody all that tonight, and I just happened to be the one who was around."

"Good comeback. Exactly what I'd expect you to say, but we both know the truth."

Hunter lay back and gazed up at that Montana sky. It seemed big even with the narrow canyon's rocky crests framing two sides of it. "I heard you gave up bird hunting, too."

Paul chuckled softly at the comment and all it implied. How the word "too" meant that Hunter knew Paul had given up hunting bears and mountain lions before they'd talked about it. "And I heard you never asked a question you don't know the answer to. I guess I should have remembered that."

"You remembered," Hunter said confidently. "You're too smart to forget something like that." A breeze drifted down the canyon. "Hey, I've got a question," he spoke up when the wind settled back down. "How did that California fire really start? We never finished that conversation on the plane."

The question had been hovering in the air between them ever since Paul had picked Hunter up late this afternoon. They both knew they were going to talk about it at some point, but Hunter had waited until now to bring it up. He figured if he brought it up too fast, Paul might clam up and stay silent on the matter. But he had to say something at some point because he felt as if he had to get Paul on Strat's team or Strat might not show up for dinner one night. Worse, Strat might never be seen or heard from again. Maybe getting Paul to work with Strat on this whole mess was how Hunter could help Strat the most, and this seemed like the question to ask if Hunter was going to get him headed in Strat's direction.

"You wanted to tell me how you thought that fire really started as we were landing at Missoula," Hunter pressed. "I know you did."

Paul took several puffs off his cigar, turning its perfect half-inch ash a glow the color of the setting sun. "I'm paid to fight forest fires," he said evenly, "not figure out how they start. That's what I said on the plane, and that's what—"

"Don't give me that," Hunter shot back firmly. "You care about how these fires start, you care *a lot* about how they start. That's why you're willing to risk your life to put them out. You hate the fact that there are so many fires this year. There's always going to be some, but this year it's like there's a new megablaze somewhere every day. There's been four times as many acres burned in the Northwest this year as last year. You can't blame that on careless campers, lightning, target shooters, or global warming. You know it, I know it. There's something else going on. Whoever's starting all these fires is being very careful not to make it look like arson, but the odds against having this many fires in one summer are astronomical."

"Hunter, don't get involved in—"

"Imagine this valley getting torched," Hunter kept going, making a sweeping gesture down the canyon at the thick cover of pine trees climbing up each slope to the crest. "Imagine all this gone in an hour, incinerated and looking like the moon, like that ridge where the Big Cat Fire started looks now. And, yeah, sure, it looks like the fire started because somebody accidentally dragged something behind a truck or a car, but Strat and I don't believe that. We don't think it was an accident at all." He hesitated. "Neither do you."

Paul's eyes flashed to Hunter's. "Why do you care so much?"

"Because Montana's my home now, and I don't want to see it burn." Hunter could tell he was getting to Paul, that the door was opening. Ever so slightly, but it was. "I love this place," he continued, "and it's only my adopted home. This is where you're from. Look, it's not like I came up with this thing on my own. My brother's the one that's been talking to me about it. He thinks there's people out here who are setting the Northwest on fire to make money. He thinks that's why there's so many megablazes this summer."

"Your brother better be careful," Paul muttered. "He's on a slippery slope."

There it was. The admission, subtle as it was, that Hunter had been looking for. Paul had engaged. Now the trick was to keep him in the game. "How do you know?"

"I don't know, I'm guessing. But it's a pretty easy guess, isn't it?" Paul kicked at a rock. "Who does Strat think is behind all this crap anyway?"

"George Drake and Bridger Air," Hunter answered directly. "The guy you didn't want to hitch a ride home with from California. Drake's got all those problems with the railroad, but maybe he can save it by using his air cargo company to make up—"

"Then there's Dale Callahan and Butch Roman," Paul interrupted. "Dale 'cause he feeds us firefighters while we're on the line, and Butch 'cause he gets to rebuild anything that burns down. Right?"

"Yeah," Hunter agreed hesitantly, taken by surprise at how Paul and Strat's analyses were the same. "Exactly."

"Well, you can scratch Butch's name off the list, and any of the other big builders out here. There hasn't been any real major property damage all summer. Some houses, but that's it."

"Not yet," Hunter agreed, "but almost at Big Cat and nearly a lot of damage out in California where you were. If Butch was too obvious about what he was doing, he might get pinned with it." Hunter was elated that Paul was starting to talk but careful not to show it. Too much enthusiasm and Paul might go silent. "And Butch has that rep for taking things into his own hands."

"So does George Drake," Paul pointed out. "Which is why you need to be careful, too, pal."

Big Bill had seemed concerned about George Drake, but not like Paul was. And Paul was probably closer to what was going on in Montana than his father, closer to what was going on in the trenches, anyway.

"There's one more person you ought to put on that list," said Paul quietly.

"Who?"

Paul waited a long time before answering. "Katrina Mason."

Hunter had been about to take a puff off his cigar. "Are you serious?" he asked incredulously, the cigar in a holding pattern an inch from his lips.

"Yup."

"What's her motive?"

"When somebody else's trees burn, it makes hers more valuable. She owns close to half a million acres of timber out here. I bet if you check you'll find out that not many of her acres have burned this year. If any."

"Did you check?"

"I didn't say that."

Hunter grumbled to himself, frustrated. "Why won't you commit, Paul? Why won't you jump into the fight with both—"

"Give me a break, will you?"

It was the first time Hunter had seen Paul's temper flare. He'd heard how Paul was tough to rile, but once you did, look out. So he needed to handle this situation delicately. "I know you've checked on Katrina Mason's timber not burning. That's why you brought it up, that's why you asked me to go fishing today, to tell me. We both know it. Come on, Paul. Why won't you help Strat and me?"

"Maybe I'm a prick like a lot of people say I am, Hunter. Yeah, they all love me to my face, but behind my back they say I'm a guy who only cares about himself."

That hurt Hunter had seen in Paul's eyes on the plane was suddenly obvious again, more than it had ever been. "You're not like that at all, you're a good man."

Paul stared at Hunter intently, then brought the cigar to his lips and puffed. "Hunter," he said, almost in a whisper, "did it ever occur to you that maybe I don't want to find out what's really going on out here? That maybe I don't want to know where the trail ultimately leads because if somebody really is torching Montana, they might have needed help to get a contract? Help from someone in . . . Washington, D.C.?"

The world froze in front of Hunter. My God, why hadn't he or Strat thought of that? It was so obvious now that Paul had said something.

"Don't get me wrong," Paul continued. "I'm not saying I have any reason to think my father's done anything wrong. I'm just saying I don't want to find out if he has." He gazed off into the distance, downstream in the direction he'd seen signs of the bear. "I'd really appreciate it if you'd never mention to anyone that we had this conversation, not even to your brother."

Hunter nodded. "You've got my word."

Paul put the cigar down on the riverbank and rubbed his eyes for a few moments. "My father saved my life twice," Paul explained. "Once when I was seven and I almost drowned, then again when I was seventeen. He shot a big female mountain lion that had me cornered against a barn, a mother with cubs that was about to tear me apart." He shook his head. "You really think I could ever forgive myself if I—"

"I get it," Hunter interrupted. "I really do."

Paul picked up the cigar again. "You know, for a man who doesn't talk much, you sure say a lot."

"Yeah, I guess."

Paul laughed. "See what I mean?"

"Actually, I do," Hunter admitted, laughing, too. He hesitated. This was a forward thing to say, but he needed Paul to know why he was pressing so hard. That it was about Montana burning all right, but it was also about something else much more important. "Paul, I want your help because I care about my brother. You know?"

Paul exhaled heavily. "I know." He looked off into the distance again. "It must be nice being so close to your brother. Jeremy and I never have gotten along, and the crazy thing about it is that it's not because we don't like each other, or that there's something between us. Or at least there wasn't. It's because my father doesn't care about Jeremy. Worse, he's never tried to hide how he doesn't care. That's what's come between us. Dad wants Jeremy to be like me, but Jeremy can't be like me. That's not his deal, it's not in him physically. Jeremy's so damn bitter about Dad caring more about me, he can't handle it." Paul shook his head. "I just wish there was something I could—"

Paul's words were drowned out by a wet, loud snort, then an angry snarl.

Hunter and Paul jumped to their feet and spun around so they were both facing upstream, so they were both facing in the direction the sounds had come from. On the riverbank just forty feet away was a massive male grizzly bear. As they stared, it rose up on its hind legs to its full height— over nine feet tall.

"How fast do you run the hundred?" Paul whispered.

"Not as fast as you, I'm sure." Hunter could barely whisper back because the adrenaline was coursing through his body so hard. "Which is a problem for me." He could see saliva dripping from the bear's muzzle, hear the heavy breaths it was taking. He'd never been so scared—or awestruck—in his life. "You take off on me, and I'll tackle you, I swear. Then we'll see what happens, Paul Brule."

"I'm not gonna take off on you, Hunter. Don't worry."

Paul was acting calm, but Hunter heard fear in his voice, too. A subtle vibration in his tone that hadn't been there a few seconds ago. "I'm not worried, I'm *terrified*."

"Oh, great. I'm sure an apex predator like this won't notice. Just don't move," Paul hissed. "Whatever you do, don't move."

"Okay."

The bear dropped slowly back on all fours, sniffed the air, pawed the ground, then charged.

It took every ounce of courage and self-control he had, but Hunter managed to stay still, somehow managed to keep his feet planted on the riverbank as if they were stuck in cement. The bear stopped no more than twenty feet away.

As the pounding in his brain leveled off, Hunter realized that Paul hadn't taken his own advice. Paul was now several steps back of where he'd been before the bear charged.

38

S TRAT CREPT ALONG an inner wall of the cavernous warehouse,
crouched behind a long line of empty fifty-five-gallon drums. He
was listening intently to the muffled voices echoing around this
end of the building, trying to understand what they were saying. It was
almost nine o'clock and the place should have been shut down for the
day. But there was a group of four men standing close together over by
a big tractor-trailer that had been driven inside through one of the large
retractable doors, which seemed strange to Strat. During the day trucks
might come inside to load or offload certain special products, but they
shouldn't be parked in here for the night. At least, he couldn't think of a
reason why they would be. There was a sprawling parking lot outside the
facility past the normal loading and unloading bays, filled with rigs. And
there was a whole string of them lined up ready to go at the railroad yard,
which was on the other side of the parking lot.

Strat reached the last drum, but he was still a long way from the men.
He could have sworn he'd heard them muttering something about where
the fire was going to be started this morning, but, of course, that was what
he wanted to hear. He couldn't trust anything he heard unless it was crystal clear and completely in context. Otherwise, it might just be his mind
playing tricks on him.

Thirty feet away from the last drum rose towering walls of products
and supplies, piled three stories high on strong metal racks. If he could

reach the aisle between the first two racks without being detected, he could easily get within twenty feet of the men and hear for certain what they were saying without being seen. But that thirty feet ahead of him was wide open, well lighted, and in full view of the men. He looked up over his shoulder, searching for cameras. Not that it really mattered if there were any. He wouldn't be recognized with his Mariners hat pulled down over his face, and he'd be long gone before anyone checked the tapes in the morning.

The men were talking louder now and one of them was getting animated, in a good way. As if he was counting his chickens and he was damn happy about how many were going to hatch. Strat's heart began to race. He had a feeling the meeting over by the truck was going to break up soon. All he had to do was hear a sliver of the conversation and get it on the tiny recording device he had in his pocket. Then he could report back positively, then he'd finally be able to pinpoint who was behind all this, and be sure to get the full support he'd been promised.

It was now or never. Literally.

He broke from his hiding place, short legs churning as hard as he could make them go. He'd never been fast, but he'd never felt slower. On top of being a plodder to begin with, he was trying to sprint quietly across the building's slab. Trying to run on his toes in his eight-dollar high-top pair of PF Flyers and not make the pounding noise he usually did with his loping stride.

Just a few more feet now, just a few more feet. He was almost there, almost to the aisle, and then he could creep to within a few feet of where the men were and overhear everything. He dove the last few feet, relief washing over him as he tumbled behind the first wall of supplies. He'd made it, God damn it, he'd made it.

Then he heard the awful words.

"Hey, what the hell was that? Hey, somebody's in here!"

39

KATRINA AND DRAKE were just about to leave her house and head for dinner in Fort Mason when her office phone rang.

She trotted back to her desk and checked the number on the phone. "It's Charlie Hall!" she called to Drake, who was still standing by the front door. She'd gotten used to Charlie's incessant need to talk to his boss and quickly recognized his number. She'd gotten used to it, but she still didn't like it. Sometimes it seemed Hall couldn't make a decision on his own to save his life. Any first-year business school student knew that keeping a chief financial officer on such a tight leash was no way to run a company, much less two companies. She hadn't said anything yet because she didn't want to irritate Drake, but she'd been tempted.

Drake limped back into the office and grabbed the phone. "Yeah, what is it?"

Katrina watched his expression change, watched it sour ever so slightly. He never let you see him sweat, but she knew him well enough by now to recognize that whatever news he was getting from Hall wasn't good. "What is it, George?" she asked when he hung up the phone.

"*Bastards!*" he hissed.

"George, what's wrong? Tell me."

Drake sat slowly down in the desk chair. "Tomorrow morning the Chicago National Trust is going to call the Bridger Railroad loan."

Katrina shook her head and moved to where he was sitting. This was terrible news for the Bridger Railroad. "But I thought you and Charlie had gotten sixty days from the bank to work things out." God, his body was so warm and his hands were shaking. She'd never seen him like this.

"We did."

"What happened?"

"I don't know."

"Are you going to have your lawyers put the railroad into Chapter 11? Are you going to file for bankruptcy protection?"

Drake stood up and moved out from behind the desk. "That would be the logical move, wouldn't it?" He stared out the window for a few moments. "Of course, I don't have too many friends left in Montana thanks to that disaster in court over in Bozeman, thanks to Hunter Lee. Judges are people, too. You can't always count on them to be fair, or to follow the law. Especially out here."

Katrina was amazed at Drake's control. A bank his railroad owed two hundred million dollars to had just torpedoed him out of nowhere, but he seemed to be back in control, and it had only been thirty seconds since he'd gotten the call. His hands weren't shaking anymore and his voice had regained its normal smoothness. He might be going crazy on the inside, but you'd never know it from his demeanor.

"I'm sorry, Katrina, but I can't go to dinner."

"Of course, George, I understand. Is there anything I can do?"

He shook his head. "I've got to get in touch with some people," he said, heading out of the office. "I'll call you in the morning."

40

I THOUGHT YOU SAID 'don't move,'" Hunter hissed. After holding up on its charge, the grizzly was just twenty feet away. It was hunched over on all fours, swaying from side to side on its massive front paws. Snorting angrily and pushing its long, pink tongue past its gums over and over, tasting the air, tasting *them*. "Isn't that what you said?" He could hear Paul's fast, shaky breathing over his left shoulder. Paul had quickly retreated a step or two when the bear charged. "Paul? *Paul!*"

"That's the theory," came the cotton-mouth reply. "But the body does what the brain tells it to do. It's a reflex action when you haven't been in a situation before, when you have no training with something. Sorry to tell you, this is a first for me."

"Jesus Christ," Hunter muttered. "I thought you were Mr. Montana."

"Hey, I don't know what the hell that's supposed to—"

The grizzly suddenly lunged toward them again, but this time neither of them gave ground. The bear stopped fifteen feet away, started to rise up on its hind legs, then dropped back down on all fours again.

As scared as he was, Hunter marveled at the animal, marveled at nature's amazing creation. It was obvious the damn thing could kill him with a single swipe of a front paw, knock him into another dimension with its incredible power or slice him into six pieces with one claw. It was terrorizing on one level, awe-inspiring on another.

Out of the corner of his eye, Hunter saw Paul slowly reaching behind himself and carefully unzipping his backpack. "What are you doing?" he asked, eyes still locked on the bear though he was careful not to make eye contact with it.

"I got you into this, Hunter, I'll get you out of it."

"Huh?"

"I never go into the woods without my .44 Magnum," Paul said, reaching around and sliding his right hand slowly into the open pack. "In case of something like this. You never know out here."

"Paul, I—"

"When I say 'now,' you're going to turn and sprint past me as fast as you can," Paul ordered, easing the heavy Colt revolver out of its hiding place. "Don't look back, just keep going until you can't run anymore. As soon as you turn, I'm gonna plug this thing with as many bullets as I can. Hopefully, he hightails it out of here after he tastes a couple of zingers. Even if he doesn't, at least you'll get out alive."

"What about no reason to take life anymore? What about all that?"

"Are you kidding me? We've got a damn good reason to take life at this point," Paul snapped as the grizzly clawed the ground. He brought the gun up with both hands. "See what he's doing? That clawing thing? It's just a matter of time before he rushes us. So, it's him or us. As far as I'm concerned, all that other crap goes out the window when it comes down to something else or me. I don't know about you, but I like being Paul. I don't want to turn into dinner."

Hunter swallowed hard. "It isn't your time, Paul."

"Huh?"

"Don't go looking for it."

"What the hell are you—"

"Put the gun down." Hunter's mind was a jumble at this point; he could only focus on one thing. Which was that he wouldn't run, he wouldn't let Paul face this monster by himself. "Right now."

"Are you out of your mind? Damn it, Hunter, I'm gonna count to three, you're going to jam the pedal to the metal and get your ass out—"

"Put the gun down," Hunter repeated.

"Don't be a hero, pal, it's not worth it. You don't know what you're doing."

"*Paul.*"

"One, two—"

"*Yah, bear!*" Hunter shouted like a madman, throwing his hands in the air and taking two steps directly at the grizzly. "*Go, bear, go!*"

"*Hunter! Jesus Christ, what are you doing?*"

"*Go, bear, go!*" Hunter yelled again, taking two more steps toward the bear and waving his arms wildly. "*Get out of here, get out of here!*"

The huge bear shook its head once and growled loudly, then about-faced and loped away upstream.

"Holy mother of Mary!" Paul shouted, leaping into the air and blasting off a few shots from the .44 just for the hell of it. "You're the man, Hunter Lee. I've never seen anything like it, never *heard* of anything like it."

Hunter watched the bear run up the riverbank until it ducked into the woods. Only then did the thought hit him. It was the bravest thing he'd ever done. By far.

He sank to his knees, still breathing hard, heart still pumping madly. Then, as he put his face into the soft grass beside the river, the tears came. Not many, but enough. All he could think of at this moment was his father.

41

S TRAT JUMPED TO his feet and took off down the valley formed by the sheer cliffs of two towering storage racks.

"Damn it," he gasped as he loped away. He'd been so close to figuring out what was going on, at least close to erasing one more name from the suspect list. Which would have left only two more names on the list, because he had it from a reliable source that the person responsible for the arson problem in the Northwest was based in this area, and Strat had already eliminated everyone else with an economic motive. If there were only two names left on the list, he was certain he'd get everything he'd been promised, certain he could be convincing enough to get all those resources and figure out which of the two left was guilty. But now he was no closer to the truth than he had been a few hours ago when he'd gotten a tip that something was going on at this warehouse tonight.

"Get out of here, Strat," he urged himself. "Make those feet go."

He'd gotten a quick glimpse of two of the men's faces as he'd jumped to his feet and run, but neither of them was familiar. They had to be out-of-towners, which only made sense. Hell, they probably weren't even from this part of the country. Whoever was burning the Northwest wouldn't want to use anyone who could be quickly identified. Of course, then people might get suspicious if they saw strangers around, so maybe whoever was in charge wouldn't want to use strangers after all. He clenched his teeth as he sprinted. He was overthinking everything. It was time just to concentrate on the task at hand, which was get out of here alive. Otherwise, all the work he'd done in the past few weeks wouldn't matter. Nothing would.

As he reached the far end of the tall racks, the entire facility was bathed in light from row upon row of big bulbs hanging from the ceiling.

"There he is!" a voice yelled.

The shout came from behind Strat, from the other end of the racks. They were closing in.

He desperately searched the exterior wall for a door to the outside but couldn't find one. So he turned right, sprinted past four aisles down the corridor formed by the end of the aisles and the exterior wall, darted right down another valley and dove in behind several cardboard boxes marked "Fragile" in bright-red block letters. Seconds later two sets of footsteps raced past.

When they faded, Strat crawled between and around shrink-wrapped cargo loads piled on pallets, made it to the next aisle, peered both ways, and rose to his feet with a soft groan. Then he stole to the end of the aisle and looked to the right, the way the footsteps had gone, but he saw nothing.

Finally he spotted a door to the outside.

Just as another voice yelled out loudly to his left.

"There's the guy, there he is!"

Strat bolted toward the exterior door. It was fifty feet away in the direction the footsteps had been going. Again, he pushed himself hard, praying the door wasn't locked as he sprinted. If he could make it outside, he had a chance. It had to be almost dark out there by now, and there'd be plenty of trees to sprint into for cover, plenty of forest to hide in. After so many years of hunting and fishing these woods, he knew them as well as anyone.

If the door was locked, well, then he had a different problem. One that might cost him his life.

As Strat reached the door, a man appeared at the end of the aisle just thirty feet away. Strat grabbed the bar handle and pushed hard, a wave of relief surging through him as the door gave way and warm air rushed to his face. He tore outside, bolted to the left, then to the right, and raced between two big semi-trucks parked with their open trailer doors facing the building.

As Strat reached the cabs, a figure darted out from between the trucks and crashed into him. Strat and the man tumbled over and over beside each other onto the pavement, then struggled to make it to their feet. With his short legs, Strat was up first. He grabbed his attacker by the collar and leveled him with a compact, powerful right cross to the chin. Then he turned to sprint away, but another body crashed into him from behind.

A lightning bolt of pain shot up his back as his face hit the side of a trailer. A strong hand clamped down on his shoulder, and he felt himself being spun around. Despite the pain knifing through his spine, Strat managed to duck, and his attacker's knuckles smashed into the trailer instead of Strat's chin. An uppercut to the guy's solar plexus, and the second attacker crumpled to the ground, facedown.

Strat reached for the guy. He was going to flip him over to see if he recognized him, but then there was more shouting in the direction of the door he'd just come tearing through. He had to get out of here, he had to get into the woods.

42

BIG BILL HAD pulled a page from his son Paul's book tonight.
Tonight Big Bill was driving a beat-up, ten-year-old Plymouth
sedan he kept at his five-hundred-acre spread north of town and
had only driven a few times in the last several years. Not any of the nicer,
newer vehicles he also kept there. But he wasn't driving the Plymouth to
show anyone who might look that he was trying to make his own way in
the world, he was driving it so no one would recognize him. It was the
only car on the place that didn't have vanity plates.

He slowed down to a crawl as he neared the Gordonsville Inn, glancing into the small, dimly lit lobby as he passed by. Someone was standing
in the foyer, but he couldn't tell if it was the person he was supposed to
meet. He flashed his lights as they'd agreed he would, then he pulled into
a parking spot a few hundred feet past the hotel entrance, past the diner
where Strat had met Ida Bach, away from any streetlights and any prying
eyes.

He climbed out and stared back toward the hotel over the old car's
roof. Someone had exited the lobby and was walking toward him through
the darkness, but he still couldn't tell if it was the person he was supposed
to be meeting. Other than this person, the street was empty. As the figure
closed in on the Plymouth, Big Bill slid halfway in behind the steering
wheel in case he needed to make a quick getaway. A moment later, he
breathed a sigh of relief.

"Get in," he called. "Door's open."

When they were both inside the car and the doors were closed, Big Bill extended his hand. "Hello, Nelson."

Nelson Radcliff shook Big Bill's hand firmly. "Hello, Senator."

"Thanks for coming. I know it's out of the way for you."

Radcliff snickered. "I don't know if 'out of the way' even describes it. I feel like I'm in another country, for Christ sake."

"Well, you won't have to stick around long," Big Bill said as he pulled out of the parking spot. "I'll have you back to the hotel in no time. Then, tomorrow morning, you can head to Missoula and get back to the East Coast. Thanks for doing this," he added. "I know it's a pain in the ass."

"It wasn't easy, but I was in Los Angeles. That made it a little better. At least I didn't have to come all the way out here from New York."

Big Bill pulled up to a stop sign, then took a right on a darkened side street. He noticed Radcliff shift uncomfortably in the passenger seat. "What's the matter?"

"Nothing. Why don't we just go back to that diner beside the hotel? We'll sit in a booth and talk."

Radcliff was nervous. It would have seemed silly to Big Bill if he hadn't seen this reaction before. Sometimes small, out-of-the-way Montana towns had this effect on people, especially when they were far away from what they were used to, especially when they spent most of their time in the biggest cities the world had to offer. "No good, someone might recognize me. We'll drive around for a while. Don't worry, we'll be fine." Big Bill pointed beneath his seat. "I always carry a gun."

"What a relief," Radcliff muttered sarcastically. "All right, let's get to it, Bill. What was so important for us to talk about that I had to actually come to Montana? What was so important that we couldn't talk about it over the phone?" He hesitated. "As if I didn't know."

Big Bill's eyes shot to Radcliff's. "What's that supposed to mean?"

"The only thing you'd need to see me in person for so fast is something that has to do with the girl. She's the only thing you would never talk about on a phone. I'm talking about Joanna Preston."

Big Bill felt his entire body tense up at the sound of Joanna's name. It was as if every muscle in his body was suddenly cramping. He thought about her every day, but he didn't hear her name spoken aloud by someone else. He whispered it to himself once in a while, but it didn't seem so bad then. It had sounded so much worse, so much more incriminating when Radcliff had said it. "Of course you're talking about Joanna Preston."

"I don't know what you're worried about, Senator," Radcliff went on. "I took care of everything. I made sure there were several 'sightings' of her in Washington, D.C., a few days after she was here with you in Montana, and I made certain her cash card was used in three ATMs near her apartment in D.C. *after* she was here. The day after she was to have gotten back, then two more times the following week. And, yes, her airline ticket from Bozeman to Washington wasn't used, but Joanna Preston took an Amtrak train from Chicago to Washington because you and she ended up driving to Chicago from Montana just for the heck of it. At least, that's what the records show. And I have those records." Radcliff smiled thinly. "The woman who was Joanna Preston on that Amtrak train won't ever have the chance to talk, either," he said ominously. "You don't have a thing to worry about, Senator. I wouldn't have even bothered to come here except that the Bridger Railroad case was a nice quid pro quo. It turned out quite well for Warfield & Stone."

"*Quite* well?" Big Bill asked, his voice rising. "You made twenty times what you thought you'd make on that case."

"Hunter Lee was amazing," Radcliff admitted. "Of course, that's what happens when one of the best lawyers around works his magic in front of a Montana jury."

"He was good," Big Bill agreed, "but I bet even Hunter would tell you that without the memo he shoved at Carl Bach on the stand the last day of testimony, the jury wouldn't have given those people forty million dollars."

Radcliff nodded reluctantly. "Maybe."

"I gave you the case, I gave you the memo, I gave you the verdict," Big Bill continued, "and big-time New York City lawyers don't always do that well in front of Montana juries. Sometimes they get—"

"You had that other reason for taking a shot at the Bridger Railroad," Radcliff interrupted. "For that business partner of yours."

"Business partner of *ours*, Nelson," Big Bill reminded Radcliff. "You wanted in on the deal, too. Just like you want in on the one I'm working on now with him."

Radcliff brushed lint from his pants. "What's the problem, Senator?" he asked in a measured tone. "Why am I here?"

Big Bill drew himself up behind the steering wheel. "I can't find any timber for my mill and I'm running out of inventory."

"What do you mean?"

"All of a sudden all the people who used to sell trees to us don't have any. My son Jeremy keeps coming up empty everywhere he looks."

Radcliff chuckled snidely. "Does that surprise you? That Jeremy can't solve a problem, I mean."

Big Bill's eyes narrowed. As incompetent as Jeremy was, Radcliff had no right to take that shot. But Big Bill wasn't going to say anything. Right now Radcliff was his lifeline, and he wasn't going to say anything that might piss him off. "I checked it out, and Jeremy's right. Everything's gone. Lots of different partnerships have bought or leased timber rights very recently, but it seems—"

"It seems odd," Radcliff finished the sentence. "You think Bruce Preston and Integrated Papers have something to do with this, don't you? You think Joanna's father is finally taking his revenge. You think she's coming back to haunt you."

A shiver crawled up Big Bill's spine. Radcliff was exactly right. "Yeah," he said almost inaudibly, "but I can't prove it. I need your help, Nelson."

Radcliff gazed out into the darkness. "All right, but it might take some time to figure out what's going on, maybe a lot longer to do anything about it. You and the mill better have an emergency plan for the short term."

43

HUNTER SAT AT the inside bar of The Depot, gazing at the stuffed grizzly bear posed ferociously in a far corner. He'd actually frozen for a second when he'd walked in and seen it for the first time. The time he'd met Strat at The Depot for drinks, he'd gone straight through the restaurant to the back deck and hadn't come into the bar, so he hadn't seen the animal. This bear wasn't nearly the size of the one he and Paul had run into tonight while they were fishing, but it was still damn intimidating. Hunter stared at the long bared canines, mesmerized, his mind replaying the terrifying encounter with the bear in the canyon tonight over and over. He could still hear its angry growls and grunts, still smell it.

"You should have seen this guy," said Paul loudly to a young couple who were the only other patrons in the bar. He pointed at Hunter as he downed his third shot of tequila. "He was amazing," Paul kept going, wiping his lips with the back of his hand, then slapping Hunter on the shoulder. "It was one of the biggest grizzlies I've ever seen, and this lawyer from New York chased him off. *He* chased the bear *off*. I've never seen anything like it in my life. I probably never will again."

"Come on, Paul." The young woman's expression was filled with disbelief. "*You* chased that bear off, not him," she said, pointing first at Paul then at Hunter, then elbowing her boyfriend. "You're joking us, right, Paul? I mean, you're the man out here."

So many people knew who Paul was, Hunter thought to himself. It was amazing.

"No, no," Paul argued, "it was this guy who—"

"What's wrong with me?" Hunter demanded, downing his third shot of tequila, then flipping his shot glass upside down and slamming it on the bar with authority. He could feel the tequila taking control of him, probably because there was a heavy dose of adrenaline still coursing through his system. "Why couldn't I have done it?"

While they were driving to The Depot, the enormity of what he'd done had hit him head on. He'd charged a grizzly bear. The question still haunting him was why? Why had he done it? What on earth had possessed him to do something so stupid? Even now he still didn't have an answer. It sure as hell wasn't because he wanted to keep Paul from feeling bad about killing one of nature's most magnificent creatures. Paul was right. When it came down to you and something else in a bad situation, you killed the something else any way you could or you died.

"Do I look like a coward or something?"

The young girl shook her head and gave Hunter a suggestive smile. "Not at all." She raised an eyebrow and leaned subtly away from her boyfriend. "You just don't look like the type who'd—"

"Hey, Karen," her boyfriend interrupted. "Let's go." The young man threw some crinkled one-dollar bills on the bar, chugged the last few gulps of his beer, grabbed her by the wrist, and pulled her hastily toward the door. "Come on."

Paul smiled broadly watching them go. "It's amazing, isn't it?"

"What?"

"The caveman approach still works out here. It's probably one of the last few places in the world it still does." He shook his head. "*Woohoo.* That boy didn't want any part of you, Hunter Lee. He saw his girlfriend thinking she might have a chance with you, even just for the night, and he herded her right outta here like he was rustling cattle." Paul glanced at the bartender. "Didn't he, Joe?"

"Like he was rustling cattle," Joe repeated with a laugh.

"But, like I said on the plane when we met, that would be a risk," Paul said. "You never know about guys out here."

"You talking about the gun thing?"

"Yup. You best be more careful. That little girl was sweet for Montana and that buck isn't going to take kindly to a guy like you giving her more than a polite hi-ho. Watch your back."

"You're crazy."

"Oh, am I?"

As Hunter watched the couple go, it struck him how people in Fort Mason didn't dress up or down. They dressed the same no matter what. The young couple was having beers at the nicest bar in town, but they were dressed in ratty jeans and T-shirts—the same outfits Hunter had seen many times on young people at nice bars in Manhattan. The difference was, the clothes this couple had on were real, probably hand-me-downs, if Strat's description of life in Fort Mason was accurate. The idiots in Manhattan were paying hundreds of bucks for their threadbares.

On the flip side, when he and Strat had run into Big Bill Brule and Dale Callahan at the Lion's Den, those men were wearing button-down shirts, cuffed dress pants and nice shoes. Of course, the guy in the booth glaring at him that day was wearing even more ragged clothes than the couple that had just walked out of here. Hunter glanced down. And here he and Paul were still wearing their grimy fishing outfits, but nobody had said a word.

As soon as the young couple was out the door, three middle-aged couples walked in. The men were wearing denim overalls and checkered shirts, and the women had on flowered polyester dresses.

"Hey, folks, this man chased off a grizzly bear tonight out in Sullivan Gorge," Paul started up again as soon as the couples were on their bar stools, pointing at Hunter. "It was the most amazing thing I've ever seen." It was as if The Depot was Paul's personal stage and the couples had bought tickets to hear him tell the story. "The damn thing was snarling at us from twenty feet off, about to charge us, and all of a sudden he goes yelling and shouting at *it*, waving his arms like a crazy man. That big furry rascal took one look at him and turned tail like a scared rabbit."

"You serious?" one of the men asked, his expression loaded with doubt. Just like that of the young girl who'd left a minute ago had been. "I got a hard time believing that, Mr. Brule."

"Call me Paul. Please." He put his hand out. "What's your name?"

"I'm Bill Perkins," the man answered, shaking Paul's hand. "This here's my wife Cathy."

Incredible, Hunter thought to himself. It wasn't as if most people knew who Paul Brule was out here. *Everyone* knew who he was. And Hunter could tell by the way they looked at him that he was bigger than life for them. A homespun hero, someone they could sincerely admire because he was one of them, just as Strat had said. They'd heard the Fire Jumper stories and how fearless he was on the line; read about his skydiving exploits; knew he was the senator's son; heard about the huge trout he caught; been told how he could knock a goose from the sky with a rifle when everyone else needed a shotgun; knew about his fight record. And they didn't take offense at the fact that he didn't know them. It was as if they were teenagers who'd pulled up beside a movie star at a red light on Santa Monica Boulevard. They were simply glad to be talking to him, simply honored to be in his presence. He was a real celebrity.

Paul slapped Hunter on the shoulder again when the introductions were over. "This man was incredible," he went on. "His new nickname's Griz. I mean, he—"

"Come on," Hunter muttered, steering Paul away from the group. Suddenly he didn't want to be the center of attention, suddenly he wanted to move back into the shadows and the comfort of the perimeter. Besides, the three couples hadn't seemed all that impressed that he was the man who'd tamed George Drake and the Bridger Railroad when Paul dressed up the introduction. Maybe because the folks who hadn't reaped millions from the lawsuit were starting to get jealous of those who had. "Let's go sit by ourselves. We'll get another round." Hunter waved at the bartender. "Again, Joe. Beers *and* tequila. On me this time."

Paul shook his head as they sat down at the other of the bar. "What's with you, Griz? Don't you want people knowing what you did? Hell, you saved our lives out there at Sullivan Gorge tonight. That's one of the bravest things I've ever seen anybody do. I'd think you'd—"

"Yeah, it's kind of like that Fire Jumper who climbs sixty feet up in a tree, hoists a friend with a broken leg onto his back, then lugs him down to the ground and up a ridge so he doesn't die."

Paul's eye narrowed as Joe served the next round of drinks.

"It's kind of like that same guy not wanting his name splashed all over the newspaper the next day bragging to everybody what he did," Hunter continued.

"How'd you hear all that?" Paul demanded, lighting a cigar he'd pulled from his shirt pocket.

"*You're* asking *me* how *I* heard it?" Hunter asked. "This is Montana, Paul. This is your neck of the woods. You know how I heard it."

"Yeah, well, I guess the rumor mill out here is pretty—"

"And I ran into Mandy Winslow," Hunter admitted.

"Hey." Paul's eyes flashed to the crowd at the other end of the bar. "Keep your voice down."

It was interesting to see how uncomfortable Paul got when he thought someone might pick up a clue to his relationship with Mandy. "She told me what you did," Hunter explained.

The fact that Mandy had told him what had happened was interesting, too. It meant that Paul had told Mandy about Hunter. Otherwise, she wouldn't have said a word about Paul saving that guy because she wouldn't want it getting around that they were dating, either. For some reason Mandy wanted to say something, probably because she wanted Hunter to know what a star her man was.

"She told me about you saving that guy," Hunter continued. "It's pretty amazing stuff." Another thought struck him. Maybe Paul wanted Hunter to know about the story and had sent Mandy looking for him. Mandy started talking about what Paul had done before Hunter had even finished introducing himself. Maybe it was really Paul who wanted Hunter to know what a star Paul was. "Way more than what I did tonight."

"Well . . ."

"Mandy seems like a great girl, Paul."

"Thanks." Paul took a long swig off his beer, then picked up his shot of tequila. He held it out and smiled. "Cheers, pal."

Hunter picked up his shot glass, too, and pushed it firmly to Paul's glass. "Yeah, cheers." They drank, and as with the other shots, Paul was finished in half the time it took Hunter. When his glass was empty, Hunter coughed loudly. How in God's name did Paul and Strat chug alcohol so easily?

"Mandy is a great girl," Paul agreed, taking a puff off his cigar. "In fact, she's fantastic."

Hunter pounded his chest. The tequila was still fighting its way to his stomach. He hoped it would stay there. "Yeah," he gasped. "I can see why you like her so much." Nothing like a day of fishing, almost being mauled by a grizzly bear, and shots of tequila to make two men who usually didn't say much start talking about things that really mattered. "I mean that."

"We're into the same things, and we have the same attitude about a lot of stuff. It's way cool." He hesitated. "But it stinks that we gotta keep it quiet."

"Because you're her boss, you mean?" Hunter asked, starting to get his breath back. They hadn't talked about it yet, but it seemed pretty obvious. "That's why you've got to keep it quiet?"

"You got it."

"Why don't you have her quit the Fire Jumpers?" Hunter suggested.

"Or have her transferred to Missoula. You could still see her up there. Not as much, but some."

Paul grimaced. "My exclusivity record with women isn't very good. Hell, what am I saying? I don't *have* a record. The longest I've ever been with one girl is a month, and Mandy and I have only been seeing each other for a little while. What if I, well . . . what if it turns out we aren't as right for each other as I'm hoping? What then? Then she gets screwed," he answered his own question. "It's not fair to her."

"I see what you're saying." Hunter paused. "I guess all you can do is try to keep it under wraps until you're sure. One way or the other."

"You and I both know it isn't going to stay under wraps for long, Griz. Not in Fort Mason," Paul muttered. "I care about her a lot," he admitted, his expression taking on a faroff look. "I didn't worry about how any of the other girls I dated felt, but I do with Mandy. It's the first time I've ever felt this way. But I still don't know if it's the real thing, Griz."

Hunter started to say something, then picked his cell phone up off the bar. The ring was on vibrate and the phone had started to dance across the dark wood. "Hey, Strat." He'd been about to warn Paul to go slow with that delicate, highly complicated thing called love, especially if his longest stint with one girl up to this point was a month. "How you doing?"

"Where are you, brother?"

"At The Depot." Hunter put both elbows on the bar and covered his ears so he could hear Strat better. The couples at the other end of the bar had broken out into loud laughter. "I'm with Paul Brule." There was a strange, unsteady tone to his brother's voice, and he seemed rushed. Usually there was at least a "hey" back. "You okay?"

"Yeah, yeah, fine. Stay put, will ya? I'll be there in a few minutes. I'll call when I'm close. Meet me outside. I don't want to come in."

"You want me to—" But Strat was already gone. Hunter made sure to put the phone back on the bar face up so he could see the screen and who was calling. Strat had sounded scared. Hunter had only heard that glitch in his voice a few times before, and not in a long time. But he recognized it all right.

"Was that your brother?" Paul asked.

"Yeah."

"Everything okay?"

Hunter didn't know how to answer that question. Strat hadn't sounded okay, but Hunter still wasn't certain he could be a hundred per-

cent truthful with anyone in Fort Mason. Even Paul Brule. Which stunk.
"Yeah, fine."

"You and he are really tight, huh?"

Hunter nodded. "We're different, we always have been. But we've always been close, even when we were young, even when me tagging along
fishing with his buddies and him was probably the last thing they wanted.
Strat never gave me a hard time about it though. He always got pissed at
any of his pals who teased me, too."

"You're lucky. Like I told you on the river, my brother and I have never
been close and we never will be. Jeremy's too far gone at this point, too bitter at Dad. Now me, I guess. He and I haven't really talked in a while."

"That's tough." Hunter took a long swig of beer. "You know, this may
seem forward of me, but I heard talking to you was like talking to one of
those big pieces of plywood your family's mill spits out every day. That
you never say much." Paul might clam up after this, might not take the
words as a compliment as they were intended. But if he was going to get
the most out of this conversation, he had to take the chance. "But that's
not how it is with you, doesn't seem like it is anyway. I'm not saying you're
a radio talk show host or anything, but the conversation's been good."

"Right back at you." Paul hesitated. "But what you heard is right. I'm
not usually like this."

"Me neither."

"You know, we need to go fishing more."

Good. Paul had taken the comment as Hunter hoped. "Sure. That'd
be great." Now Hunter needed to ask that burning question again, needed
to help Strat out if he could. But maybe he should come at it a different
way, maybe then he'd get more out of Paul than he had earlier on the river.
"You know," Hunter spoke up, "if somebody with a money motive is starting the fires out here, it's going to rock the country."

Paul ran a finger across his top lip. "Yup. It'll take some people in
Washington down, and they'll be senior people, not foot soldiers. Not to
mention the people out here who'll take a hit," he added.

"You think that's what's going on, don't you, Paul? That somebody's
starting these fires and making money off it, I mean."

Paul glanced at Joe to make sure he was out of earshot. The bartender
was talking to the couples sitting at the other end of the room while he
dried beer mugs with a plain white towel. "Of course," he said in a low
voice. "You know I do. You already knew that when we were landing

in Missoula. Look, the number of fires this year is way high compared to other years. Yeah, it's hotter, but not enough to make this much of a difference." He leaned away from Hunter and crossed his arms over his chest. "And that's all you'll get out of me."

"I heard what you said about your father," Hunter spoke up quickly, trying to barrel through the wall Paul had just put up. The same way he would a hostile witness in a courtroom. "But, Paul, do you really think Big Bill's involved? He seems like way too good a guy to get caught up in something like that."

"The other Montana senator is a carpetbagger," Paul answered after a few moments, leaning in toward Hunter. "The guy's originally from Colorado. He only moved here a year before he ran for the Senate. He basically bought his Montana seat in Washington. He didn't know anyone in Montana, still doesn't. He spends hardly any time here. Sounds strange, I know, but it's true."

It didn't sound strange at all to Hunter. People who ran for office did it all the time.

Paul held up one hand. "But my dad knows everybody out here, and he has for a long time. Anybody important, anyway. I think it'd be real hard to get one of those Forest Service contracts Drake or Callahan has' without his help."

"If it's Butch Roman or Katrina Mason setting the fires, they wouldn't need a contract," Hunter pointed out. "Your father wouldn't know anything about what's going on with them. Not that I think he would in *any* case. I think you're being—"

"Let *me* ask *you* something," Paul interrupted, puffing on his cigar. "And this answer's real important to me."

"Okay."

"Why'd you go after that bear? It was a dumb thing to do and you knew it. And you didn't do it because of what I said about not killing animals anymore. I mean, *come on*."

Hunter shrugged. "I don't know, I really don't. I keep asking myself over and over, and I can't figure it out." That last shot of tequila was doing its damage. Hunter was trying to seem unaffected by it, but that was getting harder by the minute. He heard himself slurring a few words, sensed his reflexes slowing. "Maybe I felt like I had something to prove to myself. You know, city boy needs to see his mountain-man side."

"You don't have anything to prove to anyone," Paul said firmly. "Including yourself. We both know that, Griz."

"Well, what do you think it was?" Hunter asked. "Now that I know you better, it doesn't seem like you're short on opinions. You've probably got a theory on this."

Paul watched the ash of his cigar glow for a few seconds. "I think you've got a death wish."

Hunter laughed loudly "A death wish? *Me?* Hey, you're the one who's . . ." His voice trailed off as his cell phone started dancing across the bar again. He grabbed it. "Hey."

"Hunt, I'm a block south of The Depot on Hammond. Right around the corner. I'm standing by my pickup. You can't miss me. See you in a minute."

The line clicked in Hunter's ear before he could even stand up. "Sorry, Paul, but I'm outta here." Hunter tossed three twenties on the bar.

"Going to meet your brother?"

Hunter slipped the cell phone into his pocket, then raised his eyes to Paul's. He wanted to trust this man, but it was tough. Not because Paul had given him any reason at all to hesitate. It was because his litigation experience was telling him to be extra careful with everyone at this point. "Today was great, Paul." He held his hand out. "But maybe next time I'll bring a gun, too."

Paul shook Hunter's hand firmly. "Yeah, next time."

Hunter nodded to the couples at the end of the bar as he passed them, then stopped quickly as the front door came swinging open. Zoe, then Dale Callahan appeared before him. She looked down right away, then forced herself to look back up, it seemed to Hunter. "Hi."

"Hello."

"Hi, Hunter," Dale said loudly, shaking hands. "Join us at the bar for a drink, won't you?"

"No, I uh . . . I'm meeting someone."

"Oh." Dale put his hand on Zoe's back. "Well, come on, honey, let's go."

"I'll be right there, Dale."

Callahan hesitated a moment, then nodded and headed toward the bar, giving Paul a loud greeting.

Paul started in on the grizzly story right away.

"I called you this afternoon before I went fishing," Hunter said, trying to block out Paul's voice. He liked that Paul was telling Dale the bear story. It was immature of him, but he didn't care. "I left you a message."

"I know."

"You didn't call back."

"I went up to Missoula to do some shopping. I knew you were going fishing with Paul. Remember? I was in the car when he called to set it up."

Hunter tried to keep from asking the next question because it made him seem weak, but he couldn't help it. The answer had been nagging at him all afternoon and evening. There was a lot of time to think when you were on a river fly fishing, sometimes too much. "Did you go by yourself?"

She shook her head.

"You go with Dale?"

Zoe put a hand on Hunter's arm. "I've known Dale for a long time. He's a friend, *just* a friend."

"Uh-huh. Well, I'll see you later." Hunter tried to move past her, but she wouldn't let go of his arm.

"Are you free later?" she asked quietly, clasping him tightly. "I want to see you. You know I do."

Over her shoulder Hunter caught Dale casting an obvious glance in their direction. "What does 'later' mean?"

"An hour or two."

Hunter stared into her eyes. Those lights in the middle of her pupils were burning bright. "Okay, I'll be in my room at the B&B."

"What number is your room again?"

"Three-twelve. Just come up."

"I will." She kissed Hunter on the cheek, then moved past him toward Dale and Paul.

As Hunter turned to go, he caught a look from Paul telling him that Zoe was going to hear the grizzly story, too. Every detail. He nodded a quick thanks, then pushed through the door, turned left, and jogged toward Hammond Street.

As he rounded the first corner he saw Strat leaning against his pickup truck smoking a cigarette.

"Hey, Hunt."

"You okay?" Hunter asked. He got his answer quickly. In the glow of the cigarette he spotted a big cherry on Strat's cheek. "Jesus, what happened?"

"I almost got caught tonight, had to fight my way out of it."

"What do you mean, 'caught'?"

Strat dropped his cigarette on the pavement and stepped on it. "I was inside the Bridger Air facility out near the Missoula airport tonight poking around, and some guys spotted me. I got into a little scrape with a couple of 'em, but I got away."

"You all right? Anything broken?"

"I'm fine, just a few bruises."

Hunter rolled his eyes. "Jesus Christ, Strat. What the hell were you thinking?"

"I heard the Bridger Railroad's gonna file bankruptcy tomorrow. I figured George Drake might be feeling some stress and start another fire tonight. I thought I might be there when he did his planning. I think I was right, but I didn't get a chance to finish what I was doing because they saw me."

"Who told you the railroad's filing bankruptcy tomorrow?"

"One of Butch Roman's senior execs. I saw the guy at a job site this afternoon. He said it was pretty definite that the railroad would go eleven tomorrow, whatever 'going eleven' means. Anyway, I told you about the rumor that Butch is working with a group out east to buy the Bridger. Right?"

"Yeah, you told me."

"I guess that's how his executive knew. He's probably working with Butch on the deal and they got themselves some inside information so they could be the first ones at the bankruptcy trough." Strat checked up and down the darkened street. "Look, Hunt, at this point I'm pretty damn sure Drake's the one responsible for the fires. That's what I wanted to tell you, but I didn't want to do it on a cell phone. I'm worried people are listening. Anyway, I'm almost positive Drake's behind the fires, and I wanted to . . . Well, I wanted to . . ."

"What, Strat? You wanted to what?"

Strat kicked at a piece of gum on the blacktop. "Look, if anything happens to me, make that bastard pay, brother. Go after him hard with everything you've got."

Hunter grabbed Strat by both shoulders and shook him. "Listen to me, nothing's going to happen to you. We're going to do this together from now on." He'd never seen Strat scared like this before, and it scared Hunter. It always had when he saw fear in his older brother's eyes. "Okay?"

"Yeah, okay," Strat mumbled. "I think that might be a good idea. I thought I was in real trouble tonight. I just hope nobody recognized me."

"Go home and get some stuff from your trailer," Hunter suggested. "Then come back to the B&B. You can bunk on my floor for a while, for a few days until we get all this sorted out. I'm in room 312."

"Three-twelve. Yeah, okay." Strat lighted another cigarette, then opened the pickup door. "I'll be back in a little while."

"Hey, Strat!"

Strat slammed the pickup door shut, then leaned out the window as he gunned the engine. "What?"

"We need to add someone else to the list," Hunter said loudly over the noise of the engine.

"What list?"

"You know what list."

Strat shook his head. "I told you, it's George Drake. I'm almost positive. And if by some crazy chance it isn't Drake, it's either Dale or Butch."

"There's another possibility."

Strat clenched his jaw, as if he really didn't have time for this. "Who?"

"Katrina Mason."

"What? Are you kidding?"

Strat's emotional reaction caught Hunter by surprise. "No, I'm not kidding."

"Ah, you're off your rocker."

"Think about it, Strat."

"I don't have to think about it. She's not involved."

"None of Katrina's timber has burned this summer," Hunter went on. "With each fire her trees get more valuable. If there's less supply and the same demand, then the price goes up. It's Econ 101, brother, and, it's too coincidental. And it makes too much sense."

Strat took his Mariners cap off and ran his fingers through his thinning hair. "You were with Paul Brule fishing today, weren't you?"

"Yeah, so?"

"He fill you full of all that Econ 101? He tell you how her trees haven't burned this summer?"

"Maybe."

Strat put the truck into first. "See you at the B&B in a while, brother."

"Hey. *Hey!*" But Strat roared off. Hunter watched the pickup's lone working taillight move away, then turn left and disappear. "Damn him."

"What's wrong, there, Jeremiah Johnson?"

Hunter's eyes shot to the right. Through the dim light he could see a man holding a pistol in one hand and a bottle in the other. "Jesus," he whispered. It was the guy who'd dragged his girlfriend out of The Depot right before the three couples had walked in. "Put the gun down, pal."

Hunter could see the guy swaying back and forth in the dim light. "I don't want any trouble."

"Then you shouldn't have made eyes at my girl."

"I didn't make—"

"Shut up, you prick!" the guy yelled. He took a swig off the bottle, then raised the gun slightly higher and cocked the revolver's trigger back with his thumb. "Time for you to say bye-bye to—"

Out of the corner of his eye, Hunter saw someone move swiftly out of the shadows and slam into the man holding the gun. The guy dropped to the pavement like he'd been shot, the gun clattered into the middle of the street, and the bottle smashed. He tried to stagger to his feet, but Paul grabbed him by the shirt, landed a hard left to the chin, and the guy went down again. This time he was down for good, sprawled unconscious on the pavement.

Hunter leaned over and put his hands on his knees. "Thank God you showed up." His heart was pumping, almost as fast as when the bear had charged.

"Now we're even," Paul said with a grin, retrieving the gun. "Nice piece," he muttered, admiring it. "Think I'll keep it."

"Paul, I don't know how to thank—"

"Maybe you don't have a death wish after all," Paul interrupted, slipping the barrel of the gun into his belt. "Maybe going at that bear really was what you needed to see if you had that mountain-man side in you after all."

Hunter nodded. "Yeah, I guess it was."

"Let me deal with this guy," Paul volunteered, pointing at the young man sprawled on the pavement. "I'll have a little talk with him when he comes to. I don't think you'll have to worry about him after that, but for now, you better scram." Paul grinned. "All right?"

Paul Brule was a good man, a very good man. "Yeah, all right." Hunter was about to head back to The Depot when Paul yelled after him.

"Hey, Griz."

"Yeah?"

"One more thing."

"What?"

"When I tell you that some guys out here shoot first and think later when it comes to their women? Believe me from now on, will you?"

Hunter nodded solemnly. "I sure will."

44

JEREMY SAT ON a ledge overlooking Hell's Gate, an open envelope and the letter that had called the envelope home for many years lying on the rock beside him. This was the same place he'd brought Zoe Gale when he'd thought she was serious about him, when Jeremy hadn't yet come to understand that she was simply using him. It was dark now, but in the light of a full moon Jeremy could easily make out the two peaks that formed the Hell's Gate soaring skyward above him. It was a beautiful place, but he couldn't appreciate that beauty. It seemed that he couldn't appreciate anything anymore—because no one appreciated him.

He reached down and picked up the letter, struck by how calm it was up here on the ledge tonight. Struck by how he'd placed the letter and the envelope down on the rock beside him, but they hadn't blown away. Every other time he'd been up here the wind had been strong, sometimes howling.

Jeremy had come here for the first time many years ago, as a child. Big Bill was taking Paul to see it one weekend morning, and Jeremy had begged to come along, too. Only after their mother had stepped in had Big Bill relented and reluctantly brought his "other" son on the adventure as well. That had been a cold, snowy February day, and Jeremy could still remember Big Bill warning Paul when they got here not to get too close to the edge of the cliff because the ground was slippery and the gusts were strong, over fifty miles an hour. A few minutes later Jeremy had wandered close to the edge on purpose, but Big Bill had given him no such warning. In fact, it had almost seemed as if his father was hoping the winds would whip up suddenly and his older boy might tumble off in the gale.

Jeremy opened the letter and began reading the dry, crinkled paper by the light of the moon. It was a letter he'd read many times before, a letter his mother had written to him on her deathbed years ago telling him how much she loved him and warning him to be careful of his father now that she was gone. Warning him not to depend on Big Bill for anything, pleading with him to make his own way in the world because, as much as she hated to admit it, she knew her husband was a man who could never be trusted.

Why hadn't he listened to her? Jeremy asked himself silently. Why had he assumed that a father would ultimately come around? Suddenly it had turned out to be the biggest mistake of his life. Big Bill had called thirty minutes ago to tell Jeremy that he was fired, and that he was cut off from any family money. That Jeremy was completely on his own now and good luck.

Jeremy swallowed hard as he slid the letter back into the envelope. Maybe that was why he'd resented Paul all these years. Not because Paul was better at everything than he was, but because Paul had been smart enough to take their mother's advice.

"Paul just tried to help," Jeremy mumbled. He could feel the moisture building in his eyes as he gazed up at the peaks looming above him, feel the sides of his throat closing in on themselves. "That was all Paul ever did."

Jeremy stood up and moved slowly to the edge of the cliff, the envelope still in his hand. Paul was a good man, Jeremy realized as he watch the dark water far below swirl past. Paul had always protected him as much as possible. Maybe that was where the bitterness really came from. From the fact that the younger brother had always needed to protect the older brother.

A lone tear trickled down each side of Jeremy's face as he stared at the water. A few seconds of terrible fear then a quick death. All things considered, an easy way to go. That was what Paul had always said about what would happen if his parachute didn't open.

Maybe it was time to test that theory.

45

STRAT PULLED TO a sharp stop at the end of the secluded dirt road, wishing now that he'd installed those battery-powered, high-intensity exterior lights he'd been meaning to install for the last two years. The all-weather bulbs and timer were in his bedroom closet, still packed in their boxes. And the four fifteen-foot pine poles he'd stolen from the Bridger Railroad with a friend's flatbed to put the bulbs on top of were lying beside the trailer under a thick spiderweb of weeds. They'd been lying there now for three winters.

"Damn it," Strat muttered. In addition to one of his taillights' being out, he had a blown headlight. The same one he'd gotten a citation for over a year ago. "Maybe I shoulda paid that ticket after all." From where he was parked, he still had a hundred feet to walk along a narrow trail through waist-high weeds and ten-year-old trees to get to the trailer. The one headlight that still worked wasn't very bright, so the last half of the hike to the trailer was going to be through pitch black. "Maybe I should have fixed the headlight. Maybe that's why the cops give you the ticket, you idiot." He grimaced. "Maybe I shoulda cut the path wide enough so I could drive the pickup all the way to the trailer. Hell, somebody got the trailer in here ten years ago. Maybe I should have done a lot of things in my life."

He banged the steering wheel with his fist, then sucked in his gut and reached beneath the seat for the nine-millimeter pistol he kept there.

When his fingers had made it through the empty cigarette boxes and beer cans and closed around the gun's handle, he felt a little safer. He'd never been scared to make this walk to the trailer before, even that night last summer when a big mountain lion had been spotted prowling the area. But he was scared now. That sixth sense he had about certain things was telling him he needed to be real careful. Well, as soon as he had the chance he was going to install those outside lights. He glanced through the cracked windshield. *If* he had the chance.

Strat pushed the pickup door open, cringing as it squeaked loudly on its rusty hinges. Then he took a deep breath, chambered the first round in the pistol, and headed up the path. God damn it was lonely out here.

46

AUL AND MANDY lay side by side in a comfortable hammock hanging on the front porch of his cabin, gazing up at the full moon and the myriad stars surrounding it. The cabin was built atop a ridge south of Fort Mason, on ten secluded acres Paul had purchased five years ago without any help from Big Bill.

"Oh, Paul, look, *look!* It's another shooting star."

"I see it." She was like a little kid tonight. He loved seeing her so captivated by shooting stars. "I see it, already."

"That was the fifth one tonight," she said excitedly, "and we've only been out here for a half hour."

Paul had to admit that the show had been damn good. "It is pretty cool, huh?" He'd seen better on camping trips up north during the winter when the air was even clearer. But not that much better.

"*Very* cool. I've never seen anything like it," she murmured. "There's got to be a million lights up there, but you can still see the shooting stars, too."

"That's why we call it Big Sky Country."

Paul loved the way Mandy's body fit snugly into his. Whether they were lying here in the hammock beneath the moon and stars, kicking back on the living room sofa inside watching TV, or spooning in his king-sized bed. It had never felt this good with any other woman, never *been* this good with another woman. He caressed her hair as she kept her eyes

focused on the heavens. He was falling for her harder and harder, he realized. Which was wonderful and frightening all at the same time. These
were uncharted waters for him, and the longer it went on, the tighter he
felt himself getting wrapped around the axle. She'd expect him to keep
opening the kimono wider and wider, and she had every right to expect
that. But there might come a day when he couldn't open up any more, a
day when, in fact, he had to put up a wall.

"Paul."

"Yes?"

"Why don't you and your dad ever talk?"

Jesus, she must have been reading his mind. "Why *what*?"

"Don't avoid the question." Mandy pivoted toward him so she was on
her side and her cheek was resting on his chest, then she slid her leg over
his. "Please don't."

"Look, it's no big deal. Really."

"No big deal? He's your father and you don't talk to him. To me that's
a big deal."

"You're going to miss the falling stars."

"I don't care and don't change the subject."

He'd been anticipating this question from her about his father. The
fact that he and Big Bill didn't talk was common knowledge among the
veteran Fire Jumpers, and they were worse than a bunch of old blue-haired
hens at a quilting party when it came to keeping something quiet—which
was the main reason he was being so careful about his relationship with
Mandy. He let out a long breath. She must have overheard somebody say
something about his father and him. He'd been anticipating it all right,
he'd just hoped it wouldn't come so soon.

But he had his comeback ready. "Hey, you didn't talk to your dad for
a long time before he died."

"And I regret it every day," she answered immediately, slipping her
fingers into his and squeezing tightly. "God, I regret it."

"Yeah, but—" He stopped in midsentence. This was stupid. It was
time to tell her. He had no choice. Man, the butterflies in his stomach were
going crazy. They hadn't even been this bad the first time he'd jumped out
of an airplane into a fire. "I love you, Mandy." It was the first time either
of them had said it in their relationship, and now came the part he had
butterflies about. Would she say it back?

Her eyes moved to his and she gazed at him for a few seconds, then broke into a sentimental smile. "I love you, too, Paul. I know it hasn't been long for us, but I feel the same way."

Relief washed over him, as if he was standing beneath that waterfall he'd taken her to see up in the Bitterroots, and they shared a long, passionate kiss.

"I'm sorry if I dug too deep about you and your dad," Mandy whispered when their lips parted. "It's just that I care about you so much. It seems like such a shame for you two not to be close. Everybody out here respects the heck out of you both." She put her head back down on his chest. "I'm sure it hurts him not to talk to you. Like you can't even—"

"My dad did a bad thing a few years ago, Mandy," Paul said, cutting her off. He sensed that he didn't have to explain anything about his relationship with Big Bill at this point, but he now wanted to. "A very bad thing, something I can never get past." He swallowed hard. "But he saved my life twice, and he's my father, so I'm stuck. The only thing I can do is make like he doesn't exist, so like what he did didn't happen. That's the only way."

Mandy looked up at him again and ran her fingers through his blond hair. "What did your father do, Paul?"

47

STRAT SPRINTED THE last few yards down the narrow, dimly lit trail to the idling pickup and tossed the bag he'd packed in the back beside his tool box and the crumpled-up pair of rubber fishing waders he never used. "I oughta throw them out," he huffed as he leaned over and put his hands on his knees, breathing hard, thinking about how he was a pack rat and always had been. "Like I ever will." It had only taken a few minutes to find the bag and stash some clothes and personal items in it, but they'd seemed like the longest few minutes of his life.

When the bag was packed, he'd burst through the door and sprinted to the trailhead, concerned that someone had followed him out here and might be waiting for him to come out. At least by rushing out he had a shred of surprise on his side. Now that he was back to the pickup, he felt better, though he was shaking like a leaf.

After taking a few moments to catch his breath, he raised up off his knees and shoved the nine-millimeter he'd been brandishing on the sprint down the trail into his belt. But as he reached for the truck's door, two high-powered flashlights came on at the same time, painting twin shadows of him on the side of the pickup.

For a split second he thought about bolting into the woods, but that seemed pretty stupid. As winded as he was, he wouldn't get far fast and whoever this was would track him down. Then he thought about going for the gun, but that seemed stupid, too. Nobody was going to take someone by surprise at their home deep in the Montana woods without fire-arms drawn, not unless they were idiots.

"Who's there?" he yelled as confidently as he could, raising his hands above his head. "What the hell do you want?"

"Don't go for the gun," a deep voice warned. "The one we saw you just put in your belt."

Strat squinted against the lights, pretty sure he'd recognized the voice. "Butch?" He swore the voice belonged to Butch Roman.

"You hear me, Strat? Don't go for it."

"If that's you, why would I go for my gun?"

"Just keep your hands in the air."

A moment later two men were standing in front of him. One was Butch and the other was the Roman Construction executive who'd told Strat that the Bridger Railroad was about to file bankruptcy. Both men were holding flashlights in one hand—and revolvers in the other.

Butch yanked the gun from Strat's belt and tossed it into the weeds behind them. "Move in front of the pickup," he ordered. "We'll talk there. And put your hands down."

"What are you doing all the way out here, Butch?" Strat asked when they were all in front of the truck's one dim headlight. "Why didn't you call me?"

"I wanted to talk to you face to face about something."

"Couldn't it wait until morning?"

"Nope."

Strat's eyes shifted quickly from Butch to the other man and back to Butch. Butch was smacking his gum hard the way he always did, and Strat was getting a strong blast of spearmint in his face. He'd never liked the smell of spearmint. "What is it, Butch? What do you want to talk about?"

Butch pushed his chin out, as if he meant business. "Somebody told me you were up in Missoula talking to one of the Bridger guys. An attorney named Andy Kohler. Were you?"

"Well, I . . ."

"*Were you?*"

Strat felt perspiration building beneath his clothes, and not because of how hot it was out tonight. "I uh, I ran into Kohler at a bar up there. The Rhino Bar. I'm sure you know it, Butch. We were both sitting at the bar, and we just started talking."

Christ, Strat suddenly realized. Maybe George Drake and Butch Roman were in it together, maybe they were burning Montana as a team. It seemed an unlikely match because Butch was supposed to be furious with Drake for charging him so much to bring building supplies into Montana on the railroad. But maybe that was the beauty of it. No one would ever have figured they'd work together.

Strat glanced down at the gun Butch was aiming at him. He should have put that away by now. "It was nothing, Butch. I'm telling you."

Butch took a step forward, so their faces were only inches apart. "Don't lie to me, Strat, tell me why you were talking to him. *Or I swear to Christ I'll shoot you!*"

48

"Yes, I used to date Dale Callahan." Zoe led Hunter to a comfortable love seat in one corner of his spacious room at the Lassiter Bed & Breakfast, then gestured for him to sit down. "And that was wrong." She rolled her eyes. "I should have had ESP, I should have known you were going to come to Fort Mason, win a big lawsuit, move here from back east, then sweep me off my feet with that handsome face, beguiling manner, and mysterious eyes. I should have waited for you in church with my hands clasped and my little legs crossed at the ankles. I'm very sorry I didn't, I was a bad girl. Maybe I should be punished."

"Um . . . well . . . no." When she said it like that, Hunter had to agree it sounded pretty silly. "I didn't mean it that way," he said, sitting down on the small sofa. He'd liked that last bit, though, especially the part about the handsome face and the beguiling manner. "What I meant was, are you *still* dating him?"

"But you asked me if I'd *ever* dated him."

"Yes, I did," Hunter admitted, gazing up at her as she stood in front of him in her sexy dress, hands on hips. "So, are you still dating him?"

"Why don't we see what happens tonight?" she suggested in a gravelly voice, beginning to pull the hem of her dress slowly up her thighs. "Then we'll talk about it in the morning over mimosas."

Before she could pull the dress any higher, Hunter reached out, slipped his fingers around her wrist, and pulled her down onto the couch beside him. Despite how sexy she looked, he wasn't in the mood. Strat should have been here a while ago and Hunter was worried. It shouldn't have taken him this long to get to the trailer and back.

"Why don't you just tell me now?"

49

PAUL WAS ABOUT to follow Mandy in between the soft cotton sheets of his king bed when there was a loud knock at the cabin door, a pounding that went on way longer than necessary.

"Jesus," Paul hissed angrily, grabbing his jeans off the floor and stepping into them. As a rookie Fire Jumper, Mandy only got one night a week away from the base, and she had to be back in the barracks no later than seven o'clock the next morning. Whoever this was better have a damn good reason for banging on his door. "This really pisses me off."

He reached into the nightstand and pulled out a .22 pistol. It wasn't the Colt .44 he packed when he went into the woods. That gun was locked inside a finger-touch combination safe in his closet—lying beside the .38 caliber pistol he'd lifted off the idiot who'd gotten in Hunter's grill on the street in Fort Mason tonight. The .22 wasn't as powerful as the other guns, but it was loaded with hollow-point shells, which would still rip huge holes in a human being from close range. The grizzly bear Hunter had chased off at Sullivan Gorge would have swatted these bullets away like pesky flies, but a human being would go down with one well-aimed round. And he wouldn't get up.

"Paul!" Mandy's eyes went wide when she spotted the gun. "What are you doing?"

"Protecting us," he answered matter-of-factly, making sure the pistol's chambers were fully loaded. "Don't worry," he assured her, "if this was somebody who wanted to kill me, I doubt he'd knock." Maybe it was the guy he'd belted tonight, maybe he wanted his gun back. That was the only explanation Paul could come up with. Well, this time he could shoot the idiot and the law would be on his side. If you trespassed in Montana, you put your life in someone else's hands. "I'll be right back."

"Be careful," she whispered from the bed as he padded out of the room. "I love you."

He stole through the living room to the light switch by the front door, gun pointed at the ceiling. He didn't keep outside lights on at night in the summer because bugs would swarm around the bulbs and create one hell of a mess. Before flipping on the porch light, he pulled the curtain on the window beside the door back half an inch and checked outside. When he saw who it was, he gritted his teeth and let the gun fall slowly to his side. He'd recognize that silhouette anywhere. He flipped on the switch illuminating the floor lamp in one corner of the living room, then opened the front door.

"Hello, Father."

"Hello, Paul. Can I come in?" Big Bill asked after a few seconds of strained silence.

Paul stepped back and gestured for Big Bill to enter. "Yup." It wasn't as if he could shut the door in his father's face. Much as he wanted to.

"Sorry to bother you so late, son."

"Uh-huh."

Big Bill glanced around the living room. The log walls were decorated with wildlife paintings, vintage rifles, and trophy fish Paul had caught over the years. "This is nice, Paul. A real man's home. It reminds me of my place."

"Thanks."

"I've never seen it before."

"No, you haven't."

Another uncomfortable pause ensued, then Big Bill pointed at the .22 in Paul's hand. "I don't think you'll be needing that, son. At least, I hope you won't."

Paul smiled thinly, even though he didn't want to. Big Bill Brule was an amazing man. He could charm an Eskimo out of a parka and a sled team in the middle of a blizzard. "What do you want, Father?"

"Do we have to be so formal?"

"What do you want?" Paul asked again, this time as deliberately as he could.

Father gave son an aggravated look, but didn't push. "I'll be straight with you, son. I need you."

Paul closed the door after his father had moved inside the cabin. "Why?"

"We've only got a little over two weeks of timber inventory left at the mill," Big Bill explained. "A little over two weeks and we can't find any more."

Paul didn't know much about the mill's business, but he figured that two weeks of inventory was cutting it way too close for almost any business. *"Two weeks?"*

"Yeah." Big Bill shook his head. "I'm in China thinking Jeremy's got everything under control at the mill, but when I get back I find out he's running the place into the ground. Then I have to go to Scotland, and he doesn't even do anything about the problem once I know about it."

Paul put the .22 down on the coffee table in front of the couch and stretched slowly. His ribs were still bothering him. Maybe instead of going to Scotland, probably to play golf, Big Bill should have stayed home and taken care of the problem himself. "Why are you telling me this?" He noticed Big Bill glance at the pistol.

"I need your help."

"What do you mean?"

"I need you to find me some timber."

"But there oughta be—"

"There oughta be but there isn't," Big Bill interrupted impatiently. "Everything from here to Anchorage is locked up tighter than the Coke formula in the Atlanta vault."

Paul scratched his head. "That's crazy."

"Agreed. But that's the deal, and it's all happened in the last sixty days." Big Bill leaned down and picked up the .22 off the table, examining it closely. "Nice-looking gun," he murmured, slipping his finger behind the trigger, closing one eye, and aiming it at the wall over Paul's shoulder. "Good feel to it, too."

"Look, Dad, I—"

"You know a lot of people out here, Paul," Big Bill said, refocusing on the issue at hand, waving the gun around as he spoke. "More important, *everybody* knows you. I wish I had your approval rating. If I did, I wouldn't have to worry about getting re-elected."

"Yeah, so?"

Big Bill pursed his lips and pointed the .22 straight at Paul's chest. "So find me timber, son. Call around, pull out all the stops, do whatever you have to do, but get me logs. I know you can do this if you put your mind to it." He hesitated. "You can do anything if you put your mind to it."

"I don't want to be part of the business." The thing was, Big Bill was right. Paul could get timber rolling into the mill by tomorrow. He knew exactly who to call. The guy wouldn't have an infinite supply, but it would be enough to make a difference. Enough to bail the mill out for a few months. "You know that. We've talked about it several times."

"Okay," Big Bill said evenly, "then I'm not asking anymore. I'm *telling* you to do it. Get me timber and get it for me as fast as you can."

"You can't tell me what to do," Paul snapped defiantly. "You don't control me."

Big Bill flipped the pistol in the air half a turn and caught the barrel, then held the wooden handle out for Paul. "You really like that little girl who's lying in your bed right now, don't you? You think she's the one."

Paul's vision blurred as his fingers closed around the smooth oak handle of the gun. "Well, of course I—"

"I'd hate for Captain Joe Parker up at Fire Jumper HQ in Missoula to find out what you and Mandy Winslow are up to. That probably wouldn't be a good outcome for you guys, would it? Given that he's the top dog up there, he could probably have her reassigned to the Kalispell base, couldn't he? Like, tomorrow. Maybe have her restricted to base for the rest of the season, too." Big Bill's face creased with a wry smile. "If she gets pissed off enough, you might even have a sexual harassment suit staring you in the face." He shook his head. "Boy, that all sounds so nasty, doesn't it?"

Paul's right hand contracted into a tight fist, but he said nothing.

"I was hoping we could be friends again," Big Bill continued, "but I guess that's not in the cards. I don't know what happened to us, Paul. I don't know what I could possibly have done to deserve this attitude of yours, but I'm sick of always being the one to reach out." He hesitated, then pointed at Paul. "Get me timber and get it fast. Or else."

As Big Bill headed out the door Paul's cell phone rang. He pulled it from his jeans pocket and stared at the number, not recognizing it. "Hello." God, he'd been tempted to follow his father out the door and shoot him down in cold blood. He'd never been so mad at anyone in his life. "Hello!" he barked.

"Paul, this is Jeremy. We need to talk."

50

I LIKE THE LASSITER Bed & Breakfast," Zoe spoke up, making a sweeping gesture with one hand. "I like this room."

"It is nice," Hunter agreed. "Of course, it's better with you in it. Even better now that you've told me you aren't dating Dale Callahan."

"Mmm, I had a feeling you might like that." She ran her long fingernails through his hair and smiled. "You know, I've been in Fort Mason for three years and you're the first person I've ever known who's actually stayed here."

"Well, I'm the only guest in the place, and I've been the only one since I got here. It doesn't seem like a hotbed of activity so it doesn't surprise me that you don't know anyone who's stayed here." Hunter checked the wall clock for the third time in the last ten minutes: It was after two in the morning. Where was Strat? "I think it's safe to say the couple who owns this place isn't in it to make a lot of money."

"Then why do they keep it open?"

Hunter reached for his phone. It lay on the table that stood beside the sofa arm. "I think it's got to do with something other than money."

"What?"

"I hear they like to watch their guests, especially at night."

"Oh, my God." Zoe's eyes flashed around the room. "That's creepy."

"I'm kidding," he said, chuckling. "Somebody told me that, but I haven't seen anything suspicious yet. And believe me, I checked every-where for peepholes and hidden cameras when I first got here." He had, too, including behind all the pictures on the walls. He'd felt kind of foolish doing it, but you could never be too careful these days.

As Hunter was about to try Strat's cell phone there was a knock on the door. "Hunt?"

Relief poured through Hunter. He'd started to think the worst—again. "Give me a minute, brother."

"Okay, I'll be downstairs waiting for you."

"Yeah, yeah." Strat must have assumed that Zoe was still here. He'd sent a text message earlier letting Strat know that he had company. "I'll be right down."

"Okay."

"Didn't you tell me Strat was staying here tonight?" Zoe asked.

"I did."

"What's wrong with his place?"

"Um, there's a problem with the water."

"What kind of problem?"

Hunter hesitated. "He doesn't have any." It was the only thing he could think of to say. "The well went dry because of how little rain there's been this summer. He's got a lot of problems out there."

"Well, he probably won't have to worry about it for long."

"Why not?"

"I'm sure with all that money you've got, you'll be building a mansion and he'll be living with you."

"What money?"

"You know, that money from—" She stopped short. "All that money you got from winning the case against the railroad, for representing those poor people."

Hunter's eyes narrowed. "My firm got that money, not me, Zoe."

"Oh, well then I guess the rumor mill's off a bit. So, why don't you stay with me tonight?" she suggested before Hunter could say anything. "Then Strat can have this place to himself."

Hunter stood up, then leaned back down and gave her a kiss. "Sounds like a plan."

"Then we can get wild," she said, her eyes taking on a crazy look. "Deliciously wild."

"I'll be back in a few minutes." As Hunter rose from the kiss, he realized he hadn't thought about Anne or the divorce once since Zoe had gotten here. "Oh, one thing," he said when he reached the door to the room.

"What?"

"I was thinking about taking you to New York City sometime. Would you like that?"

"I'd love it," she said excitedly, clapping her hands. "I've never been back east."

He gazed at her for a few moments. "Never been back east? Really?"

"No."

He let out a deep breath. His mind was going so fast, as it did in a courtroom when he was examining a defense witness. "We'll have a good time."

"No, we'll have a *great* time."

Strat was waiting for Hunter in the main room of the first floor. It was a big room furnished with comfortable couches and chairs where guests could read a book or play cards. There was an unfinished two-thousand-piece jigsaw puzzle on a table in a far corner of the room, and, as far as Hunter could tell, no one had made any progress on it since he'd checked in. The outside edge was finished, but that was still it.

"Well, you might have been right," Strat said in a low voice as they sat down in the two chairs at the puzzle table. "Maybe I did jump the gun when I thought George Drake was behind everything. On his own, at least."

"What do you mean?"

"As I was getting in the pickup out at my trailer to come back here, Butch Roman showed up out of nowhere."

"Oh?"

Strat nodded. "Yeah, he surprised me with one of his guys. He wanted to know what I was doing up in Missoula talking to Andy Kohler, that attorney who works for Drake."

Hunter had been about to put two puzzle pieces together, but he stopped. "How'd he know about that?"

"Either Kohler called Butch and told him about our chat, or Butch is having me followed. If I had to bet, I'd say it's the second one. Kohler seemed like a straight arrow." Strat hesitated. "I hate to say it, but I don't know about Butch now."

"What did Butch say to you?"

"He said he didn't want me talking to anyone at the Bridger Railroad because he's trying to buy it. He was basically accusing me of feeding information to Kohler about what he was trying to do. It was crazy. I'd never do anything like that, and he knows it. That's why I think he had another agenda coming out there and putting the fear of God in me like that, pulling a gun on me in the dead of night."

"Yeah, but how do you know Kohler's a straight arrow? You just met him."

"He called me while I was driving in here, at two in the morning," Strat explained. "He called to tell me he'd finally gotten that copy of the Bridger Air contract with the Feds that I wanted. He said he'd meet me later today to give it to me."

"That doesn't necessarily mean—"

"He also told me that this morning Drake is going to move a lot of cash from Bridger Air to the Bridger Railroad so he won't have to put the railroad into bankruptcy. He didn't have to tell me that, brother."

"No, he didn't," Hunter agreed. "Look, Strat, this whole thing is getting way out of hand. maybe we should—"

"Mr. Lee?"

Hunter and Strat's eyes shot to the doorway. Betty and Roger Saunders, the proprietors of the Lassiter B&B, were standing there in flannel robes.

"Is everything all right?" Betty asked.

Hunter stood up. "Everything's fine, Mrs. Saunders."

"Can we get you anything?"

"No, no. Sorry if we woke you up. I'll be finished in a few minutes."

"All right."

They turned and shuffled off.

"Maybe I should pick up that contract," Hunter whispered as he sat back down. "It might not be smart for you to go at this point. Not if you think Butch Roman is having you followed."

Strat nodded, then pointed at the TV in the corner of the room. "Did you hear?"

"Hear what?"

"Another fire broke out this afternoon. This one's in Colorado, north of Denver. It's already a megablaze, and it's already burned ten thousand acres. They think it'll burn at least thirty thousand more before they can put it out, and it's headed straight for a town of five thousand people. They're already evacuating the town. They said there's almost no chance of saving it."

Hunter gazed at Strat. "Butch Roman."

Strat nodded. "Yeah, Butch Roman."

51

Big Bill waved to the security guard as he guided his Cadillac through the brightly lighted gate area of the Brule Lumber Mill's main entrance. It was early—barely past three o'clock in the morning—but he couldn't sleep. He'd never needed much sleep anyway, but the thought of having just two weeks of timber inventory on site had kept him wide awake since making that surprise visit to Paul's place a few hours ago.

As he pulled into his personal parking space in front of the main building's front doors, his cell phone rang. He glanced at the number on the screen. Maybe the timber situation was about to change. "Hello, Paul."

"Hello," came the curt, even-toned response.

"What do you have for me, son?"

"Timber."

"How much?" Big Bill listened to the figure and his shoulders slumped out of relief. Ninety days' worth. That ought to give him enough time to figure out what was going on with the timber supply in the Northwest—and do something about it. "Good job. Tell your man to start sending trees immediately. See," he said proudly, "I told you when you put your mind to something you always find a—"

"That's all there is," Paul interrupted. "Otherwise, it's like you said. Every tree from here to Anchorage has a 'sold' sign on it."

"Okay."

"Do we have a deal?"

Big Bill knew what that meant. "Of course. You know I'd never call Missoula to tell them about you and Mandy. You know I'd never do that to—"

"I don't know much of anything anymore," Paul broke in a second time, "but I do know this. You better not break this deal. You got me? I'm telling you, if there's a problem, Father, any problem at all, I'll blame you. And I'll do what I have to do. Then being a senator won't much matter anymore, will it?"

"Hey, Paul, that's no way to talk to somebody who's saved your life twice," Big Bill shot back angrily. "I don't expect that kind of crap from a son who wouldn't be here if it wasn't for—" He heard a click in his ear. Paul had hung up.

As Big Bill climbed from the Cadillac and headed for the front door, he slipped the cell phone into his pocket. He'd heard that warning tone in Paul's voice. A warning tone that sent a chill into the heart of another man—even a father. Paul had that crazy streak in him only a few men had. The one that made him follow up on his threats no matter how dire they were. Big Bill slipped the master key into the front door lock. Well, it didn't matter at this point. He had no intention of breaking their deal. He'd gotten what he needed.

He moved past reception straight to the elevator, rode it up four stories, then hurried down the darkened hallway to his office in his Montana gait, the double-time stride he used in Washington to get from his office in the administration building to the floor of the Capitol.

A few steps away from his door he froze. A light was coming from inside his office. He could have sworn he'd turned everything off before he left last night. Even if he hadn't, the cleaning service should have turned them out when they were done.

Big Bill inched the last few feet along the wall, then peered around the corner. *"God damn it!"* he roared, bursting into the room. *"What the hell are you doing here?"*

Jeremy spun around, eyes wide open, momentarily paralyzed. He was standing in front of two file cabinets Big Bill kept in one corner of the office under heavy lock and key. "I, I—"

"What is that?" Big Bill hissed, pointing at the manila folder in Jeremy's trembling hand. "How'd you get into my personal files?" The padlocks were dangling open. They hadn't been smashed or jimmied. He hadn't bothered to call the security gate yet to tell them to bar Jeremy from the premises, which had clearly been a huge mistake. He'd just never figured Jeremy would have the brass balls to come in here like this. *"Well?"*

Jeremy swallowed hard several times, looked like he was going to completely fall apart, then suddenly managed to pull himself together enough to speak. "I always knew what you did, Dad." His voice shook badly, but he kept going. "I knew about the favor," he said, his voice getting slightly stronger. "And the payments you got for doing that favor. I just never knew who was paying you." A nervous smile broke out on his face, and he held the folder up. "But now I do."

"Put that folder back, Jeremy," Big Bill ordered.

"The hell I will, Dad. I've put up with your crap for too long, played the good son and gotten nothing for it but kicked in the teeth over and over. It's my turn to get some satisfaction."

Big Bill bristled. "You never could take the heat."

"At least I tried."

"I could have hired a bartender from the Grizzly Saloon and he would have done a better job than you." Big Bill pressed his arm to his side, wishing he'd brought his pistol with him from the car. "At least he would have told me a joke or two along the way, at least he would have made me laugh."

Jeremy clutched the folder tightly. "Gee, Dad, and I thought I did make you laugh."

"Yeah, but it was at you, not with you."

"You bastard."

Big Bill held up four fingers. "Paul got me timber. In four hours he got me ninety days of inventory when the chips were down." He nodded at the file cabinets. "What do you do when the chips are down? You steal my personal files."

"You should have treated me better."

"Put it down, Jeremy," Big Bill growled, pointing at the folder. "Now."

Jeremy shook his head and headed for the door. "Screw you," he muttered as he headed toward Big Bill and the office door. "In a few hours you'll damn well wish you'd treated me a *lot* better."

Big Bill grabbed Jeremy as he passed by, but Jeremy was able to wrench away from Big Bill's hold and race into the hallway. Despite his extra weight, Jeremy had always been fast. In seconds he'd made it to the other end of the hallway, ducked into a back staircase, and disappeared.

"God damn it!" Big Bill roared. This was a problem. A *real* problem.

52

THE SUN WAS just coming up over the mountains in the distance when Strat reached the spot where they always met. A secluded place on the ranch where a sturdy headstone marking the grave of Katrina Mason's father stood several feet high beneath a cathedral-like grove of pine trees. It was a two-mile hike in from the road, but they both felt safe meeting here. Out of sight of prying eyes. He hoped.

Strat put his hands on the smooth marble headstone and leaned over. He was starving, exhausted, worried that today might be his last one alive, and worst of all, he was stone sober. He'd moved a chest of drawers in front of the door at the Lassiter B&B this morning after Hunter and Zoe left, but it hadn't given him any peace of mind. Neither had keeping the light on in the room. He'd just stared at that stupid ceiling fan rotating above him for three hours, convinced someone was going to come barreling into the room despite the heavy dresser blocking the door.

He took a deep breath. God, he needed a drink, any kind of drink. As long as there was alcohol in it.

Strat raised up when he heard the heavy sound of hooves. A moment later Katrina appeared atop a big chestnut mare doing an easy canter. As she pulled up and hopped off the horse, he took the reins and they hugged.

"What's going on?" she asked, getting down to business right away. "I've gotta get back for a meeting so we need to make this quick."

"Sure, okay. Well, Hunter's picking up a copy of the Bridger Air contract with the Feds from Andy Kohler today. Kohler's that attorney I met up in Missoula who works for Drake."

"Yeah, I remember. But why's Hunter picking it up?"

"I told you. Hunter knows everything that's going on. Well, almost everything. He doesn't know about you helping me. Anyway, I figure it's safer for him to pick it up than me at this point. So does he."

She turned her head slightly to the side. "Are you absolutely sure Hunter doesn't know about you and me?" she asked apprehensively. "He's a sharp man. Being good in his profession depends on getting information, so—"

"No, no," Strat cut in, chuckling. "In fact, he thinks your name ought to be on the list of suspects."

Katrina gazed at Strat as if he was crazy. "What?"

"He was with Paul Brule yesterday and Paul pointed out that you haven't had any fire damage to your timber tracts this year. That your half a million acres hasn't been touched. Econ 101, I think Hunter called it. The more of other people's timber that burns, the more valuable yours becomes. Something like that, anyway."

"That's ridiculous," she snapped. "Maybe he should try going out with George Drake."

Strat put his hands up. "Yeah, I don't think that's gonna—"

"Maybe Hunter should try kissing that dry-mouth, bad-breath son of a bitch," she went on angrily. "Let him try to put up with that so we can get close to him and find out if he's the one behind it all."

"I know, I know," Strat agreed. "Did you hear that Drake's moving a bundle of cash from Bridger Air into the railroad to keep it out of bankruptcy?" he asked, switching subjects.

She nodded. "He called late last night to tell me. He was all proud of himself. Said he just wished he could see the looks on the bankers' faces when they found out."

"Butch Roman isn't gonna be happy about that."

"I know. He wants to buy the railroad so bad."

On the drive down here Strat had ruled out the possibility that Drake and Butch were working together. He'd convinced himself that Butch had been on the up and up about what he'd said during his surprise visit to the trailer earlier this morning. "Hell, he thinks I'm giving information to George Drake." Of course, Butch had picked up that pistol he'd tossed in the weeds and kept it. Strat had seen that move.

Again, Katrina looked at Strat as if he was crazy.

Strat quickly related what had happened at the trailer last night, and what Butch had said.

She shook her head, amazed. "Everybody's going crazy."

"You're telling me?"

Katrina patted Strat on the shoulder sympathetically. "Did you find out anything at George's warehouse last night."

Strat pursed his lips. "No, I'm sorry. Almost, but then they—"

"It's okay," she said. "Just get me that contract today. Get me that contract, and I'll go to my friend at the FBI."

Strat broke into a huge smile, completely erasing the naturally angry expression. "Really?"

"Really."

He hugged her hard, then took off his dirty gray Stetson and ran the sleeve of his shirt over his eyes. "Thanks," he said, his voice betraying the emotion he was feeling.

Katrina reached into her saddlebag and pulled out a flask of vodka. "Here, I figured you might need this by now."

"You're an angel," he muttered, grabbing it from her and taking several gulps.

"Jesus," she murmured, watching him drink. "So, Paul Brule thinks I'm torching the West. I could believe Big Bill saying that, but not Paul."

"What is it with you and Big Bill?" Strat asked, taking another healthy swig of vodka. "What gives?"

Katrina gazed off into the distance. "We dated a couple of times when the Senate was in recess last year, when he was home."

"And?"

"We went on a walk in the woods out at his place one afternoon. It was nice." Her expression turned steely. "When we were in the middle of nowhere, in the woods where no one could possibly see us, he tried to have sex with me. When I wouldn't, he tried to rape me."

"Are you serious?"

"When I put up a fight, I thought he was going to kill me, so I ran. Thank God I'm in good shape."

Strat whistled. "My God, I never would have thought Senator Brule could—"

Katrina grabbed the flask from Strat and took a healthy swallow of vodka. "Do you think I could burn Montana, Strat?" she asked when she'd brought the flask down from her lips. "Do you really think I could do that?"

53

AS THEY PULLED out of Zoe's short driveway in Paul's Explorer, Hunter glanced out at another hot, clear morning and the sun rising over Hell's Gate. It was a remarkable sight from any direction, but here on the east edge of town he had a particularly impressive view of the twin sentinels soaring straight up into the sky.

"So, are the rumors true, Griz?" Paul asked.

"What rumors?"

"About Zoe. Is she as wild as she likes to tell people she is? Now," Paul went on before Hunter could reply, "you don't answer that if you don't want to."

They'd only gotten a few hundred yards from Zoe's house, but already they were deep into the thick pine forest Hunter had looked out over from the back deck of The Depot. "Let me ask you something first," Hunter said. He wasn't sure this was a good idea, but he and Paul had gotten to be good friends quickly and Paul seemed like the best person to ask. He seemed to have a good line on what was going on in the area. Probably, Hunter suspected, because everyone adored him and they figured the best way to endear themselves to him was to pass along any tidbit of gossip they had because that was all they had to give. Thus, he had become a lightning rod for information without even trying.

"Sure. Anything."

Paul seemed a little down to Hunter. He wasn't his usual smart-aleck-yet-completely-charismatic self this morning. He was still doling out the probing questions, but his mood wasn't as bright as usual and his energy level didn't seem as high as normal. Of course, here it was only a little after seven. Maybe Paul wasn't a morning person.

Paul had called thirty minutes ago to tell Hunter to get dressed and be ready to go fast because they were going to a secret spot he knew of where Hunter could catch a trophy rainbow. Hunter had protested—he liked being beside Zoe in bed—but his objections had proven useless. They were going fishing and that was it, Paul had said.

"Were Zoe and Dale Callahan . . ." Hunter hesitated. "Were they ever an item? I mean, a real item."

A slight smile creased Paul's face. "You must be getting serious about her, Griz."

"Maybe."

"Then why don't you ask Dale himself?"

"What do you mean?"

Paul nodded. "His place is coming up on the right."

The only important item on Hunter's agenda today was picking up that Bridger Air contract from Andy Kohler in Missoula. According to Strat, that couldn't happen until late this afternoon because Kohler couldn't get away until then. Paul had to be back at the Fort Mason Fire Jumper base by two o'clock this afternoon, so getting to Missoula in time to pick up the contract didn't look as if it was going to be a problem. They had a few minutes to stop in and see Dale.

"I was actually thinking about getting a dog, and I've always liked yellow Labs." Hunter glanced at the sun which was starting to put some distance between it and the top of the northern peak of Hell's Gate. "It's kind of early, though. Don't you think?"

"Screw Dale. It's after seven. Any real Montana man ought to be out of bed by now." Paul hit the brakes and wheeled into Callahan's driveway. "If he's asleep, we'll wake him up. As long as you tell him you're here to look at his dogs, he won't care what time it is, I promise you."

Not lost on Hunter as they headed up the dirt driveway was how close Zoe and Callahan lived.

"You like Zoe a lot, don't you?" Paul asked as they headed toward Callahan's house. "You must if you want to know about her past."

Hunter took a deep breath. Only a short time ago he'd warned himself never to give his heart again. As he was sitting in his Bozeman hotel room the morning after Anne had served him with divorce papers. A few minutes before Carl Bach had knocked on the door. He'd taken a blood oath with himself never to let himself be so vulnerable again, but here he was, standing on the edge of the abyss once more.

"She makes me forget," Hunter admitted. "She makes the pain go away, Paul, and that's nice. Even if it's only for a little while, it helps."

Paul nodded. "I never would have understood that before Mandy. Now I think I know what you mean. I don't know what I'd do if she wasn't around." He hesitated. "Look, Zoe's a nice lady. I like her. Like I said, she's been kind of lost since she got here. Dale played her for a while, but you'll be good for her. And it sounds like she'll be good for you, Hunter."

Hunter looked over as Paul eased to a stop in front of Callahan's house. "Thanks. And thanks for telling me about Dale and her." Paul had called him Hunter, he'd noticed, not Griz. That was interesting.

"You bet," Paul answered. "Now let's go look at some dogs."

Callahan's house wasn't what Hunter expected. It was a small, brown-shingled, steeply roofed Cape Codder. Probably just three bedrooms up, and not in great shape, Hunter figured. The paint was dull, the roof needed repair, and there were several cracked panes of glass in one of the first-floor windows. The place wasn't falling down, but it didn't look like the kind of house the CEO of one of the state's fastest-growing companies would live in. In fact the Cadillac parked in front of the house and the freshly painted white barn off to the left where Callahan's prized yellow Labs undoubtedly lived seemed much more fitting for a man of his stature. Both were perfectly maintained.

"It's not exactly what I expected," Hunter said as they both climbed out of the Explorer. A chorus of sharp barks was coming from the white barn, and it was growing louder by the minute. "Know what I mean?"

Paul shrugged. "That's what makes Montana interesting, Griz. You never know what to expect. Even better, you never know what you're going to get."

The front door opened and Dale appeared. He was wearing jeans and a wrinkled shirt and his hair was rumpled. He'd obviously rolled out of bed, probably awakened by the barking. "Hello, gentlemen," he called as he tucked his shirt in. "I wish you would have called and given me a little notice that you were coming by."

"It was a spur-of-the-moment thing, Dale," Paul explained as he shook Callahan's hand, then gestured at Hunter. "We were in the area so we decided to stop by. We figured since it was past seven it was okay."

"Uh-huh. Well, hello, Hunter," Callahan said stiffly as they shook hands. "How are you this morning?"

"Refreshed," Hunter answered, making sure his eyes had a twinkle to them, hoping Callahan would wonder why. Hoping even more that he might know why they were sparkling. "More refreshed than I've felt in a long time, Dale."

"I'm glad to hear it," Callahan said hesitantly. "Well, look, I appreciate you guys stopping by and all, but—"

"We want to see your dogs," said Paul over his shoulder as he strode toward the barn, inviting himself into the kennels. "Griz here is thinking about getting one from you."

"Paul, hey, Paul!" Callahan called, trotting toward the barn after Paul. "Wait a minute."

But Paul had already opened the door and disappeared inside.

54

"WHY THE NEED to see me right away, Nelson? And why the need for all of this running around so we can be someplace private? Why couldn't we just have met in my office in Midtown?"

Radcliff gazed out over the Long Island Sound from the upper deck of his sixty-four-foot yacht as it churned smoothly at twelve knots through calm waters and a partly cloudy, humid afternoon. "I have something you need to hear, Bruce," he said calmly. "Something you need to hear immediately. You'll thank me for getting in touch with you so fast when we're done and for communicating the information in such a discreet manner. I promise you will."

Bruce Preston was chairman and chief executive officer of Integrated Papers, the forty-seventh-largest publicly held company in the United States. Preston had held those leadership positions at Integrated Papers for the last fourteen years, and he'd run the company with an iron fist. He convened quarterly board meetings because he was required to by charter, but instead of the marathon sessions most boards endured, Preston's meetings were usually completed in less than two hours because he rarely listened to anything another board member had to say for very long. He didn't have to. Integrated Papers had reported substantial profit increases to its shareholders every year for thirteen straight years, and the coming year would be no exception. In fact, at the end of this year Preston anticipated announcing the greatest per-share profit increase the company had ever recorded. The run-up in its stock price had far outpaced all major indices as well as that of any of its competitors during the last decade, and everyone was happy. Even Wall Street's top analysts no longer aimed anything but softball questions at Preston for fear that their investment bank would be shut out of some major transaction Integrated Products might execute. Preston was known to be vindictive, even for minor offenses.

Preston had a reputation in the forest products industry as an ultra-tough executive who'd rather run a competitor out of business than play eighteen holes, golf being the one hobby he loved. Though he didn't have much time for it, and he wasn't very good. So he played fast and loose with his scorecard.

He played fast and loose with his corporate power, too. Three times during Preston's reign, the Securities and Exchange Commission had investigated Integrated Papers for accounting inconsistencies, executive compensation abuses, and insider trading by management. They always threw a lot against the wall, but never uncovered anything that would stick. Preston's smug face would be plastered on the front of every newspaper business section in the country each time the SEC dropped its inquiry. The last time—a year ago—he was smoking a fat cigar in the photo and holding up two fingers in a V for victory when the SEC tried to scurry away without any fanfare, tails tucked between their legs. But Preston would have none of that, wouldn't let them skulk away quietly. He enjoyed winning too much, and he'd never been very good at it. And there were plenty of people in the press corps who liked him, plenty who were willing to put the CEO's arrogant photo in their newspaper as well as run a big article beneath the photo explaining that the SEC hadn't found anything—again—even though they all assumed Preston had probably broken a law or two along the way. He wasn't cordial to many people, but senior members of the business press were among the few exceptions. Preston understood the power of public opinion.

Bruce Preston and Nelson Radcliff had known each other for over forty years, since their days at Yale. They'd played lacrosse together there, though Preston had been a star attackman and Radcliff just a third-line midfielder. Warfield & Stone had done some minor work for one of Integrated Paper's Georgia-based subsidiaries, but Radcliff had never been able to convince Preston to give him the big-fee work for the New York–based parent. At the moment, Warfield & Stone had no mandates with

Integrated Papers because Preston had given all of the company's work to the New York firm his son had recently joined. Which was a sore subject for Radcliff, though he'd never admit it. Don't get mad, get even was Radcliff's motto. Preston and Radcliff had carried a grudging respect for each other through the years, but they'd never been friends. They'd never been enemies, either. But that was about to change.

"So, what is it?" Preston demanded arrogantly. "What's this vitally important piece of information I need to hear about on your seminice yacht? You promised to have me back at the dock in an hour," he reminded Radcliff. "Is all this fanfare to beg for my business, Nelson?" Preston shook his head. "I'm sorry, but you know the deal, everybody does. When my son joined Davis Polk, that was it for the rest of the firms in the city."

Despite the bravado Preston was doling out, it was actually quite a compliment that he'd agreed to this meeting on such short notice, Radcliff knew. No one in the business world—not even Bruce Preston—wanted to get sideways with Warfield & Stone. Specifically, they didn't want to get sideways with Radcliff. Not giving Warfield & Stone business was one thing, but ignoring Radcliff completely was quite another. A few people had, and they'd regretted it.

Hunter Lee would wish he hadn't someday. Radcliff's eyes narrowed and he almost smiled. Last night with Anne had been incredible, and he couldn't wait for their next adventure. That would have to be satisfaction enough until he had time to really focus on his revenge. At some point, he'd put Hunter in the ground. Not everyone lived to regret pissing him off.

"I understand you've taken quite an interest in trees lately," Radcliff began. "I want to know why."

"Well, trees *are* my business," Preston snapped impatiently. "Chopping them down, sawing them up, and turning them into building products, paper, and cardboard. Or hadn't you heard? Look, Nelson, I don't have time to screw around. I've got to be back in Manhattan by three," he said, checking his watch. "I've got a meeting I *cannot* miss."

"Specifically trees in the northwestern United States and western Canada," Radcliff continued. In the blink of an eye he'd snared Preston's full attention. It was obvious, suddenly written all over the other man's face. "You've tried to hide what you're doing by buying all those trees using a network of partnerships and LLCs that don't seem to be related to Integrated Papers, but it didn't take my people long to figure out what you were really doing." Radcliff had put five of his best attorneys at

Warfield & Stone on the case after meeting with Big Bill in Montana, even before Radcliff had touched down back in new York. They'd used their Ivy League connections and come up with the answer almost immediately. "I'm sure you've run afoul of several SEC disclosure rules, and I doubt your shareholders will be very happy about all the money you've wasted just to settle a personal vendetta."

"The SEC's been trying to get me for years, Nelson, and they can't," Preston shot back, "and I'm not worried at all about my shareholders. Why should I be?" He put his hands behind his head and locked his fingers. "As far as a personal vendetta goes, I don't know what you're talking about."

Radcliff had anticipated this response. Preston hadn't ruled Integrated Papers for fourteen years by being easily intimidated. "Well, Bruce, first let's talk about a facility of yours in Georgia. The one outside Athens that's been burying those fifty-five gallon drums of bad, bad stuff in the woods outside town for the last decade."

Preston glared at Radcliff but said nothing.

"Don't screw with me, Bruce," Radcliff warned. "My people have identified a couple of local truckers who are willing to cut a deal if they have to. Guys who've been hauling all that nasty stuff of yours into the woods. It'll destroy the company if it comes to light, if the EPA finds out what's really going on down there. And it'll destroy you in the process, I'll make sure of that."

"You can't use that information!" Preston shouted angrily. "You must have gotten it while you were representing our Georgia sub."

"Prove it."

"You'd be violating attorney-client privilege."

"Prove it," Radcliff repeated. "Prove I didn't find out some other way. Even if you could, which is highly unlikely, it would take years. By that time you'd already be wasting away in a federal prison because I have knowledge that you know what's going on down there. We're talking major criminal offense here for you, Bruce, and I know every important judge in the country. I'll have a conversation with whoever's presiding, a private conversation. Good luck at your trial after that."

For a few moments Preston stared at Radcliff, then his angry glare slowly disintegrated into a beaten gaze. "Why, Nelson?" he asked, his voice barely audible. "Why are you doing this to me? Because I didn't give you business? I can't believe that."

"I have an important client, a *very* important client. His name is Senator William Brule." Radcliff saw Preston swallow hard, saw the connection being made. "He owns a lumber mill in Fort Mason, Montana, and he can't seem to find timber anywhere." Radcliff leaned forward in his chair. "But then I don't need to tell you all of this, do I?"

"I, I . . ."

"This is all because you think Big Bill Brule killed your daughter, Joanna, isn't it, Bruce?" Radcliff pointed at Preston. "You think Big Bill took her to Montana and killed her out there, so you're trying to destroy him. You're trying to drive him into bankruptcy by buying all of his trees so he can't make anything at his mill. That's what this is all about, *isn't it*?"

Tears welled up on Preston's lower lids. "Joanna was my baby, Nelson. She was my baby and she was beautiful. Bill Brule murdered her."

"Careful, Bruce," Radcliff warned. "You have no proof of that."

"He took Joanna to Montana, but she never came back to Washington. He killed her in Montana. My baby's still out there somewhere."

"She was seen in Washington by several people after the weekend in question," Radcliff countered. "Her ATM card was used in Washington, D.C., after that weekend, too. Senator Brule had nothing to do with Joanna's disappearance," Radcliff said firmly. "You know it, I know it."

"I know Bill Brule's a monster, a God damn monster. He can manipulate anything. He had people arrange all that stuff in Washington for him. Her supposedly being seen and the ATM card being used, I mean." Preston lifted his eyes to meet Radcliff's, then the realization set in. "He had *you*—"

"Don't say that," Radcliff hissed, "don't even *think* it. Not unless you're prepared to go to jail. I'll call my friends at the EPA as soon as you leave. I'm warning you."

"You have daughters, Nelson. He murdered my only one. Think how you'd feel."

"The good thing about this country is that we can all have an opinion," Radcliff retorted. "It may not count for much in the end, but at least we can have it." He hesitated. He wanted Preston completely focused on what he was about to say. "Now listen, Bruce, and listen good. You'll sell the timber you've got in all of those partnerships and LLCs to the Brule Lumber Mill, and you'll sell as much as Big Bill wants to buy. You'll do it at a big discount, too. If you don't, I'll make sure you spend the rest of your life in jail. I've done the same thing to four other men, so don't screw with me, Bruce." Radcliff smiled. "Maybe you should visit them in jail and see how they're feeling these days." His expression turned steely. "The Georgia thing is the tip of the iceberg, Bruce. I've got other things on you that are worse than that. You want to hear what they are?"

Preston shook his head, then put his face in his hands. "No, I don't."

"One more thing," Radcliff said, holding up a finger. "Anything happens to Bill Brule or me and you pay." He paused to allow the warning time to sink in. "Do you understand?"

"Yes."

"As long as you play ball with us, you'll be running Integrated Papers for years to come."

Preston let out a long, defeated breath. "Thank you."

Radcliff leaned back in his chair and smiled. "See, I told you you'd thank me when this was all over."

55

ROD TIP UP, rod tip up!" shouted Paul. "You've gotta keep the line tight or that fish'll break you off, Griz."

Hunter lifted the tip of the fly rod as the rainbow trout came flying from the water, soaring several feet above the surface. Higher than it had in any of its previous jumps.

"Now down! *Jesus,* what a fish! Get that tip down when he jumps like that!"

"Make up your mind!" Hunter shouted back, trying to stay calm. But it was tough. He could feel the adrenaline pumping through his body.

After the first jump, Paul had quickly estimated the weight of the gleaming silver, red, and green fish at nine pounds. Hunter had been naive enough to yell if that was anywhere near a Montana state record. Paul had laughed and muttered something about thirty-three-pounds-and-not-even-close-but-still-a-great-fish-for-a-river, but Hunter still wanted to land this fish badly. *Real* badly. It was by far the biggest trout he'd ever seen. At least, at the end of his line.

"Now back up! Get the rod tip back up!" Paul shouted. "Come on, come on. There you go. Good man. Lean left, lean left, get him away from that rock!"

Hunter's hands were shaking when they finally netted the fish in the shallows. He'd felt as if he was standing over a four-foot putt to win the Masters, about to give a speech in front of ten thousand people, and waiting for a cop to get to the side of the car after being been pulled over for doing ninety in a forty all rolled into one. He was so worried the fish might get away at the very end and dash the experience. The last few seconds of the fight had been the most nerve-racking, and he had to admit he was damn glad when Paul shoved a small bottle of whiskey at him as they knelt in a foot of cool water gazing down at the gorgeous fish inside the net's wooden frame. Paul always seemed to be prepared for every situation out here. The way Hunter tried to always be prepared for every situation in court.

Paul patted Hunter on the shoulder. "That's a hell of a fish, my man, probably one of the biggest fish in this entire river. These things get the size of salmon in lakes, but not in the rivers. Guys come to Montana for years and years and never catch a fish like that on a dry fly."

"They don't have you as a guide, either," Hunter said appreciatively, taking a healthy swallow of whiskey. It burned when it hit his stomach, but at least he didn't feel as if he was going to throw up in the next ten seconds. Strat would have enjoyed knowing that, knowing that his little brother could finally stomach a swig of hard liquor without gasping. It was too bad Strat wasn't here to see this fish, too. He would have been damn proud.

"Are you going to keep it?" Paul asked. "Put it on your wall? Most guys would."

Hunter glanced down at the heaving fish. He shook his head. "Nah. Let's let him go. Like you said, maybe I can catch him again someday. When he's even bigger."

Paul smiled approvingly, then pulled a cigar and a lighter from his shirt pocket and handed them to Hunter. "Go enjoy yourself, Griz. I'll release it."

Hunter took a picture of the fish with his cell phone, then went and sat down on a smooth stone at the river's edge and lighted the cigar while he watched Paul revive the fish. As he took the first puff, he glanced around. The place Paul had brought him to today was like so much else of western Montana: an isolated area of pine trees, blue sky, and a sparkling-clean river full of beautiful trout lurking beneath the surface just waiting to be caught. He had twenty million dollars in the bank and no strings attaching him to anyone or anything. He could have lived anywhere in the world he wanted to: New York, London, Paris, back in Virginia. But he'd chosen here, and he had absolutely no regrets. It was all coming together, and he had one person in the world to thank for that: Strat. Without Strat pushing him to come to Fort Mason, he'd be back in some apartment in Connecticut, miserable. Probably thinking a lot of the same things Carl Bach was thinking in that hotel corridor before pulling the trigger.

Paul held out his hand and they shook as he sat down on a rock beside the one Hunter was sitting on. "Congratulations, Griz, that was one hell of a fish. You worked him great. I couldn't have done better myself."

"Thanks." Paul hadn't made a single cast today, hadn't even put his fly rod together. It had been all about showing a friend a great time. "I appreciate you bringing me here. I know it's one of your favorite spots." He hesitated. "I just appreciate you letting me fish with you."

"Don't mention it."

Hunter laughed. "And thanks for taking that detour to Dale Callahan's place this morning. I know what you were doing there."

Paul shrugged, a smug expression coming to his face. "What do you mean?"

"You were letting him know I'd stayed with Zoe last night."

Paul took out a cigar and lighted up, too. "It wouldn't surprise me if he knew that before we came by. But we put an exclamation point on the subject, didn't we?" Paul said, laughing loudly, too.

Hunter saw a puzzled look come to Paul's face. "What is it?" He assumed Paul was going to tell him something more about Dale and Zoe's relationship, but didn't know how to say it. "Come on."

Paul picked up a stone off the ground and examined it. "I always thought Dale had more dogs than that."

"What do you mean?"

"There were only five dogs in his barn today. Last time I was out there he had at least fifteen, and I heard he was up to twenty at one point. Not even counting pups." Paul tossed the stone into the river. "Did you see all those empty cages?"

"Yeah, but so—" Hunter's cell phone went off, interrupting the question. He stood up quickly and dug it from his pocket. It was Zoe. He motioned to Paul that he wouldn't be long, then walked down the bank a little ways. "Hi, honey."

"Hello, there, Hunter."

God, he loved her voice.

"Having any luck?" she asked.

"Yeah." He quickly related the story of the fight with the big trout. "Paul really knows what he's doing. The thing was huge."

"Take a picture of it for me."

"I did. I'll show it to you—"

"Hey, Griz!"

Hunter whipped around at the sound of Paul's voice. "What?"

"We gotta go!" Paul yelled, holding up his cell phone. "There's a fire and it's close to here. Come on."

56

B IG BILL WAS sitting in his office at the mill and he had the phone
to his ear before the first ring ended. "Hello."

"It's me," came the calm voice at the other end of the line.

It was Nelson Radcliff. "Yes?" Big Bill could hear his own voice shaking. He hated showing such obvious weakness, but there was nothing he
could do about it. "What happened?" he asked breathlessly.

"No problem. The shock and awe strategy worked perfectly. Your
enemy won't be a problem anymore, I assure you. He doesn't want to
go to prison. In fact, you should be contacted later today if you haven't
already—"

"We have."

The Brule Lumber Mill's purchasing manager had stopped by Big
Bill's office fifteen minutes ago to report that he'd gotten eight calls in the
last hour from people representing limited partnerships who wanted to
sell timber. At cheap prices, too. He had reported that trucks would be
rolling into the mill within twenty-four hours, and that the timber inventory would quickly be back up to its normal ninety day level with as much
more good quality timber out there as they could possibly use.

"I appreciate everything."

"Of course." Radcliff hesitated. "It was as you thought. Your enemy
believed his piece of jewelry was still out there with you. It was a personal
agenda."

Big Bill swallowed hard, anticipating Radcliff's next question: Did you kill Joanna Preston? Radcliff had never asked that question, but Big Bill expected it now, now that the issue was settled. In code, of course, but an awful question either way.

But it never came. Nelson Radcliff was far too savvy to dig into a personal issue like that. Far too savvy to put his client, a United States senator, in the uncomfortable position of having to lie to his lawyer. Instead, Big Bill got a thank you.

"Once again, we appreciate the referral," Radcliff spoke up, referring to the Bridger Railroad case. "We were just happy to be of help in return."

Radcliff was always formal on the phone, and he never used names. He was the consummate professional, which Big Bill had never appreciated more than at this very moment. "One hand washes the other."

"That communication you sent helped us a great deal," Radcliff went on, this time refererring to the memo Hunter Lee had used against Carl Bach in court to nail the verdict door shut. "I might not have thanked you enough for sending it along when we last met."

Big Bill appreciated that. In fact, Radcliff hadn't thanked him enough for getting that memo from the files of the Bridger Railroad. It hadn't been easy. "You're certainly welcome."

"All right, well, good-bye."

"Good-bye."

Big Bill hung up the phone, then leaned back in his chair and gazed up at the ceiling. Everything was coming together. He'd taken a terrible risk getting so deeply involved in the Bridger Railroad case, but he'd done it because the person he'd done it for had taken a great risk for him. He'd done it for a man who hated George Drake as much as one man can hate another man. For a friend who'd done Big Bill a great service not long ago, the service of a lifetime, really. A man who'd saved Big Bill's career, his reputation, his life.

The last piece of the favor would be to rip the contract to transport firefighters from hot spot to hot spot away from Bridger Air, and that part of the plan was already in motion. The Forest Service would be letting Drake know next week that the contract with Bridger Air would not be renewed after this fire season. The Forest Service would be letting Drake know that they would be awarding a new, bigger contract to another air cargo concern. A start-up company based in Billings, Montana.

Bridger Air would dive into a tailspin after that, because without the Forest Service contract the company wasn't a viable entity. Yes, Drake had bought himself a little bit of time for the railroad with the cash injection from Bridger Air, but it would only be a matter of time before the railroad would implode as well. Two hundred million dollars of debt was just too much for it to bear, especially with constant pressure raining down from the Interstate Commerce Commission and the National Transportation Safety Board that Big Bill would have applied. Within a year—two at most—George Drake would be penniless, and it didn't bother Big Bill one bit. For him it was simply about power and who had more of it. And about paying back his debt to a man who had saved *everything*.

Of course, he and Radcliff were going to profit from the contract being taken away from Bridger Air and awarded to that new company in Billings. Just as he and Radcliff were already profiting from the forest fires torching Montana this summer in another way. Nothing in life came free. Especially not the connections and the influence Big Bill was making available.

He turned in his leather chair and gazed out the wide window behind his desk at his now safe and secure lumber mill. Then at the Lassiter River glimmering in the distance beneath the afternoon sun. Jeremy was dead, but he felt no sorrow. In fact, it was good riddance.

Big Bill grimaced. He just needed to find those folders Jeremy had taken from the file cabinets. Then, and only then, would he feel completely safe.

57

"OME ON, GRIZ, hurry!"

"I'm hurrying already, I'm hurrying."

Hunter struggled up the ridge behind Paul as fast as he could, breathing hard, sucking in smoky air as the slope turned steeper. He was in damn good shape for a man in his late thirties, but he was no match for Paul. Paul seemed almost superhuman as he took long, effortless strides up the needle-covered forest floor, even with that backpack he always carried into the forest. Fortunately for Hunter, he stopped to get his bearings.

Twenty minutes ago Paul had picked up an emergency text message on his cell phone alerting him that the Fort Mason Fire Jumpers had deployed a DC-3 and a crew of twelve. Their mission was to extinguish a ground fire that had been spotted not far from where Hunter and Paul were fishing, but the blaze had burst out of control only minutes after the crew had hurled themselves from the plane. Unexpected morning gusts had kicked up and force-fed the fire a dose of potent flame steroids. A Forest Service ranger had witnessed the eruption from his tower atop a mountain and phoned in to Fort Mason to tell them what had happened. The blaze was suddenly too big for the Jumpers to handle. That was obvious even from the ranger's post two miles away, and someone needed to tell the Jumpers to clear out immediately. But for some reason Fort Mason couldn't raise the team leader on his IC, so the crew had no idea of the danger that was coming at them.

And one of the crew members was Mandy Winslow.

After shouting good-bye to Zoe, Hunter and Paul had sprinted from the river back to Paul's Explorer, raced down a county road to a dirt logging road, then bounced along it until Paul had skidded to a stop in the middle of nowhere and yelled for Hunter to follow him into the forest. Which brought them to where they were now.

"This way!" Paul shouted after only a few seconds rest.

Hunter took a deep breath, raised up off his knees and followed Paul deeper into the woods. The smell of smoke was growing more pungent, and he was thinking about what he'd read in those books Strat had suggested he read. How megablazes could tear along at speeds of fifty miles an hour, pack temperatures of up to fifteen hundred degrees, and change direction on a dime. At this point Hunter had complete trust in Paul, at least as long as Paul was thinking clearly. But when a woman a man loved was in harm's way, sometimes that man didn't think clearly. Hunter had seen a wild look in Paul's eyes as they were bouncing along the dirt road. A look that told him Paul might not be thinking at all. At the very least, not about safety.

Once again Paul stopped, giving Hunter time to catch up. Now Hunter could begin to see the smoke, not just smell it. He could see the slinky mist curling around and through the trees like long lithe fingers reaching insidiously into any crack or crevice they wanted to explore.

"You go that way," Paul ordered, pointing off to the left across the ridge, his eyes darting through the trees. "I'll go right." He pulled out a knife and quickly carved several Xs at eye level on the trunk of the closest ponderosa Pine so that the markings were visible from every direction. "Go five minutes straight out at a fast pace and make sure you look up in the trees as you go. Look for people in the branches, look for parachutes, and yell the whole time. Let people know you're around. We've got to get them out of here. If you haven't seen anything at the five-minute mark, sprint straight back here. If I'm not here within two minutes of that, go back down the ridge the way we came. Run as fast as you can back to the Explorer and get out of here. The keys are on top of the back right tire. Got it?"

"Yeah, I got it."

"And don't come looking for me," Paul said fiercely. "Under no circumstances should you come looking for me. Do you understand that?"

Hunter was bent over at the waist again, hands on his knees trying to get his breath.

"Hunter, did you hear what I—"

"I heard you," Hunter snapped, irritated. He didn't have any skin in the game, he wasn't a Fire Jumper, but he was here trying to help. He didn't need to be ordered around like some private first class. "I heard you already."

"Sorry." Paul patted Hunter on the shoulder, then waved in the direction he'd told Hunter to go. "If you see fire or hear a roar while you're out there, run back down the ridge immediately. Right from where you are, okay? Don't try to be a hero, because the fire won't run away like that grizzly bear did out at Sullivan Gorge. Any questions?"

Hunter shook his head. "Nope."

"You're a good man, Hunter."

"Thanks."

"All right, go."

A second later Hunter was alone in the middle of a huge Montana forest.

Two hundred yards from the point he and Paul had parted ways, the treetops directly above Hunter suddenly swayed violently against a strong gust. As the gust abated, Hunter heard a noise that made the hairs on the back of his neck stand straight up. It sounded like the wail of a ghost, like a poltergeist trapped between the land of the living and the lair of the dead. A low moan that struck such an eerie chord inside him that goose bumps rose like mini–mountain chains all over his body. For several seconds he stood statuelike in the vastness of the forest, trying to figure out what he was hearing. Then, as the moan grew louder, he realized what it was. The fire was coming directly at him down the ridge, and the moan was turning into a roar.

"Oh, my God," he muttered, coming to a halt on the pine needles as the realization hit him. "This is crazy."

But as Paul's warning about getting out immediately if Hunter saw a flame front went through his mind, out of the corner of his eye, Hunter noticed someone dangling from a tree, feet kicking wildly. The person hung ten feet off the ground and was wearing a tan jump suit and a helmet with a wire mesh face mask. It had to be a Fire Jumper. As Hunter looked higher, he could see the Jumper's arms snared tightly in the ropes of a parachute snagged in the limbs above. Without help, this person didn't stand a chance of surviving.

"Hunter!" the person hanging from the tree shouted suddenly. *"Hunter, it's Mandy.* I can't move my arms. Hurry!"

Christl Hunter's heart almost exploded in his chest. It was Mandy, Paul's Mandy. He was still fifty feet away from her and the flames were closing in. He could already feel heat on his face, hear the roar growing louder. The fire was going to engulf the tree she was hanging from in a matter of minutes, if not seconds. It wasn't clear at all to him that he could get her down before the flames swept past, probably killing them both.

"Hunter!" she screamed desperately. *"Hunter, please help me!"*

He took a step toward her, then heard another panicked cry from behind, in the direction he'd just come from. He whirled around. Fifty feet behind him and higher up the slope there was another Fire Jumper entangled in a parachute. This Jumper lay on the ground encased by the chute as if in a cocoon, and it looked as if there was blood on the cloth. Somehow Hunter hadn't spotted this member of the crew as he'd raced through the woods.

"Hunter!" Mandy screamed again. *"Help me! I'm gonna burn! Please don't let me burn!"*

For several terrible seconds, Hunter gazed at the figure struggling on the ground, acutely aware that he probably couldn't save both this Jumper and Mandy, conscious of the fact that he was probably about to make a life-and-death decision. He swallowed hard, then spun around and raced for Mandy. He was to the tree she hung from and up to her in seconds. The heat was already stifling even though the flames were still half a football field away.

"Hurry!" she shouted above the roar of the megablaze racing toward them. "I don't want to die."

Frantically, Hunter undid the clips holding her to the harness, then ripped away two ropes binding her hands together above her head and she dropped to the ground like a rag doll. He followed her down and a second later he was beside her on the needles covering the forest floor. He scrambled to his feet, pulled Mandy up alongside him, then, as she ripped off her helmet, he helped her out of the unwieldy jump suit, because she wouldn't make much time wearing the thing. Fortunately, the needle layer was so thick in here it had been like jumping onto a mattress and neither of them was hurt.

"Come on!" she yelled when she was down to her boots, nylon shirt, and pants, grabbing his hand and dragging him down the ridge. "We've got to get out of here."

"No!" Hunter shouted, pointing back across the ridge toward the way he'd come. "There's someone else over there."

"Then go, go, go!" she yelled, releasing his arm. "I'll follow you."

As they ran, Hunter marveled at Mandy's courage. She'd just been hanging helplessly from a tree, probably convinced she was about to die. But here she was, going after a crew member with no regard for her own safety as the flames climbed skyward all around her.

As they came around a thick stand of pine trees, they met a wall of flames seventy feet high. Out of reflex, they threw their hands up to protect their faces and turned away.

"Jesus!" It felt as if they'd suddenly been hurled into an oven, Hunter thought to himself. "The guy was right there," he shouted, arm covering his eyes as he turned toward the flames again, stabbing into the air with his other hand, "right where the fire is now."

Out of nowhere a massive gust blew *up* the slope, from the opposite direction the wind had been blowing, knocking Hunter and Mandy to the ground onto their stomachs. As he looked up, Hunter saw a horrible sight. The gust had momentarily blown the flame front back up the ridge about fifty feet and a blackened figure was staggering across the moonscape toward them, arms outstretched.

"Oh, my God," Mandy screamed. "That's got to be—"

Her words were drowned out as the gust faded and the flame front roared back down the slope to reclaim the territory it had temporarily lost, pushing so intensely hot a blast of air at Hunter and Mandy that they were forced to bury their faces in the pine needles. For several terrifying seconds, Hunter felt sure he was experiencing exactly what he'd read about in those books—being incinerated by a flame front that was moving so fast and burning so hot there was no escape. It felt as if the shirt on his back was on fire and his skin was melting.

But then a wave of cooler air rushed across him, and he popped his head up. The fire had retreated again, up the slope and to the right. He and Mandy staggered to their feet and sprinted in the direction they'd seen the figure. As they closed in on the spot, Hunter saw the poor man sprawled on the forest floor on his back, writhing in terrible pain, screaming for mercy. The man was burned from head to toe, blackened like some forgotten piece of barbecued chicken that had been left on a grill too long. He still wore his helmet but the jump suit had been completely burned off his body and his skin was melting before their eyes. As he reached toward them, skin peeled away from his forearms and dripped to the smoking forest floor.

"Holy shit!"

Hunter and Mandy whirled around. Paul was standing behind them.

He forced his way between them and knelt beside the stricken Jumper. "It's Duff Sparks!" he shouted above the roar of the fire, which was roaring back at them again. "My, God, it's Duff."

"We've got to get out of here, Paul!" Mandy shouted back, pointing at the flames, which were a hundred feet high now. "It's coming back."

"Don't let the flames get me again," Duff gasped feebly, blood dripping from his charcoaled lips and cheeks. Even though he was still wearing his helmet, the flames had reached inside and burned his beard completely off. "Please don't," he begged.

Paul's gaze darted from Duff to the flames to Mandy to Hunter, then he reached beneath Duff and tried to pick him up, but Duff screamed in pain. Paul stood up quickly. The flames were only thirty feet away and the treetops were bending over wildly against the gusts. "Even if we could get him out of here, he'll die in the ICU! I've seen this before." Paul shook his head sadly. "The poor guy's in so much damn pain you can't even imagine. He's got absolutely no chance of—"

Hunter grabbed Paul, spun him around, unzipped the backpack, reached inside, grabbed the .44 Magnum Paul always carried into the forest, knelt beside Duff, pressed the barrel to the man's charred skull. And fired.

"Now let's get the hell out of here!" Hunter shouted. "Come on!"

58

THE TWO YOUNG boys moved cautiously through the tall weeds growing along the Lassiter riverbank, toward the large, unusual-looking object they'd noticed swirling slowly around and around in the tail-end shallows of the large pool they were fishing. They'd noticed the object from the opposite shore and had to swim across the river to see what it was. Now that they were close, they wished they hadn't come to investigate.

When they were both certain it was a human body that was swirling around face-down in the shallows, they shouted, turned, bumped into each other, stumbled a few steps, then raced away as fast as they could. Neither one of them had ever seen a dead body. It was an experience they would never forget.

Part III

59

HUNTER SAT IN an uncomfortable metal chair across the desk from Dan Carson, the sheriff of Fort Mason. Carson was in his midfifties and of average height with a gray crew cut and a naturally inquisitive glare. He'd been Fort Mason's sheriff for the last twenty-two years, and in the last two elections he'd run unopposed. He was a modest man, the first one in line to tell you that if you were to put him in a big city, he'd be entirely overmatched as a law enforcement officer, a fish out of water. But, in the wilds of Montana, he knew exactly what he was doing. And he wouldn't be the one to tell you the good side of that story, Strat had made clear to Hunter the day on the Lassiter when they'd first discussed what Strat was doing out here in his spare time. The state cops, the county boys, the Fire Jumpers and everyone in town swore by Carson. They all had complete confidence that he was a man who could handle any situation this area could throw at him. According to Strat, Sheriff Carson was the personification of Montana: tough but fair.

On one side of Hunter sat Paul, on the other sat Mandy.

Carson leaned back and glanced around his starkly furnished office. It was an office that didn't have much character, didn't have many decorations, because, as he liked to say, if it did, he might be tempted to spend too much time in it. As far as he was concerned, sitting in his office wasn't what the good people of Fort Mason were paying him to do.

"So it was a mercy killing?" Carson asked. "That's what you're telling me?"

"Exactly," Paul answered firmly. "I was right there when Hunter—"

"Let him tell me, Paul." Carson pointed at Paul, then at Hunter. "Go ahead, son."

"Duff was dying," Hunter answered in a hollow voice. Watching Carl Bach shoot himself had been awful, but putting Duff Sparks out of his misery had been ten times worse, even though Hunter knew he'd done the right thing. "He didn't have long to live when I shot him. A few minutes at most."

"I thought you were a lawyer, Hunter."

"I am."

"Then how—"

"My mother worked as a nurse in a hospital burn unit for a year while I was a teenager. Every few weeks she took my brother and me to see those people. She said it was a good lesson in appreciating what we had, in how lucky we were even though we didn't have much money. Duff was worse off than anybody I ever saw there, much worse, and some of them were in so much agony. That's the reason I couldn't watch him suffer. Believe me, Duff wanted to die." Hunter took a deep breath. "I hear you're a good man, Sheriff. I've heard that from a lot of people. If you'd seen Duff on the ground in front of you burned so bad his skin was dripping off his arms like wax off a candle, you'd have done the same thing I did. I couldn't have left him there like that, I couldn't have left him lying there thinking he might have gotten run over by that fire again."

Carson glanced at Paul. "Is that what happened?"

"Yes. And if we'd tried to carry Duff out, we all might have died. The fire was coming at us real fast."

"That's true," Carson agreed. "I don't know if you heard, but the fire chased you three all the way down that ridge. It got to the road your truck was parked on only a few seconds after you got out of there."

"Plus," Paul kept going, "Duff probably would have died if we'd tried to carry him out of there anyway. I tried picking him up, but he couldn't handle it."

Mandy put her hand on Hunter's knee. "Hunter saved my life, Sheriff. He got me down out of the tree my chute was hung up in. If he hadn't, I would have died, too. He's a hero."

Carson's chair creaked as he rose up and moved around to the front of his desk. "Well, Hunter," he said, "I guess you're a hero to a lot of people around here."

Hunter shrugged. "Why?"

Carson shook his head. "You got my nephew's family a hell of a lot of money over in Bozeman a couple of weeks ago at that trial. I don't know how you did it, but I appreciate it. My nephew's little boy is going to be blind in one eye for the rest of his life, but at least he's not going to have to worry about working." The sheriff stuck his hand out. "I've wanted to shake your hand ever since you nailed George Drake."

"Thanks."

"We're gonna need to have an official investigation," Carson said hesitantly, as if he felt bad for having to tell Hunter that. "There's nothing I can do about it."

"I understand."

"One bullet to the head," Carson said. "That's what we're gonna find, right?"

Hunter nodded. "Yes."

"Okay, well—" Sheriff Carson interrupted himself when there was a loud knock. He moved quickly to the office door, opened it, and listened to his deputy whisper a few words. After the deputy had turned away, Carson closed the door again and moved back to where Hunter sat. He leaned down and put his hand on Hunter's shoulder. "You need to come out to the river with me." He glanced at Paul. "You should come, too."

Paul nodded. "Okay."

Hunter glanced into Carson's eyes and suddenly he had a very bad feeling about what the sheriff was going to say. He was just glad Paul had agreed to come along because suddenly he felt closer to Paul than to anyone else in the world.

60

HUNTER STOOD IN the tall grass on the south bank of the Lassiter River not far from the spot where he and Strat had fished that day a couple of weeks ago. As Paul moved to Hunter's shoulder, he watched Sheriff Carson kneel and carefully remove the sheet from the corpse's face. According to Carson, there weren't any signs of decomposition, so the body hadn't been in the water long. Hunter barely felt Paul's hand come to his shoulder as the sheet slipped over Strat's wet, dark hair, past his open eyes, then down the skin of his ashen cheeks.

When Carson looked up, Hunter nodded. "That's him," he said almost inaudibly, "that's my brother."

"Sorry, Hunter," said Carson compassionately, pulling the sheet back over Strat's face. "I had to get a positive ID from you."

"I know."

"He probably slipped on a rock or something, then those waders filled up in a heartbeat and dragged him to the bottom." Carson shook his head. "It's such a shame, but it happens like this at least once a summer. People wear these old-style loose waders, and they're at the bottom of the river before they know it with no way of making it back to the surface before they drown." Carson grimaced "I really am sorry."

Hunter didn't hear the sheriff's words. He couldn't. He couldn't hear anything at this moment. He'd just lost the only person he'd ever really trusted.

61

THE DRIVER COULDN'T figure this one out. Sure the wind was howling through Hell's Gate tonight. There probably wasn't a better wind tunnel in all of Montana with this strong, steady twenty-five-mile-an-hour breeze blowing directly out of the east like it was. Even though there wasn't a lot of dead timber in the eastern Fort Mason Valley, with the intensity and direction of this wind it wouldn't matter. With such a solid and constant flow of oxygen roaring through the narrow gorge, the fire would undoubtedly become a megablaze before it reached the east end of town, which was little more than five miles away.

And that was where the disconnect lay for him. Everything between Hell's Gate and Fort Mason would burn. It seemed like the last place on earth the boss would want to burn.

Then it hit him, and he smiled. The boss was one smart son of a bitch. Of course, that's why he was the boss.

Fifteen minutes later the fire was racing toward Fort Mason, already several hundred yards wide.

62

As Hunter raced along the darkened road in Strat's old pickup, he tried Zoe on her cell phone for the third time in the last few minutes. The call went straight to voicemail—again—but there was no other way to reach her because she didn't have a land line into her house. Like so many people these days, she just used her cell phone.

"Damn it," he muttered, feel himself starting to panic. He couldn't lose Strat *and* Zoe in one day.

Another wave of emotion rolled toward him as the ghostly image of his brother's open but unseeing eyes came to him again, but he managed to keep control, managed to push the emotion back down. It had only been a few hours since he'd seen Strat's body on the riverbank, so it was still impossible for him to fully accept that his brother was gone forever, still impossible for him to deal with the fact that this wasn't a nightmare he'd awaken from sooner or later. When that moment came, when his mind finally allowed him to acknowledge that he'd never see Strat again, it would be one of the worst moments of his life. He just hoped he could hold himself together for a few more hours.

"Jesus!" He swerved to avoid a raccoon walking along the side of the road. He hadn't spotted the thing until the last second because the pickup's right headlight wasn't working. Once again, emotion welled up inside him. That was Strat, *so* Strat. There were always so many things in his life that needed fixing, that he needed to finish, it seemed like he could never catch up. But it never seemed to bother him the way it would have bothered Hunter. Strat could handle chaos. For Hunter, that had always been one of his brother's most endearing and impressive qualities. "Don't think about him," Hunter whispered to himself as he whipped into Zoe's driveway and slammed on the brakes beside her BMW. "Not now, not yet."

The pungent and unmistakable smell of forest fire rushed to Hunter's nostrils as he climbed out of the pickup. There was an orange glow off to the east, and based on everything he'd just heard over the radio, it wasn't going to take long for that wall of flames to get here. As he sprinted to Zoe's front door, a fire truck and a state police cruiser whipped past, sirens wailing, emergency lights flashing.

Her house was directly in the blaze's path.

"Zoe!" he shouted, banging on the door. *"Zoe, open up!"* Her car was here, but she could be out with someone. He hated to think about who that someone might be. "Zoe!" He was about to break the door down when the porch light flickered on and the door swung open. Suddenly she was standing in front of him, wearing an old shirt and jeans, rubbing sleep from her eyes. Relief swept through him. She was safe now that she was with him, and he stepped through the doorway and gave her a quick hug. "I'm glad to see you," he said loudly as more emergency vehicles rushed by the house.

"What's going on?" she asked, almost losing her balance as she stepped back from their embrace. "What time is it?"

Her pupils seemed very big, and that light that usually shone so brightly in them was gone. She hadn't even seemed to notice those emergency vehicles going by, either. "It's after eleven." For an instant he thought about telling her what had happened to Strat, but that might be the moment his emotional walls collapsed, and he couldn't deal with that now.

"I wasn't feeling well . . . so I went to bed around . . ." Her voice trailed off. "I don't even remember what time it—"

"Listen," he broke in impatiently, "about an hour ago a fire broke out below Hell's Gate. It's going to be here soon if they can't stop it. You've got to throw some stuff in a bag and get going. I tried calling you, but it went straight to voicemail every time."

"A fire?" she asked groggily "Coming this way?"

It was almost as if she couldn't comprehend what he was saying. "Yeah. I tried calling Dale Callahan, but I couldn't get through to him, either." He hated thinking like the old suspicious-of-everyone-and-

everything litigator, but he half-suspected he might find Callahan upstairs in Zoe's bed. "I know he lives out this way, too, and . . . and I was
worried about him. He's alone and his place is right in the way of this
fire. Like yours is. I've heard it's gotten big in a hurry."

"I think Dale's in Billings tonight," she mumbled, still rubbing her
eyes. "I . . . I think someone told me that."

Zoe seemed out of it, as if she was drugged and it had been a big dose
of whatever she'd taken. "Did you take sleeping pills, honey?"

She shook her head. "No, I just started feeling awful around—"

"What about Dale's dogs?" Hunter asked, snapping his fingers. It had
just occurred to him that those dogs they'd seen this morning might be
trapped in their cages with the flames closing in. "Christ, I can't let them
burn, I've gotta go get them. At least let them out of their cages so they
can run away."

"They're fine, I'm sure."

"What do you mean? How can you be sure?"

Zoe ran a hand through her hair, then shrugged. "I mean, I'm sure
Dale would get them out if he heard there was a fire coming. Wouldn't
he?"

"You just said he was in Billings."

"Yeah, but I—"

"Throw some stuff in a bag," Hunter called over his shoulder as he
sprinted back to the pickup. "I'll be right back." He heard her calling to
him as he jumped in and slammed the door shut, but he paid no attention. This wouldn't take long, he'd be back in less than ten minutes.

Moments later he swerved around the corner into Callahan's driveway, then jammed the accelerator to the floor and raced toward the house,
leaning on the horn. As he skidded to a stop and pushed open the pickup
door, he held up. Something covering his shirt and pants had caught his
attention when the vehicle's interior overhead light had automatically
flipped on, and as he rose up off the seat, he suddenly realized how quiet
it was. Those dogs he and Paul had seen this morning should have been
barking like mad. They'd been barking their damn heads off this morning
and Paul hadn't been anywhere near as noisy when he'd pulled up in his
Explorer. Well, maybe Callahan had gotten them out, just as Zoe had said
he would.

After Hunter jumped out, he turned so he was facing back into the
light coming from the pickup and looked down. The front of his shirt and

pants were covered with short, light-colored hairs. Dog hairs. yellow Lab hairs. He'd hugged Zoe at her door a few minutes ago. "Christ," he whispered, reaching for the dashboard and rummaging through the crap on it until he found Strat's cell phone. His hands shook as he pushed several buttons, searching for his brother's list of incoming calls. When he found it and spied the first number, he nearly dropped the phone. Everything was starting to come together.

Strat never wore those old fishing waders that had been lying in the bed of his pickup. He'd said that a couple of times when they were out on the Lassiter that day. Hunter remembered him saying he never even wore them in winter. It was like a badge of honor not to wear them, like not cutting his Lion's Den cheeseburger in half to eat it. But he'd been wearing them as he lay dead on the banks of the Lassiter River this afternoon. Someone had killed Strat, then made it look like an accident.

Hunter gazed at the last number on the cell phone's inbound call list. It was Zoe's. Suddenly he was betting that Zoe had been an accessory to murder this afternoon. That she'd called him and figured out where he was so someone could track him down. Hunter couldn't prove it yet, but he knew in his heart it had to be true. He was suddenly pretty sure he knew who Zoe was working for as well, though he couldn't prove that yet, either.

But he was going to.

63

AFTER FIGHTING SO many blazes during his career as a Fire Jumper, it seemed to Paul that each of them had a distinct personality. Some were soft—easily beaten down. Others were bullies—they puffed out their chests but if you hit them hard enough and showed no fear, they skulked away with their tails between their legs. But a few were downright mean—you could hit them hard with everything you had and show no fear but they kept coming right at you. He had a feeling this one was going to be like that. It was burning hard and fast with a strong, narrow band of wind behind it. It wasn't wide, but what there was of it was very powerful. If it reached just a few buildings on the east side of town, all of Fort Mason might burn.

Everyone available had been called in to fight the blaze, including every Jumper at the Fort Mason base. Help was on the way from Missoula and Bozeman—by air and ground—but it might not get here in time.

They were cutting a fire line a half mile east of town. There were several homes outside the line—including Zoe's and Callahan's—but the decision had been made by the local fire chief that there wouldn't be time to finish a line outside those homes. A few people had to lose everything so that the majority of homes and property could be saved.

The fire line was already four hundred yards long and ten yards wide and growing longer and wider by the minute as two hundred people raced against time with chainsaws and axes. Fortunately a ranger had spotted the fire early on, only a few minutes after the blaze had started, and the Forest Service had quickly moved in heavy equipment—most important, several big dozers.

Paul was busy extending the north side of the line with his chainsaw, and Mandy was off to his right about thirty yards stripping branches from the trees he'd already cut down. He was keeping a watchful eye on her, trying not to be obvious about it, which was tough.

They'd just finished exchanging a knowing glance when the fire roared through the trees out of nowhere. One second Mandy was there, swinging her axe. The next she was gone—along with three other firefighters—consumed by a wall of flames.

Paul dropped his chainsaw and raced straight for the flames.

64

THE SMOKE WAS so thick now it seemed like dense fog. The fire was closing in, but Hunter didn't care. He was running on fumes, suddenly feeling like maybe today was as good a day to die as any. Zoe was a traitor and Strat was dead. Dead because of her treachery, he was sure. He swallowed hard. It was all his fault. He should never have come to Fort Mason, never have been so selfish about his own happiness. Yes, Strat had pushed him to do it, but he should have known better than to listen to his older brother. He never had before. Why had he started now? If he'd just stayed away, Strat might still be alive.

Hunter knocked on Zoe's door, three loud fists to the wood.

When she opened it, she looked to Hunter as if she were in a trance. Like Strat had looked this afternoon lying on the grass beside the Lassiter. The lights in those pupils he'd come to love seemed permanently extinguished, and it seemed as if she, too, now was looking but not seeing.

"Come with me," he ordered, holding out his hand. "Come with me now."

She nodded and took his hand. "Okay."

65

PAUL HELD HER charred body in his arms and sobbed like he never had. Several Fire Jumpers tried to console him, but he shouted at them to get away, almost pulled his .44 Magnum on one of them. Finally, they left him alone and headed back to the ambulance, resigned to waiting until he was finished saying good-bye to her. However long that might be.

The hastily constructed fire line had stopped the blaze. All of the homes outside the line had burned, but Fort Mason was safe, though at a terrible price. Four people were dead as a result of the fire.

One of them was Mandy Winslow.

66

N ow Hunter understood why it was best to carry a gun in Montana, why Big Bill and Dale Callahan had laughed that day at the Lion's Den about George Drake's probably not even owning one. As Paul had so accurately said: In Montana, you never knew. Which was how this majestic corner of the world bred its charm, and its peril. Carrying a gun was simply the smart thing to do out here.

Hunter stood beside Strat's pickup, searching the darkness for anything unusual that might signal the presence of an enemy—human or animal. He was parked in a small campground a short distance off the road connecting Fort Mason and Gordonsville. Off the road Sheriff Carson had driven down yesterday so Hunter could identify Strat's body, off the road Hunter and Strat had taken that early morning they'd gone fishing a few weeks ago, then driven back on to the Lion's Den to eat those delicious cheeseburgers. It was an isolated cubbyhole of a place to pitch a tent, past the entrance to the Brule Lumber Mill and the Murphy General Store, actually closer to Gordonsville than Fort Mason. Down a dirt road, well back in the woods, and right now Strat's pickup was the only vehicle parked in it. As Hunter scoured the area, he wished like hell he had a gun, wished he'd listened to Big Bill, wished he'd been smarter.

It was a little ahead of five in the morning, so the sun hadn't quite topped the horizon. It was smoky out here, even though it was twenty miles west of town and the fire had attacked from the east. Strong gusts had blown the thick smoke all the way out here, and though Hunter couldn't see the haze from the fire that had almost destroyed Fort Mason, he could smell it. He let out a long breath. It was eerie out here. The dark shadows from the tall, overhanging pine trees were constantly playing tricks on his mind. Every few minutes he thought he saw something lurking out there. He'd take a few quick steps in the other direction, then realize it was a false alarm and pat his chest and his racing heart.

Zoe was passed out on the passenger side of the pickup. Hunter was almost sure at this point that she'd indeed been drugged. He assumed Dale Callahan had given her something to knock her out after she'd helped him load up those last few yellow Labs and some of his personal items. Which was why her clothes had been covered with dog hair when she'd met Hunter at her door last night looking as if she could barely keep her glassy eyes open. Which was how his clothes had gotten hairs on them— they'd gone from her clothes to his when she'd hugged him at the door.

Callahan must have figured that Strat was closing in, or at least suspected he was. He must have been terrified that Strat knew he was the one torching Montana. Torching it because every time a firefighter ate a meal on the line, Callahan Foods made sixty dollars, and with thousands of people fighting a fire, sixty bucks a meal added up to a tidy sum very quickly. At least, that was what he and Paul suspected was going on after they'd spoken an hour ago by phone, what they suspected was going on after listening to each other's new information.

Of course Dale Callahan had been able to get his dogs out of the way of the fire before it destroyed his house and the kennels, Hunter realized. Callahan knew about the blaze because he was the one orchestrating the arson in the Northwest. His house and Zoe's were nothing but smoldering ruins this morning, exactly as he'd intended them to be. His house so no one would suspect him of the crimes, hers so he could kill her without coming under suspicion. He'd drugged her so she wouldn't wake up until it was too late and the fire had finished its ghastly deed—which was to kill a woman who could link him to the arson. Callahan was undoubtedly working with experts who knew exactly how local firefighters would react, who knew exactly where the firefighters would draw their perimeter. He'd played it perfectly.

Almost.

Zoe must have been Callahan's errand girl all along, Hunter figured. She'd probably been the one who'd set Strat up, and she'd always been asking Hunter about what he and Strat were up to. But now she must have outlived her usefulness, or maybe Callahan was turning paranoid. Either way, Callahan must have wanted her gone so she could never testify against him. Which meant one more very important thing to Hunter. Callahan had probably also decided to kill the other Lee brother, that litigator from New York. Callahan would assume that two brothers who were as close as he and Strat were would tell each other everything, and, of course, he was right. Which meant that every movement in the shadows—real or imagined—scared the hell out of Hunter.

Montana and the rest of the Northwest were under siege by Dale Callahan. Not by George Drake, Butch Roman, or Katrina Mason. Dale Callahan was the one setting the forests ablaze, and he was about to double his dividends from doing so—with one very important person's help. According to the information Paul was now in possession of, Callahan was in the final stages of setting up an air cargo company in Billings, and he was about to snatch that lucrative firefighter transportation contract away from George Drake and Bridger Air. The Forest Service would be contacting Drake soon to inform him that his contract wouldn't be renewed after this season. Callahan would be the beneficiary of it all thanks again to that same very important person—Big Bill Brule.

Hunter leaned forward and peered into the darkness as the sound of a vehicle coming through the trees made it to his ears. He hated to admit it, but if this was anyone other than Paul, he was going to take off into the woods and save his own ass. In her physical state Zoe probably wouldn't even be able to walk—much less run—if he could wake her, and Hunter certainly wouldn't get very far very fast carrying her. It wasn't as if he had feelings for her anymore, and there were limits to what a man would do for an enemy even if she was a lost soul like Paul said. But Hunter did have a use for her, so he was going to do his best to save her.

He moved behind the pickup when a pair of headlights came into view, and he hunched down. Now he could see, not just smell, how dense the smoke was as it drifted in front of the vehicle's high beams. A moment later he breathed a heavy sigh of relief when the headlights stopped thirty yards away, then flashed off and on three times in rapid succession as they'd agreed the signal would be. Still, he stayed behind the pickup until he was absolutely certain the oncoming vehicle was an older Ford Explorer and that the person driving it was Paul Brule.

Paul cut the engine and doused the lights, then climbed out and shook Hunter's hand. "Hey, Griz."

"Hey, Paul." Hunter could tell Paul was hurting. He could hear it in the other man's voice, and see it in his eyes, his expression, and his posture. Paul had called an hour ago to arrange this meeting and to give Hunter a boiled-down version of what was in the information Jeremy had gotten, of what was in the folders Jeremy had taken from Big Bill's file cabinet. At the end of the conversation, Paul had told Hunter what had happened to Mandy. "You okay?"

Paul slowly lifted his gaze to meet Hunter's. "No."

For the first time in his life Hunter hugged a man other than Strat. For the first time he wasn't uncomfortable initiating that kind of intimate gesture with someone other than his brother. He and Paul had been through a hell of a lot in a very short time, and he wanted Paul to know he was there for him. For the first few moments, Paul didn't respond, then Hunter felt the emotion pour out as Paul wrapped his arms around Hunter tightly and sobs overtook him.

A full minute later, Paul finally stepped back, hands to his eyes, tears still rolling down his face. "I'm sorry about this," he muttered. "I'm really sorry."

"Don't be." It was all Hunter could do not to break down himself.

"You had a huge loss yourself yesterday," Paul mumbled. "I should be helping you."

"Don't worry about me."

Paul shook his head. "One minute Mandy was there, the next she was gone. Burned so bad I couldn't recognize her face, worse even than Duff Sparks was burned. God, I've never been through anything worse than that in my life."

Hunter felt his stomach start to churn. He couldn't begin to imagine how terrible it must have been for Paul. Other than how pale the body was, at least Strat had looked normal. And Hunter hadn't witnessed Strat's death. Paul had cradled Mandy in his arms until she died. "Jesus," Hunter whispered. "I don't know what to—"

"My father's a murderer," Paul interrupted, his voice still shaking. "He killed a young woman named Joanna Preston out in the woods on our family's property north of town. He'd brought her out here from Washington. She was pretty and she was young." Paul gritted his teeth. "I was riding one of our horses that day, and I was up on a ridge overlooking where they were. My dad had no idea I was even on the property because I got to his place after he and Joanna went for their walk, after they'd left the house. I saw the whole thing happen." Paul's voice was almost inaudible. "My father tried to come on to her, tried to force himself on her. When she fought back, he grabbed a rock and slammed her head with it. She didn't move after that." He swallowed hard. "And I rode away, Hunter. I just took off into the woods." He put his hands to his face and shook his head sadly. "Everybody thinks I'm this great guy, this hero, but I let my father kill a woman and I didn't do anything about it. I let him get away with it." He shook his head again. "I can't do that anymore even if he did save my life twice, even if he is my father." Paul shut his eyes tightly. "He murdered Mandy last night, and I can't let him murder anyone else."

Hunter stared at Paul. "You mean he killed Mandy because he helped Callahan get that contract, and Callahan was responsible for setting the fire, and Mandy was killed fighting it."

"Exactly," Paul said, taking a deep breath. "My brother, Jeremy, left me a voicemail yesterday," he kept going, trying to regain his composure as he wiped moisture from his face. "He was frantic on the message, he sounded scared to death. He'd taken some stuff from Dad's personal files at the mill, and Dad caught him doing it. He said he saw a look in Dad's eyes he'd never seen before. Jeremy took off from the office with the stuff and hid it on the grounds of the mill, told me where it was on the voicemail. I got the stuff, but I haven't heard from Jeremy since he left me the message."

"Well, we better try to find him as fast as—"

"Jeremy's dead, Hunter. There's no reason to look for him."

Paul had said it as if he were delivering a baseball score or a weather report, as matter-of-factly as someone could say something.

"You don't understand my father," Paul continued, moving quickly back to the truck, then returning with two folders he'd grabbed off the dashboard. "He doesn't care about anything but himself. It's all about him, and he doesn't give a damn who he hurts along the way. Anyway, I got the stuff from the mill. Here." He handed the folder to Hunter. "It's all in there like I told you on the phone. How my father helped Dale Callahan get the contract to feed us firefighters while we're on the line, how he's helping Callahan get the new contract to fly firefighters to hot spots around the country, how he's helping Callahan get the contract away from Bridger Air. They're using some dummy corporations to hide the ownership structure, but in return for his help in Washington, my father's getting a nice piece of the action. There's another limited partnership that owns a piece of the holding company and the dox in the folders show that my father owns a big share of that partnership." Paul hesitated. "There's another guy who owns a share of it, too. His name's Nelson Radcliff."

Hunter's eyes raced to Paul's. *"What?"*

"I thought that might interest you. I remember you telling me that the name of your law firm in New York was Warfield & Stone. Well, apparently, Warfield & Stone has helped with the legal side of this thing, according to the information in the folders. Looks like Radcliff's getting his pound of flesh in all this, too."

Hunter stumbled back against the pickup, shocked by what he'd heard. Mostly by the fact that it was suddenly obvious to him that Radcliff and Big Bill had known each other for quite some time, yet neither of them had mentioned that to him. It seemed obvious to Hunter now how Warfield & Stone had found the Bridger Railroad case. "Why wasn't Big Bill investigated for the girl's disappearance, Paul? Somebody must have known that she came out to Montana with him."

"Her father tried to have him investigated, but there were reports that she'd been seen in Washington, D.C., after the weekend she was here. Plus, her cash card had been used at ATMs near her apartment in D.C. the week after she'd been out here. There were a few questions, but it stayed quiet and everything blew over fast. Nothing about it ever got into the press."

"Why would your father help Dale Callahan so much?" Hunter asked. "Just for the money?"

"Jeremy told me that Dad's taken out some loans through the mill over the past couple of years to make investments. Some high-tech things he thought were sure bets, but turned out to be dogs. So, I guess that's the answer, I guess it was for the money."

"Seems like a lot to risk just to make some cash."

"Yeah, I know."

Hunter gazed down at the ground, thinking hard. "Didn't Dale Callahan and George Drake get into it a few years ago?"

Paul nodded. "Yeah, Callahan used to work for Drake. He was a senior executive over at the Bridger companies. Then Drake fired him, and it got nasty because Callahan had a contract."

"And wasn't there some rumor about Drake's killing one of Callahan's dogs because of all that? A dog Callahan thought was going to be a champion?"

"Yeah," Paul answered, "but I don't know if there's any truth to it."

"Has there ever been any bad blood between your dad and Drake?"

"Not that I know of," Paul replied, reaching behind him and pulling out a nine-millimeter pistol.

Hunter froze.

"Here," Paul said, handing the gun to him. "You might need this."

Suddenly Hunter felt foolish. Paul was giving him the pistol, not aiming it at him. "Thanks," he murmured, taking the gun, instantly liking the feel of it and the way it fit in his hand. Mostly liking how much safer he suddenly felt.

"You know how to use one of those things?"

"I do." The naval officer who'd helped Hunter back in Connecticut had taken him to a local gun range a few times and they'd fired a number of different weapons—including a Glock nine-millimeter. Hunter had actually found it therapeutic to shoot targets, but he'd never thought he'd actually need a gun to protect himself. "Is there a round chambered?"

Paul smiled approvingly. "Nope." He reached into his pants pocket. "Here's an extra clip in case things get really tight."

"Thanks."

"What are you gonna do?" Paul asked.

"I'm going to the Feds up in Missoula."

Paul shook his head. "I wouldn't advise that. My dad knows a lot of people in Montana," he said, holding his hand out. "Go south, to Colorado. That's your best bet. There's people looking for you here. Don't think there aren't."

"Maybe you're right."

"I know I'm right. Trust me, Hunter."

Hunter shook Paul's hand and was surprised when Paul leaned forward and gave him a short, firm hug as well. "Thanks for all your help," Hunter said when Paul pulled back. He held the gun up. "For this, too."

"You bet." Paul turned to go, then hesitated. "I'm sorry about Strat. He was a good man."

"Yeah, he was. Thanks."

"Well, take care of yourself, Griz. Don't stop for anybody until you get to Colorado," Paul called as he headed to the Explorer and climbed in. "I mean it."

Then he was gone.

Hunter watched the Explorer's taillights until they disappeared, wondering if he'd ever see Paul again.

67

B IG BILL SAT in his office at the Brule Lumber Mill gazing out the wide window behind his desk at a young employee who was rooting through a Dumpster sitting beside the next building over. The sun had barely cleared the horizon, but Big Bill already had fifty of his employees scouring the thirty-two-acre facility—for the second straight day. They were searching every inch of ground inside the ten-foot-high chain-link fence for personal files "someone" had stolen from his office. They were not to look at what they found but they were to deliver anything "of interest" directly to him. They were not even to take what they found to their supervisor first.

Big Bill turned slowly away from the window. Security had apprehended Jeremy as he'd tried to run past the main gates, then turned him over a few hours later to some of Dale Callahan's associates. Men who'd shown up because Big Bill had called Callahan asking for help in getting rid of Jeremy. The same way he'd called Callahan that awful day he'd killed Joanna Preston and asked for help disposing of her body. Jeremy had shouted to the two security guards at the gate that Callahan's men had been sent to kill him, but Big Bill had assured the guards that Jeremy was on drugs, which was why he was being fired as the CEO immediately. The guards had nodded obediently and handcuffed Jeremy right away. Unfortunately, when the security people had detained Jeremy, he wasn't carrying the folders he'd taken from the office. He must have hidden the information on the grounds somewhere with the intention of coming back later and picking it up, Big Bill figured. Or of having someone else pick the information for him, he suddenly realized.

Big Bill put his face in his hands. "Oh, Christ." Those manila folders were probably already gone, and he was pretty sure he knew who'd picked them up.

Big Bill glanced at his office phone when it started ringing. Dale Callahan. The choices now: pick the phone up—or run. Right now he still had a chance to get away. If he waited much longer, that chance might be gone.

68

HUNTER BREATHED A small sigh of relief when he'd made it through the mountain pass on the south side of Fort Mason. He and Zoe were still a long way from safety, but at least they were out of the immediate area.

He'd just started to think they might actually make it, just started to think about Strat being dead, when there was a loud blast from the tree line. The pickup's front left tire blew instantly, then the steering wheel wrenched hard in his hands. The pickup veered across the double yellow line and careened over a ditch beside the oncoming lane, crashed through some saplings, and slammed into a pine tree. His forehead smacked the top of the steering wheel at the same time Zoe's hit the dashboard. Thank God they'd both been wearing seatbelts. He felt a trickle of blood running down the side of his face and saw that Zoe was bleeding from her head, too, though the impact hadn't brought her out of her sleep. Maybe it had killed her.

Hunter grabbed the Glock off the dashboard, thrust his door open, hustled to the back of the truck through the saplings, and checked down the narrow road in the direction they'd been coming from. A hundred yards back a man was sprinting toward him, clutching what looked like a shotgun or a rifle.

"Damn it!"

Hunter turned around and raced back past the pickup into the forest, then stopped, swore again, sprinted to the passenger side of the truck, threw open the door, undid Zoe's seatbelt, scooped her up, and took off into the woods. He couldn't leave her here. He thought he could, but when it came down to it, he couldn't. Even if she had been part of the crew that killed Strat. It was done and it was horrible, but now maybe she could do some good.

The guy on the road with the gun was making up ground on them by leaps and bounds, literally. There wouldn't be any outrunning him, that seemed obvious. Hunter hadn't seen any dogs, but he might have them, and that would make outrunning him absolutely impossible. The trick was to find a place to make a stand and find it quickly. Then hope the guy didn't have backup.

Fifty yards into the forest Hunter hurried around a thick stand of trees, up a sharp, ten-foot rise and down the other side. There he placed Zoe on the ground and hurried back to the top of the rise. He lay prone on the ground beside a tree and chambered the first round.

He didn't have to wait long. Moments later Hunter spotted the guy he'd seen on the road moving through the forest, swinging the barrel of his shotgun from side to side as he jogged.

It was decision time: let the guy run past or confront him now. The pickup wasn't going anywhere, and this guy might double back quickly and take him by surprise.

"Stop right where you are!" Hunter shouted when the guy was only twenty feet away. "Drop the gun and put your hands up, or I swear to God I'll blast you." The guy stopped, but didn't drop the gun or put his hands up. *"Drop the gun!"* Hunter shouted again. The only good thing about this situation was that Hunter had cover so the guy had no shot, not from where he was right now, anyway. His gun was pointed at the ground, and Hunter would be able to get off at least one shot and take cover before the other guy could even aim. "Do it."

"You're not going to shoot me," the man said calmly. "You don't have the guts." Without warning, the man pulled the trigger, blowing a shot into the ground. The deafening blast rattled through the trees and kicked up a mess of pine needles. "Now the three guys with me know exactly where we are. You're a dead man."

The guy might be bluffing but he might not be. There was no way to tell. If he wasn't, the clock was ticking and there wasn't much time. Hunter sure as hell wouldn't be able to hold off four of them. "It's him or me," Hunter whispered to himself, preparing himself to kill again.

But before Hunter could squeeze the trigger of the Glock, a shot rang out and the man went down, grasping his stomach and screaming.

"Hunter Lee?"

Hunter whipped around and brought the Glock up, but not in time. A rifle butt slammed into his chin—and the world went dark.

69

AT FOURTEEN THOUSAND feet Paul waved to Ronnie Childs, stepped through the Cessna's open door into another perfectly clear day, and headed back to earth. He was diving toward the same ridge he and Mandy had jumped to that day they'd hiked to the waterfall. Today, Paul took his time. He lay flat out on his stomach as he fell, arms and legs spread wide.

As he dropped through the azure sky, he thought about Mandy and how the only woman he'd ever loved had been taken from him so quickly and in such a brutal way. He thought about how she was perfect for him, how he'd already known that for sure by the time they'd made it to the ridge where the Big Cat Fire had started. But now she was gone forever.

He thought about his father and how in the end his mother had been absolutely right in the letter she'd penned to Jeremy and him on her deathbed. How she'd described a man who could charm you into next week without even trying, but who could never be trusted.

He thought about Jeremy and what had ultimately happened to his older brother. Maybe there'd never be an answer to that question, the poor guy.

Finally, Paul thought about Hunter. The man had endured a hell of a lot in a very brief time, but he'd still seemed completely in control back at the campground when Paul had delivered the information connecting Big Bill and Nelson Radcliff to Dale Callahan. Paul hadn't known many men like Hunter in his life, men who it seemed could handle almost any kind of pressure you threw at them, but they'd all left an indelible mark on him. As he whipped through the air, Paul crossed his fingers and said a quick prayer for Hunter. Griz was going to need all the luck and all the prayers he could get today.

As Paul hurtled toward the point of no return, his fingers closed around the parachute handle. He'd wondered all the way out to the airfield and all the way up in the Cessna if he was going to pull it or not, if he really had that death wish and if today was the day he'd get his wish. But it still wasn't clear to him.

Then he thought about pulling Mitch down from the tree and about Mitch's little baby girl and how he'd wanted kids with Mandy. About how there was still a lot of life to live and plenty of good deeds left to do. That there were more people like Mitch he could save on the fire line, but that if he wasn't there maybe kids like Mitch's little girl wouldn't have a father one day.

Then he smiled—and pulled.

70

As Hunter's eyes slowly opened, he was surprised to see a woman and a man he didn't recognize. They were peering down at him anxiously as he lay on his back on a comfortable sofa. He was surprised not to be restrained, too. Frankly, he was surprised to be alive.

"Where am I?" he asked groggily, gently touching his chin. It felt twice as big as normal and like some of it was swimming around unattached beneath his skin. "Who are you?"

"I'm Katrina Mason," the woman answered. "It's nice to finally meet you. Your brother told me a lot about you." Her expression turned a shade sad. "I liked Strat."

"Well, I won't hold that against you," Hunter said good-naturedly, forcing a sentimental half smile to his face as he struggled to sit up. "Then you must be his undercover help. That person he wouldn't tell me about who was helping him try to figure out who was setting Montana on fire."

"I am," she admitted, sitting down on the sofa beside Hunter. "I'll miss him very much."

"Yeah, me, too."

"And I'm Special Agent Cummins." Cummins flashed a large badge, then slipped it back into his suit coat and sat down in a chair opposite the couch. "I'm with the FBI, out of the Bureau's Denver office." He pointed at the lump on Hunter's chin. "Sorry about that, but my guy didn't have much of a choice. You were about to shoot him."

Hunter's jaw was killing him, but at the moment it seemed like a small price for being safe. "I'm glad he was around. Candidly, I'm glad *I'm* around." Hunter eased back against the sofa. "By the way, where—"

"You're on my ranch south of Fort Mason," Katrina explained.

Hunter felt the weight of the world finally lifting slowly off his shoulders. "The woman who was with me. Where is she?"

"You mean Zoe Gale?"

"Yes."

"She's upstairs," Cummins replied, "under heavy guard." He gestured toward the front door. "We've got fifteen agents here on the ranch with more on the way. When Katrina called to let me know your brother was dead, we came up here in force right away. We decided it was time. It took us a while to find you, but I'm glad we did. That guy who shot out your tire and chased you into the woods had three other guys with him in the area. You were in for a rough time."

"I'm sure I was," Hunter agreed, nodding solemnly. "Don't let Zoe get away," he spoke up. "She doesn't need to be protected because she's innocent. She needs protection because she's a hell of an important witness."

"We understand that," Cummins said.

"You do?"

"She started talking almost as soon as she woke up," Katrina explained. "As soon as we confronted her with the information that was in those two folders you had tucked under your shirt. And the notes you'd made."

"At least," Cummins added, "we assumed you made those notes."

"I did." After Paul had driven off, Hunter had scrawled down everything he could think of on blank pieces of paper, then stored them in the manila folders Paul had given him. In case he hadn't made it out of Montana alive, he was hoping the evidence might still make it into the right hands. "I guess that was a good idea after all."

"It was." Cummins stood up. "Ms. Gale was working for Dale Callahan, exactly as you surmised. She admitted that thirty minutes ago upstairs. The only reason we haven't taken her away yet is that we wanted to talk to you first. We wanted to make sure you were the one who'd written those notes in the folders."

"Have you found Callahan yet?" Hunter asked.

"No," Cummins answered. "We haven't found Senator Brule, either. But neither one of them will be able to run for very long. It's simply a matter of time before we catch them."

"Big Bill killed—"

"Joanna Prescott," Cummins interrupted. "We read your notes."

"Nelson Radcliff." Hunter spoke up, his eyes widening. "You need to—"

"We're all over it," Cummins assured Hunter. "We've got an APB out for him, too. Relax."

Hunter gazed at Cummins, then at Katrina. It was over, he realized, really over. Montana was no longer under siege. He really could relax.

As the emotional walls suddenly gave way, he closed his eyes, leaned forward, and put his hands to his face. Now he could finally mourn Strat.

Acknowledgments

Tremendous thanks to Terry Donitahn, who was instrumental in helping me with *Hell's Gate*.

As always, a special thanks to Peter Borland, Judith Curr, Louise Burke, and Cynthia Manson.

To the kids—Ashley, Courtney, Christina, and Ellie.

And Matt Malone; Kevin Erdman; Andy and Chris Brusman; Jeannette Follo; Jim and Anmarie Galowski; Steve Watson; Jack Wallace; Barbara Fertig; Bob Carpenter; Bart Begley; John Grigg; Walter Frey; Marvin Bush; Scott Andrews; Jeff, Jamie, and Catherine Faville; Nick Simonds; David Brown; Al Madocs; Sean Devlin; Gerry Barton; Aaron McClung; Baron Stewart; Mike Lynch; Pat and Terry Lynch; Gordon Eadon; Bob Weiczorek; John Piazza; and Mike Pocalyko.

4/10-14